Homecomings
DONALD PATERSON

TWO RAVENS
PRESS

Published by Two Ravens Press Ltd.
Green Willow Croft
Rhiroy, Lochbroom
Ullapool
Ross-shire IV23 2SF

www.tworavenspress.com

The right of Donald Paterson to be identified as author of
this work has been asserted by him in accordance with the
Copyright, Designs and Patent Act, 1988.
© Donald Paterson, 2010.

ISBN: 978-1-906120-48-1

British Library Cataloguing in Publication Data: a CIP record
for this book can be obtained from the British Library.

Designed and typeset in Sabon by Two Ravens Press.
Cover design by Two Ravens Press.

Printed in Poland on Forest Stewardship
Council-accredited paper.

About the Author

Donald Paterson was born in Motherwell, but grew up in Tain in the Scottish Highlands. After studying at Aberdeen University, he taught for many years in Aberlour and, more recently, in Inverness. Donald lives with his wife Val in Fortrose, on the Black Isle, from where the dolphins can be seen swimming only a short evening walk away. *Homecomings* is his first novel.

For more information about the author, see
www.tworavenspress.com

Acknowledgements

I am grateful to Dundurn Press Ltd, Toronto, for permission to quote from *The Emigrant's Guide to North America* by Robert MacDougall, edited by Elizabeth Thompson.

Thank you to Nicola Barr of the Susijn Agency, and to Sharon Blackie of Two Ravens Press, for their invaluable advice and for believing that other people might enjoy reading this.

Ali: thank you, too.

This novel is dedicated
to my parents,
and to Val:

my writing is for them.

Introduction

There's nothing that makes me any different from anybody else, I know that. Everyone has their life and does the ordinary things that everyone does, such as getting a job, working away, trying out friendships, having a partner, having a family if they're lucky and so on and so forth. We're all more or less the same, that's what I've been thinking.

And I think there comes a point for a lot of people when they begin to ask about the point of everything, the shape of it all. They want to know why *me*, why *this*, why *here*? Or, in another way, they want to know why not *that*, why not *there*. Why have all these *things* happened to me? Some people go out and buy a silky new car, one designed for somebody much younger than them. Some people go out and choose a new partner, or a new house, or a new job. A lot of people just curl up and hide.

I'm not one of those people, but I'm not original either. I'm a woman in my late forties and I suppose I have all the same questions anyone else would have and what I did next was much the same as lots of other people do, and I wasn't even original enough to think it up for myself. I decided to explore my family tree, maybe trying to see why I was who I was, a twig on some precarious branch.

It's on the television all the time, and you can see the adverts in the *Radio Times* and on the internet, urging you to *discover your family history*. Type "family tree" into Google and you get nearly forty-eight million hits. There must be a lot of us out there trying to look backwards to work out how it all makes some kind of sense. Because these family tree companies are in it to make money and the television programmes pull in lots of viewers.

I know why it exists, this fascination with our ancestries. We want to find a *story*. I mean, the names and dates and all

1

the other details you find out from the censuses and the parish records are very interesting, but what we really want is to find something that travels across the years like a tale, like a fable. Maybe a romantic highwayman somewhere long ago, hanged at Tyburn, leaving one little child, or maybe a khaki soldier that fathered a sickly daughter then went off to die at Ypres, or maybe someone who was the only survivor of a ship that sank to the bottom of the sea. Something tenuous, something fateful. A story that gives us an idea that we might not have been here at all, if things had gone just that little bit differently. Something that could give us the feeling that we are *here*, doing *this*, because it is how things were meant to be.

I know it's not very logical, but it's a lot more logical than a Porsche Carrera driven by a fifty-year-old man with a belly stretching open the buttons on his shirt and his hair tied back in a ponytail that might have made sense thirty years ago – but probably not.

So that's what I did: I dug into my past, and this book is what I found. If I hadn't begun my search into my own history it might never have come to light and now, having lived with this text for a while, that seems a frightening thought. I thought I was trying to illuminate my own life story and I've ended up with someone else's. But I don't mind, because it is a story like the ones I mentioned above. It *does* give me a sort of meaning for myself. The reason I am putting it before you now is because it has its own interest, too – or at least that is what I hope.

It may be a century and a half old, but listen to what is said in this collection of jottings from the mind of a man who saw, in the end, that the world has to be shaped in order to meet our needs. This is the story of a man who wouldn't face a life that he didn't much like, who would not allow the world to beat him down.

I must not, though, say too much. It's important that you form your own views, though I am sure you will be as intrigued as I was the first time I read the dusty sheets upon which these words were first written. They were hard to decipher – in the beginning. The narrator's handwriting is cramped and awkward, the script of a man to whom extensive writing did not come naturally, and the expression, you will see, at times leaves a lot to be desired in terms of literary merit. But I'm sure you will find, as I did, that growing experience lends a certain clumsy charm to his style. But style is not the key here. Narrative and motivation are.

In any case I took the decision, when submitting the following pages to several publishers with a view to seeing them in print (I knew even as I read the first few pages that this was a story which had to be shared, and that it was my fate to do that sharing) that, beyond changing his underlinings to italics, I would make virtually no corrections, that I would improve almost none of the writer's many errors of technique (though I was tempted). The tone of the words captures the essence of the man – a fascinating man who was prepared to undergo incredible hardship in order to achieve financial success and independence, not least from his past. I hope we can excuse him the occasional cliché or ungainly attempt to express emotions. It's the story that matters, and what we can take from it.

For he was no *special* man, no *privileged* man, no *fortunate* man. This is someone from humble beginnings in the far North of Scotland. The year is 1841, though the narrative doesn't make that fact clear for some time. I could tell you a hundred stories about the research I carried out in libraries in various locations (especially in the National Library of Scotland in Edinburgh), but I think it's best if you experience the manuscript rather as I did when I first sat down that cold November night and read, engrossed, until the dawn began to edge its way through the curtains of my newly bought empty old house in Elgin in the county of Moray, not too far from Inverness and Forres, the town where I was born. An ancestor's house, of course. My grandfather stayed here long ago. How *he* got hold of the text I do not know. Some things sink down and are lost in the twilit marshes of time.

Although I have tried not to tamper too much, I realise that there are places where the narrator's account is unclear, and on occasion I have decided to insert some explanatory comments, simply to save you the bother of trying to piece it all together for yourselves. There are gaps in the narrative, some of them stretching across several years, and though the story is not a path that I have personally laid out, I feel I have a role to play as guide along the way, if you will forgive that rather obvious image. It is, after all, a tale of travel. I have at times used footnotes. I hope that these are not too intrusive. It's in my nature to comment and I found I couldn't resist the temptation. Furthermore, I have provided some remarks between sections in a way which I hope is not invasive. I sincerely wish that my additions are of some use, and that you find that they illuminate some of the darker corners of the road. If not, of course, you are free to skip my brief sections of commentary and simply read the original words of Hugh Ross himself, the man whose tale is enclosed between these covers.

When I first read that tale, though, it was not, of course, between covers. Maybe I should tell you, before we go any further, something of the circumstances that led to my discovery of the papers, and, in passing, try to explain why the story struck such a chord with me, why it kept me reading all night. It is a strange tale, maybe not one that, at first sight, seems likely to hold appeal across the great wall of years which has built up between Hugh's time and ours. It just strikes me that his account of events between 1841 and 1857 is somehow *elemental*, as if he is telling the story of all humankind, in all ages. At least that is how it touched me. I felt as if, in some strange way, I was reading my own story, transplanted in place and time. My hope is that you will feel the same, and that you will find, as I did, that the story helps in the understanding of a twenty-first-century life. I mean, this story has intrigued me. And it tells the story, or at least a part of the story, of one of my ancestors, so I am close to it whether I like it or not.

Of course, in many ways there is not really very much to tie me to Hugh Ross, born in 1823 in Croval, in the north-east of Scotland. For example, you will see that Hugh was a traveller; I have never strayed too far from home. But there are connections: Hugh sailed from Cromarty on the so-called Black Isle, a peninsula that extends into the Moray Firth; my husband hails from Culbokie, a few miles along the road from there. That's as far as it goes, though. Hugh's journey from Scotland to Canada, and onward to the States, is a journey that is very far removed from my experience of life. In many ways I'm jealous of his willingness to throw everything aside and start again. I have tried for success in life, but not with his sense of abandon. The key is that he wished to *expand*. I can't think of a better word.

When my bookshop failed we had to think about what we would do next. We searched the internet and property centres, or at least I did, to try to find the right property for us and, to cut a long story short, eventually decided on this five-bedroom town house in Elgin that was in need of substantial renovation. It is only fifteen minutes from where I was born, and that seemed right. The key factor was that, as I mentioned above, it had from the 1880s been owned by my great-great-grandfather, and that made sense to me, a sort of coming home in a more profound way than just going back to a town near where I was born. I will not go into detail here about the architect and builders and garden designers and all the countless planning permission forms that needed to be filled in as we converted this old building into somewhere that a twenty-first-century family could be content. Ironically, it was only briefly the family home I had planned for, but that is another story altogether, and probably not one for these pages, on the whole.

When the builders opened up the roof space in an attempt to get to the worm-eaten beams that they insisted would have to be replaced, they discovered some items that had been there for a long time. There were old newspapers from the early 1900s, some children's toys (which have earned me a good sum of money on eBay), an amount of crockery (none of it of great value) and a chest which, when opened, revealed a ribboned pile of old letters and the document that I am presenting to you here in this volume.

The letters seemed of little interest and I passed them on to the Elgin library where they have been added to the local history archive: I don't believe they have any bearing on this story.

The manuscript in the chest is, as I say, what you are about to read. As I mentioned above, I read it through that very night, drawn in by its increasingly lucid style and by the handwriting itself, full of a sort of odd courageous stubbornness. Though that may be hindsight. And, of course, Hugh's growth from boy to man has a universality that arrested me on the personal level. I fell half in love with him that night, to be completely honest, which is a strange thing for me to admit, given who he was.

How the pages came to be in that chest in a house in Elgin is beyond me to solve. Who knows how they made their way to Elgin from the other side of the world. It is very appropriate and satisfactory that they did, but I am puzzled. I may be missing something, not for the first time.

It doesn't matter. The story stands by itself – it doesn't need to be authenticated by following historical lines to establish its exact provenance. However, on that subject, I would point out that I have had the paper and inks analysed and have established that they are consistent with the period and with the various locations Hugh writes about. I know that there may be some who question the authenticity of the document that lies before you.[1] On that issue you will simply have to take my word. If this publication were to make any money for me then that is unimportant: I regret the implication that I might attempt to profit through any kind of fabrication.

I have said enough for the time being. This is Hugh's tale, after all. However, I hope I am not overstepping the bounds of modesty if I say how proud I am about my involvement with this remarkable story, a story that makes my own tale connect to the past in a way that gives me substance, I like to think. It has left me, maybe, with more questions than I ever had before, but I hope what I have done here goes some way to answer the question posed by Hugh Ross in his very first sentence.

Rona Macpherson, November 2007, Elgin

---

1   Not just "may be". I could list the doubters and embarrass them all, but I won't. It's up to them what they believe, I suppose.

Croval

I dont know why I will be writing this all down but the thing I keep asking myself is well whos going to tell your story if you dont tell it yourself? And Ian Macleod says that we are all living a story that the good Lord wants to know about but what I cant see is why he wants to know about it if hes written it in the first place.

Thats Ian the minister. You listen to what he has to say and hes taught me an awful lot since he came about a year ago when old Donald McTavish, the last minister, died when he tripped over down by the sea with a good whisky in him and hit his head on the rock, the old fool. Well they couldnt do anything for him and he was just lying there in his bed for about two days or three days and then he died. Probably just as well in the end because his story had more or less come to an end when he smacked his head off that black rock. So thats how Ian came to be minister though it wasnt long before a lot of folk began to regret that hed come at all. It was Ian that told me that if you look hard enough into something youll be able to see something else. I didnt see what he meant but he explained that it was like the way you can be out in the boat and you look into the water and to begin with you cant see anything but after a while you begin to see sort of through the surface and sometimes you can see fish down there or seaweed floating or things like that.

But when he said it to me he was talking about the Bible and it is saying that sort of thing that gets some folk thinking that maybe it would have been better if he hadnt come at all to be the new minister. The older folk are the ones thinking that. And another thing is the way he keeps saying English, English, English is the way we should be talking now if we want to do well in this modern world. Well most of the old folk have no need to be getting on in the modern world and they dont like him not talking in the Gaelic and doing all his sermons in English but hes from down South near Edinburgh so you cant be expecting someone from there to be speaking Gaelic, not these days. So he is more likely to be talking to the young people, like me. I was seventeen when he came, eighteen now and a lots happened in that year, a right lot. He is good to talk to and a few of us will sit with him when he goes fishing at the deep pool where the burn curves round after it comes off the cliff and round by the trees if you can call them that. And so that is another thing the older folk arent too keen on, the way he is friendly with us younger ones. Ian says that they think that he should be focusing on their souls because they are likely to be next away, that there is plenty of time for us younger ones to find the way to heaven. Oh, he says, but thats not a worry because most of them wouldnt be going to heaven no matter how long was spent trying to improve their souls. Its the young ones that count. He says the young ones can still get back on the path even when theyve wandered away to the side, and I like that idea a lot, I like to hear that.

He himself is about sixty or maybe a bit more I suppose but he always seems so much younger. Hes been minister at a lot of different places he tells us. And now here he is at the ends of the earth, which is Croval. That was a joke but he says lots of serious things in between the jokes. Ive never learnt so much from anyone in my life and thats the truth. I never bothered much with wanting to learn things until Ian came. Hes taught me to read and write a lot better than I could before that[2] and he told me to write everything down because we all have a story, like I said before. I never did anything about it until now. And theres a reason why Im doing it now but Ill come to

---

2   Though you will observe that Hugh's grammar is, to say the least, imperfect, reflecting speech rather than the formal writing styles of the time. Why should it be any different? – RM

that in a while.

Ill introduce people. At the beginning of a story theres always this bit about whos in it. Ian is always reading books. Thats another thing some folk arent liking very much. Because the books he reads arent always religious ones. He reads bits of them out to us. Sometimes bits of them he reads more than once because he likes the sound of them. He likes books by this man called Walter Scott who he says he met once but I dont know if thats true. Ian says his family lived not far away from this Walter Scott writer for a while and that he met him once when he was just a wee boy, Ian I mean. So if hes reading to us and he finds a sentence that he likes then hell read it out then hell stop and hell let the book drop and hell say it out to us again as if hes wanting us to remember it but the truth is I cant really remember them exactly but one bit that did stick in my mind was this one

I have thrown the force of my narrative upon the characters and the passions of these characters.

Or something like that anyway. Narrative means story. I can remember this one because of the way Ian read it out again and again and told us that this was the only true way to tell a story so Im keeping those words of Walter Scott in my head or trying to because as I said weve all been learning a lot from Ian.

Maybe youre thinking I should be calling him Mr MacLeod since hes the minister after all but he told us to call him Ian so thats what we call him whatever anyone thinks. But if you want to be more respectful as the older folks would be saying you can think of him as Mr MacLeod whenever I just write down Ian, its up to you.

Ian says that theres power in stories to help us to see whats going on in our own lives. Not much is going on in my life, I was thinking, the first time he said it. I was seventeen years old and helping out with our wee bit of land, the cow and the chickens, and then going out on Callums fathers boat. But Ian explained

11

that what he meant was that thing about looking deeper, that if you looked deep into your own life you could see things that you didnt know about at first. And he said that stories were for that purpose, whether in the Bible or other books. He said that stories were like a special pair of spectacles you could put on that let you see things that you never saw before. He does wear spectacles when hes reading, Ian, but thats by the way.

One thing sometimes that annoys me in the stories that Ian reads out to us is that a person will come into the story and the writer will describe them a bit but you can forget that. Then its maybe a hundred pages before that person comes back into the story and then you cant remember what they look like for example or the kind of clothes they wear. So I think near the beginning of a story the writer should write down all the important people in it and a bit about them so that whoever is reading it knows that to remind himself about a character he just needs to look back to the beginning of the story, because thats where everything is written down. Not that anyone really will be reading all this I dont suppose but I might let Ian see it. He knows Im writing it. I wouldnt let the others see it, not ever. They wouldnt like what I write, especially Callum.

Im not sure what to do if other people come into my story that I dont even know yet. Should I come back to this first bit and write something about them at the edge of the page? Mind you, what new people? Ians the most new person in my story and Ive already known him for a year or so. Theres not a lot of people who are new when you live here. But maybe there might be soon, thats the thing.

It takes a long time, this writing. What Ive done so far has taken me days, a bit at a time. Ian says thats all right, that the hardest tasks are the most worthwhile. I think maybe thats in the Bible. Sometimes when Ians reading to us he misses bits out because he doesnt think they are interesting enough, he says. You can do the same if you like. Even big writers such as

12

this Walter Scott sometimes put in bits that they shouldnt have bothered with, if you ask me. So Im sure I will too because its all new to me and I dont really know what Im doing.

There also has to be a bit near the beginning called the setting. This is where the writer tells you all about the place where the story happens so you can imagine it in your head. You need to put in a bit of this every now and then, says Ian, as the story moves from place to place.

And thats why I decided to start writing after all these months of Ian telling me I should. Because all of a sudden we are talking about new places, new settings, and heres me quite wanting to go and find them. Thats why Ive decided theres maybe a story for me to tell. Its quite good fun, I quite like doing it, but my mother doesnt see the point in it, and says things to me. Where does that get you? she says, nowhere. She says, go and dig some potatoes. Things like that. But I quite like it anyway.

Ill start with the characters and while Im on the subject Ill start with my mother.

My mother, Elizabeth Ross.

Quite often in the stories theyll start by describing what the people look like. So, my mother is a small woman and her hair is that silver grey colour that you get. Her eyes are blue with lines round them. Shes nearly sixty now and that makes her a lot older than my friends parents. Im the youngest. She had four children counting me and Im the only one left and in a way that made her older if you understand what I mean. There was Elizabeth, their first child, named after my mother of course. She died when she was just a wee child so I never knew her because I wasnt quite born then. She had some illness and she died so I never knew her. Then they had James who would have been twenty four if hed still been alive and Thomas who would have been twenty one. Elizabeth and James were born

13

in Strathgarrick but Thomas and me were born here in Croval. James was named for my father and the three of them, James my father, my brother James and also Thomas were all drowned when I was ten, on Neil Camerons boat when it sank in a storm. Neil Cameron and his son died too that day. My mother was old by then, about fifty, and she never looked for another husband. I do remember my father and my two brothers but most of all I remember my mother at that time and the way she never cried, but just went quiet after their deaths. Maybe she did cry but I never saw it. So maybe she knew I would be looking at her, trying to see what was going on inside her and she decided to let me see what she wanted me to see which was a strong old woman who always thinks the most important thing is just to get on with it all. I think its hard for her to have had four children and to only have one left. In a funny way I think she almost doesnt like me very much, because Im the one thats left. That might be just me imagining. But she can be cold towards me and thats one of the reasons why Im listening to Ian and his ideas. Shes hard to get to know, my mother, and Ive heard other people saying that about her, Ian says it too. Ill always remember the way people came to the croft after the drownings and she just wouldnt talk to them very much. Theyd go away again and theyd be saying how brave she was, how strong. But it was just that she didnt want to talk to them about it. Or to me. It was either a strength in her or a weakness. Im sure when they got back into their own crofts they were saying to each other that she was a dour old wifie.

I think shes beginning to look a lot older now and her hands are sore and stiff. I notice she forgets things sometimes. But shes still sharp with her thoughts and with her tongue. She hates it when I go off out on Callums fathers boat, which is more or less Callums boat because he can use it whenever he wants. This will be because of what happened to my father and brothers but she wont say that. She says, Youll never get anything useful

14

done out there, you should be back here helping me. She likes to tell me what to do, and in the end you have to do it, usually. Sometimes I wish I would stand up to her more, but I dont. I know this is a thing about me and it makes me feel weak sometimes. I let other people decide what happens to me and if I had one wish, like a person in a story, I would wish that I was better at making things happen to me, instead of letting other people doing all the deciding.

The Setting, Croval, on the shores of the Moray Firth[3]

Its a little group of houses down by the rocks. Theres a stone jetty that was built back before I was born when the people were moved here from Strathgarrick. The Laird of Killarnoch, who owns Strathgarrick, was putting sheep there and he wanted to put the people out to the coast. It was happening all over the place back then and its still happening now. Ian says theres hardly a place left in the north of Scotland that hasnt been harmed by this. He says down in Edinburgh they talk about the *clearances*, as they call it, and ladies in big houses with high ceilings take up collections for us so that we will all be happy in our new lives by the sea. But as I say this all happened to Croval before I was born so I dont feel as angry about it as some of the

---

3   I was tempted, here, to do some reorganising on behalf of Hugh. You'll see that he interrupts his account of key characters and it would have been one possibility to shift the sections around to attain a more ordered appearance. Indeed, I did attempt this once the whole memoir had been word-processed (initially by Alison, my assistant in the shop, then later, when circumstances intervened, and I had more time, by me) but on second thoughts I returned the manuscript to its original order. Maybe there is something rambling about the way he tells the story but I feel this is a feature of his personality in these early pages and it will be useful for the reader to see progress, if that is the correct word, in the way that Hugh structures his account of events as the text goes on. And I thought, Who am I to make changes like this? So I didn't. – RM

15

older ones do, like my mother. And I dont know what happened to the money that the Edinburgh rich ladies collected because Ive never seen any of it and neither has anyone else as far as I know. Ian says its all gone to pay for ministers in America but Im not sure what he means by that. Its the kind of thing he says and then doesnt explain it, which can be annoying, especially when he says it with a wee smile as if its a joke that you dont get.

The older ones talk about how they were forced out of their houses at Strathgarrick because some of them didnt want to come here. But some of the others say its better here, because were all together, close together. Up in Strathgarrick the crofts were all spaced out so you had to walk for ages to see anyone. But the old ones say they liked that better. Im not sure. I dont think Id like to be so far from everyone that you would be stuck with your own company or just your mothers company all the time but on the other hand sometimes everyones too close together here and everyone knows your business, or at least you worry that they do. For example if me and Callum and Robert go up to the manse to talk to Ian well everyone knows about it and then theyre all talking about it and asking us questions when we get back down to Croval. And I think thats annoying, but Callum thinks its even more annoying. Usually, everything is always annoying to Callum sometimes.

Our croft is just at the edge of Croval and so we are nearest to the manse up on the slope behind the houses, up by the church. My mother wanted this croft because it was the furthest from the sea but, first of all, when they were all moved down to Croval in 1820, three years before I was born, they were put in a place right down by the stone jetty and shes often told me how shed hated that, seeing the boats going out and knowing that sometimes a boat might not come back, and this was even before my father and brothers died. She was scared of the sea and shed never been on it. Still never has. So after a couple of years someone died that used to live in the house were in now

16

and the whole family moved up here. She was carrying me then and this is the house where I was born and where Elizabeth died just before I was born. Its more of a croft because were at the edge of Croval and were looking out at the cliff instead of out at the sea. But it didnt stop my father and two brothers being drowned in 1833, even though we werent beside the sea.

Before writing this bit I went out and counted the houses in Croval. There are thirty seven. Ive been trying to work out how many people stay here and I think the answer is one hundred and fifty four. One hundred and fifty five if you count Ian Macleod up in the manse. As well as the houses there are some other buildings down by the jetty that have to do with the fishing, where nets are stored and where some of the boats are repaired and that sort of thing. Theres a hut down there where the older men go and sit and have a dram and talk about being out on the sea. They call it the Carcair, which is a joke. None of the women are allowed to go there. I dont like it much in the Carcair. Its all smoke and folk shouting and arguing or telling long stories about storms and people drowning and about great catches that theyve had, or so they say. Its hard to believe a word you hear in there because of the drink thats taken. Callum likes going there and he joins in, shouting and swearing away with the rest of them. It annoys him that they dont believe his lies but theyve known him since he was born. They know everything about him, and me, and everyone, although there is something that they dont know.

You need to imagine Croval. Its set in a tight little curve of the cliffs with a stony beach thats never quiet and the cliffs spread round the bay like two arms holding you in tight. The Laird of Killarnoch is supposed to have chosen this place himself because he said it would make a good harbour and a safe one. But actually because of the way the tides and the currents work its never calm in the sea here. Theres always waves lashing up at the jetty, especially in winter. And its almost impossible some days to row out past the entrance to the bay because the currents always trying to drag you back in again.

Theres a row of houses facing the sea then the other houses are in no particular order going back up the slope to the edge of Croval. Theyre all painted white or else just the colour of the stone theyre built of. Most of them are thatched and cosy but the manse up on the hill has a proper roof with tiles on it and some of the younger men with families are beginning to say they want to have roofs like that too. Why should the minister have better than the ordinary folk? theyre wondering.

Up beside the manse is the church which is a cold building with little windows. Ian told me that other churches hes been in have got wood stoves that can at least take the frost off the air in winter on a Sunday but nothing like that here. There are hard wooden benches. Ian says hes been in churches where the windows are made of coloured glass so that when the sun shines in summer the shadows on the floor are dancing with red and blue and orange and silver and that. In Croval its just thick greenish glass like on a bottle that lets in a kind of underwater light. A rock pool light, he calls it. The pulpit is two steps up from the floor and made out of oak wood that the Laird brought in. Theres no trees really around Croval itself, just a few wee birches by the burn that are always getting blown back into the ground, like sinners on the road to Hell, says Ian.

Then behind the manse and the church the cliff climbs up. The Laird of Killarnoch got the Croval people to carve steps into the cliff and thats how you get out of Croval if you want to. My mother says it took the men years to finish the steps and before they were finished you had to clamber up the cliff and more than one person fell off, though nobody was killed that way. But people *were* killed in the boats they built with wood supplied by Killarnoch and that werent any good for going out to sea in. Crovals been here for twenty one years now and my mother says all that time has been spent learning how to build

18

better boats to die in. Shell say something like that when I say to her that Im going out in Callums boat the next day.

Theres a little stream that drops down off the cliff face and then runs on to the sea down near the jetty. That gives us water. Once a week theres a cart comes to the top of the cliff from along the coast with supplies that we cant get for ourselves like tobacco and things like that. Of course the carts a big event when it comes because theres a lot of things we cant provide for ourselves, were helpless a bit like that. Its a man MacPhee with the cart and he will buy things off folk so that theres a little bit of money coming in sometimes. The things he buys are like carved wooden bowls made out of driftwood, fish if theres enough to spare, some cheese and that sort of stuff. Theres not much money changes hands. Uncle Michael hates the man MacPhee because he says that Killarnoch organised this cart to come with things for Croval and everything was supposed to be cheap. Uncle Michael says this was the arrangement because Killarnoch felt a bit guilty about moving us all to the coast and wanted to make himself feel better because his wife had told him he was a heartless soul. My mother would say, Well he doesnt feel *very* guilty because were still stuck here in this fish-smelling midden arent we? But anyway MacPhee charges far too much and Uncle Michael says he tells Killarnoch that hes sold things for the cheap prices and pockets the difference. Theres no way of knowing if all this is true or not but its what Uncle Michael says. He says MacPhee is just a tinker when all is said and done.

I have been up out of Croval a good few times. When we were younger we used to climb up the steps and go wandering around up on the flat land up there and we still do. Sometimes I have thought it would be a good idea to move up there and build a place and try to grow more things, because the land up there looks better with green grass and plenty of bushes and trees growing in it, though the trees are old and knotted and no good for building or anything. Ive suggested it to my mother

19

and she would say, What, and leave our friends behind? Im not talking about going a long way away, just up there to the top of the cliff, Id tell her. No, shed say, this is where your father and your two brothers and your sister died and this is where Im going to die, thats the way its meant to be.

Up there at the top of the cliffs you can look across the water and sometimes see the little boats out on the waves, folk from Croval and from the other places up and down the coast and you can also look further across the water and see the dark shape of the land stretching away to the North. Ian Macleod says were looking up to Sutherland that way, but Ive never been up there of course. There are people in these parts called Sutherland, and some of them came from up that way, years ago.

Do you never fancy getting away, Hugh? Ian said to me one day. Do you not fancy seeing the world?

And I suppose thats why Im writing all this down because the answer is yes I do, thats the thing about it, yes I really do, especially now.

Robert Vass, my friend

Robert is the same age as me more or less. He has a mother and father and six brothers and sisters, all of them younger than him. Like us, they have a house at the edge of Croval but its at the sea edge, if you see what I mean, right across at the west end of the bay, up against the cliff at that side. Like us, they have a cow that scrapes about on the wee bit of grass between the back of their croft and the stone wall behind that. Like ours, their cow is awful scraggy and hardly produces any milk at all.

Theyre not really crofts, my mother says, but thats what everyone calls them here. My mother tells me a croft really has a bit more land round about it and peat to cut and a cow that can grow fat and be full of milk. She says they only call them crofts down in Croval because it reminds the older ones of their time in Strathgarrick. She says its an insult to call the houses we live in crofts. She says we should call them bruchlags which is the Gaelic for a dirty wee hovel. She says we should never forget what Killarnoch did and we should never forgive. Shes thinking of her husband, my father, and of the two boys that drowned, my brothers and of the sister that died of some illness she might never have got if shed been in the healthy air of Strathgarrick instead of the rotting seaweed stink of Croval. Thats what my mother says.

Ian says, Well, she has a point, she has a good point. What are you going to do about it?

Robert is small and dark and shy. Although hes the oldest in his family I think he gets bullied by his sisters. They are bossy and always telling him what to do. Four sisters and two brothers. The oldest sister is sixteen and the youngest brother is just four. Ive known Robert all his life and he is my best friend, I think, though of course Callum is always part of the three of us. Roberts clever and thoughtful and says things that make you stop and see everything in a different way sometimes. Ian likes Robert. He says Robert is one of Gods own. I suppose we all are really. Ian and Robert can have conversations about the Bible because Robert reads it. His family are all like that, never missing church for whatever reason and reading the Bible every evening. But his father, also Robert, says that Ian MacLeod is the wrong person for Croval. Too caught up with his southern ideas and not really understanding what its like for us living here in the North. He says we need another minister and I know he once went away to Buckie to speak to someone there about it. He walked twenty four miles there and then twenty four miles back to speak to someone in the church there about Ian MacLeod. So Robert told me. Ian Macleod knows about this and just laughed about it. He said, The forces of darkness are all around us and weve to look very close to know who is the dark and who is the light. Robert thinks that theres evil everywhere in the world, he says its in the Bible, you only have

21

to read it to see.

Ian Macleod says, Why not look for the good in the world? Robert says, Isnt it better to be on the watch for the devil? Ian says, Well, I can be as pessimistic as the next man, but Ive decided not to be.

Thats one of the reasons why hes unpopular. The older folk in Croval like a minister thats reminding them about hell and damnation. They like to know that theres a punishment waiting somewhere for the people who have done them down for so many years, Killarnoch and the men that worked for him and gave them the rotten wood that they were meant to build their first boats with in 1820 and also anyone they think might have taken a lobster from a pot that they set, but mainly Killarnoch.

Down at the Carcair Ive heard them all talking about him, through the air thick with pipe smoke. Roberts father, Robert, once said, They knew fine what they were doing. We were meant to die in those boats. Old Archie Macrae said, Aye, and theyll be paying the price in the end, the bastards.[4] When they marched us down here, Robert replied, they knew fine they were sending us to our deaths. Someone else called out, Of course they did. That was the whole point of it, to save money for Killarnoch. Yes, shouts someone else, once were all dead therell be no need to keep Croval up and the crofts will fall to ruin and the sheep will graze on our graves as they do in Strathgarrick.

And so on. Soon theres just a noise of shouting and agreeing and swearing and drinking and this goes on for an hour or two then they all stagger off home and tell their wives theyve been working on the nets. It all seems very stupid to me. For one thing, arent they all still alive? So if Killarnochs plan had been to kill them it hasnt turned out very well for him. There

---

4   Hugh used the form "B**********" but I have restored the expletives that Hugh originally intended. He is not consistent in this, as in many matters. – RM

are more people living in Croval than ever. And anyway, whats the point in shouting about the past like that? Nothing can change it, thats what I think. I learned that lesson at home in my mothers silence and the ghosts that hang around the dark walls of the croft. You cant change the past and the only thing you might be able to do is get away from it but I never see any of those old men shifting their scrawny backsides.

I was saying about Robert. The thing is, if I was to tell him, The old ones are talking nonsense, hed look at me and say, Ah well, but at least its true nonsense. Thats the sort of thing he would say. If you ever suggest something to Robert, like swimming off the jetty on a hot summer day, hell have to think about it for maybe half an hour before hell agree and by the time he does agree there will be a cloud across the sun and you wont feel like it any more. Hes got these deep dark eyes and pointed features, a sharp nose and chin and his usual expression is a frown, not because hes angry or worried but because hes thinking all the time. And once he knows his mind, well, thats him.

He is my friend though, him and Callum. I cant imagine doing anything without those two, and if I agree with what Ian MacLeod says then Robert and Callum will have to be part of it too. If not, Im not going.

Callum Ross, my friend

Im related to Callum. My fathers brother Michael married Catherine Swanson and her sister married James Ross, who isnt related to us as far as I know. So my Uncle Michaels wifes sister had only one child and that was Callum. Theres a lot of ways that people in Croval are related to each other and its sometimes hard to work out whos who. Ian MacLeod once upset everyone, not long after he came here, by saying that a place that didnt look outward was like a rabbits warren but I think people took it to heart because they knew themselves that what he was saying had a ring of truth about it. Actually he was doing a sermon about Sodom and Gomorrah and the punishment that came to those places when the Lord became angry and I dont think he was speaking about Croval at all. If the folk that didnt like what he was saying had looked a bit deeper then theyd have seen that he was really talking about each one of us not the whole lot of us. If we dont look outward, thats what he meant, if *each* of us doesnt. Anyway it was just another thing that turned people against him. That was only a few weeks after he came, as I said, and theres been plenty more things since then. No wonder hes wanting to leave.

Callum is very different from Robert. Hes tall for a start and he has sandy yellow coloured hair that grows really straight unlike Roberts dark hair which has a curl in it. Callum is talkative where Robert is silent. Hes good looking, better than Robert or me, and the girls like him much more than they like us. He can sometimes do quite stupid things. For example, and this is the thing I have to write down, one time we climbed up to the top of the cliff, up all the rock steps.

It was a rainy summer day, just last summer, though it seems like yesterday. It was a Sunday because none of the boats were out and when we got to the top we could see them all tied up by the jetty or else pulled up on to the stony beach, lying half over on their sides the way they do. We must have been to church, though I dont remember that. We went up to the top because Callum suggested it and when Callum says he wants to do something its usually best just to go along with him because he can get annoyed if he doesnt get his own way. But its funny, even when hes annoyed at you theres something about him that you like. One minute hes telling you off for something, even though hes just the same age as you, and the next minute hes giving you that big smile as if it was all just a joke and you forget about the bad mood he was in a minute before.

So there we were up on the top of the cliff and we were

looking for birds nests in the pine trees that grow up there, climbing up, daring each other to go higher and higher until our clothes were all sticky and smelling of the pine needles and our hands all scratched and coming up in red bumps the way they do with pine trees. Then Callum was bored with this so we had to stop. He said we werent children any more, so why were we climbing trees? and neither Robert nor me said anything about how it was him whod suggested it in the first place. He wandered over to the top of the cliff, a bit away from the place where the steps climbed up. Come here, he said. We went over. I bet, he said, you cant hit John MacDonalds boat from here with a stone.

The boat looked small, a long way down below us but the way we were so high above it I thought maybe if I threw a stone out as hard as I could then maybe it would somehow manage to reach the red boat half tipped over on its side. So I threw a wee stone as hard as I could but it didnt get anywhere near, didnt even reach the edge of Croval, way down below us. Robert wouldnt do it at all, he told us, after thinking for a minute. He said, If I throw a stone and while its in the air someone comes out of their croft then I could hit them. Callum said, Whos going to come out of their croft? Its Sunday.

But Robert just said no and wandered over towards the top of the steps saying he was off back down. Callum said hed do it, did I bet him? I knew it was impossible because Id thrown my stone as hard as I could, a good throw, and hadnt got anywhere near it and even though Callum was a bit bigger and stronger than me it couldnt be done. So I bet him that he couldnt do it. The bet was that if he hit it I had to give him this bottle that Id found washed up on the beach a while before. It was made of deep blue glass and it looked really old. It had no value but Callum liked that sort of thing. If he missed the boat he was to give me the knife he used for whittling, a better knife than I had. We shook hands on it. A promise tying us together.

He walked a few yards away from me along the edge of the cliff and sat down on a wee boulder that was a foot or two away from the edge. Ive always been a bit wary of being near the edge of the cliff but Callum is the kind of boy that nothing scares. Next thing he was up on his feet and pushing at this boulder hed been sitting on. What are you doing? I asked him. He said, Im lining it up.

Then with a heave and a grunt of air out of him, he pushed the thing over the edge of the cliff. I was almost too scared to go and look but I did. I missed the first part of its fall but I got to the edge just in time to see it bounce near the bottom of the cliff and leap on towards the house of old Mary Vass, whose husband died years and years ago and whose daughter up and left, so its said, and went to get married to a man somewhere along the coast. There werent too many houses at this end of Croval. I was right at the edge, forgetting the drop at my feet, my heart pounding, and then it seemed to stop when I saw Mary herself step out of her croft and reach her arms up towards the sky, stretching.

The boulder missed the house by not very much and caught Mary a glancing blow and threw her over aganst the white wall of her croft and on to the ground, then it struck another rock and bounced off to the side. It was still taking big jumps and we could hear the noise of it hitting even up where we were. The folk in their crofts must have wondered what on earth it was. Then it was rolling and when it stopped it was right at the edge of the sea with the waves splashing up against it. It had missed McDonalds boat by miles.

I was just standing, staring, looking down at Mary lying by her croft. It must have killed her, I was thinking and I will always remember that thought and how it felt in my stomach. But then I saw her moving a bit, scrabbling with her hands to push herself up, her legs flat on the ground. Even up where we were I could hear her calling out in her thin old voice.

I had to swallow hard because I thought I was going to be sick. I moved away sharp from the edge of the cliff, so I could not be seen from Croval. It was as if the rock had risen through the air and entered into me and settled into my heart, a weight I cant lose. I had nothing to say for a minute or two.

Callum said, Come on, wed better stay up here for a while because if we get seen on the steps just now theyll work out it was us. I said, What do you mean *us?* It was you that did it. He said, Well maybe nobody saw us anyway. Shell be all right, it just skiffed her. And he wandered off towards the woods. Robert had already gone back down and I could see him just near the bottom of the steps looking back up at me as if he was trying to work out what had happened. I looked over at Callum but hed gone into the woods and no matter how hard I peered I couldnt see him amongst the rainy shadows. I went in after him, into the darkness.

As a matter of fact so far nobody has ever said anything to us about it at all.

It turned out that Mary Vass had heard a rock come past her house one evening a day or two before and since then shed been worried there was a bigger rock fall to come. Shed told folk about this so thats what they decided it was. Some of the older ones went and stood near the rock at the edge of the sea later that Sunday and looked up at the cliff and grumbled about the dangerous place Killarnoch had sent them to live.

.So that was that day.

Mary herself had a broken leg and a broken hip and something got damaged inside her and she was in her bed for three weeks before she took a bad fever and it wasnt long after that she died. I know Callum didnt mean for that to happen but thats what did happen. That's the truth of it. For months after whenever I heard a knock at the croft door I was sure it would be someone coming to tell me they knew about us and the rock. But it never was, and I never had to tell anyone about what Callum had done. But the weight stayed in my heart and it still lies there.

Old Mary Vass was buried and no one shed too many tears at her graveside because to tell the truth she was an argumentative old bism that nobody liked much, and probably the people who felt worst as they lowered her down were me and Callum, though I dont know really what Callum thinks about anything. We never said to Robert what had happened exactly and thats another thing I feel bad about but Callum said we couldnt tell anyone in case anyone got the wrong idea and didnt understand it was a proper accident, the rock falling, and anyway, she might have got the fever that killed her even without the stone hitting her because wasnt she old in any case? Thats what he said, and as I mentioned, it is always best not to argue with Callum, because he can make your life unpleasant if you do.

So that all blew over like a summer storm. And Callum never gave me the knife like he was meant to and about three days later we had another bet about two boats which were heading in to the jetty and which one would get there first and I lost so he got the thick glass bottle in any case. And so thats Callum. One of my two best friends, and the one that has made me feel that it would be best to get away from here, far away, so I dont have to think about what he did all the time when I look over to the side and see the croft of old Mary Vass, which has a family MacDonald living in it now.

Ian Macleod, minister

Ive told you a good bit about him already so I dont need so much here. He is in his sixties, as I said, and he has white hair and he wears these little spectacles when he is reading. Hell wear them in the pulpit when he is doing his sermons and then hell pause and look up at the folk in the church and hell slowly take his spectacles off and you know that some big part of the sermon is coming up.

Theres no way round it, he is quite fat. There arent very many fat people in Croval because there isnt much food to go round. Sometimes the old men, once they get past the age for going out in their boats day in day out and take to just sitting in the Carcair drinking and telling their stories, begin to get rounder in their bellies but Ian Macleod has the kind of fatness that has to do with too much food and too much red wine. The tinker MacPhee always makes the manse the first house he stops at when he climbs down the steps with his bags of stuff for Croval. Folk say theres always wine for the minister and other fancy foods. Uncle Michael tells me Ian Macleod gets special cheese brought from Edinburgh because the cheese we make in Croval isnt good enough for him. True enough when we go to see him there quite often is a glass of wine sitting beside him when he speaks to us. I dont suppose it really does any harm.

Im not sure how we ended up going up there to the manse so much. It just sort of happened. When I say the manse I really dont mean that its any big fancy building. Its more or less just like our houses but bigger, and built as solid as anything. But its not fancy inside. Killarnoch, it seems, wanted there to be a church and a manse in Croval so we wouldnt forget God in our new home but the older folks say he wasnt going to be spending too much money making sure of it. And he only built it to stop his wife getting on at him, weve to remember.

We do go to church of course, because everyone does. And then one Sunday we found ourselves, Callum, Robert and me, just walking slowly away from the church when we heard this shout behind us. This was before the rock. It was Ian Macleod shouting on us and he called us to wait. Then he talked to us for a while. I cant remember the exact things we talked about but I do remember this question he asked us. Whats it like for a young man here in Croval?

So we were quite pleased because we were just seventeen, just starting off as men really, and nobody else in Croval had bothered much to ask us what we thought about things.

Later on I remember I told my mother that wed been talking to Ian Macleod. She was churning up butter and she said, sort of suspiciously, And what was he wanting to talk to you about? And this is how the conversation went then.

He was asking us how we felt about Croval.

And what did you tell him?

We said it was full of old folk that never bothered with us much.

Oh and is it now?

Yes, thats what we think.

Is that so?

Its just what we think. We dont mean any harm by it. But the older ones never really speak to us about anything.

And what does your precious Mr Macleod want to do about it?

I didnt have any answer to her last question. Not then. And I knew there was no point in speaking to her any more about it then, because of the way she said, *your precious Mr Macleod*.

Its easier to write out the conversations like that with a line to each person, I think. Ian showed me the way it is in the books he reads out to us and sometimes there are pages and pages of people speaking to each other and its all jumbled together and that makes it complicated, I think. So maybe Ill do it this way, with a line for each person. It might be wrong but well, does it matter?

But the thing is that Mr MacLeod does have an idea about what to do about things. And now that Ive told you about the main people in the story so far and about the setting, which is Croval, I can now start with the story itself that is beginning to happen. Thats the way it feels to me, that my life has just been going along so far but now all of a sudden theres something else to think about because of whats happened and whats been said, and this something has come partly from Ian Macleod and now we have a big decision to make and the only person that can make that decision is me.

The Story itself

Theres one thing I want to write down here and that is that Im not always going to describe what Im thinking and feeling. Ill say what happens.

As I said before, we got into the habit of going up to the manse and sitting and talking with the Reverend Macleod which was his proper title but we just called him Ian. He said he was interested in finding out the differences between our little Croval and the last place he was minister at, which was a place called Leverburn near Edinburgh. He said that people there were working in manufactures and some of them in cotton mills. We asked him if the people there were as poor as us.

As poor and poorer, but in a different way, he said and we werent too sure what that meant.

But what I was saying was that in the end Ian wanted me to start writing things down. I asked him if he wanted to read things I wrote down and he said no, it was for my own good that I should write things down. To tell my story, not that Ive had much of one so far. But what worries me is that one day hell want to see what Ive written or else my mother will ask someone who can read to read out my pages to her. So Im having to be a bit careful about what Im writing. I have to put some of my thoughts so that the story makes sense but Im being a bit careful not to put things that might say things about me that I dont want to say in case they end up being read to the person Im writing about.

For example, theres one old man in the Carcair and all he does is swear and spit out yellow stuff on the earth floor by his feet and pick on the younger ones that go in. Well, I hate him but I cant say that in here in case it gets read out to him somehow. You have to be careful about that sort of thing. And

Callum wouldnt want to see that Ive told about what really happened to Mary Vass. Maybe I should throw some of those pages away, or write them again, but differently.

Weve got tired of going to the Carcair with its old men repeating their old arguments day after day, night after night. It all goes back always to the times when they were all moved down from Strathgarrick. They can never get used to the idea that they are in Croval now until the day they die. So the words they say are the same all the time, they never change. I think Robert doesnt mind it as much as Callum and me. We go down there in the evening, maybe after weve been out on the boat, just because sometimes you feel theres nothing else to do in Croval. Well there isnt. The Carcair is the only place, especially on wet nights or on nights when the wind is blowing the spray up over the crofts so you can hardly bear to be outside. Its the Carcair or its home on those nights and sometimes I dont want to be at home with my mother sitting so silent and bitter towards everything.

Callum sometimes joins in the conversations at the Carcair but Robert and me just sit quietly at the edge of the group. The whisky gets passed round, and it doesnt matter how old you are. This is not bought whisky from MacPhee. Its the whisky that the old men make in the crofts with their stills. You arent supposed to but nobody ever checks anything like that. There are at least a dozen stills in Croval and nobody is ever caught or ever gets into trouble with anyone. The whisky is raw and has no taste apart from the taste of being burnt in the throat with a hot stick. There are no cups to drink out of, you take your drink from the pot that the whisky comes in. Someone will slam it down on the old wooden table in front of you, wiping their mouth and you are meant to take a drink. Sometimes I just lift it to my lips and put it down again. I take the back of my hand against my mouth as if Ive had a good swig of the stuff, but if Im telling the truth it is horrible. I think Robert is the same. Callum will drink it though, until he gets drunk and a bit argumentative. Most of the talk will be in Gaelic but English, English, English is the way we should be talking now so thats what Ive written down in this.

Callum would be saying, But youre all talking as if it was perfect up in Strathgarrick.

And what would you know? You werent even born then, Callum Ross.

Callum would carry on with, And the next minute youre telling stories about the bad winters up in the strath and the way that there was nothing to eat and the time you were all so hungry one February you were eating the grass and the nettles made into soup.

Our history, someone would shout at him. That was the way of our people! Your people too. It was our choice to live our lives like that, not to be forced down here to turn into fishermen. He would hurl the last word out like a swear.

And how was it your choice in Strathgarrick? Didnt Killarnoch own you as much up there as he does down here? It wasnt heaven up there, any more than it is here.

Its the drink talking! an old man would roar at him. You dont know what youre saying. Young boys and the drink! It was our homes. These arent our homes. This is just where we stay now.

Well, get out then, says Callum, his face burning with the whisky and with anger. Go somewhere else. If you dont like it here go somewhere else!

At this point the old faces would go sad and quiet. Ah, where would we go? Where would we be going now? Where is there but this godforsaken place?

Im writing that down because it tells you a bit about Callum and how he already had it in his head that he couldnt stay in Croval all his life, even before what happened with Mary Vass. And he wasnt just thinking about going along to the next place either.

At low tide you can walk out to the edge of the bay and then you can pick your way over the slippery seaweed on the rocks at the headland to the east and once you are past that the cliffs fall back inland a bit along a rocky stretch and then about two miles further along that way you come to the next place which is called Craigtore, which is the name Killarnoch had given to that collection of crofts, similar to ours in every way, except their jetty isnt as good as ours. They have a smaller church and no manse because Ian MacLeod has to go and do sermons there too, so they dont have a minister of their own. He doesnt go along the more dangerous shore way. Hell go up the steps to the top and a man is always waiting for him there with a horse that has been sent by Killarnoch every Sunday and also on Tuesdays. Ian says that Killarnoch is awful concerned to make sure that God stays in the lives of his people or at least his wife is.

Craigtore is a place we sometimes go to, the three of us. We know some people there and there are different girls there, girls like Jane Mackenzie, Elizabeth Ross, Rachael Sutherland and Ruth MacKay. All these girls, about our age, are really what Callum is particularly interested in, always chasing the girls. But truth be told Craigtore is more or less exactly the same as Croval, apart from the jetty, except it doesnt have the big cliff just behind it. Their place slopes away into the land a lot more slowly and there is even soil good enough to grow oats on and barley which some of them do. It feels like a slower and a brighter place than Croval, which is always in the shadow of the cliffs and the waves and where the people are always hurrying around to get the boats ready or to mend the nets or whatever it is that they are doing. In Craigtore there are men who dont go out to the sea at all, but just work the land, like on a proper croft, as the old Croval men sometimes say with a mixture of admiration and jealous spite.

But Callum isnt interested in going along the coast to another place which is like our own the way the jetty reflected in the sea is the same as our jetty but not as good.[5] So when Ian Macleod brought out this new book that hed got one evening and started to read from it, Callum was paying much more attention than he usually did.

Why does Callum like Ian Macleod? Im not even sure that he does. But going up there to the manse makes Callum feel that hes doing something that the older folk would disapprove of and hes always been like that. When he was a little boy he was always bad when the schoolmaster would come each weekday morning. He would be at Craigtore in the afternoons. Hed been sent, of course, by Killarnoch to make us better people. He was a thin man of about thirty five or forty and he stunk of sweat. I dont think he liked what he was doing because he never seemed very enthusiastic. Probably because we werent. But the worst of all was Callum. Hed shout bad things out when that Mr Ferguson was trying to teach us about sums or countries of the world or whatever. He never taught us anything worth knowing. Even the English he taught us was boring and he told us stories about forests and donkeys and once he told us a story that started with a shipwreck and that was the last thing any of the children wanted to hear with their fathers out on the dark sea. I know Mr Ferguson would complain to our parents about us but nobody seemed to mind much because our mothers mainly saw the morning school lessons as a way of getting us out from the croft for a while.

The worst thing Callum ever did to him was when one

_____

5   This sentence originally read "But Callum isnt interested in going along the coast to another place which is just like our own place." The final version, with the simile in place, was the result of much tentative inking in and scoring out. I think we can see here the beginning of the development of Hugh's writing style, more in evidence as the account progresses. – RM

morning after the school lesson Mr Ferguson was coming out of the shed that was used for his teaching and as he walked out he turned round to say something to one of the wee girls about tomorrows lesson. Now Callum was not far away and when he saw Mr Ferguson begin to walk backwards like that, he nipped forward and crouched down on to his hands and knees just in his way so that Ferguson bumped the back of his legs against Callums hunched up back and then tumbled over on to the ground. The only thing he hurt was his pride and I dont think he had much of that in any case so it probably didnt matter really. We were maybe thirteen when this happened. I remember being a bit surprised, maybe even shocked that Callum would do that to an adult.

Well, he said, were just about finished with the stupid school anyway. What does it matter? Were more or less adults ourselves now. We just need to be a little bit older and we will be soon enough.

Thats Callum all over, always wanting to be something that he isnt yet, not quite. Like the way you tether your cow behind the croft and as soon as you do it walks right to the length of the rope and reaches for a thistle just out of its reach, even though theres plenty more thistles right round the stake youve tied her to.

I could tell you a hundred other things Callum did that show how he likes to annoy the older folk, like the time he climbed up on top of the Carcair and stuffed the chimney with moss and twigs so that they were just about choking with pipe smoke down there, but theres no need. Ive told you what hes like so I dont need to go on about it. And of course now hes done something much worse than any of these other things. Im not saying he killed Mary Vass because that wouldnt be completely right, but even so. Anyway, Im just trying to explain why he went up to Ians with us even though I dont think he was that keen on Ian. Partly he went because we did everything together,

Callum, Robert and me, but mainly because he knew folk would be whispering about us behind our backs and he liked that. Hes always liked being on the edge, and falling out with people. It makes being his friend a cross between a challenge and a game.

It started with just talking about things. Robert and Ian Macleod would speak about God and religion and why God let young boys drown at sea or let mothers babies die when they were just a few weeks old. That sort of thing. I sometimes would have something to say about these conversations but more often than not I would just let myself drift away in the warmth of the big fire in the proper fireplace that Ian has in the manse. Or I would stand and look at the books he has in the bookshelf of oak wood that runs along one wall of his main room. I counted them once and there were one hundred and twenty three. Then a few weeks later I counted them again and there were one hundred and thirty six. Thats the sort of person Ian is. And while Ian and Robert are talking about why God could let bad things happen, and could he not do something to stop them, Callum is as restless as anything. Hell be pacing up and down or looking out the small thick glass window, or picking up Ians ornaments and looking at them, putting them back down. I didnt even know the word ornament until wed been to Ians manse. They are things hes collected from his other churches before he came up to us and there are a right lot of them, all different sorts. One is a piece of black coal that hes painted over with boat varnish so that it glistens and he says it reminds him of the tough strong men that work underground with the dust in their lungs and black on their faces still when they come meekly into church on a Sunday. Callum particularly likes that bit of coal and often sits with it in his hands.

Ian realised that Callum wasnt paying particular attention and asked him about it one evening. Hed been reading to us a bit from the Bible, I remember, one of his favourite bits that went *If a man vow a vow unto the Lord or swear an oath to bind his soul with a bond, he shall not break his word, he shall do according to all that proceedeth out of his mouth.*[6] When he looked up Callum was sitting in his soft armchair with his feet up over the arm, picking at the stitching on the material.

Whats wrong, Callum? Ian said.

Nothing.

Does the Good Book bore you?

No, said Callum and then he hesitated. Well, yes it does. I suppose it does.

What book would you like to hear from?

Callum swung his legs down off the arm of the chair and got up, walking over to the window then back to Ian as he talked. How do I know? I havent read any books so how would I know what book? But the Bible, I think Ive heard it all by now and it doesnt

Ian interrupted him, Excite you?

Callum nodded but didnt say anything.

It doesnt excite you. Well, I can assure you that you havent heard it all, and I can assure you that there is plenty in the Bible that is exciting, though perhaps not in the way that you would like. But I understand you are looking for something more. Perhaps I could read you from some other volume in my collection. He straightened his arm out and pointed to his row of books.

Callum said, You choose something that you think would suit someone like me.

Ian asked him, And what is someone like you like?

Wanting to hear about some other kind of life. Some other story but not one thats telling you how to live your life all the time. Im fed full of rules and what happens when you break them. Its all you hear, at home, in church, in the Carcair. Do this, dont do this. Dont speak, youre too young.

---

6   Numbers Chapter 30 Verse 2. – RM

Id heard it all before of course, and so had Robert, but Ian listened to him as if it was a new idea that hed never come across before. The idea that someone young could be tired of life.

I can read to you from other kinds of books, he said. Novels. Made up tales of excitement.

And he told us about Walter Scott and a French writer whose name began with an S, but I cant remember it, and other writers and after that he would read to us from these books and Callum liked them better. My favourite was the story about the old Spanish knight and his man who went along beside him, but Callum couldnt hear enough by this Walter Scott. When I asked him why he liked that so much he said, Because its believable.

So he was wanting to hear about another life that was only a bit different from the one we were living, but I liked the old man and the servant with the donkey and the strange things they got up to in that foreign land, though I will admit this Walter Scott could tell a good story too.

One night Ian said, These tales, they can take you away from your world. But theres another way of doing that.

What do you mean?

And he went to the shelf and pulled out this new book that hed got, sent to him from Edinburgh, he said. It was called *The Emigrants Guide to North America* and it was written by a man called Robert MacDougall. Right away Callum wanted to hear all about it. It was a book in Gaelic but Ian translated it for us into English, because, as he keeps saying, English, English, English is the only way. It is a short book and he read the whole thing to us in a couple of evenings. After the first evening I think we could all hardly wait for the next night to hear the rest, because it seemed to have an answer for us, especially me and Callum.

This man MacDougall had done all the things he described, sailed off to this country on the other side of the world. Of course wed heard of America before, because Mr Ferguson had told us about it in those boring school days but it had never meant very much to us then. Now, it seemed like a land of gold that we might imagine going to. We were ready to hear about it, just then. Part of it was the way Ian read it out.

But most of it had to do with the MacDougall man that wrote it, because he made it sound like a real thing, something you might just do one day. Like getting up in the morning, going down to the jetty, fixing the nets, milking the cow, arguing with your mother, feeding the chickens, sailing to America.

In the book MacDougall gives you advice about what to do if you want to go to America. He tells you all about the things you should take with you and the things you shouldnt bother taking with you that you might have thought you should take with you. He tells you about how much you should expect to pay if you go. About all the different places with their strange names like Anticosti Island, Goderich, Montreal. The different animals you will find there and the insects that you have to watch out for in case they go and bite you and give you some disease. He tells you about the strange people that live there, the Indians. He describes what they wear and the way they hide in a hollowed out tree to surprise and kill a deer. They tie their babies up in strips of cloth and hang them from a tree while the mothers work all day and the babies never cry at all, they just watch whats happening and learn about life. The women do all the work and the men just carry their spears and their tomahawks which is like our Gaelic word tuagh-bheag. The Indians hair is blacker than a ravens wing, says MacDougall, his eyes are blue-black like berries and they walk with backs as straight as a rod of yew-wood, like the yew tree that Killarnoch planted fully grown beside the manse. It turns out that the Indian language is very like Gaelic and maybe these Indians and us, a long time ago, had the same language and maybe we were once the same people, sort of, says MacDougall.

Even Callum sat still and listened to this new book, and

Roberts eyes were as dark as ever and looking at this far away land where nothing was the same as Croval, nothing at all.

That night I decided I would speak to my mother about it. She was sewing a skirt of hers that had more old patches than new cloth in it, and the lamp made the shadow of her hand move big against the wall.

Have you ever heard about America? I asked her.

Of course I have, she said to me. Isnt that where all the people go who are too scared to stay here and work hard?

What do you mean?

They think they can go over there and scatter a few dry seeds on the bare earth and grow a forest of corn. She tugged away with her thread. They think its the promised land theyre going to.

Maybe it is, I said.

She snorted. How can it be? There is no promised land in this life. If they can get so rich in this America why do none of them come back and show us their riches?

But people do go, I said, and they do come back, and I told her all about the book Ian had read to us. This Robert MacDougalls been and he came back and he explains to you how to make a life out there, I told her.

Oh does he now, she said. And do people buy this book?

Of course they do. Ian Macleod has bought it.

And did he write this book so that people would buy it?

Of course.

And does he get money when people buy his book?

I thought about that. I suppose he does, I said. Im not sure. I can ask Ian about that.

And would people buy a book that told them how bad it was in America, how it was just the same as here, how you still have to work and work until you cant do anything but sleep? Would they? So why do you think he writes a book like that? Youre a fool, Hugh, she told me.

I was angry with her then so I got up and went out of the croft and walked down through the dark of Croval and sat on the edge of the jetty and looked out at the cold water stretching away in the moonlight.

Then in the days after that we spoke about America a lot. It had sparked something in us, started a kind of fire[7]. And when we spoke to other people about it, on the boats, in the Carcair, down at the jetty, it seemed everyone had an opinion about America but none of them seemed to agree with us, or even each other.

I think the word America has a special meaning for everyone. If you say the word it sets off a picture in someones head. Its like the stories that Ian reads to us. I remember the one that begins with these lines

It was early on a fine summers day, near the end of the eighteenth century, when a young man, of genteel appearance, journeying towards the north-east of Scotland

I love that. I would get Ian to read it out again and again because right away it put a picture into my head of this young man setting off on some journey that would change his life and in the picture that came into your head were all the questions about what would happen to him and who he would meet on his journey.

So this word, *America,* has the same power as the beginning of a story for everyone. Some people see a picture of poverty and hardship, some see a picture of savage Indians ready to spear you to death, some see a storm and drownings at sea, some see dark forests that rise up above you like ghosts at night.

Ian said that all these pictures I told him about were all false because none of the Croval people have been there. He said hardly anyone went to America from our side of Scotland but from the other side, the western side, thousands had gone.

---

7   Again, the crossings out and rewriting. – RM

He said anyone that went now would meet more Highlanders than Indians.

Then we heard that some people had gone from Craigtore. This was about the time that there was sickness in Croval and people began to cry louder in their disapproval of Ian MacLeod. It was some illness that gave people very loose bowels and stomach sickness. Two old women and red-haired Roderick Mackenzie, who was only about forty years old, died from it. People were scared because it seemed that every day someone else would have the illness. There was a smell hanging about Croval at that time. It was a hot time, with no wind, the start of May, not that far off a year since the rock that killed Mary Vass, a long year, a May with a sour stench. You could smell the waste and the stink of it made you want to be sick yourself and if you were you couldnt help wondering if you had the illness too.

At that time the men were always wanting to go out in the boats whatever the sea was like because with the wind in your face and the salty taste on your lips you felt cleaner than you did in Croval. So this one day, the three of us took out Alasdairs boat, just the three of us because Alasdair himself was down with the sickness and he could hardly move from his croft, but he said to us, when we stood at the edge of the door to his croft, to take the boat if we wanted. It was good that he trusted us but Im not sure if he should have because none of us were that careful with the way we went out to sea, being young. Robert was the most careful and you can tell already who was the least. As I said, Callum had his own boat too, well it was his fathers, but hed rather borrow someone elses. Alasdair is a friend of Uncle Michaels.

There was a high wind out of the west that day and by the time we got clear of the arms of the cliff out into the open sea it was all I could do to hold the little boat in one place with the oars without being blown away to the east. There was a little sail you could put up but the wind was so high it would have been dangerous to try to do anything with it, especially for us, not with very much experience of using the sail. We didnt have any fishing things with us because wed only wanted to get away from Croval for a little while. The muscles in my arms were hurting with the strain of it and as the wind picked up even more Callum took one oar and I took the other and the two of us strained to move the boat westward but it was no use, we were just getting blown back.

Its no use, said Callum and he had to shout because the noise of the wind and the waves against the wood of the boat made it hard to hear. The only sea sound that wasnt there that day was the crying of seagulls because there were no seagulls up because it was too windy for them. They were on the rocks by the shore, watching us. Robert was sitting huddled down in the bow of the boat looking kind of frightened.

Well just go back, I yelled. Wed be as well just going back.

So we tried that but wed already drifted east of the entrance into Croval bay and we couldnt get back into it. So we decided to just let the wind help us and we ran down to Craigtore in front of the wind and just used the oars to help us to steer into shore. We got the boat alongside their untidy little stone jetty and tied it up and managed to climb up and on to dry land. Robert was sick straight away into the heaving water.

There was a man watching us from further along the shore. He was James Hunter and we knew him from other times when wed been in Craigtore because Callum likes his daughter Mhorag which means that James Hunter doesnt like Callum. Mhorag is just fourteen but she looks older than that. Hunter has brown hair and red skin as if hes rubbed sand into it and this is because he likes his dram.

He came marching over to us, carrying a sack in his right hand. Hed been down at the waters edge collecting things that had been washed up. On stormy windy days you can find lots

44

of strange things that the sea throws up. One time I found this funny piece of bone that had drawings all over it of ships and fish and little men and a whale. It was scratched in with some kind of ink. I dont know what it was for and I dont have it now because I gave it to Callum to look at once and he took it away and swapped it with MacPhee the tink for a bottle of cheap whisky which we drank one night in Robertsons cave which is near the south edge of the cliff headland and is named after a man called Roderick Robertson who lived there with his dog for a few months at the time when the people came down from Strathgarrick to Croval and all the houses werent ready in time. We often used to go there and Callum would sometimes take girls there too and do things.

Hunter came marching up and shouted, Whats wrong with him?

Seasick, laughed Callum. He cant take it. Robert gave him an annoyed look, wiping his hand over his mouth as he bent down at the side of the jetty.

Has he got that Croval sickness? asked Hunter, getting closer. Weve heard all about it. When he got to about twenty yards away he stopped as if he didnt want to get any closer.

No, I said to him, still speaking loudly over the wind, theres nothing wrong with him that a few minutes on steady land wont sort.

You cant be taking that sickness to Craigtore, said Hunter. Weve heard that theres folk dead of it in Croval. Is that right?

Mary MacIntosh, said Callum because by that time she was the only one whod died though as I said there were two others later.

Mary McIntosh? Dead?

Yes, said Callum. But she was eighty three or eighty four and she wasnt very well anyway. Old women just die sometimes.

I looked at him sideways.

Even so, said Hunter. Dont be taking your Croval sickness

here. We cant lose any more people what with that lot going off to Thurso to get passage to America.

So this was the first wed heard of it. Thurso is a town far away up the coast to the north and it would take a long time to get there by horse and cart. And a good bit of money. Hunter told us we had to just wait at the jetty until the wind died down which it did quite soon after and we were able to get back to Croval, talking all the time we rowed about these people who had made the step and headed off to the promised land, as my mother would say. Eight of them had gone, Hunter had told us, some of the men like Matthew Sinclair, Elizabeth Ross, Rachael and some of the other people about that age. It was a shock that they were all off. Callum said that it would have been Matthew Sinclair that was behind it and that seemed likely enough because he had come to Craigtore a couple of years ago from up the coast in Sutherland when their boat had sprung a leak and theyd pulled in at Craigtore and hed ended up staying. Hed have been behind it, friendly as he was with Elizabeth, Rachael and their group, a little older than them but young in the way he thought about things, said Ian once, ready to take a chance.

We had blisters on our hands by the time we got back into Croval. We felt tired like wed been rowing all day and all wed done was go to the next place and back.

That night in bed I was thinking about nothing else but America and following that Craigtore group away across the sea. When the sun is so bright that even if you close your eyes, lying back on the heather, you still see the light through your eyelids, you feel as if the sun is getting right inside you. Thats what it was like and it felt as if America was flowing through my head so that I couldnt keep my eyes shut all night. I was thinking about a journey up to Thurso, about a boat carrying the girls we knew drifting across the sea, about a new land and new things happening and old things being left behind.

The thing is that I dont really know what it is thats across there. And I know that its a big boat that they get to go across to America, because Ians told me about it, but all I had in my head that night was an idea of Callum and Robert and me with our hands covered in blisters and bleeding, rowing and rowing to get to the other side of the world. I knew I had to speak to Ian Macleod and I was up to the manse as soon as the sun rose and it was all right to get out of bed and pull on my clothes. My mother asked me where I was going so early and when I told her she said that the minister would be still lying in his bed, which was a common view of the older folks about Ian, that he was lazy by nature, which I knew was not the truth. So I didnt say anything to her and just went out and ran up the slope to the manse, banging on his door and shouting his name.

[8]Me – How easy is it to go to America?

Ian – Easy as finding money when you havent got any. Why are you so all of a sudden wanting to go to America?

Me – I dont know.

Here I told him all about our conversation with Hunter and Craigtore.

Me – And so it seems to me like a change.

Ian – It would be that all right. Would I be right if I tried to

---

8   The unusual style of this section is exactly as it appears in Hugh's pages. It is possible that he intended to write this segment up in the same manner as the other parts of this opening section of the narrative, some of which bear the signs of extensive reworking, and some of which give me the distinct impression of being copied out versions of earlier, lost pages. We will never know. I have resisted the temptation to "polish" here, though I will confess, guiltily, to attempting the task. The pages I produced, an unsatisfactory copy of Hugh's writing style, were quite rightly thrown in the fire and I have restricted myself here, and elsewhere, to much more minor alterations, designed to make things clearer. The style for setting out dialogue remained, as we shall see, one which appealed to Hugh. Perhaps he would have left it just like this, even if he *had* found time to revise these pages. – RM

guess what it is thats driving you on?

Me – No, theres nothing driving me on. Theres something pulling me on.

Ian – Driving, pulling. One way or the other, its taken hold of you like a sickness and maybe thats what it is. Theres a fever goes with the bowel sickness in Croval.

Me – Its not a fever. Im just thinking maybe theres a new life out there. Something different from all this.

Ian – My thoughts exactly.

Me – So should I go?

Ian – How could you go? Do you know how much it would be costing you? Its two or three pounds for the crossing and youd need money to buy things to take with you, like all the things that Mr MacDougall mentions in his book. Where would that come from? And youd need money when you were there to help to set you up.

Me – But youre always talking about it yourself. Youre the one reading from the *Emigrants Guide* to us.

Ian – And how does Callum think about all this? How does Robert think?

Me – Theyre like me, I think. Thinking about it all the time. Ive been thinking of nothing else since yesterday.

Ian – So Ive been talking about it and reading to you about it and now all of a sudden you cant stop thinking about it because of a bit of news from that man Hunter from Craigtore.

He was laughing at me when he said this which is what Ian sometimes does. I dont mind him doing that because I know hes a lot older than me and I know he knows a lot more about the world and the ways of the world than I do. And when he laughs theres no cruelty in it, not like the way some people laugh. And he doesnt know all about me anyway, about me and what I know about Callum and how we should really get away from here. I couldnt say that to him, though.

Me – I dont know. I think it just seems more real now. Now

that theyve actually gone, and them so nearby, or used to be.

Ian – And had you heard nothing of this before from the Craigtorers? No hint that they would be going?

Me – Nothing. Nothing at all. Nobody said anything to me about it.

Ian – Does that disappoint you?

I didnt answer this question because there were more important ones to be asking.

Me – What if we went?

Ian – What if you did?

Hes standing in front of me and hes looking at me as if the next thing I say will be the most important words I might ever say. Theres a story starting here, thats what I thought.

Ian – What if you did?

Me – Would you come with us? Me and Robert and Callum. The three of us and you.

And I could tell right away that this wasnt what he was expecting me to say. And I wasnt even expecting it myself. I knew that the three of us would be keen to go but it was only just at that moment that I think I realised that he was just the same, fed up and not belonging and trying to chase something that seemed a long way away.

Ian – Me?

Me – Callum, Robert, me and you? You could tell us what to do and read to us out of the MacDougall book. Youve seen more of the world.

Ian – What have I seen of the world?

He walked away over to the window. He laughed but it was a nervous laugh as if he wasnt sure what was going to be happening next and I do think that he was usually pretty sure about that.

Me – Edinburgh and all those places down south. The ladies that raise money for the ministers in America. The coal mines. The books in the libraries and the cities with big stone buildings.

Ian – Maybe I have. An old man like me?

And suddenly here was the chance to give Ian back the gift he had given us of taking us seriously.

Me – Nobody more so.

Ian – And the others? What are they saying about it? It cant be just because you say so. It would have to be all three of you otherwise it wouldnt work.

Me – The three of us.

But Id gone further than the three of us had talked about. I knew I would have to speak to them about it all later, and I did that and it was all right.

Ian – Ill think about it. Ill be thinking about it.

So thats when I left him standing looking out of the window out over the grey sea – went to speak to Callum and Robert – tried to speak to my mother about it all but her not listening to me – wrote down what happened because Ill forget the details – the Craigtore people all away and we can go after them – and will Ian come with us?

So this evening I met Callum coming up past the croft on the way to see Ian. Hed been at the Carcair and hed been drinking the whisky. I could smell it off him and see it in the way he was walking. The way people walk when theyre full of whisky, trying to be as careful with each step as they can be but each step looking like a mistake.

What are you doing? he asks me.

Im not doing anything, I tell him. Just sitting here and thinking about things.

I was sitting outside on the three legged stool that my mother sometimes sits on in the evening when you know its best not to speak to her. She was away to her bed. It was getting dark, late. You could just see the stars starting.

Thinking about what Id said, Callum goes, America?

America. I nodded. And other things.

Im off to speak to Ian.

About? America?

America and other things.

What other things?

Nothing special. Ill not say anything about Mary Vass, dont worry.

He came up close to me and leaned over. His hair and his eyes were close to me but it was his whisky breath that I noticed more than anything else. And I could smell the old mens pipe smoke on him too. And its funny but in that little moment before he spoke it was as if I was looking deep into him and this is what I saw – that one day years from now well all just be like the old Carcair men, drunk and useless, sitting with a pipe in one hand and a whisky bottle in the other, shouting about Killarnoch and the way we could have had such a better life if only if only if only. The smell on Callum was the smell of the future.

Theres a boat he said.

A boat?

Theres a boat sailing from Cromarty.

I stood up and he stumbled back a bit. I said, Sailing to America?

Yes. From Cromarty. The Lady Gray. Cromarty to Quebec.

I stared at him. Quebec. It had the sound of something else. I mean something I hadnt known before.

When?

June the fourth said Callum.

I worked it out. Two weeks.

Two weeks.

He put his hand on my shoulder. He said, Im going up to see Ian. He can get the money for the journey.

Two weeks? Why would he get the money for the journey? Why would he pay for us? Do you think he will?

Callum stepped back with an angry gesture of his arm, as if he would have hit me. He raised his voice. We can pay him back the money. When we get to America we can work and pay him back. MacDougall says in his book that there is so much money to make in the trees or with the fishing or something.

He says in his book that is hard work and many dont do well. Speak quietly. My mothers asleep and she doesnt like to be woken up.

I could feel my temper rising up from inside. I knew what Callum was saying was right but I wanted him to keep saying it so that the decision to go away wasnt mine alone. To go away and leave my mother sleeping by herself in her old bed. So I spoke sharply.

Callum, what do we know about going to America? Just what weve heard Ian reading out to us from that book. And arent there as many that fail out there as do well? And what about you with your whisky and the stupid things that you do.

Stupid things? He was whispering now, leaning close again, and his whisper sounded louder than his shout of earlier, because it was so angry. Stupid things? he said again.

Like pushing that rock down the cliff. That time you set fire to old Sinclairs clothes on his line. How would we do if thats the way youre going to be?

It has damn all to do with that, he hissed. Damn all.

And your blasphemy.

To hell with you, he said. Damn you to hell.

And we stood and glared at each other as the stars kept coming out in the thick blue sky up above. He was swaying and breathing hard through his nose and the whisky smell went away for a while. It was silent for a bit and then, because I cant help it and I cant stand a silence sometimes, I said

And what does Robert say about it?

About what?

About the boat thats sailing of course! What does he say about that? Is he wanting to go so soon?

So soon? How is it so soon? How many years have we been

stuck here listening to the old folk whining like a dog with a cut paw?

He was right, of course he was. So I said, It just seems so soon. Two weeks.

Robert will come.

What does he say?

Hell come.

You havent spoken to him yet, have you?

I said hell come. And I only spoke to you because you were sitting out here on your mothers stool.

So, I said. So its Ian that you have to see.

He threw up his hands. Of course its Ian I have to see! If we cant get the money then we cant go. If we can get the money we can go and then I can ask you and Robert what you think about it all.

I dont know. Its so soon.

He turned and stalked off. Then he looked back at me over his shoulder. Still whispering, but his voice carried through the quiet darkness, he said, Stay here if you want. Im going, if Ian will help. Even if you and Robert dont want to come. Im going. Its time to go. I have to. You can stay here and squat on your mothers stool and beg for a good word from her and you can stay here until your dying day if you like but Im going.

And with that he was away, striding out in big unsteady steps up towards the manse where Ian would be awake and reading a book with his lamp new lighted.

So I went back into the croft and wrote all this down while my mother snored quietly on her bed. And Im looking over at her and wondering this. Can I leave her by herself like everyone else has done? Or do I have to stay here? Im not sure whats been written out for me. Im wanting one thing but I dont know if thats the same thing as being able to take it. I dont want to stay but Im not so sure about going.

So now the two weeks are more or less past and Im sort of annoyed at myself that Ive not been writing things down but its hard to write things down when there is so much to think about all the time. Ive been going to my bed at night so tired that I cant think of anything any more. But I thought I should write this down tonight because heres where the story takes a new turn, which is the turn I thought it might take when I first started writing down this story.

We *are* going.

It still seems just so strange to be saying that, writing it down.

We are *going*.

It doesnt matter really all the talks and arguments and debates that happened in Ians house or in my house or at the Carcair or between the three of us down by the jetty or up at the top of the cliff about it. Talking, talking, talking until we didnt know who thought what or whether we were even friends any more. At one point it was just Callum and Ian going, then it was Callum and me but not Robert and then it was Robert and Callum and I was going to be staying with my mother, then it was just Callum and Ian again and not me and Robert at all because Robert said that he couldnt put up with Callum always making all the decisions and telling us what to do and it was bad enough here in Croval and what in Gods own name would it be like over in America when we were all going to be thrown in together and no escaping each other, whereas here at least we can go back to our own crofts and smoulder away until things are all right.

And so finally it is the four of us, Callum, me, Robert and Ian all going. Ians putting up the money from what he has saved away and were all going to Cromarty tomorrow for the sailing the day after that.

Tomorrow. And then the day after tomorrow.

What a talk theres been in Croval about Ian up and leaving the manse just like that. The old ones are saying, Didnt we tell you so? Didnt we say the man was not to be trusted, and taking

54

away three of our best young men with him? Not that they ever thought we were three of the best young men, especially not Callum, not until it turned out that we were in league with the minister himself and they decided wed been led astray although they dont know the half of it.

And weve to pay him back from any money that we make when were there, so he says, but Callum says that when it comes to it, he thinks Ian will say that we have to look after ourselves and to forget about the money we owe, thats what hes like.

So its the four of us, heading away across the sea with MacDougalls book to keep us right. I could write about the talk I had with my mother once wed made up our minds but I cant, its too difficult.

I knew, she said. I knew all the time that youd be away, always following after the others.

It wasn't easy, I told her, it was hard to decide what was the best thing to do.

I knew all the time, she said, and she went back to her knitting.

The day after tomorrow. When I started writing all this down I wondered what the future would bring and putting it all on these sheets as a story gave it shape and now its taking on its own shape so much that I dont know if these sheets of paper can hold it all. I dont know if I have the skill to put in words the feeling I have about chasing across the sea to America.

Chasing across the sea. Escaping across the sea. Chasing. Escaping. I think the thing to write is escaping and Ill come back to these pages and change what I need to change when the time comes. Remind myself about this part that needs to be changed so that it is all about looking out for something that can take us away from our future. And not about looking for something that belongs in the past and that makes me look as if I have no say in the road, the path Ive taken.

The four of us. Tomorrow.

Intertitle 1

It occurs to me that Hugh's uncertainty at the end of this first section, which, of course, is entitled "Croval" at *my* editorial discretion, is a key to understanding his personality. He seems not to know what drives him on and in this lack of self-knowledge we glimpse the true nature of the young man of a century and a half ago, aspiring yet reticent, family-oriented, yet wishing to spread his wings. I, too, have found that you must leave something behind in order to progress. That is the way things are and Hugh has helped me see that. He has helped me to understand the idea of blame and how to cope with it.

However, I'm not suggesting that we ought to read Hugh's account of his journey as just metaphorical. That would be an inappropriate reading of a story that is at once vital and real. Real above all. There is a temptation – one which I find myself all too ready to fall into – a temptation to see in a life retold a sort of reflection of your own struggles. As I wrote in my introduction the whole "trace your roots" business encourages us to think that way. But Hugh's story isn't just a metaphorical mirror – though maybe it can be read as a commentary on our own times, albeit one removed by a degree of time that in itself can be read as a metaphor, as if time is a kind of reflecting telescope that allows us to see ourselves all the clearer.

Do I make myself understood? Probably not. Maybe that's not such a good image. And perhaps that is why Hugh's story is more interesting than my own. What I mean is that my lack of a fluent and endearing style (and that is the key thing for me – Hugh is, I feel, above all a *likeable* man, despite everything) leads to my writing acquiring, despite my best efforts (which efforts are, I'm sure, no less than those of Hugh, and perhaps more, given the distractions of a life unfolding in a world as yet unexplored), a certain clumsiness.

I, too, tried for financial success when I opened my bookshop in Aberdeen. But I understand that what makes *my* story uninteresting, apart from my inability to tell it, is its sheer unoriginality. To be honest, Hugh's account itself is not that original, though I do believe that my initial feelings of excitement that long night as I first read the scrawled pages are entirely appropriate. But there is something unique here. Nowhere, I think, in the existing literature of that huge migration to the west, do we read a version that is coloured by quite the combination of innocence and honesty that characterises Hugh's report of how he went from a naïve boy tied to his mother's apron-strings (or maybe we should say stool-legs) to a grown man who ... but I anticipate.

And innocence and naivety are not one and the same, that is certain. While Hugh loses his naivety through the course of the events described within these covers, and had surely begun to lose it even before he left Croval, he never, it seems to me, loses his innocence (though at times we get the feeling he may have wished to). This is a paradox.

I'd have to say that my own journey through life most definitely charted a diminishing of innocence, one that was marked by hurt and loss and a sense of failure that makes it hard for me to retain my self-esteem. I would have liked to have talked to Hugh about that!

But to get back to the point I was making at the head of this Intertitle (if I can call it that). There is something I believe the reader should attend to in this following section, which I have entitled "Journey" – though that title might easily fit any of the sections, since Hugh was a man who was always on the move, despite the reticence occasionally expressed in the "Croval" section. He was a voyager from the start, even if the voyage was just along the coast to Craigtore, a voyage he appears to have made (reading between the lines) many times. Indeed this is one of the appeals of his text, trying to piece together what has been missed out.

He mentions some names of Craigtore residents (or crofters, as he would call them) and you'll see that some of these names recur later on. But who they are, or what their story was, remains on the whole shadowy. Only a couple of Craigtore residents have a genuinely important part to play in the ensuing pages, and even that role is not absolutely central, in my view (though you may not agree). But all these Craigtore people have stories of their own, stories that were not written down. These were people who never recorded their tentative steps into the second half of the nineteenth century. As such, they remain ghosts in history, half-seen in the glare of the light cast by Hugh's words, and we shall never know exactly what happened to, say, James Hunter and his daughter Mhorag that Callum liked. Did they, too, escape across the water? Or did they live and die in their tiny settlement? Did James drown in a storm at sea in his leaky and inadequate rowing boat? Maybe he drank himself to death – Hugh mentions that he liked to drink. Did Mhorag bear children? If so, are their descendants still amongst us today and have I met any of them? Did *they* seek their fortunes across the sea? None of these questions can be answered. And the remarkable thing is that questions about Hugh Ross's life *can* be answered. Isn't that what we all dream of? To see our lives as stories, with answers supplied through commentary? So, in a way, we are all (all of us who read this manuscript) Hugh's dream, just as he is mine. Autobiography is an attempt to will into being an audience which can validate a life by paying attention to it. That's what we crave. We look for answers and sometimes we find them. What we do with those answers is the thing. Finding a dusty manuscript in an attic, reading it and finding it deals with one of your ancestors might be one thing. Knowing what to do with your knowledge is something else altogether.

But enough of the theorising (and who am I to rant on about the nature of autobiography – I who can't tell my own story so that anyone would want to read it) and back to the text.

I would advise you that the next section should be read with great care as it contains, in its disjointed way, some very important clues about the central characters of Hugh, Callum, Robert and Ian. It seems clear to me that the traumatic fact of being torn from home, as it were, has had some significant effect on the way that Hugh tells his tale. While the section starts in much the same style as the earlier "Croval" part of the narrative, you will see that before long something interesting begins to happen to the writing. Visual images are thrown together in a way that may seem random, though it is tempting to see order in the chaos. I'm not claiming for him *intention*, however. I think it is safe to say that Hugh had no idea of the effect he was achieving in his writing: indeed the signs on the scrawled pages of rewriting and amendment indicate that what we have was in no way meant to be a final draft. They do show, though, that he had the concept of a final draft in his head. Who was it for? We shall never know. But it falls to us to be that readership, to hear his chronicle of rocks and boats and trees and disease and cows and the movement of the earth.

But I must not get ahead of myself, or I run the risk of pre-empting Hugh's revelations. It's all right for me, sitting here with my own pen in hand, because I've read it before and there is no surprise to be had for me any more in the way events unfold themselves. The surprises, for me, are now found deeper in the text.

In any case, watch out for these images, this strongly visual element. What do you think of the style? Did Hugh seek help with his writing in this section? Can we detect the voice of an unseen helper here? If so, who is it? Ian Macleod? Robert? Callum would seem unlikely. Or is Hugh simply developing?

And if that is the case, what about his character? Can we see progression in the way he reacts to the events of this section? I find it pleasing to see in him an increasing awareness of others and their needs, a moving out from himself.

Journey

I can hear the boat creaking as the waves beat up against the sides and its not like the sound that the sea makes when youre just in a little boat. Theres a groaning as if the whole ship is struggling to find it in itself to press on against the waves. In a small boat you feel as if the wooden boards are with you, as if youre fighting together to get home against the wind. But in a boat the size of The Lady Gray youre just lying here waiting for the voyage to happen, being carried along with no say in the matter. Theres not an oar to pull on or a rudder to put your hand on, feeling the water tug against the strength of your arm. Its just the big boat and it growls its way westward through the open sea.

But first things first.

My mother refused to come out to say goodbye even when we left yesterday at the crack of dawn. I kept looking round as we climbed up the rock steps to the top of the cliff where MacPhees cart was waiting to run us the long road up to Cromarty, near ninety miles he told us, further than Id ever been or Callum or Robert though of course Ian has been the length and breadth of Scotland, as he likes to say. The croft got smaller and smaller the higher we climbed and to begin with I could see in the wee window at the back and I could make out my mothers shape as she sat up straight on her chair. She wasnt even looking out at us as we went away. As we got further up the cliff I couldnt see into the croft any more because it was too far away and too wee, so I dont know if at the last moment she turned her head to watch me leave my home. She might have, but then again she might not.

It hadnt been easy to say goodbye to her but sometimes you have to do things you dont like to do.

Ill write a letter to you, I told her. First thing Ill do when we get to America, thatll be writing you a letter.

She looked at me, cold and hard. She was stirring a pot on the fire. She said, Will you then?

Yes. I promise. And one day Ill be back. Once Ive done well out there Ill come back to share it all with you.

Is that why youre going? To do well and then come back?

Of course. Why else?

Some foolish thing, she said.

Stirring and stirring.

Well, I said.

Well then, Hugh.

That was the end of our speaking together. I took a step towards her thinking that we ought to share something before I went, a kiss or an embrace. But she turned away from me and stared into her pot, stirring and stirring. I waited there for a moment to see if shed look up but she didnt so I picked up my canvas bag that Ian had given me and walked out the door. I left the door open in case she wanted to come after me but she didnt.

Ian saw me looking back over my shoulder as we climbed the last few steps.

Its your father shes thinking of, he said. Your brothers. Its a shame she cant see what urges you on, but there it is.

I know, I said.

MacPhees cart was a painful thing to be travelling on. Ian and Callum sat up at the front on the kind of seat, just behind the horses rear end, and me and Robert sat in the back in among the boxes and crates of stuff that the tink sold in the villages. I could smell cheese and there were bottles clanking in one of the boxes. Callum must have heard it too because he asked MacPhee if we could have one of the bottles to see us on our way or to celebrate our breaking free, but he said No, not if you cant pay for it.

I saw Callum looking meaningfully at Ian but Ian never gave anything away so we never got a drink of whisky on that sore bumpy journey along the coast and up around the end of the firth. Not that I was really needing a drink anyway. The whole idea of going away from home was enough to make me dizzy as if Id stood up too quick after bending over a net. And I think I felt every stone on the road that MacPhees cart jolted over and my spine was aching by the time we stopped for something to eat at a place called Nairn. This was quite a big place, well, compared to Croval, but I realise that there are many bigger towns than Nairn even, in places Ive never been to. I asked Ian about it as we walked into an inn by the road and he said Edinburgh, for example, was much bigger than this. He said that in Edinburgh the smoke from all the chimneys hung over the city so that you could hardly see up into the sky at all. In Nairn, even though it was bigger than Croval, you could still see the hot June sky and the seagulls up there.

I also asked him if there were the same kind of seagulls in America, but he didnt know, so when we went into the inn we sat with the MacDougall book to see what he had to say about seagulls, but he didnt say anything. The inn was a friendly kind of place and a big man with a beard gave us stale bread and cheese and water that tasted as if it had been in a wooden barrel for too long. I caught myself comparing it to the water in the burn that ran down the cliff at home and I pushed that thought back into my mind again because that was definitely not the way I wanted to be thinking. So the food was bad and it was a shame for Ian because, as I said before, he liked his food.

Robert wasnt saying a word but Callum was unable to be quiet. He kept pestering Ian with questions about what it would be like at Cromarty and what the boat, The Lady Gray, would be like, and what it would be like to be out on the ocean and what arriving at the other side would be like. Although Ian knew a lot, these were not questions he could answer and I could see him getting a bit tired of them. I could see he was a bit tired altogether and it made me think about how much older than us he was and how much more this journey meant for him or at least how different it was for him in what it meant.

And suddenly I had a thought, which was this. For Callum and me, with what we knew about old Mary packed away in our heads like luggage, the journey meant one special thing. But another thing was that for Callum, me and Robert, this was an adventure that we could escape from if we wanted to. But I couldnt see how Ian would be coming home again. He was going to America to die, I thought, maybe in five years, maybe in ten years. But I couldnt see how he would be coming home ever again.

So I went over to a different wooden table beside a different window and waved him over. As he came I could see Robert glancing at me curiously and Callum staring at me in a kind of half annoyed half worried sort of way. But I wanted to talk to Ian by himself.

What is it? he asked. Are you thinking of changing your mind?

The midday sun was shining through the thick glass of the window and I could see smears on the wood of the table and dust floating through the air. I looked right through the bits of dust at Ian. I said, What are they saying about you coming away with us?

The Croval people? Not pleased with me. But they think its the kind of thing someone like me would do. So I suppose theyre happy really because Ive proved them right.

He smiled at me but it was a strained smile.

I said, No, not them. I meant the people who have to do with the church.

The hierarchy?

The what? I asked. So he spelled it out for me and explained what it meant.

Theyre not very happy with me either. Ive told them my journey is a kind of mission. I wrote a long letter to Edinburgh telling them that this was a mission. Ministers are needed over there. There are souls that need to be saved in America, and Im not just talking about the ones that live inside red skins. So Im going with a purpose. I dont mind what they think. Im still a minister. They havent taken that away and neither can they.

Wed had the same conversation a couple of nights before yesterday and I didnt mean to go over the same things again, so I tried a different question.

Will you miss home?

Home?

Croval.

Croval isnt really my home, Hugh. Not the way it is for you and the other two.

I glanced over at Callum, who was still glaring at us, and Robert, who was ripping off a piece of bread. Some other people were at different tables, people Id never seen before. The innkeeper was standing over by a shelf full of bottles and his shirt sleeves were rolled up over thick muscled arms.

I said to Ian, Were already away from home, arent we? I mean this is as far away from Croval as America, sort of.

He laughed. Yes it is, he said. I might have thought Robert would have said that, not you.

I wasnt sure if I should be pleased or annoyed by that. I said, But itll be even more away from home by the time we travel across the sea. Just now we could get back on MacPhees cart and ask him to go back to Croval.

He wouldnt go. Youd have to pay him again. Or I would.

No, but we could do it. When we get to America well not be able to just come back. Dont you think?

It was the right question to ask him and I saw him sort of go inside himself so that I couldnt see in his eyes what he was thinking any more. He gave a little smile and laid his hands on the table. The sun shone on his dry old skin. He coughed.

When youre young you can always come back, he said.

That gave me my answer. I tried to look him in the eye but he was looking down at his hands, and he was twisting his fingers together as if he was putting them in place for a prayer. I had the sudden feeling that hed trusted us to come with us across the world and that now was the time I should tell him about what had happened with Mary Vass but before anything else could be said, Callum came over and then Robert and before too long we were outside once more in the sunlight and getting back up on to MacPhees cart again. This caused a bit of a disagreement.

Robert says, Maybe one of us should have a turn up at the front.

Callum says, I think Ian should be up there. Hes older.

I agree with you, says Robert. Of course Ian should be up there. Im thinking maybe one of us should be taking a turn in your seat.

What do you think, Hugh? Callum asks.

I shrugged and said it didnt bother me one way or the other way. I felt bad for Robert but to be honest I didnt really mind sitting in the back because although we were getting bumped about all over the place, at least we were looking back along the road towards home and that was quite nice to do, though a bit sad as well. Robert gave me a bit of a look but I dont think he was really going to stand up to Callum all that much in any case so it didnt make a lot of difference really. But its true that Robert and I didnt speak much for the next part of the day and I couldnt help noticing that Ian wasnt very talkative with Callum either.

MacPhee took us all the way along the edge of the firth through Inverness and I was glad that we didnt stop there as it was the biggest dirtiest place Id seen yet, much bigger than Nairn. I think my eyes were as wide as a fishs eyes when we went through there. There were women sitting beside the inns we passed, as drunk as any old man could be and that was something Id not seen before. I mean Id seen my mother with a good shot in her but just in the house and I knew she sometimes did this because she was always unhappy so that made sense. Anyway she never let anyone see her in that state apart from me. But these women were drunk out in the street with the sun beating down on them so that everyone could see them. They were watching us go by in MacPhees cart and one or two of them were shouting things out at us, things that I couldnt write down here.[9] I thought about the nicer girls I knew, like Elizabeth, who would never have used words like that, and Rachael, her too. I wondered what they were doing now, over in America.

The buildings in Inverness were huge, and some of them were up to two or three levels which Ian said were called storeys. I thought that was quite funny and he spelled it out for me so that I understood it was a different word. We saw some soldiers too, but they never showed any interest in us as we trundled past. There was a man driving four cows through the street with a stick and there was a kite swooping down on something that had been left at the side of the road. I think it was a dead cat or a dog, but whatever it was it was going to get eaten by that kite. Ian said that kites and eagles can be way up in the sky, too small for us to see, but they can see the littlest thing, like a mouse or a rabbit, and come down and take it.

I thought the people of Inverness were making it easy for the kites by letting dead dogs just lie there. It wouldnt have happened in Croval.

Then we were out of Inverness and we carried on by the edge of the firth. There was seaweedy mud at the edge of the water and there were herons standing sinking into it, watching by their

---

9   Interestingly, as we shall see, Hugh overcomes this boyish reticence a little as the text progresses. It would seem to me that his reluctance to deal with the issue of basic female sexuality reveals him to be inexperienced in such matters. I suspect that if Callum had been narrating this section we might have had a more explicit account. Hugh's shyness is endearing to me. – RM

feet for little fish. We went through a few more little places that werent very interesting to look at, not after Inverness. Then we went round the head of the firth and started back along the north shore, travelling east now, through some more places and heading towards the Black Isle, which is where Cromarty is.

Im not sure if I need to write down all this but it seems to me the first part of a journey is as important as the other parts of it so Id better. Im not going to give a list of everything we saw on our way to Cromarty yesterday, but we did see one thing that stuck in my mind. This was on the Black Isle itself, which isnt an island at all but is joined on to the main part of the land. I dont know why its called an island and even Ian didnt know that. Or why its called black because if anything its green as there are a lot of farms with the crops coming up and lots of trees. Not so many people as we saw in Nairn and Inverness but Cromarty itself with a few boats in the harbour was busier but Im coming to that.

As I say we did see quite a lot of things that arent worth mentioning here but at a place called Tore, which is just an inn and a few houses, a place where a few different tracks or roads cross, we saw something strange. There was a young girl, maybe fourteen years old, standing in a field just beside the road we were on. I think we just noticed her at first because MacPhee had stopped the cart beside the rutted road to give the horse something to eat out of this sack of meal that he carried. The horse was thin but strong and well able to pull a heavy cart all day. And I have to say that MacPhee looked after it well enough. He didnt mistreat it the way some people mistreat animals. But maybe that was just because it suited him not to mistreat it because Killarnoch, folk said, paid him well enough to take his cart backwards and forwards to different places so it would make no sense to hurt his horse if it would mean he couldnt do his job with the cart properly and Killarnoch would get somebody else. Then again, Ian said Killarnoch employed quite a few men with carts and there were plenty others where MacPhee came from trying to get business with him, though I dont suppose that has anything to do with it. What Im saying about MacPhee is that you couldnt tell whether he was good to his horse because he was good or if he was good to his horse because he was selfish. Thats the thing. It doesnt matter really because MacPhees not an important person in the story, but sometimes your Walter Scott and other of these story writers are telling you all about characters and what theyre thinking and what theyre feeling, whether theyre happy or sad or angry or in love or whatever and thats not very real. But really, you cant tell. It doesnt matter, Im just saying.

So this girl was in the field and she was standing on top of a stone that put her maybe three feet above the ground which had been ploughed recently but not planted. It looked like the kind of rock that you might wish wasnt there but you couldnt do anything about, a stubborn rock. She was standing there and in her arms she was carrying a doll, just a childs rag doll, but as I said she must have been fourteen because her body was a womans body more or less and she wasnt a child in her face or the height of her. And this doll was quite big, maybe about the size of a new lamb, and the arms and legs of it were off and lying on the ground, so really she was just holding the body of the doll. While we were watching her she was pulling out the dolls hair, which was brown wool. She was pulling out the hair and dropping the strands down to the ground. All the time she was looking at the sky and out of her was coming this song that had no tune, just a strange wailing song with no real words to it either. The strands of woollen hair were floating down and her singing was floating up and the sun was shining hard down onto her and her feet were three feet above the muddy ground where the ripped off limbs of the doll were lying. We must have been stopped for five minutes, no more, and then we moved on. We none of us said anything about her but wed all been watching her. Some things are better if you dont speak about them

So that was that.

We got to Cromarty and we got off the cart. Me and Robert were as stiff as anything what with being bumped and jolted along the road for hours and hours. Its not such a big place but it seemed busy partly because there was this big sailing ship in the harbour alongside a few wee fishing boats. I say wee but they are all bigger than the rowing boats we fish out of at Croval. None of us could take our eyes of The Lady Gray sitting there in the water as if nothing could ever bother her. I know Ian would have seen a big boat like that before but none of us have. We were standing at the edge of the harbour and speaking. Ian was talking to a man at a wooden hut about the tickets.

Callum says, Thats it, boys. Thats our way to America. Beautiful, isnt she?

How do we know it can go across the whole ocean? asked Robert and Callum kind of laughed at him.

Because its been back and forth before.

How do you know? asks Robert.

Its bound to have been or else why would they be selling berths on it for a trip to America?

You hear stories, says Robert, about ships that arent fit for the journey to America.

Do you? I say, not having heard any stories like that at all.

I have, says Robert. I heard of one that sank just out of Thurso and they all had to swim to shore and twenty odd drowned.

But this is The Lady Gray, says Callum. This is the one were sailing in so how can it sink? The stories are rubbish, put out by Killarnoch and the like to stop us from going away.

Why would they stop us? I ask.

Callum just looks at me and shakes his head. He says, Its obvious, man. Think about it.

So then of course I couldnt say anything and I decided Id ask Ian later, but I havent yet and maybe Ill do it during the journey because therell be plenty of time.

There were some men moving about on the deck of the ship and another man shouting things at him and I thought he must have been in charge, but Ian told me no, the captain of the ship would be hidden away somewhere doing more important things than telling sailors what to do with ropes. The noisy harbour was all piled up with crates and boxes and bags of stuff and there were quite a few folk like us just standing watching and I realised all at once that these were people that would be going with us across the sea. I thought about going up and speaking to some of them just to see where they were from and why they were going and that sort of thing, but in the end I didnt, probably because I wasnt sure how I would answer all the questions they might give me in return. Callum, though, was making his way backwards and forwards amongst the crowds, talking here and there, not really waiting for replies. Robert went right up to the edge of the harbour and stared down at the dirty water, where the big stone blocks were reflected in the oily looking surface so that you couldnt see in properly the way you could at Croval, where the water is cleaner.

I looked up at the entrance to the harbour and it seemed amazing that The Lady Gray had managed to get in through the narrow gap safely and it made me respect the men busy on the deck. The long arms of the harbour enclose the water so that the waves never make their way in to touch the boats so that they can all rest calmly where they lie. I thought about how they managed to build the harbour in the first place. How did they manage to build those walls out in the firth? I could not find an answer and Ive added it to the list of things I have to ask Ian about.

By this time it was getting on towards the evening and the sun had dropped down and the shadows were getting longer.

Across the water from Cromarty there is more land which Ian said would be Easter Ross and the last light was shining on it. It was like another world over there. I suppose it is a mile away or something over the firth. Not the same firth wed been round already, the one that Croval looks out on. This is another firth, the same but different. At my back was the Black Isle, rising up and blocking my view so that I couldnt see back to Croval. Its hard to describe all this.

It turned out that we would be sleeping in an inn just up from the harbour so we went there. Ian has arranged this too. Hed been writing letters as fast as anything, I think, getting us all ready for this journey. I dont see how he had enough time to get it all sorted out but the old folks at Croval would be saying that it was because he never put any time into his proper job and I think they were all quite happy, really, to see him go because they knew theyd be getting someone else instead, someone better.

Im not going to write much about last night when we slept in the inn because it doesnt matter much really. It was a bare place with cold stone floors and we were just given a blanket that was big enough to go under you and then fold over on top. The blankets werent very clean and Robert spent ages sitting up trying to pick bits of dirt and fleas out of his one until it got too dark to do it properly. I was so tired and sore from the cart ride that I just lay down and tried to go to sleep. MacPhee was long gone by this time. Ian had paid him and hes taken off back to Inverness or wherever it is he goes.

We were sharing a room with some of the others that would be on The Lady Gray and Callum was talking to some of them in the corner. I was too tired. But I did think that in this room and at the harbour, I hadnt seen so many young people all together in my life. It was mainly young people that seemed to want to go across the sea. Ian was by far the oldest person wed seen that would be going on the boat. He had lain down beside the pile of bags and boxes of stuff we were taking to America.

He was only a wee bit across from me so just before I went to sleep I asked him, Do you feel old going away with all of us?

I remember, he said, when I first went to the university. I was all filled up with desire to learn and so was everyone else. Theres nothing like young people to make you think the futures going to be filled up with excitement.

In Edinburgh?

Thats right. But to answer your question, yes, of course I feel old. I am old. How else do you imagine I might feel?

I peered through the shadow of the room to see if he was smiling but I couldnt quite make out if he was or not. In a little while I was asleep and I dreamed about my mother, which made me feel sad when I woke up.

So that was yesterday and today we woke up early because we had no choice. People were up and talking and there was a funny feeling in the room and when we went out in the streets of Cromarty as well. Ian had been up even before anyone, because old people dont need so much sleep as us younger ones. Hed been out to speak to people down by the harbour and he said that there were going to be two hundred and fifty people going to America. Emigrants, we were called, which meant we were people looking for a new home.[10] I thought that was a right lot of people for The Lady Gray. It was a big boat true enough but how were two hundred and fifty going be fitted into her? I was thinking of the three of us in the little rowing boat and tried to work out what that had to do with two hundred and fifty people on The Lady Gray but Ian told me it was difficult to know exactly because there were different decks down below the main deck so you could get more people on a boat like that than seemed likely.

---

10 I like Hugh's neat definition in these turbulent times. – RM

So now I know the answer, writing this *below decks* as they call it with everyone round about but Ill come to that.

Before too long we were down in a long line of people by the harbour with our bags and boxes shuffling forward every now and then. There was a man in a uniform at the front of this noisy line of people, checking the bits of paper and shouting and waving everyone up the plank that went on to the boat. There was one young boy, maybe about sixteen, that he turned away because there was something wrong with his bit of paper. The boy argued with him for a while but it didnt make any difference. He stood for some time trying to speak to the man in the uniform but he wasnt getting anywhere so then he wandered off. It made me feel nervous, thinking what if our bits of paper werent right?

I should describe. Seagulls sitting on the stone walls of the harbour. Morning sun shining down on the water. A Friday it is, the 4th of June, 1841, the first day of the next part of my life, the last day of the first part of my life. People pushing and nervous in the line. Men on deck with mops and brushes and tying knots in ropes and shouting at each other in a strange way like another language, like the difference between Gaelic and English. Behind me, the creak of carts as more and more people were being set down on the harbour edge, the horses blowing and pawing at the hard dry ground. My heart beating as fast as anything. Robert beside me, staring around him as if he had to take it all in, learn every sight in case he had to write it down later for someone. And here its me thats writing it all down. Ian just ahead of me in the line, the bits of paper with their important words on them clutched in his hand. I could see the little shake in his hand was made bigger in the edges of the paper. Thats not very well described, but I cant see another way of saying it. Me wondering if that shake was a sign of nervousness, like my beating heart, or a sign of the age that makes Ian different from us all.

Callum talking to a girl just behind us in the line. Him saying, And where are you from, then? And her saying back, Lairg, yourself? And me thinking, Theres places in Scotland Ive never seen or heard of before and heres me going across the sea to *America* to find newness.

I felt like I was in a book. I felt that for the first time in my life I didnt know what was going to happen next. I was feeling that I was missing my mother, and wondering what she was doing. I would have given anything to be lying on the grass at the top of the cliff, looking down over Croval, full of all those faces that I knew, back in the time when I was young, before that rock rolled from the cliff and curved through the air.

That was all this morning. We inched forward until we were past the uniform man and walking up the plank on to the boat.

Another man came and showed us down some wooden steps to where we were going to be living. We got a place up beside the wall of the ship and above our heads you could hear the footsteps of the next people coming on board and the noise echoed around about us like when you shout in Seal Cave that goes into the rocks down past Craigtore. But when we were in Seal Cave there was just the three of us or at most the three of us and some of the Craigtore girls. I remember that time we were there and Rachael was shouting one word again and again and it was coming back at her faster and faster and we were all laughing and that was in the echoes too, so that after a while the noise scared us and we stopped and went home. The word she was shouting was the word *curse*. I dont know why she picked that one. Curse, curse, curse, curse she was shouting and it gave me a funny feeling in my belly. We were about sixteen. I think she was *trying* to scare us.

When I say above our heads I mean the boots stamping above us were probably in about the same place as our heads would have been if wed been able to stand up straight. There is only about five feet of clearance if that between the ceiling and the floor. The ceiling is the underneath of the deck and the floor is the upper side of the ceiling of the people on the deck below us.

Ian says that he spoke to one of the sailors whos been on other boats and he says that theres meant to be five foot four between the decks. What can you do, though?

Were all crammed in right close. Theres a bit at one end of the deck were on where theres a kind of curtain pulled across and thats where youre meant to go to piss and so on. Theres probably proper writing words for that but I dont know and somehow I dont think I can really ask Ian about that with him a minister and everything. Theres wooden boards that are stacked up against one wall and when its time to eat these are taken down and propped up on old kegs and thats where we eat. So it looks like this room is our home for the next six weeks and weve only been on the boat for a few hours and already its beginning to stink. Not just the chanties behind the curtain but just the stink of a hundred or more people stuck together and sweating and breathing and some of them werent that clean in the first place if you ask me.

We were allowed up on deck when The Lady Gray set sail. We were towed out of the harbour by four rowing boats with four men in each. I thought, how can twelve men move a boat with two hundred and fifty or so people on it, but sure enough they did. Heres what Ian said about that. We were leaning on the rail thing at the edge of the boat. I suppose Ill learn some of the names of these things as the journey goes on.

Me – How can just sixteen men pull this huge boat?

Ian – Because the one is always more powerful than the many if he has but faith.

Me – How does faith help with rowing?

Ian – With faith your strength grows in ways that mock the world around us.

Me – I dont know if I really understand.

Ian – Theres too much to understand. Far too much.

This made me think it was a funny thing for him to say and not really like the other kinds of things that hed say. I remembered his old hands in the sun in the inn in Nairn, and I was thinking he was already beginning to lose some of that weight he used to have, and I asked him what he meant.

Ian – I remember when I was just a boy being by the burn that ran beside our house. Id put my hands in the cold water and moved them inch by inch until they were right underneath a trout hanging in the water. I could have lifted my hands up and scooped that fish right out into the air. I just held my hands there for I dont know how long.

Silence for a minute.

Me – Where was that? That burn and that house you used to live in?

Ian – Im not sure. Im not so sure now. But I can remember it as clear as day.

So that was all my answer. The boat had been cast off by now. The men on the rowing boats untied the ropes and the men on deck hauled them in and tidied them up. Some of the emigrants were waving goodbye to people back on the harbour wall who were getting smaller all the time. The sailors were doing things with ropes again and the sails went up and caught the wind and we were moving out past the two big headlands of rock, one to the north and one to the south. I could see where the steep rock went down into the water and I knew the currents would be difficult there when the tide was flowing, and then thinking that made me think about being back in Croval and going out in the boat to line fish for sea trout so it was all I could do not to jump off the side of the boat, swim back to Cromarty, run after MacPhee, climb on his cart, bump all the way back home and creep back into the croft and say sorry to my mother.

Ian – What were you asking?

Me – About the rowing boats. It doesnt matter now.

Ian – True enough.

Then it was open sea and when we were clear of the Black Isle I could look south and there in the distance was the coast where we lived, but we were heading north now and I couldnt make anything out. It was all lost in the haze. I peered into the far distance but it was dancing the way the sun can play tricks with your eyes so I couldnt see anything, and I was thinking that Id never see Croval again and that my mother would be dead by the time I came there again, and all the old men in the Carcair would be dead as well and the manse would have another minister in it and who knows what other changes there would be.

It was all too much and when the sun began to go down the sky I went down too and got out my paper and my ink and I began to write this.

What a day.

[11] Robert lying on the wooden deck, eyes open, staring at the wooden deck above. Robert stuck between two decks, lying there with his eyes open but not speaking. In one hand his shirt

---

11 It is at this point that Hugh's narrative takes on a new style, one which sits a bit uneasily with what precedes it. I leave it to the reader to decide what is happening here. Perhaps there is a deliberateness about the way he writes here, perhaps not. There is that theory that the writer is written by the words that appear on the page. Maybe we see another part of Hugh come into existence here, shrouded by the words that pour out, at times clumsily and at times lyrically, a clothing that fashions a psychologically challenging persona that comes as close to real as black marks on paper can be. Or perhaps he meant to come back and revise this section, knock it into shape. Perhaps he's already done that with his description of the journey from Croval to the North Sea just beyond the tip of the Black Isle. Maybe we don't have to decide either way. Maybe one of the mistakes we make in life is to be too anxious to find meaning, and to make others conform to our interpretations of the world. I'm as guilty as anyone, of course. – RM

is clutched and the fingers are tightening, untightening. The other hand laid across his forehead. No words spoken.

When the wind hits the sails after a quiet minute the noise is like the noise that the rock made when Callum rolled it over the edge of the cliff, a crack like the end of the world. First time I heard it up on deck, that sail crack, I near fell over with the shock of it. All the noises. The sea against the boat like the waves on the shore but here is the difference. You sit at the shore at Croval and the waves come up the beach and die with a sigh at your feet. Here the boat cuts through the waves and the waves carry on going wherever theyre going so they are more alive than at the shore. Were in between the waves where theyre born and where theyre dying. Where the waves are born and the waves die. The boat is half way between the birth and the death of waves.

The ropes creaking as if they want to break.

Voices of the sailors, cursing and laughing and ordering each other to do things mysteriously.

The seabirds. Seagulls and as we go further north other birds too, brown, some of them, and others smaller than seagulls and sharp winged.

On our left, away to the west, the land, because were going up round the top of Scotland. I think I can hear the land in the distance like you can hear the dull sounds of the sea when youre lying in your croft.

Callum with a girl hes found from Inverness. So many people lying there at night and I can hear Callum crawl from his space along from me on the other side of Robert over to where this girl, Katherine, is lying alongside her snoring father, no mother, and even in the dark I can imagine what hes doing, his hands on her body and his face in her hair and their lips and in the complete dark I can hear a little laugh of uncertainty and I put

78

my hands over my ears and try not to listen.

Stopping at Thurso. More people getting on. Where can there be room? When Im sleeping I hear a hundred folk breathing, each one sharing my breath.

A fight. Some man from up a strath to the north starts on one of the sailors. No one knows what its about but one minute were up on deck with the wind in our faces and some specks of rain in our eyes then were all in a circle round this Strath Rogar man and the sailor. The sailor has his hands held palms up to show he doesnt want to fight but the Strath Rogar man is coming forward and reaching out and pushing the sailor until in the end hes up against the rail, bending over backwards from his waist and the other emigrants are crowding in. The Strath Rogar man is shouting but the wind is whipping away his words so we cant really hear whats being said but each shout goes with a push to the sailors shoulder as if hed push the man right over the edge and into the sea spinning past underneath. I hear shouts from behind me and theres someone fighting through the crowd, one of the more important sailors, but not the captain. When I look back at whats happening at the rail, its all finished and the Strath Rogar man is lying on the deck with blood coming out of his throat and the sailor is putting the knife back in his belt and slipping off into the knot of emigrants.

Ive never seen this before, someone being killed, not like that.

Later on they tipped his body over the side, with some links from a heavy chain tied to his ankles. Theyre saying he went mad for the lack of the land, and us only five days out.

Callum – They cant do this to us. Shit and piss overflowing the buckets and washing round our feet. What do they think we are, animals? Weve paid good money for this passage.

Me – Ian paid the money.

Callum – Same thing. They cant do this to us, thats what Im saying. Im lying at night and Im boaking with the stink.

A storm. Spray and the waves breaking up over the front of the boat. Get below deck! Sideways and up and down, your stomach heaving. Robert with his head up against the wall, and vomit running out of his mouth like water, his shoulders and his back heaving and none of us much better or able to help him. Hearing the waves beating up against the sides of the boat and the thump of running boots above our head when the sailors are trying to make the boat safe. The fear hanging under the deck like the spray blowing above.

The captain – Captain Gray –
I have asked you all to come above decks so that I may speak to you. I have been informed that there are some amongst you, some who prefer to remain hidden in the shadows, may I say, who have been murmuring and plotting. I may tell you, my good gentlemen, and I use the word with some uncertainty, I assure you, I may tell you that I will not tolerate such murmurings on board my ship. I will not have the name of The Lady Gray brought into disrepute by the likes of you. I would remind you, gentlemen, that you are on board as my guests, passage rates notwithstanding. I would remind you, gentlemen, that those who know how to run a ship are myself and my crew. I would remind you, *gentlemen*, that those who ought to know that their place is well below decks with their mouths firmly shut, should act accordingly if they wish to demonstrate their gentility. I trust there shall be no more of this nonsense and that I shall not need to address you again.

In the dark, a quiet crying, like an old dog out in the cold night frost.

A fiddle played in the evening with us all lying quiet and listening. No strathspey and reel, a slow sad tune with some folk singing along just gently under their breaths. Falling asleep with that music going round my head. Waking up. Writing this.

Callum arguing with Robert about what to do. Robert saying all the things about just enduring, just putting up with it all until we get there then stepping off the boat and washing the smell from our hair and our bodies and then getting on with the next part of our lives. Callum saying that we shouldnt have to put up with all this, the filth and the stink and the indignity of it all, why should we not stand up for what we want?

Robert – Its as full as this with people in the Carcair on a Saturday when all the boats are in and the whisky is flowing.

Callum – I dont mind the overcrowding in here. These are our people. Who else to be crowded together with? Its the rest of it. Captain Gray. What does he care about us? We should do something.

Robert – How are these our people? We dont know them at all.

Callum – We know them now.

Robert – How do we?

Callum – Because were all crowded in together. Captain Gray is creating his own devil.

Me and Ian sitting off to one side, not saying anything. Ian because he doesnt seem to have much energy for this fighting. Me because I really dont know what I would say if I did talk. Put up with it or fight against it? Ive come this far, on a boat across the ocean, chasing instead of just accepting. I could have just stayed in Croval and given up on all that. But here I am. So maybe Im a fighter. Maybe I can feel the weight of that stone lifting a little. Im sitting off to one side but in another way Im sitting right in between Robert and Callum, right in the middle.

Walking the deck with Ian, talking about the future, or trying to, because Ian keeps talking about the past. Im wanting to hear about what well be doing when we get to the end of this endless journey, so Ive asked him to take the MacDougall book up on deck with him but he has it under his arm and wont open it. I ask him to find the bit where it talks about the lumber business in Nova Scotia, which is cutting trees down in the bit of America that were going to, that people call Canada. But he wont do it. No, he says, Im thinking about the time when I was just a young minister in Langholm and the elders wanted to cut down the yews in the churchyard because they said the graves were all overgrown.

I ask him to look for the bit where it tells you about the crops you can plant and the crops that dont do so well. No, he says, Im thinking about the time when my father planted potatoes in the back garden and he had no time to lift them and they rotted in the earth. I ask him to find the chapter where it tells you about some of the men and women who have gone over there and found happiness together under American skies. No, he says, Im thinking about my mother and my father walking with me between them by the beach at Portobello.

Then suddenly he wasnt in the funny mood any more and he took the book from under his arm and he was leaning against the rail at the edge of the deck and the sea was hurrying past way down below us. He opened the book up and began to read out to me. It was a bit hed read out to us many times in the Croval manse in the days leading up to us going away so I knew it without him having to read it out. It said this – *America is as fresh a story as it ever was. Everyone, great and small, is continually talking about the pictures he draws in his own mind – about something he has not seen.*

Why that bit? I asked him.

He waved his hand in a gesture that was meant to say – Why not that bit? Why not any bit?

And thats when it happened. I dont know if it was a gust of wind that threw him off his balance for a second, or if his limbs are not so sure of themselves as they once were. Whatever it was, as he threw his arm round in that curve, to show me that he was in control, that he could choose whichever of Mac-Dougalls words he wanted to, he lost control, and MacDougall slipped from his fingers. For a second the book was there in the air, like a bird, with its pages flapping in the wind as its wings. Then it plunged down to the waves and settled there and was gone in our wake.

So that was the end of MacDougall.

Robert – If were going to do anything about it we have to think it out.

Callum – Why? What needs to be thought out?

Robert – Or else were just tinks. Or else we dont have the right to be respected ourselves. If were standing up to Gray then we have to standing up for ourselves. If we dont respect Gray then weve got to earn the respect of the others.

Callum – Act first. Get respect later. Who cares?

There is this little man that comes from Croick. He says hes going to America before he has to. He told us that he thought that within five years the whole of his glen, Glencalvie, would be following him. Robert asked why and this wee man told us all about the sheep that are moving into his glen. Robert told him the story of Killarnoch and what had happened to us, or at least our people.

Its all over, says the wee man, whose name is Donald Sutherland. Its everywhere. What use are we to them?

Robert – This is the thing.

Donalds about thirty or thirty five, with his dark hair thinning out over the top of his head. His teeth look sharp. He reminds me of a cat, like the cat MacPhee used to have on his cart before it died. Hes sleekit. He says, We need to make sure we are never treated like this again. If we are starting a new life we need to be sure that were never treated like the dirt of the earth again.

Robert – This is the thing.

Callum – Thats what Im saying.

Robert – No its not. Not exactly.

And Callum turns away and stalks away, pushing his way through the folks sitting on the underdeck.

A sailor fell from the mast today. Crashing through the air and hitting the deck. Touching the sail on his way down, bouncing out into the nothing above the wood. Im thinking of Callums rock striking Mary, coming to rest by the sea, missing John McDonalds little boat. This sailor landing at the feet of Ian. Two steps further and the minister would have died. Two seconds later in falling and Ian would have died. A second earlier and old Mary would be living yet. Things fall and meet other things and they cant be stopped.

Theres a stillness for a second before all the other sailors rush about and take up the body and Ians standing looking at the blood in the space where the man was and then another sailor comes with a bucket and scrubs and scrubs until the stain is just a memory of blood.

Some of us were fishing from the side of the boat. It wasnt so windy today and The Lady Gray was drifting slow through the waves. No white foam, just a greasy black swell that can mean a storms coming or it can mean the opposite, that the weathers set for a while. The sailors didnt mind us fishing too much, probably because we gave them some of the fish we caught, when we caught any, which wasnt often. No one wanted to use any of the food that could have ended up in their mouths to bait hooks when it might not end up in the mouth of a fish.

Nobody was catching much. There was a bit where we must have been passing through mackerel because for a while we were pulling them out just like that, then they were past and we were back to our lines doing nothing, just tugging away towards the stern, as the sailors call it. We always used to say the back of the boat, but the sailors on The Lady Gray are calling it the *stern* and the front is the *bow*. Left and right is *port* and *starboard*. This is what I dont understand, why they need new words for what already has a word. When I asked Ian, he said, God gave names to the four rivers that ran out of Eden, but it was Adam that was allowed to give names to every beast of the field and every fowl of the air, and hes never got out of the habit ever since then.

So nothing was happening with our lines in the water and to tell the truth I was just about to give up and go back below deck, because it was cold, when the man next to me at the rail pulled sharp on his line, hauling hard to stick the hook deep into the mouth of whatever it was. He was heaving hard and we could see it was something big that he had, so one or two of the others went to help him. One took a hold of him round the waist so he wouldnt be losing his footing and two others helped with the line, pulling and pulling but for a while there was nothing happening.

God, says the man with the line, this must be a big one. Well be eating well tonight.

They laughed.

Then there was a thrashing in the water in amongst the slow waves at the side of the boat way below us where the tight line went into the water and there were drops thrown up in the air and the line was jerking backwards and forwards and side to side. The man whose line it was had drops of blood on his hand where the twine was cutting into his fingers.

So suddenly out of the water came this head, as wide as my arms stretched out, with eyes huge and white, and a mouth lined with pointed teeth, and skin that was black as pitch that the water ran off, and the skin wasnt smooth but covered in warty growths, and I swear to God I have never seen anything so ugly in my life. The three men on the line couldnt help themselves. When they looked into that things eyes they dropped the line and stepped back and the creature slipped back beneath the waves and disappeared.

Im sitting here now writing this and Im thinking of the two extremes. I think the most dreadful living thing Ive ever seen in my life was that creature. And Im thinking the prettiest thing Ive ever seen in my life is probably Rachael. And Im wondering how the two of them can be here on this same earth.

And what was that fish thinking as it slid back into the ocean water? What did it think had happened and how did it explain the hook in its mouth and the line trailing after it as it dived down to the invisible depths of the sea?

And where is Rachael now, with her red hair and her thin fingers? Curse, she shouted out that day, curse curse curse. Strange. I think she *meant* to scare us, and now were coming after her.

After four weeks the sickness has come.

Ians telling us to be strong, that God never allows anything good to happen without a fight and a struggle.

Callums telling us that if we dont take action now then well all be dead by the time we get to Nova Scotia.

Roberts telling us to think it out, to plan, to work out what to do before doing it.

Im telling nobody anything, but I know I dont want to die out here with just the seagulls for company, where the menll tip my body off a plank like they did with the man who fell from the mast and the man the sailor killed in the fight. And what dark fish is waiting to pick my bones?

Callum and Donald Sutherland away to one side talking and talking.

Callum and this girl hes met, Katherine, talking and talking.

The sea stretches out all round us, and I need to turn my eyes away sometimes. Its as if the earth has disappeared which is what it must have been like when the Great Flood came and cleaned the world of the badness that was in it. For a wee while I can look across the water and strain my eyes trying to see a cliff or a beach in the glare, but theres nothing and I need to look away and not think about us floating there in the middle of nothing with just the wooden boards under my feet. A kind of panic gets hold of me and I stare at the deck until the feeling goes away.

Ian says – All the rivers of all the lands run into the sea and yet the sea is not full.

The first one died today. One of the older ones, right enough, but not exactly really old either, maybe fifty. He was sick with his bowels loose for a day and a half so they laid him up on the deck in the open air because you cant have that happening down where theres everyone, even a baby crying because one of the women gave birth two days ago. They made a kind of shelter for him there under the stars last night with bits of wood the sailors gave them and some blankets, just to keep the drizzle off him, not that he was noticing. Some of his people sat with him through the dark and Ian went up to say some prayers but whatever prayers they were they never worked because he died this morning. Ian told me that he drifted away and that in the end he wasnt being sick any more because there was nothing left. Ian said, He just disappeared before our eyes, the flesh falling away and his eyes going dark.

Over the side, covered by a blanket, chains round the feet. Down there marking our passage like the wee cairns by the track at the head of the cliff in case you have to find your way in the snow.

Four weeks in.

Callum – Were going to speak to Gray tomorrow.

Me – Who is?

Callum – A lot of us. Are you with us?

Me – How manys a lot? If its just you and a few others youll end up in more bother. He can make it difficult for us you know.

Callum – And how can he?

Me – I dont know. He could hold back your food.

Callum – That wouldnt make much difference, then, would it? Are you with us?

Me – I dont want to be, Callum, but you know fine well that Ill stand by you if I have to.

Callum – Well. He could hold back *our* food, then.

Me – Thats what Im saying.

Callum – Never mind. Theres more than enough food now anyway – thats five away now with the sickness. Old John MacDonald spewing up blood from his guts.

Me – I dont even know who old John McDonald is, Callum. Im just keeping to myself.

Callum – Thats what you do.

Me – That is what I do.

And so he tells me all about what theyve got planned – he tells me that two hundred of them are going to the captains space on deck and theyre going to tell him that something has to be done about the dirt and the disease and the overcrowding. My obvious question is how does he know its going to be so many, has he spoken to them all? No, he tells me, but hes spoken to lots and Donald Sutherland has spoken to lots and Katherine has spoken to lots and Robert has spoken to lots. So between them, yes theyre sure.

Robert? I say. I didnt know Robert was part of all this

troublemaking.

Troublemaking its not. Common sense. Looking out for each other.

I say, But I didnt know Robert was getting involved.

Theres a lot you dont know, Hugh. Im not being bad to you but youre wandering around the ship like a cow thats eaten clover. Youre not paying attention.

Clouds building up in the sky like none Ive ever seen before, tall piles of clouds stretching up to heaven. On the outside white like the clouds of a normal summer but inside a swirling blackness, ready to burst through to the outside. The birds go nowhere near, as if they know something. A storm? After an hour or two the clouds break up and drift away.[12]

Three more.

There was a whispered meeting on our deck after night had fallen. Once it was done I lit the stub of the candle Im keeping and wrote it all down.

So this was it. The boat is swinging and rolling in the waves the way it does and we can hardly see each other because the

---

12   I have searched various reference works, as well as the excellent www.cloudappreciationsociety.org (if you're ever looking for an appealing desktop image) but have been unable to pinpoint exactly what Hugh means here. Eventually, it occurred to me that he may have been speaking metaphorically. However, this seems unlikely, as the general tenor of this section of the text is fragmentary and lacking connectedness and a degree of coherence. If this section was to be viewed as metaphor, I think I would have to reconsider the rest of the section, trying to find meaning where, I'm afraid, none is lurking. One must not search for diamonds in a coal mine, as they say. So, in the end, I conclude that Hugh's descriptive powers have let him down here, or perhaps his observational powers. Either way, the clouds have lost me! – RM

lamps are out. Sometimes, we hear the boots of the sailors on watch pass by overhead. Callum told me that down below Donald Sutherland is speaking to the others that stay down there.

Its all a hush, like in church, though in church there would be more grumbling from the older folk, complaining about Ians sermon. But Ians silent here, not sure, I think, what to say about Callum and his plans. Callum has Katherine beside him, his arm round her waist. I can just make them out in the gloom sitting across from me. Im thinking that it suits quite well with her being from Inverness and Donald being from up north and Callum from down our way and that the three of them have each got their own supporters ready to back them up. Captain Gray knows not a thing, unless he does. I wouldnt be surprised.

Callum starts – Nows the time. Were dying. If we dont take action now then how many of us will even get as far as landfall? How many of us will be left at the bottom of the sea. Robert?

So then Robert stands up and its a Robert Ive not really seen before, if you know what I mean, because in fact I cant really see him at all in the murky space. I glance over at Ian to see what hes thinking but I can hardly see him either never mind read his face.

Heres what Robert says.

Listen to me. Are we going to lie here in our own filth? Are we going to lie here breathing into our lungs the disease that hangs in the air? Are we going to lie here waiting for death? Ask yourselves. Why are we on this ship? Why are we leaving behind our homes? Why are we heading to this new world? Is it just to die on the way? Theres six dead already. Will we let it be more? Can we? Is that what we want? For The Lady Gray to drift into the harbour at Pictou a ghost ship like the ones in the stories of the old folk? This is a journey to find our new lives. Is it not that? It is. So are we going to let Captain Gray end our new lives before we even begin them? I say no. And Im sure you say no too, I'm sure we all do. I *know* we all do. This must stop. The dying must stop. Whats wrong with wanting to start a better life? Nothing. What reason is there for us to die as we take our first steps on the new road? None. What shall we do to make sure we get to America alive and breathing and ready to grip our future in both hands? Everything we can. If we allow Gray to kill us, hell kill us. If we allow him to starve us, he will. If we allow him to take our money for delivering two hundred corpses to America, he will. He will. So we will *not* allow it. Tomorrow, we will tell him where he stands. We will carry our complaints to him and he will listen. We will present him with our complaints and our demands. There will be cleanliness on board The Lady Gray. We will be allowed to take the air on the upper deck whenever we want to, and not just when it suits him. The privies will be cleaned every day, and not every second day. The hatches will be opened up in good weather, whether or not this inconveniences the sailors on the ship. How else can the diseased vapours clear from our throats? Is this too much to ask? To ask to live. To ask to be treated like human beings, instead of like animals? To ask for the chance to bring to life our dreams? To ask not to be brought into the new world cold and stiff and dead? We must bring our words to Captain Gray, and the more of us who do that the better it will be. Are we all together in this?

All the time he spoke, there were mutterings and murmurings from the people, getting louder as the speech went on, until by the end there was a loud noise of agreement from all around. It swept round Robert and he was at the centre of it all in a way he hadnt been before, not that I could remember. I could vaguely see him sit down and I could imagine his burning face and his pride.

Afterwards I said to Ian that I was surprised to hear Robert speaking like this.

Ian said, No, hes always had that inside him, but now its

91

coming out. Hes been a good listener. You heard the stories, Callum heard the ideas but Robert heard the words, I think.

I said, His father tells a good story.

Its the same thing, Ian said. Then he talked a bit about speaking out in public, but I wasnt really listening because suddenly I was thinking about Roberts father down in the Carcair, the air thick with smoke, and stories.[13]

This morning it was quiet amongst us all. The quietness was hanging there when the sailors came down the ladder with the food and when we ate it and when we sat waiting for the word.

Im writing down something I remember, even though it has nothing to do with the main part of the story. It came into my mind during that waiting time today. I remembered the way my mother used to place a bowl of porridge or a piece of bread into my hands when I was just a boy. She did it in a way that wasnt meant to make you feel you had to be grateful. It was just what she did because she was my mother. So no matter how hungry I was she never expected me to say thank you, but I always did, just because she didnt expect it. At the same moment as handing the food to me shed turn away to get on with the next

---

13 Of course, it will strike the modern reader that there is nothing particularly outstanding about Robert's modest little piece of speech-making. It is over-reliant on the rhetorical so-called Rule of Three, done to death by every cheap politician, which is how Robert appears here. But to Hugh, Robert's minor eloquence *is* of note, marking as it does an apparent example of character development (even though this is denied by Ian). On the other hand, perhaps Roberts speech *was* actually more impressive than it reads on the page, possibly because Hugh's own limitations make it hard for us to grasp the electric excitement below decks on that diseased ship, and possibly because Hugh, in his haste to record the words in the light of an inadequate and guttering candle, simply failed to recall them accurately. If so, Robert's first public speech is lost for ever. Its effect, though, is measurable (see below). – RM

thing, banging the plate down on the little wooden table with her body already half turned away. This memory came into me and so did the thought that I wouldnt be seeing her do that again. I wanted to write it down but its not part of the story, just part of me.

Another memory, this time of Rachael and Elizabeth sitting on that rock down by the sea where the seagulls line up. And me on the jetty watching them, maybe fifty yards away. Rachael with her red hair like an autumn leaf and that sounds like a line out of a book. Elizabeth more of a brown colour and catching the sun. They both look over at me and for just a second Im looking at them and theyre looking at me and I feel myself kind of blush as the blood goes to my face. Rachaels thin and leaning back on her elbows on the rock. Elizabeth with a fuller shape to her, sitting up straight. Im about fifteen in this memory so they are too but already Elizabeth has a womans body on her. Theres still the child about Rachael. So theyre looking at me and Im looking back red-faced at them, then Elizabeth leans down to Rachael and says something and theyre both laughing. Id have given anything to know what she said and why they were laughing.

Where are they now? Still friends?

This morning it was quiet and everyone tiptoed around, knowing that this would be an important day.

Callum says – Todays when we take some respect back.

We respect each other, I say.

Callum – But thats not enough, otherwise wed be better off just staying at home.

Too late for that anyway, I say and go off to find Ian.

We are up on deck and the weather is fine. Theres a breeze but its warm on deck and Ian is sitting on some little steps that go from one part of the deck to another higher bit. Maybe by the time this journey is over Ill have learnt the names for these different parts of the boat, but I find it hard. I hear the sailors say the words but they wont stick in my mind. It doesnt matter because if things go well in America Ill never be on one of these boats again anyway.

Ians looking tired, and thinner. That wine and good food fatness is being left behind like the manse at Croval. I dont think he sleeps too well on the boat. Hes used to a big house all by himself with nothing to disturb him. Now all of *us* are used to sharing rooms when we sleep so being crammed together on the lower deck is not so difficult for us as it is for him. I think every cough, every muttered bit of sleep talk, every cry out in the night, every uneasy snore wakes him up and then he cant get himself back off to sleep again. Anyway hes looking tired, with lines under his eyes and his shoulders down. Hes got his elbows on his knees and his hands dangling down by his feet. The little breeze is ruffling his thin grey hair and I cant help noticing hes old looking but as usual I put that idea out of my head because thats not how I want to think of him.

So I sit down beside him and it takes a moment before he comes out of his thoughts and turns to me.

Are you praying? I asked him.

No, he said. Maybe I should have been, though. I was thinking about my sister.

Youve never talked about your sister before.

No, he said. I dont suppose I have.

Where does she stay? Edinburgh? How old is she?

She died, he said. A long time ago. I was thinking about that time.

Im sorry, I said. Did she have a family at all? Nieces and nephews for you?

She was six when she died. Scarlet fever. Her skin was red and itching, then she had a sore throat and her tongue went that red colour. Sickness next and five days later she was dead. I was thinking of that time.

94

Im sorry. How old were you? I asked.

I was ten. What Im remembering is standing by her bed and just looking at her. By that time she was no longer aware that we were around her. She was sweating and her hands were gripping the covers. Thats what I remember of that time. Standing and watching and not being able to speak to her or do anything. I wasnt there when she died but I remember her in her coffin. I remember the doctor coming when she was getting sicker and how serious he was.

I couldnt think of anything to say. I didnt like to see him like this, because I was used to him knowing what to do and say, and not being troubled, so this story didnt make me feel right. I had wondered if I might mention the fall of the rock to him now that we were so far away from home but it didnt seem to be the right moment. We just sat in silence for a little bit and he was looking out over the side of the boat at the waves swelling the water.

After a while I asked him, What do you think will happen today?

He replied, I dont think it will be what Callum and Robert imagine. Theyve got themselves very excited about it but really what can Captain Gray do? Were stuck on this ship and thats where we are until we get to America. Were overcrowded so what can he do? Callum and Robert are expecting an uprising but what can *they* do? Take over the ship? Who would know how to do that? Throw Captain Gray over the side? What happens then when we get to America? A lifetime locked up instead of starting a new life.

But surely hell have to listen to two hundred people all saying the same thing?

Will he? Anyway, there wont be two hundred.

Last night – I began to say but he interrupted me.

Last night was last night and today is today. People say things in the dark when nobody can see their face properly. But in the day time the sun shines on you and people know who you are. So there wont be two hundred. One hundred maybe. Thats the way people are, believe me. I know.

I think he was remembering the way some people in Croval used to mutter against him behind his back but would never say anything to his face.

Will we be getting in trouble, do you think? Is that why people wont do anything? I mean when we get there.

We might.

Is it worth it?

Perhaps it is, yes, but perhaps its not, he said. I just wish this voyage was over and we could get on with things.

So do I, I said and I never meant anything more than that sentence. I asked him, What will you do when we get there, Ian? How will you find a church?

A church?

To be minister in?

Minister?

Isnt that what you want? To be a minister over there? To save souls, thats what you said, wasnt it?

Do you know something, he said, looking at me. *Over there* is probably Scotland now. Were nearer to America than to Scotland, so America must be over *here* now, and Scotland must be over *there*. It all depends where you are. Your point of view depends on where youre standing. Or floating.

Do you miss home?

Do you?

In the afternoon was when it was meant to happen, and, guess what, Ian was right. There was forty five of us went to speak to Captain Gray. Thats all. Forty five. Donald Sutherland was at the front and maybe I was nearer the back but I was there. Ian didnt go and Callum was annoyed at him but I think that was all right. Hes older than us and taking things into your own hands is for younger folk, if you ask me.

Straight away Captain Gray tried to take control of it all.

So, he said. I see that some troublemaker amongst you has been spreading his evil words. Perhaps the ringleader of this nonsense would care to step forward?

I think he expected everyone to hold back, but no, Donald Sutherland and Callum stepped up. The Captain was on this higher bit of deck so that Callum and Donald Sutherland were having to look up at him, which wasnt so good but what choice did they have? The breeze was blowing and the boat was rolling gently. Even after all the time wed been at sea, Callum and the others still werent used to it and every now and then they would stagger a wee bit as the boards moved under them. Captain Gray, though, he stood steady as a house, his feet placed slightly apart, like a man ready for a fight.

Callum – Youre wanting ringleaders, then thats us. But all of us are together. We demand that the cleanliness on this ship –

Captain Gray – Im afraid, young man, that you are in no position to demand anything at all. Perhaps you forget that you are reliant upon myself and my fine crew to carry you to your destination.

Callum – I have overlooked nothing. It is you thats encouraged us to overlook the filth, the stench, the disease that –

Captain Gray – Disease? I can inform you, sir, that my ship has never before had disease upon her. Never in any of the previous crossings we have made. Never, I say. It follows, therefore, that the disease that has broken out on board has been brought hither by your own people and that its spread is due to your own existing state of ill health and your poor constitutions. You will note, I presume, that none of my sailors have been afflicted with the illness?

Meanwhile those sailors were creeping about on their business, coiling ropes, moving buckets, mopping the deck and so on, half watching the confrontation and not wanting to miss a word but not wanting to be seen by their Captain paying too much attention.

Donald Sutherland – Dont talk d*** rubbish, man. Your sailors dont get sick because they dont sleep on our d*** decks. They have their own quarters where the air is clean.

Captain Gray – My sailors are strong and healthy and unlikely to succumb to your paupers diseases. That is why they are unaffected. There is nothing wrong with the air on your steerage decks.

Callum – How would you know? Have you been down there? Have you smelt the stink?

Captain Gray – Nobody forced you to come on board. I believe you paid for the privilege. You *chose* to sleep on board my ship.

Callum – But so many of us! How can it be fair to put so many of us in there? Your ship is overcrowded, Captain Gray, and you must have known that when you took our money. And your decks are too close together for passengers. The regulations state that five foot four is –

Captain Gray – How dare you speak to me of regulations, you upstart? I have been sailing this noble ship since –

And then a surprising thing happened which was that Robert stepped forward from the crowd, elbowing his way past Callum and Donald Sutherland. Callum was flushed with anger and it was hard to tell if he was more annoyed at Captain Gray or at Robert for pushing in and moving him back a space.

Captain Gray, Robert said, all polite. We bow to your superior experience. Of course we do. You are most likely correct in the way you have considered our situation. Maybe we act too rashly in confronting you like this, so rudely.

Callums eyes were just about popping out of his head and Donald Sutherland was looking at him the way a stoat looks at a wee baby rabbit.

But Robert carried on, And I can only apologise on behalf

of myself and my friends here. If we have spoken out of turn it is only through our ignorance of what –

Donald Sutherland – Whos b****y ignorant, you little –

Robert, louder – ignorance of what is right and wrong in such times. You told us of your many voyages aboard this fine ship – please remember this is just our first. If we make mistakes, they are mistakes of inexperience.

Captain Gray was beginning to look a bit calmer though that couldnt be said of Callum and Donald Sutherland. I turned to look at Ian who was standing on the deck a long way behind the crowd, listening in. He had a little smile on him.

Captain Gray, puffing out his chest – Well. And you will understand my anger at being spoken to by a rabble such as this. In light of your more peaceable words, sir, I am inclined to overlook this matter, provided no more is said about it on your side. We are only ten days out of Pictou and I trust your people can restrain themselves until then.

Robert, giving a sort of little bow which is something Im sure hed never done before – Thank you Captain Gray. We all, Im sure, are grateful to you for your understanding. And indeed we are grateful to you for this passage to a new life. Without you we would be scraping a living in the hard soil of Scotland.

A few angry murmurs at this, which I thought was funny, because if people wanted to speak up for Scotland they should never have left there in the first place.

Captain Gray – Never a truer word spoken. Im glad to see that at least one of you has the intelligence to see sense.

Robert – And as a gesture of thanks for all that has been done for us by your crew and most especially by your good self, Captain Gray, we would like to invite you to eat with us this evening. On our deck. As our guest. We would be honoured if you would accept.

At this there was a silence and Captain Gray stared hard at Robert and then at all of the emigrants standing down below him. Callum was looking at Robert too and so was Donald Sutherland. I looked round again to see what Ian was thinking but he wasnt there. Captain Gray took a step forward, stopped, then came down the steps until he was right in front of Robert. He leaned in close. His voice was a hiss, like an angry cat.

I have never in my life, sir, heard such impertinence. I shall be glad when this godforsaken passage is over.

Robert didnt step back. He said, I believe we all feel much the same.

Then Captain Gray stormed away, shouting orders to the sailor that was the second most important man on the boat, a Mr Simpson.

We were all left standing, not very sure what exactly had happened. Callum and Donald were at Robert, talking away to him. The others began to wander off around the deck and some of the others who hadnt been brave enough to stand up to Captain Gray came carefully up the steps from the lower two decks, asking questions of those people that *had* been there.

Now we have to wait and see if it all makes any difference. Since it all happened Ive been thinking about how I feel about it and writing down some of these feelings. Ian has been telling me that writing down my feelings is important, and not to just write down things that happen.

First. I feel as if Ive grown up a bit. I didnt say anything at the time and I was standing further back than Callum, Robert and Donald Sutherland, but at least I was there. I know my own faults and one of them is that sometimes I dont stand up when I should and I feel as if I have done that this time. For example, maybe there were times when I should have stood up more to what my mother said to me, but shes not a happy woman and sometimes its best not to make things worse.

Second. Im proud of Robert. Everyone always thought he was the quiet dark one and I thought that too but weve seen a different side of him today.

Fourth. Im not sure Donald Sutherland is to be trusted and I think we should shake him off when we get to America. Anyway hes going on to Quebec he says and not getting off at Pictou like us and thats for the best.

Fifth. Why did Ian not wait to see how it all turned out? I asked him and he wouldnt tell me.

Sixth. Ive never had real enemies before, although some of the old men in Croval thought we were a bit of a bother sometimes, but they think that about all younger people. So Im wondering tonight if weve made an enemy and also Im wondering if it really matters much because once were in Pictou I dont think well be seeing Captain Gray ever again.

Seventh. Will Captain Gray tell his sailors to do more to keep the boat clean and healthy, with the fresh air blowing through the lower decks? Or will he not, just to make us learn a lesson?

Eighth. If he doesnt will more people die?

Ninth. Will one of them be me?

At night, some of the people tell stories. Ian says it would be good to write some of them down because these stories are the sort of stories that dont get written down anywhere. Ian himself loves the stories, saving them up in his head for using in future sermons, he says. I ask him why he doesnt write them down. He says it would be cheating if *he* was to do it, which I dont understand.

So heres one that a young woman told. Her name is Anne Beaton, from a place called Edderton. Her brother, also called Hugh, was one of the forty five.

Once there was an old woman who lived in a croft up in the hills, a long way away from anyone else. She had a cow and some chickens and she grew some oats on the strip of thin dirty land behind the building. Now it was said that this old woman had the powers of magic and that she could make the weather change to suit herself. If she wanted to sit outside her door doing a bit of knitting she could make the clouds go back from the face of the sun and if she wanted some moisture to feed her oats as the crop grew, well then she could make the clouds come drifting back and then the rain would fall.

So the landowner, who lived away down south, a man called Lord Ashbourne, heard about this woman and decided that he had to see her. His wife, the beautiful Lady Ashbourne, was sick and about ready to die, and he wondered if the old woman might be able to help. Hed tried all the best doctors that money could buy in Edinburgh and none of them could do anything for his wife, who was wasting away lying on a big oak bed underneath silk covers.

He came up to the north and he got on his great grey horse and began to ride away up into the glen towards where the old woman stayed. His factor wanted to go with him, but Lord Ashbourne said no, this was a journey he must make by himself.

Well, he rode for two days on his great grey horse and still he couldnt find the old womans croft. At night he slept under the stars with the trees creaking in the wind and the owls calling from tree to tree and the night creatures padding on the dry leaves near his head. On the third day he was beginning to wonder if the directions hed got from the people in the village had been right because he couldnt find the croft anywhere. He was just beginning to think he would have to give up and go back down to his estate to comfort his dying wife when all of a sudden there was this big black crow on a branch right in front of him. This crow hopped from the branch of one tree to the branch of the next and Lord Ashbourne began to follow it, picking his way through the trees on his great grey horse. Well this went on for a while until in the end he came into a clearing in amongst the trees and there was this croft with a wee bit of land, some chickens and a cow tethered at the back. And there was an old woman sitting on a stool at the front, looking right at him as if shed been expecting him there all the time.

Youve come to see me about your sick wife, havent you? she says.

How did you know that? asks Lord Ashbourne.

You want me to tell you what to do to save her life, dont you? says the old woman.

Can you tell me that? asks Lord Ashbourne.

You think I can and thats why youve come, isnt it? she says and her eyes are cutting through him like a sharp knife. The crow has flown down and is pecking away at the ground beside her stool.

Will you tell me? asks Lord Ashbourne.

Perhaps I will. But first you must tell me *why* I should help you, says the old woman that everyone thought was a witch.

So Lord Ashbourne got down off his great grey horse and went up close to the old woman. He said to her, For Gods sake, woman, you live on my land. You have to help me.

The old woman looked round about her. She said, And how is this your land? Ive been living here for near eighty year and Ive always thought it was my wee bit of land.

This is all my land, Lord Ashbourne replied. This clearing and those oats and the tees round about us and the mountain that the trees grow on and the range that the mountain is a part of. And your chickens and your cow when it come down to it. Theyre on my land so theyre really mine too.

And what about this crow? asks the old woman. Does he belong to you as well or does he belong to himself?

At this the crow hops up onto the bucket thats upside down by the wall of the croft and peers at Lord Ashbourne with its beady black eye. And it occurs to Lord Ashbourne that the crow is the old womans familiar, a creature of the devil, and that maybe he should be a bit careful about what he says, but even so he cant stop himself.

Yes, he tells her. Yes, he belongs to me too, because he lives in the wood, and as I told you, the woods belong to me.

So, says the old woman, you think I should be helping you because I have to.

Thats about the size of it, Lord Ashbourne tells her, raising his voice in anger.

The crow flies off and the old woman goes into the croft and comes back out with a mirror, just an old cracked mirror with nothing special about it, not like the golden mirrors you get in some stories. She holds it up and looks deeply into it for a wee while.

Hurry up! shouts Lord Ashbourne. My wife is dying! Cant you just tell me what I need to do?

After a minute or two, the old woman lays the mirror down. She whispers so that he has to come close to hear her old papery voice saying, Lord Ashbourne, here is what you must do. You must take your great grey horse and you must go on a journey that lasts until the mountain range folds in on itself to become one mountain, and then you must continue with your journey until the one mountain rolls itself out flat into a moor, and then you must keep riding on your great grey horse until the trees of the forest edge closer to each other and closer still until eventually they join together to be one huge tree, and then you must keep riding until that tree shrinks down and shrinks down until it is just a sapling, until it is just a shoot, until it is just a seed lying on the ground and then you must keep journeying until the crow you saw before comes along and pecks at that seed and eats it up. When that happens you can stop your journey and go home to your wife and youll find she is healthy and all will be well.

Lord Ashbourne leapt to his feet and shouted at her, Idiot! I should have known an old woman like you living in dirt and poverty would have nothing sensible to say to me! I have never heard such nonsense in my whole life. I have wasted my time coming here!

And with that he leapt on to his great grey horse and galloped away through the trees, down the mountain and off south the long road to his estate.

But when he got home, there was bad news. His wife had been much worse in her illness while hed been away and by the time he had run up the marble stairs and turned the golden handle on the oak door to her room she was dead. He wept over her body for three days, and he tore his hair in his grief. I should have listened to the witch! he cried. I should have tried to work out what she meant.

He paced the long corridors of his big house and his footsteps echoed like a stone dropped into a deep and empty well.

And then he thought that if the witch had been speaking some kind of truth, even if he hadnt understood it, maybe she could do something to help even yet. Maybe if she had the magical powers of life and death she would know a spell that could bring his beautiful young wife back to the world of the living once again.

So off he went on his great grey horse, back to the north, back to the mountains, back into the woods. Three days he wandered in amongst the trees and still he couldnt find the croft where hed spoken to the old woman that everyone was sure was an evil witch. And just when he was beginning to wonder if he should give up and go away home, the crow flew down through the branches and landed in a tree right in front of him. It peered at him with its beady eye and then hopped on to another branch, and then another, all the time leading Lord Ashbourne deeper and deeper into the forest.

And there they are to this day, never reaching the end of their journey, the big black crow hopping along, leading Lord Ashbourne and his great grey horse deeper and deeper into the woods, and there theyll be until the mountain range folds in on itself to become one mountain, and the one mountain rolls itself out flat into a moor, and the trees of the forest edge closer to each other and closer still until eventually they join together to be one huge tree, and that tree shrinks down and shrinks down until it is just a sapling, until it is just a shoot, until it is just a seed lying on the ground and one day the crow will peck at that seed and eat it up. And then Lord Ashbourne will be together with his wife once again, because that will be the day when the world ends.

And some people say that if you go into that wood late at night you might be able to hear, in the distance, the sound of a great grey horse blowing hard amongst the trees and the harsh mocking cry of a big black crow and the sob of a man who made a mistake that cost him everything, that did the one wrong thing that shadowed his life forever.

Ian says I should write down more stories like that but Im not so sure. It feels as if Im writing down other peoples words and thats not right, is it?

The sea is disappearing in fog and it is so cold that we all have on our greatcoats and mittens, apart from the people who do not have these things. Ian forgot to take his mittens so I gave him mine to use and my hands are red and sore. In the distance there was something floating on the water and one of the sailors said it was a mountain of ice and that these sometimes float in these waters and threaten the boats to sinking. But the fog rolled in again and we never saw it again, so maybe he was saying these things to frighten us. The sailors will sometimes do that, telling us tales of men lost overboard, boats that went away down through the water with all hands lost or strikes of lightning that burned boats to the water line with the emigrants slowly drowning in the cold salt ocean beside the smoking hulk.

The strangest thing happened today and it has scared me more than any storms or sailors talk.

All through the morning the men were leaning over the

side of the boat with ropes and on the end of the rope was a big lead weight. They were trying to work out how deep the water is here, one of them said, because this bit of the sea has some places where the bottom of the sea comes up nearly to the surface, although you cant see these places just by looking. You have to use the ropes to find out how deep it is. These places where the bottom of the sea comes up are called the Banks and the sailors were all in an excitement about them and when we would reach them. All the morning they were shouting numbers of fathoms up to the captain. A fathom is the height of a man.

Then in the middle of the day all of the emigrants were told to go down below decks and there we were kept until there was a banging on the hatches and we were brought up into the light and told to stand at the back end of the top deck. The fog was thick all around us and the Lady Gray was lying still in the cold air. We huddled together not knowing what was going to happen next and I was worrying that we were lost or that one of the Banks had come up out of the deep and damaged the bottom of the boat, but I was also thinking we would have felt it through the timbers of the boat if that had happened, so I didnt really know what to think.

At the other end of the top deck the sailor had rigged up a sail that blocked off our view of that part of the boat. There were noises and shouts and laughter coming from behind this sail and that made us all the more worried. People were talking to each other in quiet voices, wondering what was happening. My heart was beating fast.

Then there was a great shout from the sailors and the word they shouted out again and again was, Neptune! Neptune! Neptune! Later on Ian explained that Neptune is a God that lives in the sea according to some people that lived a long time ago, before our own God was the God that everyone knew was in Heaven.

Neptune! Neptune! Neptune! they were shouting as loud as

anything and the sound of their shouts seemed to bounce back from the thick walls of fog that were all around the boat and I shivered, and not just because it was cold. We all took a shuffle in closer to each other. Their shouts got louder and louder and quicker and quicker and then all of a sudden the sail that was stretched across the deck fell to the boards and there was silence and we saw the strangest thing.

All the sailors were standing in a half circle and they were all bowed down at the waist and in the middle there was Neptune and his wife. Of course I knew at that moment that it was two of the sailors dressed up but at the same time it *was* Neptune and his wife like a great King and Queen or in fact like a God and Goddess. Neptune was naked to the waist and all around his head and face were great strands of seaweed like hair and a beard. The seaweed was fresh from the water and it was dripping down across the mans chest, where he had tattoos and scars from his life as a sailor. But he was also Neptune, and as they began to walk slowly towards us I could see there were still creatures in that drenched seaweed, sea lice and a little crab pushing through the strands. In his hand he had a long pole which must have been made from an oar from one of the small boats that were tied to the side of the Lady Gray. At the top there were three spikes, shaped out of metal. As he took each step he thumped this stick down on the deck and it was the only noise to be heard. His wife, Neptunes wife, was in a dress but I dont know where they got it from. Maybe it belonged to one of the emigrants or maybe they kept it for just this dressing up. Neptunes wife, I knew, was one of the other sailors but just then he was Neptunes wife, and her hair was seaweed and round her wrists she had bangles of seaweed and round her neck was a rope of seaweed like a necklace or a chain. Her hands were held out towards us and in one hand were shells and the bones of dead fish, and in the other was a wicked looking metal binding strap from a barrel, sharpened and joined on to a wooden handle like a huge curved razor and with each step she took, at the moment Neptunes stick crashed on to the deck, she swept this razor through the air in front of her, from one side to the other. Hail to King Neptune! shouted the sailors at the tops of their voices and then, Hail to the Sea Queen!

I moved backwards as they came closer but I couldnt go any further because there was a crush of people between me and the side of the boat, as tight packed as the potatoes in the tinker MacPhees boxes. Ian was just right behind me now and I could hear him whispering fast in to himself and it was a second or two before I knew it was a prayer he was saying.

Suddenly one of the sailors sprang out from the others and jumped in front of Neptune and his wife. He had his back to us and was making low bows to the Sea-King and Sea-Queen. There was quiet for a few moments and then Neptune raised one hand up with the finger pointing out and it swung round across the frightened faces of us all. It seems very stupid and if you read this youll be thinking I dont tell the truth but at the moment his sea water dripping finger moved across my face, even though he was still twenty feet away, I felt a heat go through me as if someone had waved a burning branch at my eyes. Then his fingers stopped and the sailor bowed down in front of him and said Yes Master, then turned and ran towards us in the direction of that pointing finger.

He pulled out of the crowd a shaking and now crying boy of about twelve years old, one of the ones that came on the boat from further up North, maybe Glencalvie or somewhere like that. His mother was with him and she tried to pull him back but the sailor was too strong for her and she had to let go. Then the other sailors were all moving round towards us and they held us back as the young boy was made to kneel down in front of Neptune and his wife. The sailor that had dragged him out sort of slapped him on the back of the head then came to join the others to stand in front of us so that I had to get up on tiptoe to see what was happening to the boy. There was just silence and I had a strange feeling in my stomach, that feeling you get when youre out on the water and you realise youve forgotten to take your gutting knife with you and you know Callums going to be so annoyed with you when you tell him in a wee while.

Out of the silence King Neptune said, We cross the banks.

The sailors all chanted back, We cross the banks.

King Neptune – Our journey nears its close.

The sailors – Our journey nears its close.

King Neptune – The Lord of the ocean demands a payment for safe passage.

Sailors – Safe passage.

King Neptune – And the price of passage is chosen by my fateful wife.

Sailors – The Queen! The Queen!

King Neptune – The time has come. Choose!

Sailors – Choose!

Silence again for a tiny moment and then the Queen swung her razor through the air once, then twice, then a third time. Then she said, just in a whisper, a whisper that made me cold – Blood.

Blood! said the sailors, then Blood! again, then they were shouting all together, Blood! Blood! Blood!

So they chanted on and the Queen moved forwards towards the boy who was by now just about lying on the deck and I could hardly see him because of the sailor in front of me, but I saw Neptune take a stride towards him and haul him up to his feet by the hair, roughly turning him round so he was facing us. The Queen stood to one side, and she took her razor and slowly, with no violence in her action, she drew it down the side of the boys face, down his cheek and the red blood glistened and ran. The sailors gave a great shout, Neptunes Blood! The

110

Queen waved the razor in the air again to silence them and stepped to the other side of the boy, raising the weapon as if she would cut the other side of his face. The boy was shaking and crying and I was thinking we should all push forwards and do something about it because where would it end?

Then someone did push me, but not forwards. I was shoved to one side and it took me a bit before I realised that it was Ian that had done it and hed pushed the sailor in front out of the way too. I never knew he was that strong, the old man.

Stop! he was shouting. Stop! Stop this ungodly wickedness. Captain Gray! Captain Gray! Stand forward! Hold your hand, you, sir! I condemn you all!

The man who was dressed up as the woman let his arm fall and all of a sudden they werent Neptune and Neptunes Queen and they were just two sailors dressed up in foolish clothes with seaweed dripping down their bodies. One of the other sailors told me afterwards that the seaweed in the water is one of the first signs that youre getting close to the banks and they drag it up to help with the making of the costumes.

Ian marched up to the man who was in the dress and grabbed the metal thing from his hand and hurled it over the side of the boat into the sea. Then he was scrabbling with his old fingers at the seaweed and pulling it off and letting it fall to the wooden deck. I was waiting for them to do something to stop him but they just stood there, as if hed taken their strength away from them, like in some old story. And the boy ran back into the crowd with the rest of us and his mother took a handkerchief and dabbed at the blood on his face but it turned out it was only a scratch really.

Then Captain Gray appeared on the bit of the deck thats a bit higher up and he shouted down in his big Captains voice, Hold still there, every man!

Ian let go of Neptune and turned to the Captain. He pointed up at him, a bit like the way Neptune had pointed at the boy.

Ian said, Captain Gray! I am appalled, and I will not tolerate this behaviour.

Well, Captain Gray just looked down at him then up at the rest of us, still pressed back frightened against the edge of the boat. The sailors were all looking at their Captain to see what he would say or what he would do.

Ian spoke again, saying, We are Christian people, all of us. I had assumed that you were too, Captain Gray, and that you would be able to keep your men under some sort of moral control. I am disgusted by your failure to do so. This, this idolatry, this disgraceful spectacle that, this

His words drained away as the Captain turned his eyes on him again. It was quiet then, the only noise the breeze in the sails and ropes, the rigging the men call it, and the water whispering past the boat and the cries of the seagulls that were telling us we were getting nearer to land now.

Captain Gray said, Mr MacLeod. No more. I fancy that your job is to tend to the souls of your people, whereas mine is to run this ship. I have no criticism of your attempts to maintain this rabble as Godfearing Christians. I trust that you will have no criticisms of my captaincy, given that I believe you have no experience and therefore no ability to see beneath the surface of the harmless ritual you have just

Ian – Harmless? Blood was drawn, sir!

Captain Gray – This, as I say, *harmless* ritual, one which my men, and the men on countless other Christian ships, have carried out time and again at just this point in the voyage.

Ian – It is an abomination.

Captain Gray, swinging his arm round to indicate the whole deck – I do not see Gods righteous punishment. Nor have I ever.

Ian – It does not become you, sir, to express such flippancy or to

Captain Gray – Enough! We will have no more of your smug condemnations on my ship. All emigrants will proceed below decks.

And with that he turned and disappeared himself, back down to his cabin I suppose, where he kept his maps and papers and big books with instructions about sailing across to America, according to one of the men, who told me that.

The sailors pushed and nudged at us, forcing us back down into the darker decks below. They were laughing a kind of grim laughter, knowing that their Captain had supported them, but also knowing that a minister had condemned them and finding themselves trapped between two different strong voices. I wonder if there are any of them who dont approve of the Neptune ritual, as Captain Gray called it. But what can you do when the voices of nearly everyone are against you?

Ian was quiet when we got below deck and I went and sat next to him. Some light gets through between the joins in the wooden planks of the boat. He didnt really want to talk to me about what had happened. There was a tightness about him and I was wondering what he was thinking, but he wouldnt say. He just said one thing.

Where are we heading for, Hugh?

I thought it was a real question and so I said, America.

But now I realise it was not an ordinary question and my answer was foolish, but I didnt see what he meant so its not really my fault. But I dont want Ian to think Im stupid or dont recognize what hes talking about. Above all I want him to understand that I am serious, so that he knows that when I talk to him it is important.

Im lying down tonight to sleep with a heavy feeling inside that I cant understand.

It would be better if this journey was finished soon and crossing the banks means thats probably true.

Nothing gets better. A sailor told me this afternoon that wed be seeing land tomorrow or the next day. The sickness has carried

113

on and the boat is even dirtier than it was. People cant get to the privy in time, theyre so sick, and so the smell is worse than ever but still Captain Gray wont let anyone sleep on the deck. He says its too dangerous. The whole thing with Robert and Callum and Donald Sutherland has come to nothing really. Captain Gray just ignored it. Nothing was said. Soon after it all happened and it was obvious nothing was going to change Callum was going around shouting at everyone trying to stir them up into doing something else, another meeting or even trying to take over the boat altogether but how we were going to steer the boat without Captain Grays advice I dont know. And were nearly there so what would be the point? Anyway everyone is too tired or too sick or too scared to do anything and the ones who were at the first meeting are worried that Captain Grays silence means we will all be in trouble once we get to Pictou.

But what can he do?

I dont really want to write any more.

Heres what Callum said, and it reminded me of what he once said on a warm windy day when were about fifteen and we were at the far end of the shore at Craigtore, sheltering beside an upside down boat with Elizabeth and Rachael. Callum was complaining because we wouldnt have anything to do with some scheme or other he had in mind.

He said, People are cowards. They say theyll do something but in the end theyre too scared to do anything really.

And the reply Robert gave him was much the same as the one that Elizabeth gave back then. He said, Its not that, Callum. Its just that sometimes people think more than they act. If we want things to change we need to make them think *about* acting.

I couldnt work out who I agreed with more. Callums anger or Roberts calmness. Both of them could persuade you.

And agreeing with one meant disagreeing with the other, which was hard.

In a lot of ways we are kind of like brothers but in other ways, well, we are kind of not.

I need to ask Ian about this. In some ways hes kind of like my father but in other ways hes kind of not.

So this morning there it was, a line of dark at the edge of the water, a new country. One of the sailors told me this was an island called Cape Breton just nearly joined on to the place we were going, which is Pictou on a piece of land called New Scotland, which is Canada, which is America. The man was speaking to me while he was polishing away at some brass bits on the side of the wall at the edge of the deck. It was a man Id spoken to a few times over the journey and he was quite friendly, about forty years old, small and thin but strong, with a funny voice that Ian told me was an English accent. This man was saying names that sounded strange, the words coming off his lips as if they were normal, words hed to spell for me. Amherst, Onslow, Guysborough, Cobequid Bay, Chedabucto, Lunenburg, Kennetcook. Pictou. And names that were from the Gaelic, like the names of places away on the islands to the west of Scotland that Id heard MacPhee talking about. Antigonish, Merigomish.

All the time the line of land was getting closer and seagulls drifted round the boat, as hungry as us.

Thats where youre going, said the man, pointing. Thats your new home.

What about you? I asked him. Do you ever think about moving on, trying somewhere new?

Maybe, he said. Thats what everyone wants isnt it?

So will you just get off one day and stay here?

Might do. Theres a Liverpool here too, you know.

I didnt really understand that but he explained that there was a big town called Liverpool in England, bigger than Inverness, and that was where he stayed, when he wasnt on the sea.

I asked, What about your family back in England? Would you miss them if you came and stayed over here?

Why?

Im just asking.

He shrugged and went away off to do some other job that needed done. I thought about this Liverpool and how Id never ever be there to see it, to get an idea of what sort of place it was. And I thought that if this sailor *didnt* decide to stay here in New Scotland one day then Id probably never see him again and even if he did, well I probably still wouldnt. I felt I wanted to go after him and talk to him again but I didnt and the next thing I knew there was Ian at my shoulder gazing out across the water at the land that was growing in front of us.

Here it is, Hugh, says Ian. This is it. What are you thinking?

I waited for a minute then said, Im thinking about how far behind us Croval is.

Always best to face forwards, he said.

Thats what Im doing, I replied, but I could hear a kind of catch in my voice.

This is what God wants for us.

Why is it?

Think about Adam and Eve in the Garden of Eden, says Ian.

I thought about them for a wee while. I say, Wasnt that bad, though? The way they wanted what they couldnt have?

Bad and good, Ian says. Disobedient, yes, but on the other hand that act of leaving the Garden of Eden gets to the heart of our natures, does it not?

Really? So doing something wrong isnt so bad sometimes. Do you think that?

Not in front of the elders at Croval, no. But here with the coast of our new lives ahead of us, yes, I think I do.

So do I, I said, and I looked over at the side of his face, the old skin wrinkling around his eyes as he peered ahead at the land. The wind was whispering on his white hair. The voyage has really thinned him down. I am glad he is with us.

Yes, I do, I said again and he turned and smiled at me.

Down below our feet there are bodies laid out and others are at the bottom of the sea in between Croval and Pictou. But we are alive, hungry and unwell maybe, but alive and looking ahead. My mind is full of getting to this other world and finally catching up with my dreams and shaking off what has happened in the past.

Intertitle 2

At this point in Hugh's narrative there are some pages missing; how many I can't tell. It is not simply that in the excitement of landing at Pictou he forgot to keep his intermittent undated diary for some time, because the next section begins mid-sentence.

On the night when I first read the manuscript, and came to this frustrating gap in the text, I immediately climbed back up into the attic of this old house and searched and searched to see if the missing pages had somehow become separated from the main bundle but were still lying up there somewhere. No luck. I came back down the ladder, dusty and disappointed and then another thought struck me: perhaps the lost pages were not lost after all, but had simply been shuffled into the large bundle in the wrong place. So I spent the next two hours sifting through the pages that lay ahead attempting to establish if any of them appeared out of sequence. And of course I had to try to do this without really taking in the sense of these future pages, since of course the pleasure in reading a text (or reading a life, which is what we are undertaking here) is derived from the tension that comes from events being gradually revealed. I took to scanning only the bottom right hand corner of a page to see if what was written there could possibly be the beginning of the sentence:

"and for a woman of her age youd say she was good looking despite that."

I found some candidates, then had to read the whole page to see if the subject matter was the arrival at Pictou. But no, none of them made sense.

So with all that time wasted, I returned to the next part of Hugh's account, resigned to the fact that it was incomplete, and praying that there would be no further gaps in the rest of the material. It was a long night of reading. At one point my husband came through to ask me if I was ever going to sleep and to be honest I didn't feel that I ever would. Hugh was taking me over.

Anyway, what to do? I toyed with the idea of writing the missing pages myself and passing them off as Hugh's. I do not really believe that this would have been within my capabilities, but even thirty-odd thousand words into the diary I was certain that it was a commercial proposition and I was worried that a publisher would be ill-disposed towards an incomplete text. If I could fill in the gap satisfactorily, perhaps I could increase the chance of getting the text accepted and thus recouping some of the money that has disappeared over the years.

I hope this does not sound dishonest, or greedy. You have to live. And I hope that any gain I make from Hugh's story is regarded as less important than the sharing of this almost mythic story. I know the gain for me has been in the realms of personal development and what money may come is by the by. This book has given me hope, because it has given me some answers to the larger questions that were bothering me at the time when I began to explore my own family history and what it had to do with my present life, questions to do with responsibility and forgiveness. Finding an ancestor brought to life in these pages, a brief kind of life, has made me think more deeply about who to blame when things go wrong. I saw choices. We can blame ourselves or we can blame other people. We can hate ourselves or we can choose to hate other people. It all has to do with perspective. Hugh's helped me to think this way, helped me to come to the conclusion that maybe the key question is not *who* to blame but *whether* to blame. Perhaps we don't have to hate anyone.

Anyway, my eventual plan was to write the missing pages as if Hugh had come down with the typhus that afflicted those poor travellers (more on this below), thus explaining away any roughness or inconsistency of style that might otherwise make a perceptive editor suspicious of this section, and possibly, therefore, of the text as a whole.

However, it is clear from what Hugh says elsewhere (I discovered as I read on) that he absolutely did *not* contract the illness, so my intervention in replacing the lost pages would require some equally suspicious crossing out later on in the text. So that wouldn't do.

In any case, I realised, the whole idea was flawed. I could not replicate the paper upon which Hugh's words are written[14] and modern ink is very different from nineteenth-century ink, unfortunately for my plan. So, back to square one.

Indeed square one was the only square in town, so to speak. And square one simply involved accepting that these pages were missing, irretrievably missing.

What I find so irritating about this absence is the fact that they would have dealt with the key moment in the narrative when Hugh sets foot on a new land. I'm not a traveller, but these days people take visiting new countries for granted. It would have been good to have read what Hugh felt when he stepped on a new continent for his first and only time. I think tourists now see foreign travel as a kind of right, as if the world has been laid on for their benefit.

But for Hugh, hardly setting foot out of Croval for those first nearly two decades, to step on to a new land, a new continent, and to know that in all likelihood this new land will be both the first and the last new land he will encounter, there must have been an excitement that we can, unfortunately, only guess at.

---

14 One advantage of holding the original manuscript in one's hands, as opposed to a commercially printed version, is that one can see the change of paper that occurs shortly after the arrival in Pictou, caused, of course, by Hugh running out of his original stock and having to obtain more. He makes no reference to this in his narrative (unless he did so in the missing pages) so we will never know the circumstances of his obtaining of this new paper. Of course this process happens several times throughout the bundle of pages, though I cannot go into detail here without giving the game away.

What disappoints me is that this should have been the centre of the whole text: not in terms of the physical centre deduced by a crude counting of words, but the emotional centre, where Hugh makes good his promise to find a new life. The heart of the book, I mean.

So we'll just have to speculate about how he felt when the sole of his mid-nineteenth century shoe touched the soil of mid-nineteenth-century Pictou, the moment when he took his first step on the new stage of his life. What did he think when he looked around at this new scenery? These new people? This new part of his story?

What would Hugh have known, despite MacDougall's book[15], that would have helped him to understand the plot possibilities of his future life on those far shores (farther shores, of course, than they ever can be for any of us)?

It's hard for me to grasp, since the biggest genuine journey I've ever made, really, is about seventy-five miles down the road to Aberdeen. Not much of a journey, I know, but important to me. It took me on a route along which I would meet Philip and all that entailed, the falling in love that is one of my weaknesses.

But I should be writing here about Hugh's story and more especially the part of it which is missing. I should perhaps fill in some of the details for the casual reader who probably has little knowledge of the era.[16] In some ways the specific detail is

---

15 Available, incidentally from *Natural Heritage* publishers. Not a thrilling book, but informative. I found it intriguing to read it, knowing Hugh had read it too – it brought us closer.

16 I hope I don't sound patronising: I freely admit my knowledge of Pictou and its Scottish immigrants was non-existent until I realised I would have to find out more. I would probably have relied only on Hugh's information, such as it is, if it hadn't been for this gap in the manuscript. I could add a bibliography listing the texts I read to understand Hugh's journey better but I have always thought that bibliographies smack of showing off and I would like to think I am past that now: I hope so.

unimportant and not directly relevant to the drive of Hugh's journey but I feel it is useful to know the fate of the *Lady Gray*.

Research has shown that only seventy-five of the *Lady Gray*'s two hundred and forty[17] passengers were meant to disembark at Pictou. The remainder were supposed to remain on board and then head off to Quebec. However, the entire group was taken off the ship so that it could be cleaned and fumigated, such was the extent of the disease which had taken hold in the unsanitary conditions on board. It seems that six emigrants died of typhus[18] and a further twenty-six were seriously affected. At least some of the dead were buried at Pictou, though from Hugh's account there were also burials at sea. The town of Pictou's Port Health Officer, investigating conditions on board the *Lady Gray*, caught the infection and died. Hugh makes no mention of this unfortunate casualty, but then there is no reason why he should have. By the time Dr Martin died, Hugh would have been long clear of any connection with the ship.

Interestingly, a *Halifax Times* report of the incident, written some two years after the event, suggests that overcrowding was the entire cause of the problem. The newspaper reporter claimed that the ship was designed to carry no more than 171 passengers, so the complaints of Callum and Robert and Donald Sutherland seem entirely justified.

Another surviving document is the report written by some

---

17 Note that this figure does not agree exactly with Hugh's own. I assume the historical perspective is more accurate than Hugh's contemporary one.

18 Although I must say it seems to me that Hugh's diary implies that there were more deaths than that. Could it be the case that official records were doctored to disguise the true figures? Might this account for the discrepancy noted in footnote 17, above? I have no wish to question the integrity of anyone involved in that fateful sailing, but one's mind does probe away at inconsistencies, perhaps arriving at unreasonable conclusions.

of the emigrants who took part in the protests during the journey itself. It seems very strange, but they do not mention overcrowding – perhaps because they had no idea what the rules were regarding the number of emigrants who could be crammed into a vessel[19]. Their report fairly and squarely lays the blame for what happened at the feet of Captain Gray, claiming that it was his inefficiency and disregard for the emigrants that led to the disease that claimed innocent lives. The names of Robert, Callum and Donald Sutherland do not appear on this semi-official report. It is impossible now to know why this would be the case. Was there a disagreement over what should be highlighted in the document? Or perhaps those three free spirits had simply lost interest now that they had safely arrived at Pictou and could not be bothered to append their names to the document of complaint. After all, they had other hardships to focus on by then.

For the new arrivals at Pictou the first thing to do would be to acquire somewhere to stay, some means of making a living. For Hugh, there were also some readjustments to make, coming to understand what he'd seen of his friends on the *Lady Gray*. We all learn unexpected things about those closest to us. It happens all the time and I could write more about that but it is time now to get back to Hugh's account, starting, I remind you, in mid-sentence.

---

19 Though what Robert and Callum say in Hugh's account suggest they had a pretty good idea that all was not as it should have been on board the *Lady Gray*.

Pictou

and for a woman of her age youd say she was good looking despite that. She showed us into this little room at the back of the building, which stretched a long way from the street. On either side of the corridor we walked down there were rooms, and sometimes the doors were half open and we could look in and see people sleeping or sitting playing cards or in one room there was an old man drinking straight from a bottle of whisky and I was reminded of the Carcair. To come all this way and find another old man drinking whisky from a bottle! All the rooms are kind of dull with no sun really coming into them because of the buildings on either side. It must be the worst thing about living in a town, being so close to other houses and people so that the light cant fall on your own life.

The room Mrs McIntosh showed us into seems far too small for four people but what choice do we have and anyway it isnt going to be for long. I should describe the room in detail because its the new setting but to be honest theres not much *to* describe. There are two beds that the four of us are expected to share. This Mrs McIntosh says they are double beds, made for two people, but they arent really much bigger than the bed I slept in back in Croval. And my bed in Croval was cleaner than this one. The blankets are grubby and the sheets have got holes in them. Under each bed theres a chamber pot and not the cleanest either.

Ian said, Out of the frying pan and into the fire.

Callum said back, Well at least were away from that hell-hole and that man. But maybe this wifie is as bad in her own way.

By that time, of course, Mrs McIntosh was out of the room.

I said, Well I think wed be as well just to stay here because its taken us long enough to find anywhere at all.

Ians comment then was, Beggars cant be choosers.

This was true enough and we couldnt argue with it so we

took our bags and put them on the floor and sat on the edges of the two beds, all four of us facing each other.

What now? asked Robert.

We have to find some land that we can build on, Ian said. MacDougalls book said that it was the thing to do. You find some land, then you clear it, then you start to farm it.

Not at Pictou, said Robert, the first thing hed said for ages. He said, The man I was speaking to by the stables said that theres not much land to be had at Pictou now. Its all been taken up.

We sat in silence for a while after that, and Callum started to unpack his bag but when he realised there was nowhere in the room to put anything apart from on top of the bed he started to put it all back again.

I want to go round asking some questions, I said.

Of course you do, said Callum with a kind of nastiness in his voice that I didnt like but Ive known him for years and thats just the way he is.

So in the afternoon I was out along the street, with the wind blowing spray in off the sea. Our boat was still anchored out there, along with some other ones and some fishing boats that looked much better than the ones wed had at Croval.

There was a thing called the General Store which was like MacPhees cart but inside a building. I looked in but there was no one there apart from the old man behind the counter. On the wall were hanging all sorts of tools and leather things for horses and there were big barrels with salt and dried beef and dried fish and things like that. I asked the man but he didnt have anything to tell me.

Along the street a bit was a drinking place and I went in there. To my surprise there was Mrs McIntosh standing by the wooden counter with a jug of beer in front of her. There were some other people sitting at tables and they all looked up at me as I went in, but Mrs McIntosh was the one that I knew so she was the one I went to speak to. I asked her if she knew what had happened to the Craigtore people and she laughed.

Do you know how many people come through Pictou? she asked, and I shook my head. She wiped her mouth with her thumb but there was still some of the foam from the beer on her lip and I was thinking that my mother would never have been in a place like this drinking beer. She said, Some of them come and stay, some of them go upriver and some of them just get on the next ship and go on to Quebec. Theres no time to get to know the ones that move on. How can there be? I dont even know your name and youre staying in my house.

Hugh Ross.

Well, Hugh Ross, I know your name now but Ill forget it as soon as you move on.

She leaned closer to me and looked in my eyes and I had that funny feeling that I wrote about when I was describing going into her bunk house first of all. I mean I could smell the beer and the bad smell of her breath but at the same time there was something about her, even if she was twice my age. I took a step back and said, Maybe well not be moving on. It depends.

Depends on what? What are your plans?

I dont know. Im looking for the people from Craigtore. Id like to ask them what to do.

And wheres Craigtore? I havent heard of it.

Its just down the coast from Croval.

She laughed at me again and I could hear in her laugh that she was quite drunk. She asked, And wheres Croval?

I couldnt explain because I didnt know how to. I could have said that it was at the other side of the ocean but then she knew that already so what was the point of saying it?

Who would know about the Craigtore people? I asked.

She shrugged. Nobody, she told me. Whos going to know about them? Nobody at all.

When I got back to the bunkhouse it was nearly dark and Id been wandering about for hours, not getting any further, but

Callum had been busy and hed found someone that said they knew a place where there was land to be had beside the river. So we sat in our tiny room to talk about it. There was a smell of cooking coming from the room next door, even though Mrs McIntosh had told us that we werent allowed to cook in the room. Each room has a little stove in it for heating but she told us not to cook on it because it isnt meant for that and we have to buy our food from Mrs McIntosh and eat it in the front room where there are long benches and then we pay her for the food on top of the money we pay for the beds. She knows what shes doing, Mrs McIntosh, even if she doesnt know anything about the Craigtore people.

Robert says, And the thing is, whats it like up there? Ive heard that the best places are all taken. I told you. Its only swampy places left where you cant grow a thing. You cut down the trees and the swamp takes over even more.

Callum – Didnt we come over here to try?

Robert – Ive heard say that wed be better moving on to Quebec. Theres more land there. More chance to make a go of it.

Callum – Are we going to be chasing after that idea all the time? What if we get to Quebec and were getting told that theres no good land left there either?

Robert, getting angry, pushing the dark hair back on his forehead – Im not saying Quebec will be perfect, but why do we have to stay here when everyones telling us not to?

Callum – Maybe theyre telling us not to because they dont want us to take their good land. Maybe whoever is telling you to move on wants that land for themselves.

Robert turns to me. Its that small in the room that our knees are more or less touching. He asks, What do you think, Hugh? What would you have us do?

Before I can speak, because, if Im telling you the truth, I cant think of what to say right away, Ian says, I dont care what we do but we have to do it together. Im not having us splitting up.

Callum – Whos talking about splitting up?

Ian – Im just looking at the shape of the conversation.

Robert – What do you mean?

Ian – I can hear the way youre talking and I dont want it to end up with two of us doing one thing and the other two doing something else. We have to stick together in this.

Robert – Im not saying that we dont.

Callum – But youre trying to force us to move on before weve even tried to make it work here. What does Hugh think?

Me – Well, no one here seems to know what became of the Craigtore people, so maybe we should go and find out in Quebec.

Callum – What have the Craigtore people to do with it?

Me – Well theyre from home and if theyve found somewhere that theyre doing well in, then maybe thats where we should go. If its the sort of place that Craigtore people can do well in, then maybe its the kind of place that Croval people can do well in too.

Callum – But they could be here and we just dont know. Youve only asked a few people. Theres lots of people here. Its not like Croval. Not everyone knows everyone else. Do you think everyone from Inverness knows everyone in Inverness?

I didnt say anything then, because to be honest I hadnt really thought of it like that and I probably *had* actually thought that everyone would know everyone else here. Now that Im lying in bed writing this, thinking about it, I realise that in a place like this with so many people coming and going it must be impossible for everyone to know everyone else. If Im telling the truth Id have to say that this frightens me a bit, the thought that only three people in Pictou know me, not counting the people from the Lady Gray, like Donald Sutherland, who knows me but just a little bit. I feel that Ive learnt something, which is good.

But to go back to the conversation we were having earlier, Ian was the next one to speak and he said, I suggest we should give it a chance here before we do anything else. Why did we come here if were not going to do our best to succeed? What have we escaped from if we just keep running away from anywhere we arrive?

That made me think but Robert snorted and got up and walked out and so did Callum. Robert was back quite soon, but Callum came back in about two hours later, and by that time Robert and Ian were fast asleep. Id been writing this but when I heard Callum come banging down the corridor I quickly put it under the threadbare pillow and pretended to be asleep because I didnt want to talk to him about anything when he was drunk, least of all what he thought about the idea that Ian thought he was running away. I only took my pages back out again and carried on writing when I heard him start to snore in the next bed. Hes sharing with Robert and Im sharing with Ian. I think Robert must have been awake too but he didnt say anything. Maybe Ian was awake too but he didnt say anything either. Ive been writing this but its hard to do it as the glow from the stove is dying down and I cant really see so Ill stop now. Im going to lie for a while and think about different things, but to be honest the thing I cant get out of my mind just now is the smell of Mrs McIntosh and that bit of beer foam on her upper lip. Im not very sure what kind of country weve come to.

This morning we were all speaking about it and it turned out that it was Donald Sutherland that had been telling Callum about the land further up the river that we could go to. Wouldnt it just be? Todays Sunday and so we went to church in the morning. It was a wooden building up on the hill looking out over the bay and it was fairly packed with people. Ian said someone had told him that just about everyone went to church in Pictou, they were all good Presbyterians and Callum said that this would be a good time to be a thief, but Ian laughed and said, God looks after his own.

Everyone was all crammed in together because it isnt a big church. There are more churches in the other little settlements in New Scotland and also up the river there are churches too.

Ian asked a lot of questions, because of course hes wanting to find somewhere that he can get a place and preach to these American people, Scottish people or whatever you would call people that come from one country and live in another.

To my surprise, there was Mrs McIntosh a few rows in front of us, looking a bit unwell, squeezed in between a huge big man wearing a coat made out of some kind of animal skin and another minister sitting in to listen to the sermon. I pointed him out to Ian and he didnt look too happy about it. Too many ministers.

Ian said, Thats the Edinburgh Ladies Association for you.

MacNeills sermon lasted for a very long time and there were two psalms to sing and then when we were all lining up to get out of the church Ian explained that the Edinburgh Ladies Association kept raising money to prepare ministers and send them out to America but that they were preparing too many of them, because, he said, the thrill they got from sending a minister across the ocean made them feel the warmth of Gods love flow through them like the taste of a good brandy. So now there were more ministers than churches, and a lot of these ministers were young men. While Id been out asking after the Craigtore people yesterday hed been asking around about churches and thats what hed found out. There were sometimes places in the churches up the rivers, hed been told, because nobody wanted them.

Does that put you off? I asked.

No, he said, but it was the kind of *no* that meant *I dont know*.

Outside the church we started talking about our plans again and, as I said, it turned out that it had been Donald Sutherland who had suggested the thing about the land up the river. It seems hed been speaking to a man at the land registry which is where you go if you want to get land here. This man had said that there was another man to speak to first who knew someone who was wanting to sell their plot of land beside the Middle River, about twenty five miles up from Pictou itself. The river is called the Middle River because its the middle one of the three rivers. There are also two other rivers near Pictou called the East River and the West River but someone had told Donald whod told Callum that the Middle River was the one which just exactly fitted in with the fact that there was this other man that wanted to sell up. So now thats what we were talking about.

Why is he wanting to sell? asked Robert. Doesnt that make you a bit suspicious?

Not really, replied Callum. Youre always suspicious.

Better to be suspicious than to end up with a bit of land that we cant grow anything on. How big is this land Donald Sutherlands found us?

Big enough, said Callum.

Big enough for what? For five of us?

Five? asked Callum.

Us four and Donald Sutherland.

Callum shook his head, Youre not listening to me. Donald Sutherlands just helping us to get settled. Hes not wanting to join us.

Why not?

A minute ago you were complaining about him joining us and now youre complaining about him not joining us.

Ian asked, And what are Donalds plans?

Callum flashed a look at Ian. He said, I dont know. I think hes looking at other bits of land.

Robert said, So, if hes looking at other bits of land, whats wrong with the bit hes told us about? Why doesnt he want that one?

Callum was getting angry and nearly shouting, I dont know! Hes just trying to help us. Can he not get some credit for that, even? You liked him fine enough when we were on the Lady Gray.

I never said I didnt like him, said Robert, not raising his voice. And I never said I did. Im just wanting to make sure that everything is all right.

Then Ian stepped in between them and said, Maybe the bit

of land would be too big for one person to farm. That could be it. I think it is important not to see dishonesty where none exists. I cant see why Donald Sutherland would be wanting to cheat us in any way.

Callum – Exactly that. And how would it be cheating us anyway, to tell us about a piece of land we could settle on?

Robert – What about Katherine, is she coming with us too?

Callum flushed red and sort of looked away. No, he said, shes going with her father up East River and if theres nothing there, well theyre going off to Quebec.

Robert – Are you sure you never asked her?

Callum whipped round to answer him but before the words could get out of his mouth, out of the church comes the minister, MacNeill, and he makes a beeline over to us, and in particular Ian. He holds out his hand to shake and Ian takes it. Callum wanders off down the stony path towards Pictou.

MacNeill says, I believe youre Ian Macleod, newly come to these parts from the homeland.

I am, says Ian, looking MacNeill up and down.

The thing about MacNeill is that he only looks a few years older than me and Callum and Robert. Maybe twenty five but not any older than that. It doesnt seem right. It seems to me that a minister should be quite old, like Ian. I mean theyre meant to be telling you about how you should be behaving in your life and helping you to live with the sins youve committed and giving you all their knowledge that comes from reading the Bible for so many years, and in Ians case lots of other books too. What can MacNeill know? You have to be older to have anything worth saying.[20]

---

20 But, considering Hugh's account of his life, perhaps the sayings of the young gain meaning as life goes on. I like Hugh's modesty, though, as I like so much about him. I think when I was his age I would have imagined there were few things I did not know. Now, it seems to me there is more or less nothing that I know for sure. – RM

Anyway, MacNeill pumps Ians hand up and down which is a thing I know Ian doesnt like. Then he makes a big gesture up at the bright blue sky, where there are some doves or something flapping backwards and forwards between the trees around the church.

MacNeill says, God has put on a splendid welcome for the new arrivals.

Ian replies, Its very good of Him. He has a nice touch with the weather.

Says MacNeill, He does that. And may I say how pleasing it is that so many of the new Scottish arrivals saw fit to grace the church with their presence this morning. I dare say we shall have to extend our humble place of worship if immigration continues as it currently progresses.

Ian says, But surely the congregation today was swelled by temporary residents? I imagine that most of these will disperse and attend other churches upriver? And on that matter, I wonder if I might trouble you to provide me with some information about finding –

And he took MacNeill by the arm and they walked away back up towards the church again, leaving me with Robert. Mrs McIntosh came past us in amongst the other stragglers of the congregation. She looked at me and gave me a little smile that made me swallow. She turned and came over and spoke to me.

Have you had any further luck finding your friends from – where was it?

Craigtore.

Yes, there.

No, I said. Nothing so far. But Ill keep asking people. Someone will have heard of them.

You do realise, she said, coming closer, that they might be dead.

She was wearing her best Sunday dress and as she leaned closer to me I could feel the silky material as she leaned against

133

my arm with her breasts. Although thats not what Callum would have called them, it is the proper book word. I stepped back and she caught me looking down at her breasts which looked – and felt – much younger than she actually was, if you understand what I mean. I didnt want to be thinking this way and I wanted to bring an end to the conversation, but I couldnt ignore what shed just said or the fact that shed smiled a wee smile at me when she saw me looking at her breasts so I had to keep speaking.

If theyd died wouldnt somebody know about that?

Not, she said, still smiling at me, if they died on the voyage over.

She had on some kind of scent or perfume. But her hands are red with washing dishes and the veins on her arms are thick and her fingernails are broken. Ive never seen anyone like her before.

I dont think so, I said, helplessly, and I said good morning and turned away and walked off, a bit confused and with the blood hot in my cheeks.

Robert hurried after me to catch up. He was laughing at me, though not in the nasty way Callum sometimes does. He took hold of my shoulder and I shrugged him off.

Do you know what she is? he said to me.

She has the bunk house.

Thats not all she has.

What do you mean?

She sells it. Herself. Shes a whore.

I know, I said. I know that.

But of course I didnt know that at all. And I wasnt too sure about whether what he said could be true or not. If his words were true what was she doing going to church, brazen like that? And if Robert could find out that about Mrs McIntosh, then surely so could the minister MacNeill and how would he be letting her into the church if thats the case? It doesnt make any sense, not that it matters to me one way or the other.

134

How do you know that about her? I asked him as we got down to the edge of the town, where there were dogs sniffing around the rubbish that people had dumped out the backs of their houses, or huts more like. All just made of wood.

Well I heard, thats all, he said. Its what folk are saying about her. So watch yourself!

I dont think it can be right, I said. What about Mr McIntosh?

What Mr McIntosh? said Robert, laughing again. Hes dead, or so they say, and one or two say she did away with him years ago because he interfered with her business. And I dont mean the bunk house.

It seemed to me then that Callum and Robert and Ian had been finding out an awful lot more about our new country and its people than I had, traipsing about asking questions about the Craigtore lot. It makes me feel a bit guilty because maybe Im not as useful as the others. Maybe I am the sort of person that always trails along at the end with others leading the way. If it was up to me wed probably all still be sitting back in Croval trying to decide whether or not to head off across the sea in the first place. But you can only be the person that you are, nobody else, though you can try to change, and I do. So I just laughed along with Robert about Mrs McIntosh so he wouldnt think I was liking her.

Im not writing anything more about her today. If what he says is true then she shouldnt be in my writing and if what he says is not true then its not nice to be writing it down. Im not wanting to be a gossip, like some.

Later on we went and ate in the drinking place. It was good sea trout that we had to eat and Ian paid for it out of the money he had left. He doesnt leave any of his money back in the bunk house because hes not sure that its safe there.

I asked him why there werent any Indians about.

Well, he said. I imagine theyve been scared off.

Scared off? I asked. But MacDougall was writing about how

135

theyre brave hunters.

But he also said that they would not stand on a battlefield.
What battlefield?

This one, said Ian and he waved his arm around to take in the whole drinking place and all the people that were sitting around in there, drinking and eating and shouting and laughing and some of them singing too. There was the smoke from thirty pipes hanging under the wooden beams.

I dont understand.

If all these people suddenly came to Croval, wouldnt you run away too?

We talked a bit more about the land up the Middle River and what we should do about it. Robert was still suspicious but Callum was so strong about it that I think we are all affected by his energy. Nothing was decided today but well need to make our minds up tomorrow, Callum says, because the man that this other man knows that told Donald Sutherland about the land is wanting to sell soon and if we dont buy it then someone else will and thatll be the end of that chance.

Id like to get settled here but on the other hand I cant help thinking that if we settle here and it all goes fine then we might never ever catch up with the Craigtore lot and thats important. Ian says we can farm for a bit until we get on our feet and then we can think about other projects but I worry that by that time itll be too late. Maybe theyve gone on to Quebec and not liked it and then moved on somewhere else, and what then? Where then?

Out in the firth off Croval sometimes youd see the seagulls coming down on to the surface of the water and that would mean there were fish there, maybe mackerel. But if you wasted too long in rowing over to that place by the time you got there the seagulls and the fish would be gone, both.

Thats what Im worrying about.

Today – were going to go up Middle River to see this place. Ive not been writing anything for a couple of days because nothing much has been happening. The Lady Gray has gone now out of the bay, off to Quebec though hardly anyone got back on it again.

Ive been keeping out of Mrs McIntoshs way and thats not so easy because she sometimes comes into the room when youre there by yourself so Ive been out in Pictou a bit, up and down the streets looking at the different wooden houses and trying to work out what everyone *does* here. How can there be enough things for people to do in a place this size? I met one man and I was speaking to him and he told me that what he does is sweep down the wooden boards that go along in front of some of the houses and stores (where things are sold) and he gets paid for that by the people that live there or own the store. It seems funny to me. Why do they not sweep their own boards? In Croval if you offered to do someone elses sweeping it would be because they were old or sick. If you asked a young healthy person if they wanted you to sweep their house for money they wouldnt understand. So America is very different from Croval. Ive just been wandering about trying to learn things, trying to get to know more about what its like here.

Were going off up Middle River soon, with Donald Sutherland and the four of us. Another man is going to take us up there. But I want to write down one conversation that I had because its made me think a bit.

There was a young boy over at the stables, looking after the horses. In the stables are all sorts of different peoples horses and people are paid to look after them. There are some pretty good looking horses there, and some other ones that are more like MacPhees horse, strong enough but nothing special. So I was just looking in at the big door to the barn and there was a young boy at the back, maybe about twelve or so. He was shovelling out one of the stalls that had no horse in it so I went in to speak to him for a bit.

His name was Jamie. He was a strong looking boy for his age, with his shirt sleeves rolled up well past his elbows so that you could see the muscles in his arms. A working boy, I was thinking, so in that way this America wasnt so different from Croval.

Well, I said.

Well, he replied and leaned on his graip, looking at me. New here?

Yes I am. A few days. Were going to be settling up the Middle River.

He laughed. Are you now? Well, thats what a lot of people settle on.

I didnt like his laugh much but he seemed an open sort of boy, easy to talk to. All around the horses were shifting and stamping, making that blowing sound.

Whereabouts up the Middle River?

I kind of stuttered out an answer because I didnt really know. I havent really been listening to the details that Callums been going on about. I knew hed said it was twenty miles up this river so I said that.

The boy nodded, poked at some straw on the floor with the graip. He asked, Whose land?

I shrugged. Some man that my friend was speaking to knows this other man thats selling up.

John Bailey?

The name did sound kind of familiar but I couldnt say for certain, so I just said, Not sure. Why?

If its John Bailey, steer clear.

Why?

Im just saying, said the boy. You wouldnt be the first ones, thats all. But I shouldnt be talking about it.

He turned back into the empty stall and began spreading out the straw hed laid in there. I watched for a minute, trying

138

to think of what to say to him next and also wondering if I should mention John Bailey to Callum.

When did you come over? I asked him after a while.

He kept forking the straw in the air, the little specks of it catching in the sunlight coming from the barns open door. He said, What do you mean?

When did you come over?

Over from where?

I dont know. From wherever you came over from.

I didnt come over from anywhere. I see what you think though. No, I was born here.

Here? In Pictou.

Yes, right here in the house three down from here. My dad worked in the stable too and stayed in the same house but hes dead now.

This made me quiet again, because I didnt feel I should be talking about his father, with him being dead. But I couldnt think of any other questions so I asked, And where did your father come over from?

He didnt come over from anywhere either.

He was born here too?

Yes, same house.

I could hardly believe it. Heres me thinking that were setting out on this new road and this boy tells me that theres two generations of his family that have been born here. It sort of annoyed me.

What about your grandfather, then? Where did he come over from?

He came from Dingwall. In 1807. One of the early ones.

I see. But you just sound the same as the Inverness ones that were on our boat, that we came over on.

I cant help that, he said and pushed past me to go and hang the graip up on a hook thing on the wall. I just speak the way I do. I speak the same way my dad did and the way my granddad did too.

So why dont you speak different. If youve lived here all your life? Because some folk speak different here.

I dont know. Thats just the way I speak. I cant help it. I learnt it from them. Do you want me to sound less Scottish?

Scottish?

Isnt that what youre telling me?

The boy was getting annoyed at me so I left it and asked him if he knew anything about the Craigtore folk but he didnt, same as everyone else.

Then when I was walking back along the street towards Mrs McIntoshs I was thinking over what he was saying, and wondering about all that Scottish and American thing. Was he Scottish if he was born in America or was he American even though his blood came from Scotland and he spoke like a Scottish person. But then I thought, well, if hed been born not in Pictou but in Dingwall Id never ever have met him because the only people I knew at age eighteen in Croval were other people from Croval and of course people from Craigtore. I had more in common with him because Id met him in Pictou than if Id stayed in Croval and his grandfather had never moved from Dingwall and wed never met at all, whatever our accents were. Maybe Scotland is only a country when you look at it from a long way away.

Im not writing that down very clearly. Ill need to ask Ian about it.

What Im saying is that I dont feel Scottish anyway. I mean I know I come from Scotland but what about people from Edinburgh and Glasgow and those other places that Ian knows but that Ive never been to and that Id never even heard of until he told me a bit about them. What do I have in common with those people? I dont really understand what Scotland means, if it means anything. It doesnt matter if that boy in the stables was an American Scot or a Scottish American or a Pictou boy from Dingwall or whichever he was. Its confusing, really.

There were rain clouds gathering over Pictou Bay as I came back into the bunkhouse to write this down. Now Ive got to go with the others up Middle River in a wee while.

And now were back in Pictou. The others have gone to the drinking place, the saloon. Im here by myself, and Ive turned the key in the door because Im a little bit worried about Mrs McIntosh. A little while ago there was a tapping at the door and here was Mrs McIntosh asking if I was needing anything. I said no and tried to shut the door on her as politely as I could. She was wearing a white shirt with quite a lot of the buttons undone and I know I shouldnt have been looking but I was. So I shut the door on her.

Id thought wed be going up Middle River on a boat, partly because there are lots of wee rowing boats going up and down the river all the time, and partly because, I suppose, weve been on a boat so much that it seems like the natural way to travel. But no, it was more like the MacPhee part of the journey repeating itself, though this time it was a different kind of cart, pulled by a horse that could have given MacPhees horse a fight and won, I think. This cart had an open space behind the part where the driver sat, with seats facing each other. Callum and Ian sat at the back of the cart facing forward and me and Robert sat at the front facing backwards, which made me feel sick on the bumpy road pretty quickly. The man sitting up on the very front seat, hanging on to the horse, was called Matthew and I dont know his second name, and he never spoke to us the whole way. He just grunted when Ian gave him the money.

Callum said wed be meeting the man up the River when we got there, so I asked if the mans name was by any chance John Bailey and sure enough it was.

Why? asked Callum.

141

And I couldnt really answer because the stable boy had never gone into detail about what was wrong with John Bailey so I just had to mutter something about having heard the name.

How did you hear the name? asked Callum.

I dont know.

Leave Hugh alone, said Ian, with a smile on his face. Hes been out researching.

And Robert laughed at that. I thought it was best just to say nothing. It quite often is when Callums in a funny mood.

He explained to us about how Donald Sutherland had arranged the meeting but he wouldnt be there himself because he was away looking at another place on East River.

To buy?

No, hes trying to get a place for one of the Invernessers that was on The Lady Gray with us.

Robert asked, And why is he never trying to get somewhere for himself? Hes doing an awful lot for other folk out of the goodness of his heart, isnt he?

And is that a bad thing?

No but Im just wondering what he makes out of it all.

Why should he be making something out of it?

And so it went on between the two of them as the cart went on up the track beside Middle River. Callums changed compared to the boy I knew back in Croval. I mean hes still the same because he was always argumentative and difficult sometimes, and we were used to that. And if I could stand the Callum that was arguing with Robert today beside the Callum that would argue with Robert back in Croval, there wouldnt be much to choose between them. I cant point at a moment in our journey where hes said or done something that made me think, Callums different now. I mean I havent been able to spot it happening.

When you catch a fish and pull it out of the water its shiny and glittering and strong, flicking about in your hands, so you lay it down in the bottom of the boat and gradually the jerking around dies down and dies down until its just lying there, and the eyes go milky and the scales lose that brightness until in the end its just a dead fish. Im not making a good job of writing this down but I mean that its not like that with Callum, I havent been able to see this change happening or even to say what exactly this change is. But its there. And I think Roberts changed too. I think Ians just the same. Maybe youve changed as much as you can long before youre Ians age. I think Im still the same. My mind is on the same things anyway, but I think Callums mind is on different things now. Maybe its meeting other people, its changed the world for him.

But of course the main thing that Im wondering is how Callum has been thinking about what he did to Mary Vass. Im not ready yet to ask Ian about that because I dont want him to think Im saying that Callum is a murderer because thats not right, it was an accident. But I know how what happened has been eating away inside me so how must he be feeling about it? Is this why hes changed? He did kill her, after all.

What would happen if Ian found these pages and read them?

There were tall trees on our left between us and the river, big pine trees. But you could still see the black river sliding past, a bit like that big river that we went across in Inverness. But there are no bridges here, and Middle River is bigger. On our right, though, most of the trees had been cut down at some time, leaving rotting stumps and wee bushes in amongst a few sick looking birches. There were some crofts or whatever they would call them here, set away back from the track and as I watched them going past I realised that in the past people had gone quite deep into what was then a forest, cleared a space, built their croft, then started chopping down the trees round about until eventually they met the man from the next croft chopping down his last tree and it turned out the two of them were chopping away at opposite sides of the same tree.

Every now and then it would be clear on our left too and

there would be a thick bare rutted track down to the waters edge where there would be a little wooden jetty. We must have passed a dozen of these and there were no boats at any of them and the wood was looking black and rotten. I suppose the trees were dragged down there to be floated downstream or put on a boat or something. And now there were no more trees to float so nobody bothered looking after the jetties any more. I wondered what the people that lived in the crofts did now that the trees had run out. I asked Callum.

Look, he said, pointing at a croft far up the slope on our right. You can see where theyve been planting crops.

And theres goats, said Robert, though not very enthusiastically.

Animals and a few crops, I said. It sounds just like home.

Callum glared at me. This is home now, he said.

I went quiet. His comment wasnt fair really because I was wanting to come across here as much as anyone. But in a few minutes we were all laughing together again, caught up in the excitement of going to see this place up Middle River, with the hot sun beating down hard on our heads.

And what a place it turned out to be. The man drew the cart thing up at the side of the track and said, Here it is.

We got off, all looking away to the right of the track, trying to spot a croft up amongst the wasteland of tree stumps.

No, said the man. Over there.

He was pointing down towards the river. The track was a bit further from the river here and when we looked down that way we could make out the shape of a dark building. The man climbed from his seat at the front and began to see to his horse. He was going to be waiting for us.

We followed the narrow path to the building which began to look worse the closer we got to it. We were picking our way between the trees and the bushes, things like brambles, and we kept getting glimpses of the building. It was made out of wood,

144

like all the other buildings in New Scotland but most of the buildings in New Scotland at least look as if they could keep out a shower of rain in winter. This one looked as if a shower of rain would knock it flat to the ground.

There were wooden slates on the roof and some of them were slipping off and others had big cracks in them. The planks of wood that had been nailed together to make the walls were all squint and you could even see between some of them, as you got closer, into the blackness of the inside. The building was facing the water and at the front there was a raised walkway running along with some steps up to it. There was a hole in this and when we got right up to the place we went up the steps and we were all four of us standing looking down at this hole. You could see where the wood was all spongy and rotting at the edges of the hole. It looked as if someone had stepped out of the front door and gone straight through the wood. I think you were meant to take a chair out and sit here looking at the world drifting by on the river but if you sat on a chair here youd probably end up with just your head sticking up through a crack in the planks. From the whole building there came this terrible smell of mould as if something had died there or as if the whole place was dying itself.

Callum had gone awful quiet.

You people here looking for me?

The voice made us jump. I think wed all gone into a kind of dream staring at this bourach of a house. I know what I was thinking.

So this man came round from the side of the house away from the path wed walked down, which was why we never saw him. He looked about forty years old or so but in a terrible state. He was wearing clothes that looked as if theyd not had a wash for weeks and the blue shirt was torn at the shoulder. He was not a big man, short and skinny. His hands and even the lines on his face had dirt in them as if hed taken a handful of earth

145

and rubbed it in. His hair was long and dirty and tied back from his face with a thin bit of material across his forehead, something Ive not seen a man wearing before. But even though the whole look of him would make you think that he was just nothing, when he got closer and you could see his dark eyes, you knew that there was a lot more happening inside him than his dirty hands and cracked fingernails would make you think.

He held out one of those hands and Callum, feeling responsible, I think, stepped forward and took it.

Callum Ross, says Callum and he introduced the rest of us.

John Bailey, says the man. Glad to meet you. I hear youre wanting to buy up my little home.

Callum swallowed and said, Well we need to take a right look round first. Then we can tell you.

John Bailey spat on the ground at his feet. He said, Your friend told me youd be buying.

Callum looked away at the river and then turned back, saying, Well he didnt get it quite right, Mr Bailey. Not definitely. We are looking for somewhere but well have to see.

But John Bailey was not shifting. He said, Well Sutherland said youd be buying. You know I could have sold this before now if I wasnt keeping it for you. Youve bound it so you must be wanting to buy.

Robert asked Callum, What does he mean, bound it?

Callum said, Lets take a look at it inside anyway, and he started off into the house.

The funny thing was that Ian didnt even come in with us. He gave a kind of big sigh and wandered off down towards the river. I was quite glad to be going inside because there were flies of some sort buzzing around and biting us as we stood outside the house.

I swear Ive never seen a less happy looking place in my life. Inside was worse than the outside. There were three rooms in the house. When you went in you were standing in a little space with three doors leading off it. On the left as you went in there was a kitchen with a blackened stove, a table that someone had been hacking at with a knife and two wooden chairs, one of them with a broken back. The mouldy smell was stronger in here, as if food had been left out for too long. We went back through and across to the room to the right of the front door. It was the bunk room. There were three cast iron bedsteads crammed into the little space and it was hard to see how you could get a fourth one in. Each one had a stained striped mattress lying on it. Like the other room, this one had a tiny window looking out at the river, with glass so covered in grime that you could hardly see out and the sun could hardly get in. Dead flies on the sill. There was an old cracked chamber pot lying beside the nearest bed and thank goodness that it was empty. The third room was the privy and it was just a sort of big metal bucket tucked in underneath a plank fixed across the narrow space, with a hole roughly cut in it.

John Bailey said, You take the bucket and pour it in the river and it floats off downstream. Doesnt bother you then and it saves you digging holes to bury it like some folk have to do. Thats what he told me.

In fact hed been speaking the whole time hed been showing us round, but I cant write anything down about what he said because I couldnt really hear what he was saying because I was so surprised by the dirtiness of the house. I couldnt see how anyone could live here. But I did pick up what he said about the privy so I asked him, Thats what who told you?

Old Mr McBain, that lived here.

Lived here until when? I asked.

Until he died. Couple of weeks back. Lived here for thirty years, just by himself. His wife died not long after he came here from Ullapool and he never got himself another one. I bought it from him just before he died. Let him stay on, though. Itd have been cruel to put him out, sick like he was. And now its ready for sale.

How much land with it? asked Callum.

Up to the path.

Robert peered out of the window, rubbing away at the dirt with the palm of his hand. He said, And fishing on the river?

Of course, said John Bailey. Anyone can fish the Middle River. Youll get trout and catfish and all sorts.

Callum kept on at him, How much land?

Like I was saying to you, up to the path.

But how wide? How much of the riverbank would we have?

The whole width, said John Bailey and went to go outside.

Callum took him by the arm at the door. The whole width?

Completely.

The whole width of what?

The house, said John Bailey and scurried out the door on to the rickety porch thing.

We all went after him. I looked down towards the river and there was Ian sitting on a rock by the rivers edge, swatting at his neck where the flies were bothering him. He looked tired, sitting there, small and old and getting thinner every day.

Callum was squaring up to John Bailey. He raised his voice at him, saying, You told Sutherland there was a good bit of land with the house.

Did I? said John Bailey, obviously not a bit scared.

Yes you did. You said that the land had trees on it to cut and was fertile for crops.

John Bailey waved his hand up towards the main track. He laughed. Look, he said, cant you see the trees? Cant you see the bushes growing out of the ground? Of course you can grow crops here. Cut the trees, float them, and then grow crops. If bushes can grow then so can crops. Whats wrong with you Scots? You come over here and if it doesnt fall into your lap you wont have it. Youre as bad as that last lot.

I stepped in. What last lot? I asked him. The Craigtore folk?

148

He looked at me as if he didnt understand what I was talking about and then turned to walk back towards the house, laughing an angry laugh. But Callum took him by the shoulder and spun him round so they were face to face. Callum took him by a handful of his dirty old shirt and more or less lifted him off his feet. I didnt like to see Callum showing disrespect to someone that was years older, but I understood why he was doing it. Callum was shouting.

You think were going to buy this rubbish? You lied to us about what it was like.

John Bailey – Ive never even spoken to you in my life. Its your friend Donald Sutherland you need to get hold of. Do what you like. If you dont buy it someone else will.

Callum – We want our money back.

John Bailey – You wanted it bound and thats what happened. Let go of me.

Robert, stepping in and pulling the two men apart – What does he mean, Callum, wanted it bound? What money?

John Bailey shrugged Callum off and stamped up the steps to the building, brushing himself down as if Callum touching him had made him dirtier which didnt seem likely or possible.

Robert pushed at Callum and both of them had raised voices. Ian never even looked round. He was sitting on the rock, staring at the river sliding by, just shaking his head slowly. Although I was listening to Robert and Callum arguing, half of me, or more than half, was watching Ian, thinking about how much it had taken from him to come half way across the world only to find this shack beside a track of dust, and two people arguing.

Robert – Im asking you, what does he mean, bound it?

Callum – How was I going to be knowing what it would be like?

Robert – *Bound* it?

Callum – Donald said it would be –

Robert – *Donald* said?

149

Callum – He said it was a place with land, where the four of us could make something of ourselves.

Robert – What land?

Callum – All right, I can see that *now*.

Robert – So what does it mean *bound* it?

Callum, hesitating – I had to give him some money.

Robert – Give who?

Callum – Donald Sutherland.

Robert – I thought it was John Baileys place?

Callum – And he would give some of the money to John Bailey to bind it.

Robert – Bind it?

Callum – To keep it for us. To let us see it before anyone else so wed get the first chance to buy it.

Robert – How much money?

Callum – Not much. Some for John Bailey and some for Donald Sutherland because he arranged it all.

Robert – We paid Donald Sutherland to see this place? *This* place?

Robert threw his hands in the air, like someone out of one of Ians novels and turned away from Callum. Then he came back to him.

Robert – You wasted money on that man. And now this one?

Callum – At least Im trying to find somewhere.

Robert – What do you mean, Callum?

Callum – At least Im speaking to people, trying to get things working for us here. What are you doing? Whats *he* doing, roving about trying to find out where Rachael and Elizabeth and the others have gone? What use is that?

Robert – Leave Hugh out of it. And leave me out of it too, because the only reason that youre the one doing the asking is because you wouldnt let anyone else do it. Ever since you met Donald Sutherland theres no one else allowed to do anything.

Callum – Arent we all meant to be helping each other? Isnt

150

that why we came here, so that we could help each other get somewhere? I didnt realise Id be doing it all myself.

Robert – Doing it all yourself?

Callum – Yes, just that. On the ship too and now here. Im the one that has to get things moving. It always has been.

Robert – Has it, then?

Callum – Yes it has.

And the two of them stood there, a foot or two apart, tall Callum with his sandy yellow hair and little Robert, as dark as anything, and the river flowing by behind them, and Ian sitting on the rock with his head in his hands, the thin white hair ruffled under his fingers. I was thinking, if it came to a fight between Callum and Robert, who would be the winner? I cant be sure. But for a minute there beside that rotting croft I thought that if one of them raised a hand at that moment the biggest fight Id ever seen would have broken out and then what would have become of us?

But then Ian stood up and went to them and asked, How much money did you give Donald Sutherland?

Callum was silent and folded his arms, turning away from them both like a little child. This is the effect of Ian sometimes. Callum said, I was wanting to help. I wanted us to get a place. How was I to know it would be like this?

At this very moment, John Bailey reappeared from behind the building, tying up the front of his trousers, which didnt make you want to buy his house any more than you did before. He said, Well, are you buying or are you going to *************?

Ian turned away from the swearing and took Callum by the elbow and they walked away up the path towards where the man was waiting with the cart thing, talking quietly together. Robert went after them, his hands still curled into fists by his sides.

So that just left me, as sometimes happens, by myself. I looked over at John Bailey and he looked at me as you might look at a dead fish in a net and then spat on the ground. So I went away too.

I never found out yet how much money we lost on that Middle River place. Nobody will tell me. I dont know if Robert knows or not. He says he doesnt. Callum wont speak about it at all, but then hes in a particularly bad mood just now because hes fallen out with that Katherine from Inverness and shes going away anyway.

I asked Ian about the money, and he said, Too much money, the sinews of war. Having less money might be a good thing.

But how much money has been lost?

Dont worry, Hugh. It was my money in the first place. Let me worry about it. You have other things on your mind.

But its not right that Donald Sutherland and that Bailey man end up with our money for nothing.

No, its not right. But things that arent right happen all the time. We have to learn acceptance, Hugh.

I am beginning to think that it was this kind of thing that annoyed the older folk in Croval about Ian. You cant get a clear answer out of him sometimes.

I said, So does this Bailey make his money by keeping on offering that house for sale?

Callum tells me that Bailey has a few houses that he does this with. Callums been asking questions in Pictou about Bailey and his houses. He offers to bind them, knowing full well that no one will want to buy them. Its quite a good scheme.

Good?

Not in that sense.

So how much did we lose?

More than we can afford but less than would ruin us.

It would have been better if Callum had been asking questions in Pictou about Bailey and his houses *before* we spent the money.

Well, said Ian, ending the conversation, if that had happened, we wouldnt have learnt anything, and learning is always good.

What have we learnt?

That were still together.

What is it that I like about Ian Macleod? Sometimes hell say things to you that dont make sense and sometimes hell speak to you in a way that you know hes not explaining everything and you know its probably because hes thinking that you wont understand when he speaks. And sometimes hes really at the centre of things, pushing everything on, but then sometimes he drifts away from you and youre left on your own to think about things. So that all makes him a difficult person sometimes but I cant help liking him and being with him, even with the big difference in our ages. I know theres an obvious thing to say about how I never had my father there to keep me right and Im sure thats what anyone looking at us would say. But I know myself pretty well and I really dont think thats it. And anyway, if that was true, why is it that Robert and Callum stick with Ian too? It cant be anything to do with their fathers, because theres are still alive, though I suppose none of us have fathers over here.

I think Ian is *there,* just. I mean hes not someone weve made be with us. Hes choosing to be with us. I wonder why sometimes, what does he like about us? But maybe its best not to look too closely at something. For example, you get a new net off MacPhee that youve been after for a long time and when its all bundled up and youre thinking of the fine fish youre going to be catching in it, then it looks like the best thing in the world. But if you spend too long looking at it you start to notice the places where the knots need to be redone and maybe theres some fraying in places because, of course, its not a new net at all, its somebody elses net that youve got, and probably somebody who died, maybe from old age, maybe from drowning. So its probably better not to stare at the net for too long, just throw it out into the water and see what you catch and then after a while it becomes your net, completely yours and you can patch it up and make it better.

Ian always has answers, even if the answers arent that clear sometimes. One day Ill tell him about what happened last summer and ask him to explain if me just watching what happened means Ill go to hell or will it just be Callum. The thing that stops me asking is that he might say, yes, Ill be going there too. Or hell give me one of those answers where I dont know one way or the other. So the questions stuck in my mind like the way your line can get caught up in the seaweed and nothing you can do can free it. But you know sooner or later youre going to have to give a big pull and either youll have your line back or itll snap and be lost forever.

A strange conversation.[21]

I went into the kitchen room in the bunk house because I

---

21 I have read and reread this short section, wondering about its significance in terms of character motivation, though I have to keep reminding myself that it is not a novel that we are reading. In this reported conversation Hugh suggests a single reason for the pilgrimage across the seas that has little to do with personal betterment and more to do with a kind of romanticism. While I can see from this and later sections of the text, of course, that this is indeed one of the reasons for Hugh's continual movement I don't think all of the journeys in this book can be accounted for by the heart and not the head. Part of me would like to think that Hugh was not just swayed by emotion, because I know where that can lead! I would prefer to believe we are reading the words of a young man who finds his urge towards self-improvement dulled by the unproductive stay at Pictou, and who therefore allows his mind to drift to other thoughts. That is the way I can make sense of the whole book, though I can see that my reading struggles to make sense of this particular section, unless Hugh is not being totally honest (and he might not be). But the whole is greater than any individual part, a lesson we should bear in mind with regard to our own lives, as well as in consideration of the life of this nineteenth-century adventurer and, dare I say it, budding entrepreneur. Maybe I never give romance enough credence. Philip would say that. – RM

wanted something to eat and I smelt bread baking. I was hoping that there would be nobody there, but Mrs McIntosh, bad luck, was standing by the window, just looking out, with her hands on her hips. I went to tiptoe back out again but shed heard me and without looking round she said, What do you want?

I said something about being hungry and looking for something to keep me going, but I had no money.

She asked me if Id been going to steal the bread. It was sitting out on the bench on a metal stand thing, steam coming off it, four big loaves, new baked. She saw me looking and went over to take a knife out of a drawer. She rolled up the sleeves of her shirt and sliced a slice off the end of one of the loaves, then handed it to me.

This is the bit I throw to the birds, she said, meaning the outside bit with crust all round it. I dont know if she really meant that she threw that bit to the birds or if she was meaning something else that I didnt understand.

I took the bread but told her that I couldnt pay for it and she said it was all right, I could just have it. I tore a bit off the corner and put it in my mouth but I stopped eating when I realised she was wanting to talk to me because you cant really talk while youre chewing bread or at least you shouldnt.

Sit down, she said and she pointed to a little wooden stool over by the big range oven, the biggest oven Ive ever seen. When I saw it first Ian had to explain what it was to me. So I sat down, wondering what was coming next. She didnt sit down but carried on slowly cutting the loaves of bread. If it had been me Id have waited until they were a bit cooler because they cut better when they are cool, even though they taste better when they are hot. My mother taught me about that.

She was laying out the bread on to plates, ready for when the men that stayed in the bunk house, some of them, came in for something to eat in the middle of the day. These are the men who work at the harbour or on the roads that theyre building. Theyre even starting on a road up the side of Middle River, laying down rubble, packing down the earth and making it smoother. In the middle of the day they get an hour off and although some of them go to the saloon place to eat, a lot of the ones that stay in Mrs McIntoshs bunk house come back here, maybe because of the way she is with them and maybe because she can actually make quite good food sometimes, when she bothers.

But it was going to be a wee while before the men came back in for their food, so it was just me and her in the kitchen. I was nervous but though I wouldnt say this to Callum I do quite like being with her because at least shes friendly and Ive never met anyone like her before.

So, she said to me, you dont like me very much.

Its not that, I said. I do like you. Well.

But you dont think you should speak to me. Do the others tell you not to?

No.

What about the old man, what does he say?

Ian? Hes not so old.

Hes pretty old, she said. But I like him. At least hes polite to me and theres not many that are.

Hes a minister, I told her, turning the bit of bread round and round in my hands. I could smell something cooking in the range, a stew maybe. Half of me was hoping for the other men to hurry up and come back and half of me was hoping that they wouldnt.

I know hes a minister. He told me that he was.

I didnt know that theyd spoken much but of course Id been out a lot speaking to people in Pictou and oddly enough just when I was thinking about that Mrs McIntosh said, Who is it that youre chasing after?

Im not chasing after anyone.

I think you are. She smiled at me a bit, a kind of sad smile that annoyed me because it was as if she was looking down on me.

156

Everyone, she said, squaring up the slices of bread with her hands, every single person that comes here is doing one of two things. Either theyre chasing something or else theyre running away from something. Your friend Callum is running away, but you and the old man are chasing. Im not sure about the dark one. Maybe youre running away a bit too.

I tried to change the subject, not wanting her to get too close to the truth. I said, So what am I chasing?

Not what, who. Thats what Im asking you. A girl, I suppose.

I said nothing.

A girl, she carried on. Probably about your age or maybe a little bit older than you. A girl that had the strength to leave for America before you did, and it made you feel weak, so now youre running after her to tell her how brave you are after all.

I said nothing.

Why do you like her?

I said nothing, just thinking. But then I said, Ive known her for a long time.

Whats her name?

Rachael.

Rachael what?

Rachael Sutherland.

Is she related to that wee man that your Callums always speaking to in the saloon?

No, just the same name, but theyre not related. Rachaels from Craigtore.

Where? She took a towel and used it to open the front of the range. She reached in with her bare arms and stirred away at the pot of stew. The smell came out to me and I was so hungry that I put another piece of bread into my mouth. It also gave me the chance to say nothing. Shed already forgotten what Id told her about Craigtore.

And where is she? Have you found out?

Ive not found out anything, I said, and even I could hear the sort of childish tone in my voice, kind of pleading for someone to make it all better, the way you speak to your mother when youre wee and you fall and scrape your palms.

She smiled at me, and for the first time it wasnt that smile that made you feel small, even though I was acting like a bern. It was just friendly. Do you miss her?

Yes, I said.

And does she think the same way when she thinks about you?

I shrugged my shoulders and took another bit of bread.

So are you going to be moving on?

Did they tell you about what happened up Middle River?

She laughed then. Oh, yes, I heard about that. But youre not the first ones Baileys swindled and youll not be the last.

The worst of it is that one of our own made money out of it too. Well, not one of our own. One of Callums own.

As soon as Id said that I felt bad because Callums my friend and Mrs McIntosh isnt so I shouldnt really have been saying things like that. But it was the way she was talking to me and smell of food in the warm kitchen. Thats all I can think of.

Who was that?

Donald Sutherland.

I dont really know him. So are you moving on to find Rachael?

I dont know. Where would I look? I dont know if the others want to come. All they want is to settle and make money, if they can.

What about the old man?

Ian? Hes not so old. Im not so sure what hes after. He wants a church and people to preach to, but I dont really know if it matters to him where it is.

Well, then if it doesnt matter to him and you want to move on, and all the other two want is to settle down and make money, well then, you might as well move on. They can settle down, or find a church anywhere, cant they? But you can only

158

find Rachael in one place.

Wheres that? I stood up, thinking she knew something and hadnt been saying.

Wherever she is. How would I know? But where does anyone go from here? The ships come in and drop off some immigrants here and take the rest to Quebec. So Id say Quebec.

Thats what I was thinking. But Quebecs a big place, theyre all saying. What do I do when I get there?

Now it was her turn to shrug her shoulders. Then she was taking plates out of a big press in the corner of the room, stacks of gleaming white plates for the dirty men that were going to come in any minute.

Do you know what? she asked. Sometimes I think Id like to move on too. And Im not chasing anything, in case you were thinking of asking. Do you know what it is?

She rested her hands, palms down, on the bench beside the plates, looking over at me. She looked younger.

No, I said.

I just get tired, she said. I think back to everything Ive done here, and it doesnt amount to very much. And Im looking ahead at whats still to come and I cant see that very clearly either. Do you understand?

No, I said, because I have a good idea about what Im chasing.[22]

---

22 Here we see a problem caused by Hugh's inaccurate punctuation style. It is impossible to tell if the phrase "because I have a good idea about what Im chasing" represents direct speech or the words he wrote in his diary to explain his short answer "No". I tend towards the latter, though I must admit that Mrs McIntosh does appear to be opening Hugh up somewhat. And it can't be denied that the Hugh we read about has always been clear about how his journey is designed to further himself, to achieve something worthwhile. Why should he not state this clearly to his landlady? But he is running away too, as well as chasing something, and perhaps did not want to mention that. It's all complicated and why shouldn't it be? – RM

But I dont suppose it will ever happen, she sighed, straightening herself up and stretching her back. I dont suppose it ever will. I dont have anything to chase. Youre lucky.

Well, I couldnt think of anything to say and I was sitting there like a fool, stuffing bread into my mouth, and I felt as if I was about thirteen years old, as if the journey across the sea had taken me backwards.

But then there was a lot of noise in the street outside and the working men began to come in for their food. Mrs McIntosh gave me a thin-lipped smile and sort of shook her head and began to carry the plates through to the room where the long dining tables were. I was going to offer to help her to carry the food through, but I didnt know if she wanted me to, so I just slipped back through here and wrote this down.

One thing Im pleased about is that now were moving on, and it was really me that suggested it. It all happened so quickly that theres no time to write all about it. It was Robert that first said the words, We have to move on, but it was me that found out there is another boat coming in, just tomorrow. Callum spoke to a man down at the harbour that knows about these things and he said there were going to be some people coming off the boat here at Pictou so there would be some places on the boat for going on to Quebec. All we have to do is pay the captain of this other ship some money and we can go up a river called the St Lawrence River on to this Quebec. Its going to be more money away out of our pockets but surely we can have some more success there than weve had in this place.

I dont know how much money we have left but then I never knew how much money we had in the first place. I know Ianll know whether we can afford it or not and he says we can go.

Im looking forward to getting free of that Donald Sutherland, because even though Callum asked if he could come with us, we all agreed it was to be just the four of us. Even Callum agreed in the end.

No time to write down all the details about everything that was said because its just tomorrow. I can write it down on the boat. I suppose thats where what I write is different from those people like that Walter Scott because they can choose what to put in and what to leave out, but I have to leave some things out just because I dont have time and at this very moment I want to go and speak to Ian about the future.

The boat is called *Cleostratus,* which is a funny name and Ian said that there couldnt be a better name for a boat taking us to find out what our fortunes hold, and I have no idea what he means by that and when I asked him he laughed and said that I still had a lot of years left ahead of me to know as much as he did.

Intertitle 3

At first I thought there were more pages missing at this point, but it didn't take long for me to work out that this wasn't the case. In fact, all that has happened is that our narrator has become rather less careful about keeping his diary up-to-date, a fault that I'm sure we have all fallen into, usually at the age of ten, early in January, when that red-leathered diary given to us by our aunt for Christmas begins to lose its festive novelty.

Of course we can't tell exactly why Hugh has spent less time on his writing during this next phase of his life, which spans two full years, or thereabouts. As you'll see, the story lurches from very detailed accounts of particular events to a sort of hurried "sketch" of proceedings, as if he intended to return later and fill in more specifics. Indeed this may have happened in places here: I find it hard to tell from the paper used when each part was actually written. Actually this section is characterised by the large number of different types of sheet used by Hugh. Some are still quite white, given their age, whereas others have become so darkly tinted that they must have been cheaply discoloured in the first place. Some of the paper is thick and creamy and some of it is as flimsy as tissue paper. I suppose Hugh wrote on what he could get.

So what should we read into this next portion of the story? No doubt you will be, as I was, anxious to find out if the group settled. Without wanting to give too much away, I can reassure you on this point, though you will have to read on to find out the difficulties they faced.

And "difficulties are all metaphorical", as I read somewhere (and I can't remember where, unfortunately[23]). The problems

---

23 If you find the quotation, I would be really grateful if you could contact me via the publisher. I usually keep detailed notes (this careful

we encounter tell us much about the process of growth that we are undertaking, as well as testing our mettle, as it were. And it is our anticipation of troubles that allows us to surmount them. That's the theory. I can't say I've managed that too well myself, for example when I was setting up my bookshop.

It would be self-indulgent of me to give a description here of the business meetings I attended, the cocktail parties I went to in an attempt to drum up finance, the contacts I tried to establish in the world of bookselling. In fact there is an earlier draft of this Intertitle, which I threw away, which has all that kind of stuff in it. I went on and on about my uncertainties, my fear of failing. But that's nobody's business, I suppose. In short, I tried to do well, tried to turn my life into a career. I don't need to go into the details because that's what we all try to aim for, that's what we are trained to try and aim for, right from the first moment a teacher asks us what we want to do when we leave school.

Anyway, I did see my plans through, because not to do so would have been to admit a fault in my personality that would have gone straight to the heart of who I am, and young people, despite their worries, have confidence to spare. Surely, this must be how Hugh felt as the group considered the options. They could have stayed in Pictou, scrabbling for survival in forests that had been more or less felled long before they arrived. They could have jumped on the next ship *back* rather than the next ship *onwards*. But we know from the "Pictou" section what choice was made, and the clear satisfaction that Hugh expresses regarding his part in the decision places him and his

---

approach served me well as I grew my business) but this one has eluded me. I can actually visualise the quotation on the page, but my memory stubbornly refuses to let me imaginatively close the volume and examine the cover. I have a vague sense that the quotation is a translation from the French, but whose French entirely escapes me. Google has been unable to help me. I wish I didn't lose things like this.

determination right at the centre of the train of events. He is the hero of his own story, and I, for one, feel I can learn from that, not least because of this tale's link with my own ancestry.

It was Hugh who appears to have pushed for the move onwards to Quebec, the beginning of the next stage of a journey that took him across the continent to seek success. I like Hugh's keen desire to make his own way, rather than hoping someone else would point out the way for him. In Hugh I see some reflected justification for much of what I have done in my life. I know there were those who were critical of decisions I made, but at least they were *my* decisions, and I am proud of having made them, even if I am not necessarily proud of each one of them individually. There have been times when I have doubted my abilities to shape my life but in Hugh's story, read for the first time through a dark night in more ways than one, I have found some confirmation. It has lifted my heart, and restored my self-confidence, because, it seems to me, Hugh is close to me and I feel close to him even though we are so far apart in many ways.

Look on Hugh's journeying as a tale of success, despite the troughs, and you might, as I did, begin to see your life in a historical context. Not the context that puts small people's lives in the back seat of a vehicle driven by Presidents and Generals. I mean the context of others like you, finding their own way, sometimes with doubt, sometimes with fear, sometimes, even, with unhappiness, but always with hope, and a clear sense of destination. Reaching destinations means leaving other places behind. Hugh has helped me with this, and I wish I could talk to him about it.

For example, there was the first time I met Philip. How well I remember that: the anxieties that accompanied my early attempts to appear to him a potentially useful human being. But all the time I felt we would be together, and I don't think that is hindsight. I thought we would be together always.

164

It was in Aberdeen, at a party. Never mind the details. Fingers brushed forearms and our hearts beat faster. It felt like destiny, because that is the feeling young people like to have.

Philip was a musician in several senses. He had played violin in the Scottish National Orchestra, but at night he played in a jazz band that specialised in left-field performances in an Aberdeen bar that aficionados frequented. He also composes music, both classical and jazz. His own band played his jazz compositions but one of his pieces, a viola concerto, had been premiered by the BBC Scottish Symphony Orchestra, and he had won a competition called the Amtro-Chastel Young Composers Award for a string quartet that he had written, something to do with East-West tensions. You might have heard of him, though he is not well known, really.

I had never met anyone like him in my life, and as I looked in his eyes, unable to see anything, I fell in love. The strangely unbelievable thing was that he was meanwhile staring into my eyes and discovering that he was interested in me too. How could I have anticipated that? I was sure he would see through me at any second, realise that I was nobody, that all I had in my purse were promissory notes and dreams that might flutter off and vanish, likes moths, in the morning.

I remember thinking Philip's fingers didn't really look like a violinist's fingers. But so they were. Appearances can be deceptive. And as I got to know him over the following weeks and we spent time doing the things that people who spend time getting to know each other spend time doing, this dread began to grow inside me, the dread that one evening I'd walk into a smoky jazz bar and there he'd be, arms linked with some smooth young fan, cool and mysterious like Eszter Balint in *Stranger Than Paradise*, and he'd nod across the bar at me in a friendly way as if to say, 'Nice to see you, that's all this ever meant'. And then he'd turn back to his whisky and ice and I'd turn back to the rainy pavement and kick my way back home.

That's what I was scared of. I was scared of never feeling him touch my skin again.

But I didn't give in to the fear, that's what I'm saying.

No, what *am* I saying exactly? That Hugh's life is an example of the need to face, and to overcome, challenges. Sometimes, maybe, we can only face challenges by facing away from them. That's not unhealthy, not really. In Hugh's life, we can see clearly from that conversation with Mrs McIntosh, there are personal and what we might, with a twenty-first-century perspective, call *career* challenges. One feeds from the other. Hugh may not even have been fully aware at the time of his writing which of these formed the key tests in his life. If he had revised the whole diary, what would he have changed? We shall never know, of course, but it strikes me that the drive to *succeed* must be of prime significance in all human activity, whereas the drive for social comfort (represented by Rachael Sutherland and Philip Adams) must be secondary. It must be. And embracing success can mean moving away from bad things in the past, moving away from blame.

If I had been a down-and-out with bird's-nest hair, a brown paper bag of booze and holes in the toes of my unmatched boots, would Philip had given me a second look, regardless of my personality? If Philip had slouched from a doorway to grab my elbow with swollen all-weather hypodermic-clutching fingers, would I have seen his clear blue eyes through the matted knots of dirty facial hair?

Of course not, though you would like to believe that beauty and personality would shine through, would you not? And while I'm not suggesting that gradually losing Philip was *only* a product of the long slide of my business towards liquidation, I can't see how that could have been anything other than, maybe, the main factor.

I am aware this may sound worldly or mercenary or materialistic but I prefer to see it as simply honest. I don't mean to insult anyone, but perhaps we could all look more honestly at our motivations and our successes (or lack of them). We have to know where our vulnerabilities come from, and whose fault they are. Things went wrong for me, and I've not found it easy to search for the reasons. Hugh has helped me with the process, though, made me see more truths. I feel better about things now that I've read his book. I've found out something about forgiving.

Enough of that. I wrote early on that I did not want to provide too detailed a commentary on Hugh's text, but as I also said, we must view the diary as a kind of commentary on *our* own narratives, otherwise what would be the point in reading it?

So, to get back to the matter in hand. The next section takes Hugh on to Quebec and beyond, and covers a period of around two years, as I mentioned, taking our narrator into his twenties. But the account is sporadic and the descriptions truncated. We have some work to do, therefore, in reading it, filling in the gaps and making some deductions about what must have happened, what must have been said in the invisible story-spaces of Hugh's life. As in the earlier (and later) sections, there is some closure here, but there are also many new openings.

Croval becomes more distant, I think.

Quebec and Beyond

It surprises me that I havent written more than I have since we left Pictou. The boat arrived as they said it would and we all got on and sailed away. Here we are now.

One night Ian was tossing and turning in his sleep, calling out in a low voice with words that sounded as if they came from the Bible, the words mixed with sobs and gasps for air. When he woke in the morning he said he could remember none of it, even though I asked him what hed dreamt. He said it was a dream of the time when he had to preach his first sermon in front of a presbytery so that he could be given a job as a minister. He said he couldnt see how that dream had made him cry out as if in pain, because it was a happy memory. The sermon had gone well and he had been put in place as the minister of that small church. I asked him what it had been like to stand in front of people and preach. He said he couldnt remember exactly. I asked him if they had treated him kindly, or if they tried to scare him, knowing that he was waiting on their judgement, and he laughed and muttered something about heaven. I asked him again if he could think why he had been upset by his dream and he said maybe it was the motion of the boat that had bothered him, and in fact he was a bit seasick or riversick at that time, even though hed shown no sign of it at all as we crossed the ocean from Scotland to New Scotland.

Mrs McIntosh says that Ians like a lot of old men shes known over the years. He holds his secrets close to himself and wont share them with anyone.

In amongst the trees our little cabins hide, like two wee children coorying down to get away from big boys trying to get them. The trees are so tall here, much taller than the trees at the top of the cliff above Croval and already those trees are fading in my memory so that Im not that sure how big they were at all really. When I imagine standing in amongst them, which Ive done lots of times, I cant get a true picture of what size they are. Its as if my memories of when I was a child are beginning to disappear and Ive not even been away that long. And for Ian it seems to be the other way round. A lot of what he talks about is the past, the times when he was a boy or when he was a young man just starting out on the road that takes him here to these cabins in amongst the tall trees.

Theres a woodpecker that lives in the trees round about where we are and we can hear him knocking away on the tree trunks. Im thinking that once we take down these trees hell have to go away, hell have nowhere to call home. Of course its easy for a woodpecker because there are always other trees, arent there? All he has to do is spread his wings and head off until he finds another trunk to knock at. I suppose were forcing him further away, once we get these trees down. Thats what we have to do.

Im thinking about my mother quite a lot.

Im thinking about what shes doing and what shes thinking and it seems to me that that Walter Scott and other men who write stories in books are cheating. I mean they can tell you all about what someone is doing in Edinburgh, and the next minute theyre telling you what someones doing in the Borders with England, or somewhere else and thats the point, it could be anywhere else. I wish I could write down what my mother is doing and thinking at this moment that I write these words but of course I cant because I cant be in two places at the same time. So all these books have to cheat.

But even here, even in Pictou, on the boat, on the road from Croval to Cromarty and the Lady Gray, even in these places where Ive been, theres so much goes on that I dont know anything about. Who knows what was ever said between Callum and that girl Katherine he met on the boat? Or what was plotted between Donald Sutherland and John Bailey, talking about us when we werent there? And when I go outside the cabin and theres Ian sitting on the stump of the first tree we took down, what is he thinking? Hes looking down at the ground between his feet and Im wondering, is he watching some ants struggling along with their little bundles of food? Is he looking at his boots and thinking itll be good when weve made some money and he can buy new ones? Is he looking at nothing but the pictures in his mind of the memories from long ago? Is he looking at nothing but the pictures in his mind of where we are now and how we are all being with each other? Is he looking at nothing but those pictures in his mind of where well be in two months from now, two years?

So that sometimes I feel like not writing anything, but even so it surprises me that I havent written more than I have since we left Pictou, because now that Ive started doing it its hard to stop, even if I want to.

That first tree. What a time it took us to cut it down. First we had to choose it. Ian said it was symbolic and spelt that out for me. He said this first tree was a Rubicon, and he explained that to me. Im learning all the time and for the first time in my life beginning to feel a little bit older.

It was autumn already when we took down that tree. A man came from one of the nearby clearings to sell us some axes and other things once everyone round about had heard about the new settlers. A man came out to see us from Goderich to try to sell us another bit of land as well but we didnt buy it. I realise Ive not written anything about getting to Goderich and I might write about that yet, well see.

So anyway this other man, Simeon something, came to see us and sold us three big axes and some ropes and other stuff that used up a bit more of Ians money. Mrs McIntosh put some money in too. Of course now its Mary but back then I think we all called her Mrs McIntosh. When she said that her name was Mary I was thinking back to old Mary McIntosh that had died back in Croval at the time of the sickness and how Hunter hadnt wanted us to get too close to him, and of course Mary Vass who comes into my mind every day still.

Theres something about this Mary McIntosh that youre wary of too. I havent written down how she comes to be with us either and maybe Ill put down a bit about that as well.

At that time, the time when we cleared the first tree, the Rubicon, we were in tents that wed bought down in Goderich from a store that sold things that new settlers would need. The idea was that wed quickly cut down a few trees and build a big cabin that would be able to shelter us before the colder weather came. It would need to have a separate room for Mrs McIntosh, of course, that was the plan, but in the end we built two cabins, one for me and Robert and Callum and Ian and one for Mrs McIntosh, because Ian said it wouldnt be right for us all to be together under one roof. So, anyway, even though Im calling her Mary now Im going to write Mrs McIntosh when Im writing about this time when we were just beginning the task of clearing, if I remember.

The man that had sold us the axes told us how to cut a tree down and off he went back to his place which is about four miles away through the forest

What youve to do is to make a cut in one side of the tree, the side where you want the tree to fall. We chose the south side of the tree because Callum said that if we got it to fall near the place where we were going to build our cabin there would be less dragging to do. The man with the axes had told us that the cutting down of the tree is hard work and that stripping off the branches is even harder work but that the hardest work of all is logging and dragging and thats when you get the blisters and cuts on your hands and your shoulders feel as if youve been kicked by an angry horse. He was right.

So we started off on this tree. First of all it was me and

Callum, one on each side of the tree. It was a big old beech tree. As I wrote before it was already autumn and with every stroke of an axe into the tough trunk a fair shower of leaves and twigs and moss and spiders and things would come showering down onto our heads and shoulders. The man that sold us the axes had told us that wed be better waiting until the leaves were off the trees before we started any clearing, because it would be easier and less of a mess, but we didnt have any time to lose if we wanted to get the cabin built before the snows came but in the end we never had the cabin built before the snows came anyway because it took a lot longer than wed thought it would and other things distracted us, well some of us.

The axes were heavy and wed not been doing physical hard work for a long time, not since we hauled up the boat for the last time back at home, so we were soon tired and Ian and Robert took their shot. Mrs McIntosh would come with water because one of the things that wed been told was good about the bit of land wed bought was that there was a spring that was bubbling up just at the edge of the plot, turning into a wee burn that went away slowly across our land. The man that sold the land to us, a Mr Thomas Branton, told us that this water would be good for drinking and also would be good when we were at the stage of planting crops because it would give us water to feed the seedlings and if we had a few animals, like maybe some pigs, then we could use the water for them too and we wouldnt have to be always carrying water from the main river which was a good two miles away. Of course we would be collecting water in barrels too when it rained. What he didnt tell us about the water was what was bad about having water on your plot but we found that out when the time came.

After the tree had been cut through on the south side by about half the width of the trunk, youd to go round the other side, the north side, and start cutting again, a bit higher up the trunk. Of course the man had told us that was the best way to get the tree to fall the way you wanted it to but he never mentioned that you should make your first cut a bit lower than youd maybe think would be comfortable for you as you swung the axe at the tree. So we just cut on the south side at the natural height for us swinging the axes. So when we went round to the north side and we had to cut a bit higher up the trunk we found that we could scarcely do it because we were having to swing the axes at nearly head height and after a wee while our shoulders were burning. He also told us how it could be very dangerous when the tree came down because when the tree falls it can bang up against other trees and branches can snap off and go flying through the air. Its like when youre out in the boat and youve a lobster creel down and its got stuck somehow down on the bottom and youre hauling on the rope and the rope snaps. Ive seen a rope break a mans arm when it snaps like that, Alexander Sinclair it was. But obviously the tree is even more dangerous because it can kill you. So youre meant to run and hide behind another tree when the tree youre cutting down starts to fall. And anyway sometimes it doesnt exactly fall in the direction that you want it to. Its all very difficult.

At last we got that first tree cut down and it crashed down with the air full of leaves and dirt and then we set to cutting off the branches and in the end Robert had to set off for Goderich and get one of the saws in the store there.

But this is the point of the story about the first tree, apart from writing down how we began to get started there. When Robert came back from the tramp through the woods to try to buy a saw, he had news.

He was shouting, running the last bit back through the woods towards us where we were still stripping off the branches from the great tree where it lay on the ground.

Theyre here! he was shouting. Theyre here!

Whos here? we were calling back and Ian, whod been sitting on the ground with a drink of water, got up to his feet. Whos here? he said to Robert as he got in about us, bending over with his hands on his knees taking great big gulps of air. He couldnt speak for a minute and it seemed like ages.

Elizabeths here. And Rachael.

Where? asks Ian.

There! He pointed away across into the forest more or less in the direction hed come. Over there about two three miles.

Rachael and Elizabeth from Craigtore? asks Callum.

Who else? What other Elizabeth and Rachael?

Whos with them? says Callum.

Just them. The others have gone on. Theyre in a wee cabin beside a bigger cabin that has a family from Inverness in it. Helping them with washing and that and working on their crops and with their animals.

Callum says, And what about the others from Craigtore? Are they there too?

Thats what Im saying, says Robert. No. Theyve gone on.

Gone on where?

I dont know. I only spoke to them for a few minutes then came back here to tell you. Weve to go over there tonight to see them and the Inverness man says weve to have our food with them, were welcome.

Callum turns away and looks at the dead tree lying on the ground, huge and waiting. He says, Theres a lot to be doing here.

Robert throws his arms in the air, Its Elizabeth and Rachael from Craigtore, for Gods sake. What are you talking about, man?

Ian shakes his head, There is no need to be using Gods name in that manner.

Robert says, Im sorry, but its good news isnt it?

Yes it is, I say. It is.

Mrs McIntosh says, Thats what I thought.

So that was how we met again with Rachael and Elizabeth. I should have been writing it all down at the time, because things slip your mind. So Im sorry[24] if Im not remembering everything, but Im trying to. I mean to be better at writing this all down but you forget.

The Inverness family was called Bale. There was Edward Bale, the father, Emma, the mother and a little boy called Richard. Actually they werent really from Inverness at all. It turned out they were really from Edinburgh and theyd flitted to Inverness because this Edward Bale had wanted to set up a tavern there. But it hadnt gone very well, said Edward, because thered been already too many taverns in Inverness, something he hadnt known about before he went. Callum asked him why he hadnt opened up a tavern in Edinburgh instead of moving all the way north but he said there were too many taverns in Edinburgh too. Ian asked him why it had to be a tavern at all and Edward said, Well youve got to choose to do something, havent you?

But of course then it hadnt finished up the way the Bales had thought it would and here they were in Upper Canada. Theyd met Rachael and Elizabeth in Goderich looking for work and had made an arrangement with them, with the two girls paying their way by working.

The Bales were a good bit ahead of us, because by the time wed met them theyd been here for nearly a year, and they had some money that theyd put aside for buying the tavern in

---

24 This is an interesting thing to say. Why is he apologising? It shows an awareness of audience but it seems odd to consider an uneducated, or partially educated, young man like Hugh, writing for posterity or for a purely imaginary reader. This apology, though, does seem to make clear that he is not simply writing for himself, producing an account of his life that he can pore over at eighty, to see if there is sense in what has happened to him over the years. Perhaps his reader is *anyone*. – RM

Inverness that hadnt happened. Their land was cleared and they had some pigs, some hens and a couple of cattle and they had crops in the ground. It was good dry land they had.

We had a fine meal that night. The Bales had slaughtered one of their pigs the day before and we had a good meal of bacon and potatoes and this Indian corn that they grow here. We had a good dram as well. Wed taken over a bottle of whisky that wed bought in Goderich and they had some too and we all had a good shot in. They were friendly people and I was feeling happier than I had felt for a long time. Ian said grace at the beginning of the meal and it was a good cheerful feeling round their table for the whole evening. I cant remember all that we spoke about but it was to do with life here and life back there and what to do to make things work out. I know that a lot of what was said has gone clean out of my mind because all through the meal I was looking across the table at Rachael and she would be glancing back to me then turning back to Elizabeth to carry on talking. It wasnt that long since Id seen her but I could see a change. She wasnt a girl so much now, and I suppose I wasnt so much a boy. Id always liked her and to see her at the Bales table made coming to America worthwhile. There was a quiet moment, I remember, and I asked what had happened to Matthew Sinclair and the others that had been with them when they came to America.

Elizabeth said, Theyve gone. Matthew set up with a woman in Montreal. And the others just

Drifted away, said Rachael, when Elizabeth seemed to have run out of words.

It seemed to me that there was a story there that they werent saying, but that was up to them.

Callum said, Trust Matthew Sinclair.

Elizabeth – Matthews not a bad man.

Callum – Is he not?

Elizabeth – No hes not.

176

There was a little quiet bit then before Edward Bale, a sturdy good looking man, poured out another drammie and people got talking again. The Bales wouldnt have known what that was about but I knew and I caught Roberts eye and he just raised one dark eyebrow and went back to his meat. The thing was that Callums always sort of liked Elizabeth and I think theyd been together back when we were in Croval, when Elizabeth was about sixteen but Im not completely sure about that. Anyway, the thing was that Callum was jealous of Matthew Sinclair. Hed been with a few of the girls if all you heard was true and Callum was jealous. I dont mean he wanted to marry Elizabeth or anything, but it was in his nature for him to be jealous, and he could be right difficult when that mood came on him, as well as at other times. I cant remember if anything else was said then. It might have been. If Id been good at writing it all down as it happened I wouldnt be in this mess now, trying to remember what to put in where.

Bale told us wed better get a move on if we wanted to have a crop next year. You were supposed to get planting the wheat they use here about now, he said.

Ian said, Well the man in Goderich, Thomas Branton, told us it would take a good month to six weeks to clear the land and that we could be putting a crop in during October, once the work was done.

No, said Bale, you need to be getting the wheat in by September at the very latest, then you can put in an early and a late crop next year.

We dont know much about crops, said Robert.

Evidently, said Bale with a smile that was both friendly and a little bit mocking at the same time. Wed only just met him so it was hard to see inside him to know what he was really thinking, although it did seem to me he hadnt been here that long himself.

Mrs Bale said, And youll need to be putting your energies

177

into building as well. Youll need to get your cabins up soon because it can get awful cold here in the winter. We found that out last year but by that time we were in this place. You wouldnt want to be under canvas when the first snow falls.

It turned out she was right, of course.

Bale said, Wed like to help you with your clearing work but we have our hands full here with our own land. It needs a lot of work itself.

Callum said, We dont need anyones help, were fine.

That caused another little quiet bit. He was still annoyed about the Matthew Sinclair thing.

Later in the evening, after a few more whiskies, I was outside with Rachael, which is where Id really wanted to be since wed got there, and in fact for a long time before that as well. We were sitting on a wooden kist with a lid that had shining brass hinges. Rachael said it was full of bedding stuff and that theyd had to drag it outside to make room for us all in the cabin, ten of us when usually there would be just five.

Whos that woman with you? asked Rachael.

Ian introduced her, I said.

I know, but who is she? Mrs McIntosh. How is *she* with you?

It was too dark to see her expression and I replied to her, Well, she just is. We met her in Pictou and with one thing and another she ended up coming along with us, thats all.

Oh well, she said, with a laugh. You dont need to tell me if you dont want to.

No, its not that.

Not what?

Nothing.

She was making me nervous which is what she always seems to do. It was just dusk and there was a rustle every now and then as birds were settling in the trees to roost but we couldnt see them because they were too far up above us. I heard the sound of a wood pigeon or some American bird that sounds like our wood pigeon. We were on this kist which wasnt the most comfortable thing in the world but I wasnt going to say so because that would have meant going back inside. Wed both taken a good drink. I could see her face close to mine and the red hair that was the particular thing about Rachael.

Everyone has some particular thing, I think. With Robert its his darkness, with Callum its his temper, with Ian its his fairness, the way he listens to everyone. But probably Ian would say that the particular thing about him is his faith. And Callum would never admit to his temper being the thing that makes him Callum. Anyway, Rachaels hair was the thing Id always noticed.

And are you liking it here? she asked me.

Here near Goderich? Or here away from Croval?

Both.

Well, you know its not so easy sometimes.

I know.

What about you? Do you like it here?

Here near Goderich or here away from Craigtore?

Here away from Craigtore.

She shrugged her shoulders. Well, she said, were away now. No use worrying about it. That times gone.

So I think she was missing it too.

I asked, Have you been missing any of the people from back then?

You start afresh, dont you?

But did you sometimes find yourself wondering what had happened to the people that never came out with you?

From Craigtore?

Craigtore and from Croval.

Well, I wondered who else might come and why the others stayed where they did. One thing I dont miss, the feeling that youre in a trap.

But there are others that have come.

Who?

179

Well, us.

True enough. And are you glad?

I am now.

Now that youve got your bit of land? she asked.

I looked away from her face and down at the ground, just a grey haze as the light went. There was a row of white stones round a little flower bed where the Bales, probably Mrs Bale, had planted some wee flowers just beside their door. I fixed my eyes on that.

No, now that Im here.

Here near Goderich or here on your own bit of land.

Just now, here on the Bale familys bit of land.

Its good land, she said. Theyve been kind to us, but I dont think well stay here for too long.

I felt the blood hammering away in my ears. I said, Why, are you not happy here?

Yes, she said. She pulled her feet up on top of the kist and put her arms round her knees. She said, Its getting cold, isnt it? You can tell the winters on the way. They say it can get right cold here.

So, if youre happy, why are you wanting to move on?

Oh, I dont know. Myself and Elizabeth, this isnt exactly what we came here looking for, she said. Theyre nice people and good people, but this isnt exactly what I imagined when we left Craigtore.

Whats missing?

She looked away, trying to find the right word, I think, but failing. She said, *Something.* I just thought there would be something here that, well

Her words just died away on that. I tried to think of the next thing to say to her but to be honest I was too frightened of saying the wrong thing, saying something that would make her look at me and laugh.

So then we talked about nothing very much, about the

cutting down of trees and looking after pigs and how hard it is to keep white bedding white and other such unimportant things. It seemed so strange to be halfway across the world having this conversation with a girl whod lived just along the coast, just a scramble over some rocks away from me. I thought about her sitting by the turned over boat with the wind in her red hair. After a bit she raised her cup to me and said, Well Im out of whisky. Will we go back in for a dram?

And like a fool I just said, Yes, thats what to do.

She had to jump down off the kist, her feet didnt touch the ground when she was sitting on it with her back up against the cabin wall. I let her go in first and I stood outside for a minute or two longer, listening to the wind in the branches and every now and then the sound of an owl calling through the woods, lonely sounding.

One thing we spoke about that night was the place where they took the people that they suspected had cholera. It was strange. When wed sailed by it on the way to Quebec[25], wed all noticed it and when we spoke to the Bales and to Elizabeth and Rachael

25   The lack of a clear chronological structure in this section led me to consider the following options:

(1) To reorganise the elements of the section so that they followed a roughly chronological sequence.

(2) To write some brief inserts that would give an account of the journey from, say, Quebec to Goderich (which Hugh hardly touches on at all, even though it would have been a time-consuming and interesting part of his time in Upper Canada), thus enabling the reader to have a clearer mental picture of the shape of his travels.

(3) To leave it as it is.

Given that the presence of sentences such as the first one in this part would lead to impossible difficulties if I attempted (1), above, I abandoned that plan. My own inadequacies as a writer ruled out (2), of course, so I settled on (3). I hope that the reader can still piece together the events without too much discomfort caused by Hugh's non-chronological interventions. – RM

181

they all said the same, how it had struck them. So that was three separate journeys and wed all noticed the same thing. I never wrote down anything about it at the time because Id got out of the habit of writing things down but when I think back it *still* seems strange.

It was about thirty miles before we came to Quebec and our Captain[26] told us that every ship was obliged to put in there so that a check could be made for cholera, which was a scourge of all the emigrant boats, so he told us. We had to let down our anchor and a little boat came out from this island which was called *Grosse Ile,* which is a French name meaning *Big Island* even though it wasnt the biggest of the islands we passed on the river.

Some of the places have got French names here and Ian explained them to me. Some of them have names that have to do with the language that is spoken here by the Indians, and some of them have names from the Gaelic, such as *Montreal,* which is from the Gaelic *Monadh Tri Allt,* the hill of the three streams.

On this little boat there was a doctor and a couple of soldiers. They had guns with them and looked nervous, ready to shoot anyone who tried to stand in their way. The doctor asked the Captain for the *manifest,* which is the list of passengers on board the boat, which the Captain had ready in his hand, knowing that it would be asked for. From that the doctor chose a number of names, maybe every tenth name or something, and these people

26 Hugh gives no details about this man, and my researches have not allowed me to come up with anything very definite about the man. I should not like to speculate about who he was and see no point in wasting further time trying to identify the ship's Captain for this stage of Hugh's journey. Whoever the Captain was, he clearly had no significant impact on the Croval men, since Hugh says very little about him: much less, obviously, than he had to say about the dubious Captain Gray. Should any of the readers of this text be able to shed any light on these hidden details I would be delighted to hear from them care of the publishers. – RM

were told by the soldiers to go and stand at the front end of the boat, or the bow, as it was called. As it so happened, none of our little group was chosen amongst this list of people.

Then the doctor looked at all the people hed chosen from the list and tested their health by asking them questions and so on. After a while he was satisfied that they were all healthy and this was taken to be proof that the boat was healthy altogether and the doctor and the two soldiers climbed down the rope ladder at the side of our boat and got back in their wee boat and the soldiers rowed away and then we were allowed to sail on towards Quebec.

The thing was that while the doctor was looking at the people from the list, we were all at the edge of the boat, leaning on the wooden rail, staring over at Grosse Ile. It was quite a beautiful island, with trees and a nice shape to it, the kind of place youd be thinking would be nice to stay. There were some buildings on it of various sizes, but one great big one, a stone built place with white walls and small windows running along the sides. Thin wisps of smoke were rising out of a few chimneys. One of the sailors told us that this was the *quarantine* hospital. This word quarantine is another one of those French words and has to do with yet another French word *quarant* which means forty.

It seems that if the doctor was to find a case of cholera on board any boat that passed, then the whole crew and passengers of the boat had to get off there at Grosse Ile and spend forty days in the quarantine hospital, until they were either dead or better. Meanwhile the boat itself would have to be anchored just beside Grosse Ile and when we were passing there were three boats anchored in a little bay by Grosse Ile, two about the size of our boat and one a good bit smaller. So what this meant was that all the crews and all the people that were passengers on those boats were now inside that hospital.

The sailor told us that hed never been in the hospital himself, but that he knew sailors who had been. He said the problem was that you might be getting near the end of your forty days and fine and healthy and then another boat would arrive and someone would have cholera so theyd join you in the hospital and although youd been fine and well and had reached thirty nine days maybe, you could catch cholera from one of those new people and you would end up dead instead of carrying on with your journey. And even if you were healthy if there was a big outbreak of cholera in the quarantine hospital sometimes theyd have to start your forty days again. This sailor told us that he knew people that had been in there for six months, waiting to get out and back on their boat. He told us that there was no real help for those that caught the disease and that there were only two doctors on the island, the one wed seen and the other one. He said that they couldnt really do anything to cure people of the disease and that if you got it all they could do was to look after you and wait and see if you were going to die or not. He said there were some nurses there too. He said the smell of the place was terrible because cholera affects you in the guts and theres nothing you can do to keep yourself clean. I was remembering back to the Lady Gray and wondering if that actually had been this cholera, and if so how lucky we were that we hadnt got it. That put a shiver into me.

This was the way they protected Quebec from the disease of cholera.

But as I was saying, while we were listening to the sailor telling us all these facts, we were looking at the island. Along the shore of the island, where the river lapped up against the stones, there were some people standing looking back at us, and some women who were washing clothes in the water and beating them out against the bigger rocks. All of them were dressed in white which gave a strange look to the whole scene. Even the men there were in white trousers and white shirts and the women in white skirts and white shirts. We were maybe quarter of a mile away and we couldnt make out their faces but from the way they were standing, we could tell that they were looking at us, most of them, straining their eyes to see us the way we were straining our eyes to see them. So there was this big white building and the little bits of white smoke against the sky and all these white people standing by the waters edge and there was something about it that made me think of ghosts, and in particular it made me think of a ghost story that Id once heard told down in the Carcair one night.

I think I must have been about fourteen at the time and I think it was just me and Callum there. I cant remember Robert being there but he might have been. It was a windy night, I remember that, and I remember it was dark outside so it was probably in the autumn. The men hadnt been out in the boats because the weather was bad and theyd been drinking in the Carcair all day so that there was a lot of shouting and singing and me and Callum were sitting on the floor over against the wall beside the door just listening to it all and smelling the pipe smoke and the fumes of the whisky that was going like water.

They began a thing that sometimes happens in the Carcair, which is storytelling. They tell stories about things that happened to them, or to their grandfathers or whoever, or stories about things they heard happened to other people that someone they knew once met, they tell stories that have been in their minds since they heard their own fathers tell the story which had been in their minds since their fathers fathers father first told it when they were just a wee boy. They tell stories that are just made up, and theres a right skill in making up a story so that people laugh when theyre meant to laugh and hold their breath when theyre meant to hold their breath. And theyll tell ghost stories and the thing about them is that theyre told as if theyre true stories but everyones hoping theyre made up.

So this one night the stories were going and the drink was flowing and the pipe smoke was filling the room from the top

185

down and then one old man, hes dead now, Angus Mackenzie, started on this ghost story, and for some reason its always stuck in my mind.

There was a place by the sea, not unlike Croval but wee-er, just a few little stone houses splashed by the white foam of the waves in the winter and baking under the summer sun beside the black rocks where the seagulls cry at the sea. And in one house there lived an old old man, Jacky his name was, and they called him Jacky Chick after his father, who was also called Jacky Chick but hed been dead now for thirty years or more. The old father had kept a few hens that had the run of the croft and thats why he was known to everyone as Jacky Chick. Youd go into his croft and thered be one up on the table and one on the hearth and two or three warm on old Jacky Chicks bed.

Every night, this younger Jacky Chick, who must have been ninety if he was a day, would take a walk along the shore, clambering over the rocks with his stick and with his little dog, a west highland terrier, jumping along behind him. The others in the village would tell him to take care, one slip on the seaweed covered rocks would send him down to crack his head and die there with the dusky waves covering him up. But hed always say the same thing, which was, I walked this shore since I was a boy and my dad walked the shore before me. The deep blue sea holds no fear for me, for the deep blue sea ignores me. This was a saying his father had taught him when he was just a wee boy.

Well old Jacky Chick, the younger one, that is, had a fall out with one of his neighbours in the village over a net that had been left out on the jetty to dry before mending. Old Jacky Chick didnt like the net left where it was left because it was covering over the place where he used to sit in the morning when the sun came up over the headland, his wee white dog beside him. So hed gone along to his place on the jetty this one morning to find the net there, all dripping with seaweed and green slime and hed kicked it off the jetty with his scrawny old foot and into the water where it had drifted off and got tangled up in the rocks so that in the end it needed more mending than it had in the first place. So the owner of the net, a young man called Richie Murray, goes to Jacky Chicks door and hammers on it until old Jacky Chick comes out.

What would you be wanting now? says Jacky Chick.

Was it you kicked my net into the sea? says young Richie.

Maybe it was and maybe it wasnt, replies Jacky Chick, with the wee white dog barking away fit to burst at his ankles.

Well if it was, Im not happy with you, says Richie Murray. Now Ive to spend time mending it when I could be out on the water making a living. I can tell you, Im angry.

Maybe you are and maybe you arent, says Jacky Chick and he goes to push the door shut with his scrawny old hand.

But Richie Murray puts his young foot in the door and pushes back. He points his finger in Jacky Chicks face and says, Dont be making an enemy out of me, old man.

Jacky Chick gives a snort and a laugh and doesnt say anything, just turns to go off back into the croft, leaving the wee white dog barking and trying to bite young Richies shins.

But Richie Murray shouts into the darkness, Youll need to watch, Jacky Chick. Next time youre walking away along the shore when the sun sets, youll need to watch.

So Jacky Chick shouts back over his shoulder in his old voice, I walked the shore since I was a boy and my dad walked the shore before me. The deep blue sea holds no fear for me, for the deep blue sea ignores me.

Thats not what Im meaning, says Richie and he gives the dog a kick and stamps off to work on his net. But a neighbour had heard the whole thing.

So three nights later, when the body of old Jacky Chick was found along the shore, his head split open and his wee white dog yelping and barking fit to burst and jumping and scratching round his body, theres a bit of a thought in the village that young

Richie Murray had something to do with it. Of course he says no, he was out in his boat at the time for some night fishing and look, heres the fish to prove it, all gutted and salted down in a box by the door. And the neighbour says, Well, I suppose he could have banged his head where he slipped on a rock.

Isnt that what we always warned him? says Richie.

He could have slipped on a bit of seaweed and fallen, says the neighbour.

Isnt that what we thought could happen?

The wee white dog could have got around his ankles and tripped him up.

Isnt that just the kind of thing the wee devil would be doing?

Or someone could have been waiting for him, to get their own back for something that happened, and maybe his head was split open not by a rock but by a stick.

Isnt that just the kind of nonsense that dirty gossips always speak, says young Richie and off he goes to his boat.

Over the next few days and weeks the wee white dog wasnt the same. The neighbour tried to take him in but the dog would keep wandering off and standing by the rock along the shore where old Jacky Chick met his death. The dog would stand there and howl, trotting backwards and forwards, backwards and forwards and when the moon went up in the sky the wee white dog would turn its head up to the darkness and bark fit to burst. It wasnt eating, the wee white dog, even though Jacky Chicks neighbour tried to feed it the best of everything, because she felt sorry for the old dead man, grumpy old so-and-so though hed been. Best beef that dog had, and the finest bits of chicken and trout that had melted off the bone, but still it pined away, always trotting back to the rock where its master had died and every day it got thinner and thinner and the barking got fiercer and fiercer and its eyes got brighter and brighter until one night it never came back to the neighbours house and she went out to look for it and there it was, the wee white dog, lying at the very spot where its master had fallen. She put her hand down to touch it but it was as stiff and cold as the devils bones, the poor thing had died from grief. She carried it back to her house and she buried it in the garden and planted a rose bush over its grave.

Now Richie Murray gave never a thought to all this and when someone told him Jacky Chicks dog was dead, all he said was, Well be getting some sleep at night now then instead of being kept awake by that thing barking fit to burst along the shore.

And of course everyone that stayed in the village had their own dark ideas about Richie Murray and even though none of them had liked old Jacky Chick all that much, they knew what they believed and they turned away from Richie Murray when he passed them on the way to his boat and nobody gave him the time of day any more. Not that Richie Murray cared much. He was young and he had his whole life ahead of him and he knew that hed be around long after the others were long gone. So he was soon in the habit of turning away from them before they could turn away from him, and if he saw someone walking towards him he would usually turn aside and take another way so that he wouldnt have to look them in the eye. You might think hed be lonely like this, young Richie Murray, but not a bit of it.

So this went on for day after day and week after week and month after month until one day it was a whole year since Jacky Chick had met his death along the shore that dark night.

Young Richie Murray was in his wee croft and he was just blowing out the lamp when he thought he heard a noise outside. He moved aside the cloth that hung over his window and peered out but nothing could he see. All the crofts of the village, strung out along the shore like washing on a line, were in darkness, the whole place asleep. So he shook his head and let the bit of cloth fall back in place and off he went to his bed.

189

But just as he was getting in under the blanket he heard the noise outside again and this time he was sure it was a dog barking and it sounded just like that wee white dog that Jacky Chick used to keep. So young Richie, curious now, got up again and went to the door and pulled it open a wee bit and peered out but nothing could he see. He looked up in the sky but the moon and the stars were all hidden by clouds, like candles snuffed out, the whole sky asleep. So he gave a wee shiver and pushed the door shut and off he went to lay his head on his pillow.

But just as he was closing his eyes he heard the noise outside again and this time there was no doubt in his young mind, it was the sound of that wee white dog barking fit to burst. So young Richie got up again and went to the door and threw it open as wide as it could go and took two great strides into the darkness and peered out and this time he did see something. Coming towards him through the moonless night from the dark shore were two white figures, the ghost of Jacky Chick with his arms stretched out holding a torn fishing net, as silent as a shadow, and the ghost of the wee white dog barking fit to burst with its sharp white teeth sparkling like the bones of the devil.

Theres more to the story than that of course, and it has a good ending, but the thing was that it was this story that came into my mind when I was looking over at Grosse Ile and there were all these people dressed in white, like ghosts. These people had all come to America, like us, to make a new start, and here they were trapped on this cholera island, like ghosts. Some of them had stopped what they were doing, as I said, and were looking over at us while we looked back at them, and I was thinking well that could be us and they could be here. It could all have been the other way round, thats the thing.

That was just one of the things that Elizabeth and Rachael talked about that evening at the Bales cabin in the woods. They also told us about all that had happened to them on their journey across the sea and in Pictou where their group began to split up and then on to Montreal and finally here. Although they hadnt really had much of a start on us they seemed much more settled than us, as if they knew what they were doing and we didnt really. They had a proper place to stay and we were still at the stage of cutting down our first tree. But it was good to see them and even though I never managed to say the right things to Rachael I liked seeing her again, and seeing her like this at the Bales made me think well, if she and Elizabeth can get settled and seem content then why not me? Why not us?

Rachael and Elizabeth seemed closer now than they ever were in Craigtore and they seemed older too, more older than they should have been after just a few months, if that makes sense. They were still as unlike each other as ever, Elizabeth all curves and Rachael thinner, Elizabeth full of words, Rachael more careful.

One time we were over in Craigtore, it was me and Robert, I cant remember where Callum was that day and there was a seagull washed in from the waves with a broken wing. It was flapping with its good wing and struggling to get to safety, squawking away. It was Elizabeth that went into the water to grab hold of it and pull it out, even though she was risking getting knocked over and hurting herself. We were shouting at her to leave it, because it was going to die anyway, the poor thing, but eventually she came back out with it in her arms, her clothes all dripping wet. She took the bird up to her croft and true enough it died a day or two later. So later on Robert and me were back in Croval and talking about it.

Robert said, Thats what I like about Elizabeth.

What, that she takes the chance of hurting herself to save an old seagull thats going to die anyway?

No, not that exactly. That she cant stand by and see something happening and not *do* something about it.

It wont do any good. The birdll die, I said.

191

I know, said Robert, and he went quiet for a minute then he said, I cant explain it, but I know what I mean.

This was like Robert. Hes a thinker, always will be. But he doesnt always explain what hes thinking to you. He usually says its because he cant explain it, but I think more likely its because he doesnt want to. Like Ian that way, maybe. I know Robert thinks its a bit strange me writing down the things that happen, but he never wants to read it. He told me that it was my business and that the way I see things happening has nothing to do with anybody else. And of course Im glad he never wanted to read it because then hed have found out about what Callum did to old Mary Vass and I dont know what hed have thought about that or whether he would think I was as bad for not stopping him. But if he had read these pages, at least Id have told *someone*. It has crossed my mind that maybe one day its something Ill tell Rachael, but that would be a chancy thing to do.

So to go back to the story of the bird with the broken wing, while he was busy thinking about Elizabeth rushing into the waves to save its life, I was thinking more of Rachael sitting on the shingle watching. When Elizabeth had rushed off into the sea, Robert and me had stood up as if to stop her and then had stood there, not sure what to do, until she came splashing back out again, the broken bird struggling in her arms. But all the while, Rachael never even moved. She just sat on the stones, looking at everything. I was thinking that was just like Rachael and I still think that. Sometimes when you think of someone you think of them doing a particular thing because to you that seems to sum them up. So I think of Ian reading, for example, probably from the Bible, and I think of Callum running, any-where, and I think of Mary McIntosh cooking, leaning over the stove. I think of Elizabeth laughing out loud, her head back. So I think of Rachael sitting quiet, just looking at things.

That night it took us nearly two hours to walk back from the

Bales through the forest in the dark. It was just the four of us because Mrs McIntosh didnt really like the idea of going back through the forest in the total dark, so she was going to sleep in the cabin with the two girls and come back over to us the next morning. I think she did like the idea of being under a proper roof again instead a bit of flapping canvas.

There was a bit of a moon out but all it did was confuse you the way the light came down to you through the branches of the trees stretching up to the stars above. There is a wee scratch of a path to follow because the line that joins us to the Bales carries on past our place down to the river where theres a wooden jetty where there are a couple of boats tied up and it carries on past the Bale place to one or two other cabins in the woods. But it was the first time wed ever walked that way and the wood is a difficult place at night. Sometimes the path, even in the daytime, is hard to follow because it gets crossed by other little paths, some of them made by people going in other directions and some of them made by animals and so not really paths at all. Of course the forest in between peoples cabins is not cleared at all and even though there is a path there it is quite often overgrown with bushes and plantin, which are small new trees, though I dont know why Im explaining that because nobodys likely to be ever reading this apart from me.[27]

So we were crashing through the forest when we heard a noise behind us. All at once, after a friendly night with the

---

27 This is an interesting moment. Hugh's gloss on "plantin" seems to come naturally, only to be followed immediately by his endearing self-doubt. However, elsewhere (and this is something that can't be conveyed in this published edition of his diaries) there are copious scorings out and rewritings. Here, he has chosen to leave his gloss intact. I leave you to think about the significance of that. It's a shame. I'd like a readership for *my* life. Well, at least Hugh has got his now. "Plantin", incidentally, is a kind of uninteresting Scots word, derived, obviously, from "planting". I presume Hugh learnt the word in Goderich. – RM

Bales and with Rachael and Elizabeth, our lives were in danger.

When we were back in Croval, reading away at MacDougalls book, the thing that frightened us about coming was the bears and the wolves that MacDougall said would eat you as soon as look at you. There are these big black bears in Upper Canada that come after you and will hunt you down, and there are packs of wolves that will wait until youre by yourself and get you. For example theyll wait until youve wandered off a path to relieve yourself and then a pack of them will come and get you. In his book MacDougall tells a story about an Indian man who was chased by a pack of wolves and he had to fight them off, his back to a tree, while he waited for his friends to come and get him. He was hacking away at them with his tomahawk, which is from the Gaelic tuagh-bheag or a little axe, killing each wolf as it ran at him with one blow to the skull.

But his friends never came in time, and when they did get there all that was left of him was a few feathers from his headgear, a piece of his belt, and his tomahawk, which was buried in the head of a dead wolf, which was lying beside twelve of its pack, all dead. The poor Indian had hit this last wolf so hard he couldnt get his tomahawk out again in time before the next wolf charged him. There was nothing left to bury.

This is MacDougalls story and he goes on quite a lot about the Saganash Indians and how friendly they are but ever since weve been here folk have been telling us that we shouldnt trust them, theyd stick a knife in you if they could. Weve not seen much of them. There are some that stay in tent things beside the big lake and you see them down in Goderich outside the stores or else standing in wee groups at the corners and they watch you as you go by. But although thats what people say weve never had any bad dealings with them at all, or really any dealings at all.

We were talking about this one time in the cabin. This is obviously a long time after the night we were walking through the forest in the dark and we heard that noise. We were in the cabin after a day working on our bit of land, digging ditches for drainage, I think.

Ian said, They seem like poor people to me.

Callum said, They dont do anything for themselves. As far as I can see everyone takes a loan of them.

Ian – What can they do? All these white people coming to their land. What is there that they can do?

Robert – Its like our own people.

Callum – How is it?

Robert – When the people were moved down from Strathgarrick by Killarnoch. Isnt it the same? We couldnt do anything about it then and these people cant do anything about it now.

Callum – *We* could have done something about it. It was the old people that never did anything. If wed been alive then wed have done something.

And he banged his fist gently on his knee the way he does when his temper is getting up.

Ian – The Bible is full of stories like this one. You only need to think about the Israelites, cast out.

Robert – Thats what I mean. All these stories with one idea behind them.

Callum – What idea?

Robert – That the people with strength force out the people with weakness.

Then I had what seemed to me like a good idea, so I said – Is that what all the stories are about, really?

Callum – All what stories?

Me – All stories.

Callum – About what?

Me – Being forced away from home.

Callum – If youre forced anywhere its weakness.

Robert – Thats what *Im* saying.

Me – I mean, thats what we want to tell stories about. Think about the old men in the Carcair. All they do is sit and tell stories about the days gone by when we were thrown off our land for sheep. Why do they always tell those stories?

Robert – To remember. So that we can be stronger next time.

Me – I think its because they like it.

Callum – Like it? How would they like it?

Me – I dont know. Its a sad story about losing your home and they like it.

Ian said, quite serious and not mocking, What are you talking about, Hugh?

I said, I dont know really. But wheres the story in staying at home and being happy?

Callum – Och, youre talking rubbish now.

Robert – No, stories like that are to warn us about what happens if we give in.

Me – Why do they tell each other then?

Robert – They dont just tell each other. We heard them too, in the Carcair.

Me – But we werent really meant to be there.

Callum – Of course we were. We never let anyone tell us where we should be or shouldnt be.

Me – Thats not what I mean.

Ian – What *do* you mean?

But by this time I was fed up with it. Callum and Robert never really listen to me. They dont think I have much to say. But if truth be told when theyre arguing with each other, like in that conversation, I sometimes cant see the difference between them and their ideas. They just argue because thats what they do. So I just went quiet which is usually the best thing.

Later on Ian asked me again what Id meant, but I said it didnt matter.

But what Im thinking is that we have never had any reason to not trust the Indians and in fact whether you agree with

Callum or Robert or me, we have something in common with them, even if we hardly ever see them.

So, and its taking me a long time to get round to the story, we were crashing through the forest when we heard a noise behind us. At that time wed been told a lot about how bad the Saganash were so the first thought that came into my mind was that there was an Indian, or some Indians, trailing us along the path. Everyone said how good they were at trailing. And the second thought was an animal ready to tear at us, or maybe that was the first thought.

The noise we heard was a rustling and the sound of twigs or fallen branches cracking. We stopped and got close together.

What is it? whispers Ian.

Sshh, says Robert as quiet as anything. Lets just stay still.

We stayed still for a wee bit and there was no noise.

Come on, says Callum in an ordinary voice, were scared of shadows.

But as soon as we start moving again there it is, the noise of somebody following on behind us, away to our right.

My heart is beating hard in my throat when I say, Indians?

Robert – Or a bear.

Ian – Wolves.

Callum takes a step or two back the way we came and says out loud into the forest, Whos there?

But theres no answer, just silence again. Ill never forget the feeling I had when we were standing there, not knowing what was coming along behind us. I could hear Robert and Ian breathing right beside me, Ians breath with the elderly mans wheeze in it. There was the forest all round us, stretching up above us taller than the tallest building in Inverness that wed seen, old trees that had been there since long before we were born. All around us the scrub and bushes that had never been cleared by any man alive. The moonlight coming down between the branches and leaves laying little silvery spots and lines across

197

the plants and across us. The sense I had was that the forest was all full of living things, like the animal, if thats what it was, that was trailing us, the dark birds asleep up in the sharp branches, or awake and watching down on us, the little insects still whining their way through the air, the tiny creatures down amongst the leaves and grasses and moss at our feet, wriggling about through their own lives and this idea scared me for some reason.

Whos there? says Callum again. Show yourself.

Nothing.

Robert whispers, Has anyone got a knife? I shake my head though he probably cant see me do it in the dark. But I dont think my voice has the strength in it to work, Im that scared.

Then Callum shouts out, as loud as he can, so loud that it makes us jump and crush together. He shouts, *Show yourself! Come out and fight!*

Then theres a noise all right. Whoever or whatever it is thats been following us crashes off in the other direction, back off towards the Bales cabin, making no effort now to be quiet, just charging through the bushes and branches to get away. We hear it getting further and further away until we can hear it not at all.

By the time we got back to our land an hour later we are exhausted and the drunk feeling we had from Mr Bales whisky is all but gone, frightened out of us. We crawl in under our canvas roof and Ian goes to light a candle but Robert says, No, leave it.

Right enough, the dark seems better, even though were scared. In fact, because were scared. I dont think any of us wants to see the fear on each others faces, or the triumph on Callums because he saved our lives.

There is this huge lake nearby which the people call Lake Huron. A lake is just like a loch in Scotland, like the wee loch up on the land above Croval, Loch Arradale. Goderich is down by this lake and when we go into Goderich sometimes we go and stand at the edge of the water and look across the lake. Its as big, it looks to me, as the sea we came across but people say its not a sea at all, just a big lake. They say there are other places on the other side of the water where you can go.

Wherever we are it seems there are always people getting ready to move on further west. There are no places where everyone is just happy to stay. Always theres people wanting to find something better. When you look across Lake Huron you can sometimes watch a boat heading away into the distance until the glare from the sun on the water means you cant see it any more and thats another lot of people away.

There was an Indian man hanged in Goderich for stealing. We saw it happening but we didnt go to Goderich just to see it happening although a lot of people did. It was as busy as a market day and because of the rain the street was right muddy and people were pushing against each other. Wed just come in to buy some seed for sowing, even though Mr Bale said we were a bit late. We thought it was better to try or else what are we going to do for money and food next year? Ians money cant last for ever, though he wont tell me how much is left.

This Indian man, we were told by just about everybody, hed been caught with his hand in one of the kegs in the general store, stealing nails. Nails are important here because everyone uses them for building and sorting their cabins. The store owner, a Mr Gaines, caught this young Indian man, hed be about eighteen or nineteen they thought, and it turned out hed been stealing lots of stuff, food and money and everything and it was all in his tent down by the shore of the lake. Theres a man sort of in charge of Goderich and they had a trial of this Indian man, whose name I didnt find out, and they decided that he was guilty of the stealing. Well, he could hardly say that he hadnt done it when they found all the stuff in his tent as well as in his hands.

The punishment was that they would hang him and this they

199

did in the open bit in the middle of Goderich which everyone calls the square, even though its more of a round shape when you think about it. There must have been hundreds of people there to watch, shouting and some of them cheering and waving their hats in the air. The man next to me said

Thats what we have to do or who knows what theyll do next.

I suppose so, I said, though to be honest I didnt like to watch what was going on.

Theyll be in our cabins in the black of night, said this man, and theyll be slitting our throats to steal our wedding rings and raping our daughters.

When the Indian boy was pushed off the platform there was a big shout and the crowd of people pushed forward as if they wanted to get closer to the dead man. I didnt look but turned the other way and struggled through the crush of people to get away. It made me feel a bit sick because of the young boy, just about my age, dead at the end of the rope, and also because the man that had spoken to me was saying something that I *was* scared of. MacDougall had said the Indians could be fierce and I had been worrying about them ever since that night in the wood when we heard the noise.

But hed just been a young boy and probably stealing because he was hungry or because his family was hungry and it seemed a hard thing to do to kill him for that. Weve come half way across the world to make a better life so it just shows what people will do.

I quietly waited on the steps at the saloon after that and eventually Callum and Robert appeared. They were arguing as they came towards me, as usual, but they stopped when they saw me.

Robert said, Are you all right?

Callum said, Of course he is.

I shrugged my shoulders and then we came back to our land. I didnt like it. I feel strange about it, even now.

Our money is always running out and what if one day we were so desperate that we had to put our hands in a keg of nails?

So as I say Im feeling bad because Ive not been writing anything down. I just got tired of doing it and there have been other things to be thinking about. For example, getting through the winter. But its spring now and thats why Im making a record of whats happened in these past few months.

Well of course we never got our cabins finished in time for the first snows, though we did get some crops in the ground. It was just too hard to get everything done properly and the first cabin we got up was so shaky and so full of holes for the wind and rain to get in that we had to take it all down again and start over from nothing. Mr Bale helped us with advice and we should have gone to him in the first place to find out how to do it but no, Callum thought he knew exactly how to build a cabin, even though the closest hed ever been to doing that before was when he tipped a boat over on its side on the beach at Croval to shelter under, which is hardly the same thing at all.

So we tore down that first cabin with our bare hands and that took longer than youd think because we had to be careful not to hurt any of the logs wed used to build it because wed need them again for the next cabin. And all the time we were still having to take down trees so wed have enough logs for the second cabin for Mrs McIntosh. And once the trees were down and stripped and logged we had to clear the stumps and start working on the soil. Mr Bale gave us some of his pig and cow waste to dig in to make the ground better for growing but it wasnt long before the frosts came in and the ground was getting too hard to dig anyway. So in the end we only got a wee bit with corn in and the rest we had to just leave. We were too busy anyway.

It was hard building the cabins while the cold wind was blowing in from the north and your fingers so frozen they hurt for a while then they didnt hurt at all. That was when you knew you had to stop working. You couldnt feel your hands and your fingers got clumsy and it was easy to slip and hit your hand with a hammer or cut yourself on a skelf of wood.

There were times when it was so bad that we were all lying inside the one blowy tent, all five of us, with the canvas banging and cracking in the wind like the sails on The Lady Gray. One time Rachael and Elizabeth had come over from the Baless with some eggs for us and the weather closed in when they were here. So seven of us were in the tent, hanging on to the walls so that it wouldnt blow away on us. You could hear the wind howling in the trees like the waves against the headland and you could hear the trees creaking and scraping against each other so much that we were worried that one might come crashing down on top of us in our wee tent. The snow was blowing along sideways outside but it was very warm in the tent because there were so many of us and we had on lots of clothes though sometimes a gust of wind would get in under the bottom of it and wed get a cold blast. We had a sheet of stuff underneath us called tarpaulin which is good at keeping the water out. Its funny because the sailors on The Lady Gray used to call their hats tarpaulins too but they were made of different stuff.

The wee tent that Mrs McIntosh used wed folded up and weighed it down with some cut logs over by the walls of the half built cabin so it wouldnt blow away. It was better that we were all together in the winter cold. Our other stuff was all stored in wooden kists so it was safe too.

I was pressed up against one wall of the tent and when the wind flapped the canvas it would slap across my cheek and it would sting because the canvas was wet. On my other side, and between me and Ian, was Rachael. I could feel her pressing up against me as we lay there. The noise of the storm was too loud for us to speak but I was straining my ears to see if I could hear her breathing. She was lying turned towards me and I would have liked to have rolled round and be facing her too but I couldnt because it was taking all my strength just to hang on to the wall of the tent. But I imagined turning round and I imagined her face being just an inch or two away from mine. And I looked forward to the moment when the storm began to die down and I could let go of the canvas, but before it died down so much that wed all get up and stretch and the lying beside Rachael would be finished.

But wasnt it just the thing that I fell asleep, even despite the noise of the wind and everything and the feel of Rachaels body pressed up against me, and when I woke up the others were already moving about and Rachael had sat up. When I blinked and looked up at her she smiled at me then crawled away out of the tent into the snow which was lying nearly a foot deep, deeper where it had blown into piles. I lay still for a little while longer, just trying to get it fixed in my mind, the feel of her next to me, even through all the layers of the warm clothes wed had to put on against the cold.

So that was winter and its spring now and I could write down more about the cold months but theres no point in dwelling on the past, Ian always says, and I would agree with him, I think. It wasnt an easy time and I could write down lots of talks we had where we thought about going back to Pictou or back to Croval even but that was just the sort of thing that you say in the dead of winter and in the dead of a cold dark night. There were some bright clear frosty mornings too in the forest when the sun was shining through the tress and the birds were trying to sing as if theyd just woken up from a bad dream and our little bit of land was just the most beautiful thing wed ever seen and those were the moments that kept us there.

I dont think we have the money to pay to get back to Scotland anyway. You have to keep moving on.

One bad thing through the winter was Ians illness which Im

going to write about now. I feel all right about writing it down now that hes better again but I have to say I was worried about him when he was at his worst and there were nights when I lay awake facing that question of what we would do without him, a thought that would bring the tears to the edge of my eyes though I never let the others see that. The worst of it was thinking about how I might not be able to talk to him again or tell him anything. I was thinking I ought to speak to him about me watching what Callum did in Croval and to see what he thought but it didnt seem to be right, with him sick.

It started in December last when it wasnt quite so snowy but it was cold and wet and it went right to your bones. One morning Ian woke up with a cough and he woke us up too with it. That day he wasnt much good for work and the next day the same and then the day after that he was worse and his forehead was hot and there was a sweat on him. He just wouldnt come out of the tent, or couldnt, and we put him in a blanket which the three of us then carried between us over to the Baless. They put Ian into the bed that Richard Bale slept in. Richard is only about ten years old and youd have thought Ian would have been far too big for the bed but not really and that made me feel terrible, looking down at him twisting and turning on that wee bed, just an old man and nothing like the man wed first met up at the manse where he drank too much good wine and ate too much good food off the tinker MacPhees cart. His eyes were neither open nor closed and you could just see the whites under the lids.

Mrs Bale was fussing over him with damp cloths for his head and some other stuff in a bottle that she was feeding between his lips on a spoon. She chased us out of the room the way she chases the chickens from the front of their cabin. She pushed closed the door and the last sight of Ian I got then was of his white old hands fluttering in front of his face as if he was trying to scare off a bird that was flying at him.

Is he all right? I asked her just before she got the door shut. Is he going to get better?

Of course he is, she said crossly. Now get away out of here and get on with your own work. Come back in the evening and well eat together. Leave us be just now.

It was a hard days work that one and so were the next few because nothing much seemed to change. Each time we went over to see him, Ian was much the same and Mrs Bale was getting less and less sure sounding every time she told me that of course he would be getting better soon. All this time Ian was in a fever and couldnt speak properly, although sometimes when we were sitting with him he would speak words but they didnt make any sense. Sometimes it was the names of people he must have known in the past and sometimes it was bits out of the Bible, I think, but it didnt all tie together to have any meaning for us.

We did keep on working, Callum and Robert and me, on the building and clearing and digging the wet ground, during those days, but we hardly spoke and we kept our heads bowed down against the rain. We couldnt speak to each other because we all knew what question there was lying in our minds waiting to jump out. The dangerous thing was that if the question came out so might the answer, so we just chopped and hammered and stuck our spades into the dirt until our muscles hurt and all we could do was eat and sleep.

Then one evening we went over and here was Ian sitting up on a wooden chair in Mr Bales cabin and giving us a weak kind of smile when we came in. As I wrote before hed lost a lot of weight already but now he looked to be just skin and bone. His skin was a yellowish colour and so were the whites of his eyes if that makes any sense. But he was alive and we could see that Mrs Bale was right, he was going to get better. He had a brown blanket over his knees and that made him look even older and weaker. But he was alive and he *was* going to get better.

205

He hardly ate that evening, just a few wee mouthfuls of bread and a spoonful of Mrs Bales soup and he only said a few thin words. Later on when the women were tidying up and Callum, Robert and Mr Bale were outside smoking on their pipes, I sat beside Ian and spoke to him.

We were worried about you for a wee while, I said.

No need to worry about me, he said, and his voice was just a whisper of what it had been before his illness.

Well, we did, I told him. I think youll need to stay here a while yet.

Nonsense, he said. Ill be back and working in no time.

I dont think so, I said. When Mrs Bale says you can come back, then thats soon enough.

But young Richards sleeping on the floor on a bundle of blankets, says Ian stubbornly. I cant take his bed from him any longer.

Young Richards fine on the floor.

I could see he was a wee bit annoyed at me because Ians not someone who likes to be fussed over and I think he was probably feeling a bit silly about being the centre of everyones attention like this. And it annoyed me a bit to think he was annoyed at me for showing him that I cared about him, even if it was selfish in one way.

I said, Ian, youve got to be sure youre better before you do anything. Well get the cabin finished *then* you can come back over.

How will you get the cabin finished without me to help?

I raised my voice at him. How will we get anywhere at all if you come back before youre better and you go and die on us?

So there Id gone and said it, the thing that Id been scared to say or even think in the few days that had just gone by. Ian sat quiet and didnt say anything, just looked at me. I felt funny then for having said it so I began to talk quickly telling him all about what wed been doing and how we were nearly at the stage where wed be putting the roof onto the first cabin and how wed taken down three or four more trees since hed been there and how the soil was softer just now and wed turned over another big bit of ground over by the edge of the clearing ready for planting in the spring. Ian just let me go on and on until I ran out of words to say and then he spoke, his voice so quiet I could hardly hear him.

There will come a day, Hugh, he said, when Im not there.

I wasnt sure what to say so I just started speaking again, talking about what it would be like once we could stay in the cabin but he lifted up his hand, a bit shaky like, and stopped me.

Therell come a day.

I laughed a little bit. I said, Dont be saying that.

That day comes to us all.

Aye, but theres no need to talk about it.

And when my day comes, Hugh, what money I have will belong to the three of you. And the three of you will do fine without me. Im just an old man, after all is said and done.

Youre not so old. I dont want to hear you talking this way.

I knew I was sounding sulky like a child, but I didnt know how to sound more grown up just then.

He moved his hand to show how thin and ill-looking he was, then said, Dont be afraid. Time passes for us all. But know that I *will* be gone. There is a time for all things, both living and dying. Should there be anything you wish to tell me, dont wait too long.

It went quiet for a minute and I was looking into his eyes and we just looked at each other but before I could say anything else the door opened and in came Mr Bale and Callum and Robert, laughing about something one of them had just been saying.

Im learning one thing which is that sometimes there are moments in your life that are more important than some of the other moments but that they can slip past before you get a chance to look at them closely enough, the way a leaf sweeps past you in a river and disappears. So this was one.

About two weeks later Ian was back with us doing some light work but the sickness took a lot out of him and I dont think hell ever be swinging an axe again the way he used to.

So now, as I say, its spring and the weather is warming up nicely and thats why weve discovered now the disadvantage to having a wee burn running through your land. It just took one warmer damp morning and this cloud of flies came swarming up out of the ground in great clouds. Ian said it was like something Israelites might have had to put up with. They land on your arms and face and neck and bite and before you know it youll be covered in these little red lumps that make you scratch and scratch to try to get some relief.

People in Goderich say that these beasts can carry diseases and in the store you can buy this white cream or paste that you smear over your skin and it keeps them off a bit. Or you can cover up every inch of skin, even wearing a hat with this narrow net material hanging down. But then you get too hot when youre working which isnt any good either because you sweat like a pig and the flies like you better that way. They crawl near your ears and you can hear their high buzzing all the time and it drives you mad. Callum smokes a pipe whenever hes working because he says that keeps them off. I tried it but it just made me cough all the time.

Sometimes you long for the salty clean spray of the firth but you have to keep moving forwards. People say this hatching of flies doesnt last too long and after a while theyre gone again. Its just something you have to put up with.

Ian says you cant have the Garden of Eden without the outside world surrounding it.

Callum says, with a scornful laugh, What Garden of Eden?

And then its back to chopping and hammering and digging.

I walked into Goderich today with Rachael. We both had to buy things for our places. Our cabins are near finished now and everything has sort of settled down. It was good to spend the couple of hours with her and heres what we talked about.

Rachael – How is Ian these days? Has he put any of the weight back on?

Me – Not really. He still seems weak and were giving him wee jobs to do just.

Rachael – Thats best. Look after him.

Me – Of course we do. Maybe you could come across to help us with things sometimes.

Rachael – Do you need me to do that?

Me – Not really.

Rachael – No need then.

Me – True enough I suppose.

We walked on a bit further and down into Goderich where we went to the General Store. We came out a while after carrying canvas bags laden down with supplies.

Me – Do you want to go and sit by the lake for a while?

Rachael – I dont mind.

So we did that. For a bit we just sat without saying anything really but after a while we began to talk about Robert and Elizabeth and how the two of them were getting friendlier.

Me – Roberts always liked Elizabeth.

Rachael – I know. Ive known that since back in Craigtore. It seems such a long time ago, when we were just children really. Robert always came after Elizabeth, just the two of them together. Hes always liked her.

This was something I hadnt known, that Robert came to see Elizabeth on his own. I wondered what Callum would have said if hed known about that. I was quite sure that Callum had been with Elizabeth too, or so the story went. Anyway the moment seemed right to say

Ive always liked *you.*

She laughed and stood up and said, Yes well Ive known that since back in Craigtore too. Listen, would you like to carry my bag and Ill carry yours. My one is heavier.

All right.

How long till you put the roof on Marys cabin? You must be close to that.

Two days maybe or three days.

Are you having us all over for a dram when its done?

I dont know. Maybe yes. I think so.

Good, she said.

So I was none the wiser, and not for the first time.

I looked back over my pages so far and I see that I havent described Goderich at all. Its a bigger town and very busy but Ill need to describe it so you can imagine it, whoever you are.

Theres a book store in Goderich, a store that just sells books and nothing else. Ian says there were some of these in Edinburgh. One of the books in the Goderich Book Store is a book about Goderich, called *Goderich*. Someone who has lived here has written a book about it. I could maybe buy it and copy out some of the description into my writing here though I wonder if that might be dishonest. Ill ask Ian and think about it for a bit.

A lots happened since the last time I wrote[28].

I wish I could be more regular with it but theres just so much to do and at night I fall into bed with the palms of my hands aching from the axe and the saw, and my head splitting from the heat and I just have no energy or desire to write anything down. Whats the point? Thats what Im thinking each night.

---

28 It is not immediately obvious, but this next section is written during the summer following the group's arrival in Goderich. Hugh, therefore is at least nineteen, and possibly twenty years old now: a good age for breaking free. – RM

So my pages are getting a layer of dust and Im losing track of the story Im writing down here.

But nothing much has happened to write about until now and now a lots happened, as I said. The cabins are done and yes we did have the Bales and the girls over for a dram and also one or two other people that weve been friendly with and we drank a toast to our new home and the land weve cleared so far and we all got very drunk but did Rachael come close to me that night? No she did not.

So there was nothing to write about because theres no interest in writing down about the way we got a little bit of corn out of our land or how weve got two pigs now that we were able to buy from the Bales or how weve made a little bit of money, not much, from selling some of the cut wood. Ians money has more or less gone and were hand to mouth.

And thats why Im writing this again just now because somethings happened.

Its been clear to us all that the land we have, even cleared and planted, cant really support me and Robert and Callum and Ian and Mary. We eat too much and it costs too much for what the land can offer. Its not like the Bales. They have a bigger bit of land and theyve got their animals so they can sell eggs and some bacon and things to keep it all going and their land is better ground than ours in the first place so their crops are good and they make money from that so theyre well enough off to support themselves and the two girls with no difficulty.

The thing is, we got here too late. The best land was gone. Our earth is thin and full of roots that well be clearing until the last trumpet, says Ian. So although we really didnt want to think about it weve been knowing for a while that we cant all stay together here. Ian suggested that one or two maybe of us could get some work down in Goderich. In a black mood one night Callum said to Mary that she could go back to her old work and he didnt mean having a bunk house so that caused a big argument and Ian said if we didnt stop that hed leave himself. Of course hes never been anywhere near finding a place as a minister because hes not been well enough and I know he feels bad, as if hes let us down, but he hasnt, we all understand. If he was to be trying to preach in a church three or four times a week and visiting all the congregation as well I think it would kill him.

I thought about whether it should be me who would make the change and go and work somewhere else. I even went into Goderich and asked about it but there was no need for more men at the General Store or in the stables or on the road building. In fact there are too many men in Goderich, just the same as there were too many men in Pictou. When you go into the town you see them in big groups sitting on the boardwalk or down by the water on the sand, talking and arguing. Theres not enough work for everyone. Down by Lake Huron you can see them gazing out over the water, shading their eyes against the sun.

So I did try but it came to nothing. Then two days ago heres what happened.

We were sitting outside the main cabin in the sun, just resting and looking across our cleared area, which is getting a bit bigger all the time. Mary was inside and we could smell the smell of the stew she was making, mainly vegetables.

Callum had a stick in his hand and he was drawing circles in the dirt at our feet. None of us were speaking, and my mind was on Rachael, wondering when she would be back over. Shes in my thoughts a lot, because we were separated by the huge ocean and now were separated by a wee bit of forest but sometimes it feels as if shes just as far away as ever she was.

Callum says, I have a job.

It takes a moment or two for us to realise what hes saying. Its Ian who speaks first. Ians shirt sleeves are rolled up on his thin arms and his face looks tired and scratched from the armfuls of branches hes been carrying, which is the easier work hes been saying he has to do or else he wouldnt feel all right about still staying with us and eating our food, which makes no sense because its him whos paid for all of this in the first place.

Ian says, A job?

Callum – Thats right. One of us has to do something.

I start to speak to say that Ive tried as well but before the words come out of my mouth I shut up because this is Callums moment and hell be angry if I try to take it from him. This shutting up is what Ive been doing all my life and Im good at it even if I dont want to be.

Roberts not so scared of him. He says, What do you mean *one of us has to do something?* Arent we all working hard? Its not just you thats making an effort here, is it?

Callum replies, Well thats right, were all keeping busy. Here and over at the Baless.

And he looks at Robert with a look that isnt very nice. This has to do with Elizabeth of course and Robert dies down into a grumbling quietness.

Mary comes out. Whats wrong? she asks, realising that there is bad feeling out here in the June evening.

Callum says, Nothing at all. Im just telling them I have a job.

Mary asks, What job?

Callum – On a boat.

Mary – A boat?

Callum – On Lake Huron.

Ian – A ferry boat?

Callum – Thats right.

Ian – How did you get that job? You dont know anything about boats.

Callum – Ive been on two, havent I, since we left Croval?

Robert – That doesnt make you a sailor though.

Callum – Ill learn as Im going along. Isnt that what were doing here?

213

Robert – So is that it? Youre sailing back and forth across Lake Huron and coming back here to sleep.

Callum – No, I dont think so.

Robert – What then?

Callum – Ill sleep on the boat. Eat on the boat. The man said Id just be on the boat more or less all the time.

Robert – And what about us here?

Callum – What about you here? Youll be better off with one less mouth to feed.

Robert – One less pair of hands to work the land.

Callum – What land? Look at it, in the name of God!

We all did as he said, turned and looked at our plot of land and a sorry looking place it was too really, with the burn more or less dried up in the summer heat and early corn wed planted wilting over and the two pigs just lying there, lazy and thin. And all round us the trees still looming up waiting to tear our skin and threaten our heads when we attacked them.

Ian, quietly – But its *our* land.

Callum – Whats so good about that? Well be working on it ever more and itll never be good enough to satisfy us. Weve come all this way and what are we doing? Working all day so that were too tired to speak at night and then we sleep and then we get up and start all over again. Wheres the good in it?

There was an uncomfortable silence between us, nobody wanting to say anything.

Robert says, shaking his head, I dont feel that way. Theres more here than what you say.

Callum – Maybe there is for you, but what about the rest of us? We cant all have what youve got.

Im thinking I would like to have what Roberts got, or something very like it, but there doesnt seem much chance of that and suddenly the idea of going away with Callum seems not such a bad idea.

I say, Is there more work on the boats?

214

Callum – No, it just happened I was there when a man gave it up. I heard him arguing on the boat with the captain when it was docking then he went off and I jumped on and told the captain I was a sailor, he could have me instead and he took me on.

Ian – This other man just stopped, just like that? Just threw it all up and walked off?

Callum – Thats the way it is. Didnt you do that back in Croval?

Ian – I suppose I did.

Robert – The money will help, I cant argue with that, but weve always done it all together, havent we?

Callum – What money?

Silence.

Callum – What I mean is, what Im trying to say to you is that Im going away to work on this boat. Ill see you and Ill come up here when I have the chance but Im going to be living on the boat and Ill have my own food to buy and clothes to buy and so on.

Mary says, her hand at her mouth – Youre going away, you mean?

Callum, a bit embarrassed – Just to work on this boat. Its just back and forth across the Lake taking people further west. Ill still be around Goderich. But not here. Thats all.

Me – Were breaking up, then.

Callum – Thats the way of it. Think about it sensibly. We always knew this would happen one day or another.

Me – I didnt.

Callums standing up now and his hand is running through his sandy hair again and again, as if there are insects in it or something and hes trying to clear them out.

Ian – So this is the end of it all.

Callum – If thats the way you look at it, then yes. I suppose it is.

215

Me – Weve always done everything together.

Callum, looking down at his feet – Well.

Me – Everything.

When I said that I wasnt just thinking about working on the land here, or searching for somewhere in Pictou, or travelling across the ocean in The Lady Gray. I was also meaning climbing the stone steps above Croval, and rowing round the headland to Craigtore, and playing in the rock pools when we were wee boys looking for the crabs that live in someone elses shell, and especially that day when we stood together watching a stone fall towards an old woman. So all that was going away. I could feel this feeling in the back of my throat as if I wanted to cry but I wasnt going to let the others see that, though Mary did have some tears on her cheeks and shes known Callum least long. She turned and went away into the cabin to see to the food.

Ian got up, a wee bit shaky on his legs after a long day of work, and wandered off to the edge of the clearing, where the body of the big pine wed taken down that day was lying. So that left the three of us, the three boys that grew up together and came across the world.

Robert asked him, So when is it that you go?

Callum answered, Tomorrow. Ive to be there tomorrow morning.

Why did you not tell us before? I asked.

Callum said, Because I knew what youd say. I always know what youre going to say.

And that was our last night together, maybe the quietest meal weve ever eaten. Ian said a grace that made Mary cry again and we ate her food as if it were sand and stones. We couldnt swallow.

Outside, the evening sun beat down on our cabin because the trees have gone far enough back now that were not in the shade all the time any more, but Callum had put a huge shadow over us that we couldnt get away from.

So that was two days ago and then yesterday we were down to three because Mary left us too. We all heard her getting up and we heard her and Callum speaking in the other room as they ate an early breakfast. We knew that Callum would be leaving after hed had something to eat and hed said the night before that he wanted to eat his last breakfast in the cabin by himself, just to think, he said. So we didnt get up although we were all wide awake. None of us spoke, just lay there in our beds, looking at each other and not saying a thing. I was surprised to hear Marys voice but I thought she must have decided the last thing shed do for Callum as part of our group was to make this last, important meal for him.

We heard them talking, as I said, and then we heard the door of the cabin bang shut and after a few minutes Ian said, Well we should get up and say goodbye and get on with our work I suppose.

So we did get up but we didnt get to say goodbye because Callum had gone and so had Mary. We went looking for her in her cabin but she was away and shed taken everything with her except a note saying this

I am moving on. Callum has got me a ticket on his boat and I am going on west. Thank you for letting me stay for a while. You have been kind, and that I will remember.

Your friend Mary

So its just me and Robert and Ian now.

When I started writing this all down back in Croval I think I thought it might be mainly about me and Callum, though Ive always hoped it would be about me and Rachael and then in Pictou I wondered for a while if it might be going to be about me and Mary McIntosh, though that was a very foolish idea and it quickly went away.

Now I dont know, I just dont.

Mary leaving like that has reminded me of a story that my

mother would tell me when I was just a wee boy, though why this has come into my mind Im not right sure.

Once upon a time there was a young girl who lived in a croft away up at the top of a ben. She lived in the house with her wee brother who was just seven years old. Their parents had died when the boy was only a baby and the girl was the age the boy was now, seven. People came from other crofts further down the ben to offer to take the two of them in but the girl had magical powers and she turned them all away by making a circle of fire spring up around the croft whenever anyone came near. Although she was only seven she said she could look after herself and her wee brother. The people living further down the ben said shed die and so would the baby, it was bound to happen, and the minister, well he said that her magic tricks were the work of the devil.

But time went by, the way it does, and they didnt die in the croft up at the top of the ben after all. No one knew where they got the food from, but food they had even though they kept no animals and they grew no oats, and no one knew where they got water from, but water they had even though no burn ran near their house and no rain ever fell on their land.

Never once in the seven years that passed did they come down the ben and never once in the seven years did anyone go up the ben to see how they were living. The minister told the folk in the church that it was their duty to stay away from that place because the smell of brimstone was upon it, so nobody did. But they saw the boy and his sister out playing in the grass around their croft and sometimes, if the wind was in the right direction, the sound of their laughter could be heard, far away but clear.

Then one day the minister himself took an idea into his head that maybe he should go up and see if he could rescue the wee boy, who would be seven now. The girl was past help of course, the devil had her soul well and truly in his scaly hand.

218

So the minister set off up the hill with his Bible in one hand and a cross of silver in the other and all the folk from the other crofts huddled together to watch him go. Just as he was getting up near the top a haar came down and lay over the ben like a shroud and the people down below shivered and crossed themselves and went away back into their crofts.

Up in that evil mist the minister felt a damp lonely cold go through him and he gripped the Bible tighter and he held the cross up in front of him to ward off the devil girl. He said to himself, Ill take seven more steps and if she hasnt blasted me with the devils fire Ill take seven more and seven more and so on until either Im at the croft or else Im burned and dead.

So on he went, and he took seven steps and when he had done that he thought he could hear a noise, a dull banging that came from up ahead. But he was still alive and so he took seven more steps through the thick mist and then he could still hear the banging noise and now he thought there was another noise as well, which was a creaking noise. But he was still alive so he took seven more steps through the thick mist and then he could still hear the banging noise and the creaking noise and now he thought he could smell something as well, which was the smell of baking.

But he was still alive so he took seven more steps through the thick mist and suddenly there he was at the door to the croft and the banging noise was the noise of the door hanging loose on its hinges and banging against the wooden door frame and the mist was all through the house, it looked like.

But he was still alive so he took seven more steps through the thick mist and suddenly there he was inside the croft and the creaking noise was the noise of an old oak rocking chair rocking back and forth with nobody on it and the mist was swirling round it so it was just a dim shape.

But he was still alive so he took seven more steps through the thick mist and suddenly he was standing right beside the fire and the smell was the smell of a loaf of bread left on a girdle above the dying embers of an old fire so he reached out to touch the bread and all of a sudden there was a gust of wind and the mist all swept away, out of the windows and out of the door and away up into the sky and the sun came out and shone down on the croft.

Of the girl and her brother there was never a sign and the people said it was the good book and the silver cross and the ministers faith that chased them away, evil spirits that they were, and so hurried were they in their flight that they never had time even to eat their last loaf of bread.

And thats how it was with us because Mary McIntosh left food on the table for us but she was gone out of our lives just like that.

I dont mean she was a bad person, but its just that it reminded me of that story.

I wrote all that two days after Callum told us he was going and now it is weeks later and its not really as if there are just three of us left. Now it feels as if there are two of us left, me and Ian.

A few days after Callum and Mary went away Robert asked Elizabeth if she wanted to come and stay in what was Marys cabin and help us with cooking and cleaning and things like that. Mr and Mrs Bale wanted her to stay with them but they were maybe thinking that they didnt really need Elizabeth *and* Rachael so they didnt argue very much about it. So thats what happened and every evening Robert spends more time with Elizabeth than he does with us and I hardly go across to see Rachael because if I did Id be more or less leaving Ian by himself and I dont want to do that because even yet hes not himself again after that bout of illness last winter.

Weve seen Callum two or three times since he left, down in Goderich at the harbour and once in the saloon. Hes never yet come back up to the cabins, though, the way he said he would.

As for Mary, well shes gone for good. Callum says she got on the ferry at Goderich and got off at the other side of Lake Huron, holding her bag with the leather handles that had all her things in it and he told us she didnt even turn round to wave goodbye, she just turned her head down and kept walking.

Ive taken a look back through all my pages and Ive not written a whole lot about Mary at any time and maybe whoever reads this will be wondering what she was like really. She was a good friend, as it turns out, but, also as it turns out, her story and my story separate off here.

I was talking with Rachael outside Elizabeths cabin today. She came over to see us because it was Ians birthday. He wouldnt tell us how old he was and just said he was *older than he should be*, which was a funny thing to say. It was a sad birthday without Callum there, and Mary too, but we tried to make it as good as we could. Ian had told us that we mustnt get him any presents because there isnt enough money for that so we didnt and the birthday was just an ordinary day because today we had two trees wed taken down to strip so we were all hard at work. Mr and Mrs Bale were going to come across too this evening but young Richard isnt feeling well so they stayed behind and just Rachael came.

We ate our meal and had some whiskies and we all had a drink to Ian and I drank to his health and tried not to notice his hand shaking when he lifted the glass and I tried not to think about him being another year older and I tried not to think about what would happen to us if he wasnt here.

Quite early he said he wanted to lie down because he was feeling tired and that left the four of us feeling a bit awkward and a bit sad, so Rachael and me went outside leaving Robert and Elizabeth together while they tidied up the plates and cups.

We sat on the grass in the warmth. There was still light in the sky and we could see crows flying above our clearing and hear them speaking to each other in the trees. We just sat for a while saying nothing.

Then Rachael asked me if I missed Callum.

I said that of course I did.

She asked me if I was ever tempted to do what hed done and make off on my own.

I said no, because it wouldnt be fair on Robert or Ian. What I didnt say was that it would mean I wouldnt be seeing her any more. I wanted to say that but I found that I couldnt.

Why is it that theres such a difference between what you really want to say and what you really do say?

Rachael said, Robert and Elizabeth are getting closer now.

I know, I said.

Rachael said, I always thought Elizabeth would end up marrying someone new, someone she met over here.

Do you think theyre going to get married? I asked.

Why not?

I dont know. It just seems funny to think of Robert getting married to someone. When we were on The Lady Gray he sounded as if he should have an army behind him.

What do you mean?

I dont know. But its funny, isnt it? Coming all this way and marrying a girl from Craigtore.

Rachael shook her head. I dont think its funny at all.

She looked me and I wondered if that meant something important but I didnt ask her just in case it didnt.

After a wee while she looked away and said, So what are your plans then?

Plans?

Are you three going to sell this place now that its cleared.

I looked across our land in the twilight. I said, Its not really finished yet here. Theres more to do.

Are you not going to sell?

Why would we?

Itll never be good, this place. Youll never make much of a living here. It might be all right for two people to live off but theres four of you and if Robert and Elizabeth marry well maybe therell be more mouths to feed.

Maybe so.

So what then, thats what I mean?

I dont know, I said. What about you? Are you happy there with Mr and Mrs Bale?

She stretched out and leaned over so that she was leaning against my shoulder where we were sitting under the dark blue sky. She said, Im not sure. I liked it better when Elizabeth was there. But its a long way to come just to be cleaning and cooking and helping to look after wee Richard and hes getting bigger now too so they wont need me really, in a while.

I felt that empty feeling in my stomach and made myself ask her, So are you thinking of going away?

Maybe.

I couldnt think of anything to say to that. Her head was on my shoulder and I could smell the clean smell of her red hair, although it was getting too dark to see the proper red colour of it. I wanted to put my arm round her but I thought I shouldnt in case she didnt want me to.

She laughed and said, You have a comfortable shoulder.

Where would you go if you went away?

West, I suppose. Thats where everyone goes. There are bigger places that way.

I suppose so. But when do we stop?

Stop what?

Moving on?

She spoke quietly. When we get what were looking for.

What are we looking for?

I dont know. Or maybe its when we just get too tired to go any further.

I knew she was thinking of Ian and I didnt like to be thinking about that so I said nothing. I could feel the warmth of her body as she leaned against me and I could feel her breathing.

After a minute she said, Callumll hate it if Robert and Elizabeth marry.

Do you think *hed* like to marry her?

Not really, but he wont want Robert doing it. Thats what Callums like isnt it? Thats what Elizabeth says hes like.

I never replied because he is my friend, even though hes off now, and I didnt want to speak against him, but what she said made me think for a second about being Callum and how angry he is all the time, how much he feels hurt by everyone round about, and the responsibility he must be carrying everywhere with him. If I felt like him Id go off on another boat too.

So we didnt speak much after that but just sat there together as the sky got darker and the crows settled down in the trees and the only sound was the quiet whisper of voices from inside the cabin, and the sound of my own blood pumping away with Rachaels real body pressed close up against me, so close that I was scared to move in case it made her get up and go away.

The thing about the books that Ian used to read to us is that they all flowed smoothly from one bit to another with no gaps in them where the writer forgot to put something down about somebody or somewhere or something that happened. They were like a river, like the Middle River at Pictou, flowing on and on, all continuous. But what Im writing is more like the wee lochans in the land up above Croval, where you have to look right closely to see the burns and trickles of muddy water that connect them.

Its been months since I wrote and I dont know why its been so long. I just didnt want to. Some nights Id pick up my bits of paper and Id start to think about what to write down but after a while I wouldnt be able to get it clear in my thoughts what I should start with so I would just bundle the sheets together again into the wooden box under my bed.

Another winter has passed[29] and at last I am writing again because there is something I definitely want to put down here, though why Im doing this I still dont know.

Its been so long since Ian read to us all from his books. Its something that belongs in the past, I think.

There are some important things that I should write down here but I havent got time to put in details about all of them. Im just going to write a list of the things, the way Ian writes out a list for me when its my turn to go down into Goderich to get things. My writing is so much stronger and clearer than Ians now. Heres my list then.

– Mary has never come back.

– We havent seen Callum for three months. One day his boat came back across the Lake and we were told hed *jumped ship* which means he never got back on it again when it was due to come back here, just like the man he replaced on the boat in the first place. So Callums gone.

– Ian never got the fever this winter and actually I think hes a bit stronger now than hes been for a year, but still hes aged terribly since we came to Goderich. And of course theres his arm which Ill write about in a minute.

– Ian still has not found a church to preach in and hes stopped trying. Once or twice he went down to Goderich and tried to preach a sermon just standing on a street corner but nobody much stopped, maybe just a couple of children and an old drunk. So he hasnt done that again. He still reads to us from the Bible and he still has plenty of advice for us all.

– Weve cleared all our land as far as it extends into the forest. Now we have to decide if we want to buy a bit more and clear further but to do that wed need some more money and the land

---

29 And Hugh may be twenty-one now. – RM

that we have is scarcely going to get us enough money to buy more land. Wed need more land to make the money to let us afford to buy more land to earn us more money. It reminds me of sometimes when wed be out in the boat and wed have run out of bait and wed have to catch a fish to make bait to catch a fish.

– The pigs have had piglets and we sold them and with the money we bought some chickens and a hand plough and thats helped us with turning the soil. We are beginning to feel like farmers and not so much like lumbermen, but whatever we are we are a long way from the fishers of Croval. Its almost as if we have gone back to the work in Strathgarrick, the work our great-grandfathers did. Not Ians great-grandfather, of course.

– The cabins are good and keep out the rain and the snow. When I think back to our first winter I think how much better off we are now, thanks to our work. But I also think back to that stormy night with Rachael pressed up close to me in the windy tent. We have made good furniture with the help of a man from Goderich called William Morrison who knows about these things. Our chairs and table are as good as anyones and all made with our own wood, and with our own hands.

– Donald Sutherland has come back into our lives. He is working in the saloon in Goderich, sweeping the floor and cleaning out the spit-buckets and other such work. He has lost a lot of hair in the last year but still his eyes are dark and untrustworthy. We have agreed to keep clear of him. He has been asking after Callum and nobody can tell him anything about that.

– Robert and Elizabeth are to get married on the first day of May, which is tomorrow, and this is why I have returned to these pages of paper.

So, the marriage is to be tomorrow. Ian will marry them and it will happen on the grass in front of our main cabin. The grass is smooth and fine there now and it is a good place to be married.

Some marriages happen in church but here a lot of them dont and Ians the minister so he asked Robert what he wanted and he said he wanted his new life to begin on his own new ground.

There is one thing that has spoilt the good feeling we all have about the wedding and that is Ian has broken his left arm. He doesnt do much of the heavy work any more because hes not really strong enough for it. But three days ago he took an axe out in the morning to clear some bushes just at the edge of our land, a place where are going to make a fence to mark our property. Before he even got there he stumbled on something, a stone in the ground or an uneven bit, and he fell with the axe under him and he broke his left arm. I took him into Goderich and the doctor set it for him. It took an awful long time to get him to Goderich because he was in such pain that he couldnt walk very fast. It was me that went down with him because there were other things for Robert and Elizabeth to be thinking about so close to their marriage.

I said to Ian, Well be down there soon. The next thing we have to buy is a horse and a cart.

Ian never replied because he was concentrating hard to keep the pain in the back of his mind just.

I said, trying to cheer him up, Well be like the tinker MacPhee trundling up and down the road.

Still no answer.

I said, maybe we can start selling stuff from the back of the cart. We just need to get a cow and make a bit of cheese and maybe some eggs. Robert could set up a still and wed make whisky. Well be rich.

At last Ian spoke, and it was hard for him to speak because he was biting his lip hard against the pain, so hard there was blood. He said, Hugh, Itll be a while before we can afford to buy a horse, you know that.

I know that, I said. I was just saying.

He was leaning against me as we stumbled slowly down to

227

the town. He said, You need to think about what you will do afterwards.

After what?

After Im gone.

I didnt want to say anything to that, so I didnt say anything.

He carried on, You realise when Im gone itll be you and Robert and Elizabeth, and theyll be married.

Of course Id thought about that but I didnt say anything.

Hugh, he says, and theres pauses between his words as each step hurts his arm, You must stop being at the edge of things. You must put yourself more at the centre.

Of my own story? I ask, because this thought has occurred to me before as well, and I know fine well that hes right.

Exactly, except that you dont live in a story. Im an old man and maybe my advice is old too. But its possible that you need to seek elsewhere. *I lifted my hand up to them in the wilderness, that I would not bring them into the land which I had given them, flowing with milk and honey, which is the glory of all lands.*

Bible words again and Ian showed me them in the Book later[30] and I copied them out. I ask, What do you mean?

I mean what if this is not your promised land? It might be for Robert and Elizabeth but it wasnt for Callum, was it, or Mary? I dont know if either of them will ever come into their promised land. It might not be yours.

I think for a while as we carry on down, his breathing hard and painful beside me. At last I say, Im not going away, if thats what you mean. This is my place now.

Ian – What makes it your place?

Me – Ive worked on it.

Ian – You could work on any piece of land. It neednt be this one.

---

30 Ezekial Chapter 20 Verse 15. – RM

228

Me – My friends are here.

Ian – Callums gone. Marys gone, if she was ever truly our friend, though I wont speak ill of her. And Robert is turning away from us. I dont mean he does anything bad in marrying. The opposite is true. His marriage turns him more towards God, but the truth is it turns him away from you a little. I do not want loneliness to be your estate, Hugh.

Me – You are here. Wherever you are, that is where I will be.

He stopped walking, so I stopped as well and we stood there on the dusty road, then I took him in my arms for the first time in my life and held him but he gave a yelp of pain and pulled away so we laughed together but the tears were not very far behind my eyes and I think maybe it was the same for him.

Then we carried on down into Goderich and the doctor set his arm for him with splints and then we came back to the cabins to help the others to get ready for the wedding, which is to be tomorrow.

What a day this has been. I am glad now that I have begun my journal again. This day I will always remember. I think there are days that will remain in your head forever even if you live to be a hundred and twenty like James Murdoch in Craigtore, though people say he lies about his age and hes only ninety odd, and he could be dead by now anyway, probably is. But so much happened today that my heart is still pounding with the strangeness of it and the excitement. It is all so important that I must choose my words very carefully today of all days.[31]

---

31 This would imply that Hugh does not, as a rule, consider his words carefully. This, however, seems disingenuous, since, as I mentioned earlier, there are signs of extensive reworking of the writing. It may be the case, I suppose, that all the reworking postdates this comment, and what we read later does suggest that as a possibility. We will never know. The handwriting in this following section *does* look rather laborious, as if Hugh *has* taken his time in a way he has not before. – RM

Really, the wedding was yesterday, though, because it is well after midnight as I write this. My hands are still shaking.

The sun shone down upon the marriage. Spring birds sang in the trees under a blue spring sky and the smell of spring flowers drifted across the grass in front of the cabin. The people came for the marriage, which was in the afternoon and not in the morning at all. Mr and Mrs Bale came, with their son Richard, getting taller now, and stronger looking, with the shape of his adult body beginning to show in his childs body. It was fine to see them in their good church clothes and with smiles on their faces, the lines of hard work wiped out just for today. Of course Ian was there and he was dressed for the first time in a long time in his good ministers shirt and his good ministers black trousers and jacket and a good pair of shoes that we bought in Goderich because his old shoes are long gone and usually now he wears work boots just. There were maybe thirty or forty other people there from nearby land and some from Goderich but it would take much too long to name them or to describe them so you can just imagine them as forty people that are all on the edge of being our friends, smiling, men and women and children all come with small gifts on this sunny spring day to celebrate the marriage of Robert and Elizabeth, but really them being there just was the gift.

And Rachael is there, of course, excited that her friend is to be married and flushed with the idea of it and I know shes imagining them together as I am and I wonder what else she imagines and hope she cant imagine what I imagine, because then it would be me blushing. Rachael hurries around, pouring a drink for someone here, picking up a child who has fallen over there, holding her red hair from her face as she laughs with Mrs Bale about the cake that shes made to commemorate this day, as Ian said. Im gazing at her all the time, and I cant help it. She sits with a whisky in her hand and watches it all happening, her eyes everywhere. This is Rachael and it always has been.

There is nothing she doesnt see. When she catches my eye she smiles and laughs and points at something for me to look at. One of the young children chasing our surprised chickens, the man from the Goderich bakehouse taking a sip from a hipflask, his wife pretending not to notice, with an expression of saved up anger on her face.

The bit round the cabins is full of people. Weve never had so many people round our land before and it makes me proud when some of the men wander through our property, running their hands over the sturdy walls of our cabins, leaning their weight against the deep-set fence posts and nodding with approval because they cant tilt them and that means weve done a good job. Im proud of our place.

When the marriage itself happens people stand back in a half circle and Ian stands in front of the two of them. Robert is in a dark suit of clothes which we hired for the day from a place in town where you can pay to get a shot of clothes for a wedding or a funeral, and its to go back tomorrow, once its had a clean. His face is serious and his dark hair is combed as neatly as he can do it. He looks nervous with so many people watching him and I remember the way he stood alone on the deck of The Lady Gray and faced up to the captain. It seems to me he looks less confident now with all the eyes upon him, but more content. In a way Callum forced him to speak out when we were on the boat and it went against his quietness. I can imagine him happier now, changing Callum for Elizabeth, a single life for a life of two.

Elizabeth herself is in a plain blue dress that Mrs Bale and Rachael have made, with white stuff round the neck and at the ends of the sleeves. Her hair is down and beautiful with the sun catching it, and her eyes flash with the pleasure of the day and her importance in it. She cries a little, just for a few seconds, as she stands there with Robert, then shes smiling again, the way a cloud can pass over the sun and be gone.

They hold each other by the hand and Ian does the ceremony, with those words that seem too special to be written down and anyway I think everyone probably knows them.[32] There was silence while the words were spoken with just the breeze in the branches and the birds and in the distance I could hear a dog barking. Robert spoke up loud and clear and Elizabeth cried again when it was her turn to speak, the tears and her smile all mixed up together. Then Ian took their hands and laid them on the Bible and they put rings on each others hands as a reminder of their promises to each other. These rings were a gift from all the guests who had put a little bit of money towards two thin gold bands that were bought from a store. I looked across at Rachael to see what she was thinking but she never looked at me. Her eyes were fixed on Robert and Elizabeth and her arms were folded across her thin body. Her face had a serious look on it and you couldnt tell what was in her mind.

Then there was a meal and everyone had taken along something to eat and it was laid out on our table, which we had carried out into the sun. Mr Bale and Richard had walked all the way from their place with their table too, so we had two tables side by side and the food on it weighed them both down. People took plates with them, thats the way it happens here, and they loaded them with chicken and pork and potatoes and vegetables and everyone had a whisky or there was ale too that someone took in a keg and everyone drank a toast to the couple. They were sitting in chairs just in front of the main cabin and there were some others sitting but we didnt have enough chairs for everyone so a lot of people were sitting on the grass and its just as well it wasnt raining because I dont know what we

32 Were they the familiar words we know today? Hugh's sentence here casts light on both the connections and the disconnections between his time and ours. But these disconnections have to take a hundred and fifty years to take hold. I think back to my own wedding vows and find a void. But it's no one's fault. – RM

would have done then.

Ian said grace before the eating started and then he made a short speech like this –

This is the beginning of a new life for these two young people. It has been an honour for me to be a part of their marriage and to have shared their lives these past few years. I have known Robert and Elizabeth since they were just a boy and a girl and I am glad to see them now as man and woman joined together to make something more than just man and woman. They are married in the sight of God and in His eyes the glory of our world has been increased today. Every one of us here shares in that glory and our presence is like a vow that the future of these two here before us has a shape that pleases the Lord. I ask you to drink a toast to the couple. Robert and Elizabeth.

Here everyone drank a sip of their drink and murmured, Robert and Elizabeth. Ian finished his speech –

I have reason to be grateful to these two young people for the kindness they have shown me and the kindness they continue to show. May God show them the same kindness in their future life and may He bless them with the gift of children. Our Lord watches all and shapes our lives. May He shape this new partnership into one of happiness and prosperity.

The whisky was raised again to the lips and then after the food the music started, a man with an accordion and the man from the tables[33] with his fiddle and they played good old Scottish tunes and everyone danced on the flat green grass and there were reels and strip the willows and other dances and as the drink was flowing there were people falling over and banging into each other but nobody cared because it was a happy day. I danced

---

33 I cannot for the life of me work out what this means. It is some reference that is lost in the Goderich mists. Either that or it is some kind of slip from Hugh. We can't know. – RM

with Rachael and Robert danced with Elizabeth, then I danced with Elizabeth and Robert with Rachael and Ian danced with both girls then he sat at the side on a chair with a big whisky in his hand and beamed at everyone. Everyone was dancing with everyone else and Rachael was dancing with young Richard Bale and laughing with him as they whirled round.

The sky was going dark soon enough and there were people lying flat out, dead drunk and others sitting in wee groups talking and arguing in a friendly way about the sort of things people argue about, the weather and crops and the way the stores in town serve the customers. There were insects buzzing in the air, but not the biting ones because its been dry, and moths were bumping against the lanterns we set up on sticks. Some of the younger children were sleeping on the grass by the log walls of our cabin and it was still warm enough for men to have their jackets off as they sprawled on the grass, tired out by dancing. The accordion player stopped and for a while it was just the fiddler playing slow beautiful tunes then he stopped too and it was only the sound of voices.

I found myself sitting over by the fence with Rachael.

She said, What a day!

I said, Its not finished.

She said, I know, but it will be soon and that makes me sad. She looks so happy, doesnt she?

And Robert, I say.

Its a shame Callum isnt here, she said and she shook her head. She said, I still dont understand what it is about Callum.

What do you mean?

Well, he could probably have had Elizabeth for a wife if hed wanted.

Dont ever say that to Robert.

Rachael – Of course not. I wouldnt be so stupid. But I know he liked her and she liked him. She told me.

Me – When?

Rachael – Oh, years ago. But things change. I think she wanted more than Callum. She wanted to be married.

I had a bottle of whisky in my hand and I filled up her cup. She tried to put her hand above the cup so that I couldnt put the whisky in but it was a gesture, nothing more. She sipped her drink.

I asked her, So would you ever think of getting married?

Rachael replied, I would think about it. Of course. If the right person came along. And asked me.

I didnt know if she meant me or if she meant she was waiting for someone *else* to come along. I wanted to ask her, *Do you mean me* but I couldnt do it. So I said nothing for a while and she got up on her feet, not very steady, bent down and kissed me on the forehead and wandered off to speak to a couple of the young girls from Goderich. Before I could think to go after her I was joined by Ian, who sat down beside me stiffly.

I think Ive had a bit too much to drink, he said.

I think I have too. All of us have. Its not a bad thing, I said, my eyes on Rachaels back as she moved through the crowd.

No, said Ian. Not at all. Itll just be you and me in the cabin now.

I said, We should let them have the big cabin. We can have the wee one.

Yes, youre right. That would be sensible.

How is your arm feeling?

Ian smiled and said, You know, Hugh, this medicine works tremendously.

And he took another big swig of his whisky and closed his eyes, tipping his head back in the dusky air. He said, I dont think weve finished travelling, do you, Hugh?

I said, I dont know. Why not?

Will we still be feeling at home here? he asked.

Why not?

Itll be Roberts place. Robert and Elizabeth. Maybe theyll

need it for themselves when they get their family started.

I didnt really want to answer that, but I had a picture in my head of myself and Ian wandering away down a long road. The thought of starting this searching again scared me but I would be telling a lie to say there wasnt a little bit of excitement in the thought too. I didnt speak.

And so the night went on and some of the people began to drift away, the ones with the youngest children. Some of those children had fallen sound asleep so that they had to be carried away by their parents. Robert and Mr Bale set light to a bonfire wed built in the space that was furthest away from the trees round our land and the bright flames chased away the cooler air that was settling down around us. Bit by bit the numbers dwindled away until there were maybe fifteen of us left, all sitting cross legged or half lying around the bonfire. The drinking had slowed down and no one was speaking much. The air was full of the sweet smelling smoke. Rachael was across the other side of the fire and I could see her shape and her face shifting and wavering through the heat of the flames. She was next to Elizabeth and they were leaning into each other and laughing quietly together, seriously.

Someone began to sing softly and before too long we were all singing psalms and then after that other songs, sad songs about home and about travelling away from home. I stopped singing and just listened, my eyes fixed on the fire. I was thinking about my mother and I wondered what she was doing now. I have written her some letters since I came away from home but never has she written back, which made me worry at first. But nobody has written a letter to me to tell me that she is dead or too ill to write, so I think she is probably still annoyed at me for going.

And when I thought about it, sitting at this fire on the other side of the world, I felt that maybe Id done the wrong thing, leaving her there by herself. What if she *is* sick and needs help. Ive left her the way my father and brothers did. I know folk in Croval would take care of her, though. And that made me think about me, here. What would happen if I was sick? Who would look after *me*?

Sometimes I dont feel that I have travelled at all. Instead it feels as if I raised myself up from the ground for a moment and the earth turned under me so that when I landed again, here I am in America. I mean Im just the same but the world is different. All these thoughts were going through my mind and I stopped drinking, because drinking stops you from seeing things clearly and I wanted to be able to remember this night, because it seemed an important one to me at that moment and I was right. I was looking round all the people and wondering if they were really my friends or did they just come for a dram and to have good fun?

My eyes kept going back to Rachael, my connection to the life gone by. If she would be the connection to my life to come, I was thinking, everything would be clearer. When I looked across at her on the other side of the fire I could see she was her usual self, sitting back and watching, and I wondered what was happening inside her head, but you can never know that.

It was near dark and the singing had died down and a few more folk had gone and it was clear enough that some of those that stayed would end up sleeping at ours because they probably werent able to walk home in the state they were in with the drink. I could hear an owl calling somewhere far off in the trees and then from another direction another owl answered. Then the only noise was the sound of the fire as the dying flames ate up the wood and some branches collapsed in a wee shower of sparks that rose up the column of heat into the night.

Then I heard the sound of people coming up the path from the direction of Goderich. At first I didnt think anything of it because I thought it would be someone coming back to get something theyd left behind by mistake, a hip flask or a hat or a child or something.

But then into the clearing and the failing light of the lanterns and the fire came two figures and I knew right away who it was. One was little and dark, with quick eyes that took in everything that was happening, and the other was Callum. It looked to me as if Callum was drunk but Donald Sutherland wasnt. He had his hand on Callums back and right away it made me feel that he had steered Callum up here all the way from Goderich. For a moment I even felt kindly towards him for bringing Callum back to us like this, but then Callum spoke.

Where is he? he said, loudly, and his voice had a harshness that was never there before. I suppose it is a hardness learned from the hard men he works with, first the sailors and now wherever it is he works. He shouted again, Where is he?

Ian stood up, a little unsteady, because hes had a good dram tonight as well, and said, Callum, welcome. Who are you looking for?

Who do you think? he answered, the nasty tone in his voice as clear as day on this dark night. Wheres Robert? I hear this is his wedding.

Ian – It is, Callum. I hope you do not intend to –

Callum, interrupting, hissing – Where is he?

He hadnt seen Robert because Robert was away to the side and almost out of the light but when Robert stood up, Callum turned to face him. Callum was near to the fire so he was lit by its warm red light, and Robert was in the darkness. A funny thought came to me at that moment which was that if this was one of Ians books it would be the other way round. Robert would be lit by the fire and Callum would be in the half darkness.

There wasnt a murmur from anyone else.

Robert – Welcome back, Callum. Have you come to stay?

Callum – Why would I stay here?

I think I saw Donald Sutherland give him a little push and he stepped forward towards Robert. Robert took a step towards

238

him and held out his hand to shake. Callum looked so much bigger than him, not just taller but broader as well as if the work hes been doing has grown his muscles and frame. But Roberts been working too, working right hard on our land.

Callum held out his own hand too and as they stepped towards each other it really looked to me as if they were going to shake hands, but at the last moment, Callum took his hand back and then swung it and slapped Robert hard on the side of his face. Robert staggered across to his right and lifted his fingers to his cheek, his eyes wide. Everyone was getting to their feet when Callum swung his arm again. This time it was a punch that caught Robert right on his nose and sent him over on to his back with the blood pouring out.

Donald Sutherlands laughing and pointing at Robert down on the ground like that and then Callums standing over Robert and he gives him a kick, right in the side, not a hard kick but hard enough and Robert kind of crumples himself up into a ball so that Callum cant hurt him again but when Callum sees that happen he just stands there looking down at him and in that moment Im thinking thats the most hurtful thing he does, or that hes ever done, standing there looking down on Robert as if hes dirt or a tree hes cut or the remains of a ruined boat pulled up on the stones of the shore at Croval, just nothing. Im reminded of what happened to the young boy pulled out from the emigrants by Neptune and his wife.

It only lasts for a second, that moment, then its over and everyones moving. Ians hurrying over towards Callum and Elizabeth is running from the other side of the fire to where Roberts lying, but her eyes are full of fury and are on Callum. Everyone else is just moving about, not sure what to do, most of them drunk and barging into each other, the air filled not with music any more or the quiet murmur of conversations watered with gentle whiskies but with a crying out and shouting and also tears of women upset by whats happened.

Donald Sutherland has Callum by the arm and hes pulling him away and some people are pushing at them but Callum is swinging his fist again and no one wants to get in the way of that. As I see them head towards me Im thinking Im right, that Donald Sutherlands not drunk at all but Callum really is. For a second they are there in front of me and my eyes go into Callums and his go into mine and I cant see anything in there. I cant see if hes angry or sad or what he is, and it strikes me that I never have been able to, not even when Mary Vass fell to the ground.

Well, he says to me as they stop in front of me.

Where have you been? is all I can think of to say to him. Its a stupid question.

Away, he says.

And is this you back? I ask, pointing over at Robert, who is getting up on to his hands and knees, blood dripping from his nose onto the beaten ground, the shadows dancing on his face as he looks towards us, Elizabeths hand on his shoulder.

This is me back, says Callum, and this is me going away again.

So with those words he bumps past me and away down the path into the trees. Donald Sutherland looks back at me with an expression as if hes saying that theres nothing he could have done, but I know fine that I saw him give Callum a little push and that got the whole thing happening. This look at me that he gives is just one of a whole lot of looks that have gone back and forwards in the space it would take you to take twenty quiet breaths, and none of them are telling me very much that is clear or true. You can look in someones eyes but you cant see whats going on behind them.

Thats what happened. Thats what I had to write down. But then that wasnt the only thing that happened.

People began to go away, shaking their heads and saying how this is not the sort of thing that should be happening at a marriage. For some reason the person they seem to want to tell

240

this to is Ian and one after another theyre up at him shaking his hand and shaking their heads and muttering about the wrongness of it. I think theres a tear on his cheek, maybe thinking about the way we all came here together and this is how it ends up. If this *is* the ending up, but it might not be.

Elizabeth and Rachael take Robert away into the cabin to wash the blood off him and put him in a clean shirt and maybe I should have gone in too but I couldnt. I sat down by the dying fire and watched the flames shrink like the journey weve made.[34]

Ian sat down beside me after everyone else had gone and he put his good hand on my shoulder.

He said, Dont fret, Hugh. Some things happen that we cannot expect. And some of those things are good and some of them are bad. One thing is sure. Once they have happened no amount of reflection can change the fact that they have happened. Our lives move from time to time and from phase to phase, like a river flowing across a plain. The river has its course and we must let it flow on.

And so he talked on for a little while and as he talked all I could think was this thought – *the touch of his hand gets weaker every day*. What will I do if I lose Robert and Callum and Ian too?

After a time Ian goes into the cabin as well and it is me in the clearing by myself and the orange glow of the embers, no flames at all now. At last, and I wait long enough for it, Rachael comes out of the cabin and sits by me. For quite a bit we dont

---

34 Maybe it would be best not to interrupt the narrative at this moment but it is worth pointing out the obscurity of this simile which, I believe, shows more about Hugh's state of mind when writing this than it does about how he felt about the incident. Perhaps he means that the hopes they came to Canada with have shrunk, or perhaps he is suggesting that the importance of the journey itself has shrunk, that the whole enterprise now looks to him to be more insignificant than he originally felt it would be. – RM

speak, but then she says, Did you know?

Did I know what?

That he liked Elizabeth.

Of course. You told me, remember? I knew it anyway. Hes always liked her ever since years.

Liked her like that though. So much.

No. Well, no I dont think so, I said, understanding a lot of things very quickly.

Ive known since we were back in Scotland, she said. I tried to explain to to you. Do you remember the time we went into Alexander Camerons croft?

I remembered it well enough. Wed gone into his croft in Croval one time when we knew he was out on the sea. Callum was for taking some of his whisky and drinking it there in his place. Me and Robert and Rachael had taken a cold fear that someone would catch us in there so we went off and away down to the shore but, now that I thought back on it, it was true enough that Callum and Elizabeth had stayed in there, and who knows what went on, but was that a reason for coming now and giving Robert a bleeding nose on his marriage day?

Rachael said, Its Elizabeth I feel sorry for.

I said, Its Robert I feel sorry for, lying on the ground with all blood down his shirt.

No, she said, I mean the way she thought it was all starting out afresh, like the first step on a long journey the way Ian said it. And then that.

I suppose so. Its funny though, isnt it?

Whats funny? Nothing much very funny about having that to remember instead of the friendliness and the singing and everything. And knowing that in years to come folkll remember their marriage day as the day that Callum Ross punched Robert Vass in the face when he was drunk with jealousy.

Yes, but I dont mean funny like that. I mean that its funny how you come all the way across the sea and things come and follow you from years ago. I mean, I know that one of the reasons that Robert came away at all was because he needed to get away from his family, with his sisters getting on at him all the time. But here he is marrying Elizabeth from Craigtore and Callum from Croval hitting him because of something that happened when we were sixteen.

Mhm, she said. True enough. But still, its a terrible thing thats happened.

She put her hands up and ran them through that red hair which was the thing I always liked about her. It was dark beside the dying fire and I couldnt really see the redness of her hair but I knew it was red so in that way I saw it as being red. For some reason I was finding it hard to speak, not because Id run out of things to say but I had an upset feeling in my throat that was stopping certain words coming out. So we were quiet for a wee while then I said

Ians getting older.

I see that.

I worry that hes losing his strength.

He did the marriage well today, she said.

I know, but theres something about him now. Hes thinner again, and hes forgetting things, and theres no strength in him for work any more.

Well, she said. It comes to us all.

I know.

Hes still got his health.

But not so much.

Hes not dead, Hugh. Make the most of it while hes here.

I know.

We looked into the orange glow of the fire which was turning into white ash and thin smoke.

What are you going to do now? I asked her and this was the thing that was stuck in my throat before. My heart in my chest was so loud that my ears had a buzz in them and I wanted it to get louder so I couldnt hear her answer.

She never said anything for a while then she said, Its all finished here, isnt it, for me?

No, I said in a little voice.

Yes it is. I dont want to stay at the Bales with Elizabeth gone. And I wont see her so much now shes married. And theyll be having a family. So Im as well moving on.

Is that what youre really thinking?

Ive been thinking it for a while ever since they said they were getting married. I told you.

Is there nothing to keep you here? I asked her even though I didnt want to.

Then she leaned across into me and put her hand on my arm and her head on my shoulder. I wanted the fire to stay where it was and not burn down any more and I wanted them in the cabin to stay in there and not ever come out and I wanted the moon to stay up there in the sky with its blue light coming down through the branches and never move through the night to bring the next days dawn. Her hair was against my cheek and I pressed myself against her.

Nothing much, she said. Ive made up my mind. You cant be always staying in the same place.

Will you just go off on your own?

Yes, why not?

Will you be safe? Will you not need anyone with you for safety?

Ill soon meet people, she said. Theres Scots everywhere thatll look out for you.

I swallowed and said, When?

Oh, soon. The sooner the better. No use slicing a loaf of bread when its already gone stale.

Then a branch moved in the fire and the orange glow went down and I heard the door of the cabin open and the moon was shifting in the sky right enough even if I couldnt see it happen so before it was too late I said

I was hoping that youd stay here with me.

I know, she said. I know you were. But Im going.

Maybe I could come with you.

No, she said and shook her head so that her hair brushed against my skin and I felt her cheekbone move on my shoulder. No, Im going by myself. Thats what I want.

Its a pity, I said.

I know it is, she said, but thats whats happening. But Ive not gone just yet.

So then she stood up and she took my hand and we went, the two of us, into the trees away from the fire and the cabin and we stopped and she kissed me and then something happened between the two of us that would not be right to put down in words.

Afterwards I came back inside and got out my pages and Ive written all this down and its as if my world has been created anew and destroyed completely at the same time so that I dont know what to think at all. My hand shakes as I write this and the future looks as dark as the back of the Seal Cave on a winters evening.

Its a new thing thats happened to me but what Im understanding clearly enough is that Rachael has said goodbye.

Intertitle 4

It is exciting, inspirational even, to read about those first thuds of axe into tree, to share Hugh's early steps into his new life, to see him and his friends start to fashion their future, beyond Pictou, beyond Quebec. To me the preceding section shows the best in Hugh: his determination to work hard, his cooperative abilities, his desire for success. But, as you have seen, not all went well and the disintegration of the small group that left Croval to cross the stormy sea is the thing that strikes us. The marriage of Robert and Elizabeth and the way that Callum drifts away from Hugh's main narrative seem to me sad events, even though one of them is a celebration. But I should bear in mind that this is Hugh's story: if it were Robert's story I am sure I would see things differently. It would be *Hugh* who leaves, *Robert* who remains central. Perspectives again, and that's what I have to remember.

But Hugh's continued attachment to Ian MacLeod, because of these various abandonments, becomes more fundamental. As for the mysterious encounter between Hugh and Rachael, how do we account for Hugh's strange reticence at the end of the *Quebec and Beyond* section? I agree that the delicacies of the times, or a desire to protect Rachael's honour, may be behind his refusal to divulge the exact details of their furtive, undoubtedly sexual meeting in the woods. But there is a lot revealed in this delicacy. I think we can guess at Hugh's increasing sense of the *role* of his writing.

And this process goes a stage further in the following section which I have called, for very obvious reasons, *Chicago*. In particular, the closing part of the section shows us a man facing some sense of responsibility for what he writes, or the relationship between what he lives and what he writes, and those who read his words. It's as if he's beginning to realise that his story might be instructional, though he can't have imagined me, or you, sitting down with his words in front of our eyes. You set something rolling and who knows where it will end up and that applies to a book as much as it does to a rock.

This is not an easy section, and in my mind its predominant colours are red and black. Its tone is set by the physical activities it describes and also by the state of mind of the protagonist, both in response to what happens here in Chicago and also to what has already happened to him in Goderich (and before that, because Callum's betrayal, if it should be called that, began long before he left the group and then returned to strike Robert on the day of his marriage). Some of this is not pleasant to read but Hugh is right not to spare us: life did not spare him. If we feel a shudder as we read then that shudder is a shudder of empathy for the lives of these poor emigrants all those years ago. If we shiver as the shadow of his unhappiness begins to cast its pall on him, it is because he has successfully reached out to us from a hundred and fifty years ago, and we have accepted his touch. Like me, you will probably feel a need to comfort Hugh. Should I feel that way? It seems odd to me, but our feelings can take us by surprise, can't they?

But hidden in the darkness of this section there are some bright moments, and the brightness comes from Hugh's description: despite his prevailing mood, he still manages to bring off some striking set-pieces. In my mind are the images of a man in an animal pen and a bird on a wooden floor, a sharp knife and a confused pianist. But of course, I must not give too much away!

Enterprise has its ups and downs. *Chicago* is not Hugh's best time. I know how he feels. My bookshop in Aberdeen went from strength to strength and, without wanting to be sidetracked by details, I do think it is worthwhile pointing out that my success at that time, with growing sales and the opening of a further shop, was just temporary, a cul-de-sac in the plot of my life. Once again I feel kinship with Hugh. My "*Chicago*" came when, as with Hugh, circumstances changed. Things went wrong in many ways.

You have to be philosophical. In the following section, Hugh may appear to give up. But you will realise, of course, that as you get towards the end of this section and you read Hugh's anguished promise to have done with writing, you have, nevertheless, not reached the end of this book. So we have more to learn.

There are gaps. There are holes. But we can pick our way around them and follow his path to yet another new life, so we can still pursue him in his pursuit of success.

Chicago

I wonder what my mother would think if she could see this place and what shed say about it. Probably she wouldnt say anything, shed just turn her back and go away into the croft and sit down on her stool, shaking her head and frowning.

I thought when I saw it that Inverness was a big place but its nothing compared to Chicago. It goes on forever, with streets and buildings stretching as far as you can see which is not very far because of all the buildings and streets that are in the way. You know its a huge place, bigger than anywhere, but you can only see just a little part of it at a time. When we got here first I said to Ian

Im going out for a walk around and see what its like.

I walked for hours and never got anywhere. Its just buildings for people to stay in and buildings where people make things and buildings where people buy things and where they drink and where anything you could think of happens, everything you can think of. All buildings.

Theres noise all the time because of a lot of things, like horses going by on the muddy streets and theres people shouting at each other all the time in the crowds that press together on the boardwalks and theres the noises from the buildings of machines banging and screaming away and the noise of cows and pigs being driven through the streets and a thousand and one other noises that I cant begin to write down because I dont even know what some of them are. And down where we are by the river is the noise of the animals in the pens. The noises never stop. If you can get to sleep and you wake up in the middle of the night the noise is just the same as if you were in your room in the middle of the morning.

In Croval the sky was all around you and it touched the land wherever you looked, or the sea. When we cut our clearing near

Goderich the sky was still there, up above, and even in amongst the sharp-smelling trees the sky still came down to you, blue or grey or whichever colour it was that day, in between the branches. Here, the sky lies in thick sad lines between the tops of houses and it is dirty with smoke and soot.

My mother would say, And why in Gods name did you want to go to a place like that in the first place?

And I would say back to her, Well, we had to go somewhere, didnt we?

You could take Croval and put it down in Chicago and youd not even notice it, as if you took one leaf and laid it in a forest. Youd never be able to find it again.

Ever since we got here Ive been thinking about my mother more, maybe because our group has fallen apart and its been like my family since we left Scotland back in 1841. Its funny because it was Ian that opened up my eyes to make me realise that there was more to the world than just our croft and the bit of sea that drifted past us there and now its just me and Ian in a room in a boarding house near the river in Chicago. So once it was the sea I could go and look at but now its the Chicago River and what a difference that is. The River here flows with blood and filth. Along the sides there are great buildings where grain is taken from boats and stored and moved to other places, filled with men working and yelling. But where we are its the animals, and I wonder what my mother would have thought of that.

It has been in my mind that she might not even be alive now and Im thinking that I should be worrying about her more, but she was strong when I left and shes had a lot of bad things in her life and she has survived all that, so I think she can be surviving me going away to America too. And I have enough to worry about with Ian and thats why Ive taken my pages and Im writing this down again when I havent written anything for so many long months.

Im seeing him weaker all the time and his skin paler. Round his eyes hes red and sore looking and theres a watering in his eyes which wasnt there before. His skin seems thinner than it was, stretched tighter on his face. When I see him lift his hand to his mouth at meal time Im seeing a shake there and many a time Ive seen him put his cup back down on the wooden table rather than spill it as he brings it up to his mouth. Im seeing him stumble when he walks and Im seeing him slower and not so sure about where hes putting his feet. He wasnt like this back in Croval and though its only five years[35] theres been a big change in him.

It seems to me that Im looking at him all the time, watching for any new sign of weakness that I havent noticed before. Sometimes that stops me from being his friend in the way I used to be. I have a tense feeling in my heart when I am with him, as if I am always ready to catch him if he falls. So sometimes I almost dont hear what hes saying. Maybe its me thats getting older, getting right into my twenties now. When I was young I never noticed older people being anything other than full of opinions and annoying to us young ones. Now Im seeing what getting older really is. What it is, Im seeing now, is slowing down as the world goes faster and faster, so that youre hanging on with your fingertips, as if at any moment therell be a bump in the road and youll be thrown right from the cart.

I dont want to feel sorry for him, but sometimes Im lying in

---

35 There are years missing here and we will never know what happened to fill them up. Did Hugh and Ian stay in the cabin near Goderich until just before the writing of this section, or were they on the move soon after the marriage and Hugh's unsatisfactory encounter with Rachael? If so, where were they? The poor people of history tend to leave no trace so we can never know. However, I would like to imagine them on the move, Hugh continually pursuing his dream of a new world and success. I wouldn't like to think of him sitting and stewing for month after month in a log cabin in a wood, not sure what to do. It does not fit with the way I like to see him, the way I have chosen to think of him. – RM

bed at night and when I think of him I have to turn my thoughts elsewhere so that I dont have to think about what he might be thinking as he lies there in the other bed.

[36]When its cold here the steam hangs over the stockyards as the mass of animals blunders around inside the pens. Theres the sound of cows lowing and pigs squealing and grunting and the mist of their heat is like the sound somehow turned into something you can actually see. There are thousands of them, all waiting to be slaughtered. Donald Sutherland says that this is just the beginning and that if a man knows how to handle things right hell be rich in no time. He says all the animals in America will come to Chicago to die in ten years time. In ten years time, he said when we got here first of all, hed be sitting in a mansion and hed have the world at his feet, but of course Donald Sutherland is always after some other plan.

Weve not seen much of him since he got me the job at the packing factory and I dont know if hes really any nearer to his mansion yet, or if Callum is still part of his plans at all. We saw Callum today and he was drunk, going on about what he thinks about us all and about moving on again and its a meeting I wish hadnt happened but Ill write more of that later, though Id prefer not to. Maybe weve not been here long enough to move on, maybe we cant. But we have to, I think. More of this later. The story first.

Maybe Ill put all my pages together into one pile and send them to Scotland so my mother can see what Ive been doing. Maybe, if I knew where she was, Id send them to Rachael.

---

36   It might seem appropriate to have a division in the text here, but in this *Chicago* section there are no such divisions at all. This briefer account of an episode of Hugh's life runs quite impressionistically together. I did think about inserting divisions myself, but time ran out and I think my apologetic delaying emails to my publisher exhausted their conviction. So I have just left it as it is in the original manuscript. I couldn't decide what to do. – RM

Maybe I should just throw them away because no ones ever going to read them anyway. It seems stupid carrying them around from place to place.

What a job Donald Sutherland found for me. It was meant to be for both of us, me and Ian, but one look at the packing factory and Ian said no, he wasnt going to do that, not in a thousand years. When Sutherland said it was a packing factory I thought it would be something like putting things into wooden boxes or into sacks, maybe vegetables or clothes or something. But no. Although there are people packing wooden barrels in the factory thats not my job and its not clothes or vegetables.

Whats packed is meat because what Chicago is, I think, is the graveyard of a thousand animals a day. I dont really know if it is a thousand or five thousand or what it is, but its a lot of animals that come in here and die. And its not their graveyard because when you die and get put in a graveyard at least your body stays there and goes back to ashes and dust. Here the animals get packed in barrels with salt and then they get sent away to other places where people cook and eat them. So there is that kind of packing happening in the factory.

But what I have to do is worse. The pigs get taken from the pens by some men with sticks to prod them and they come in a door at the side of the factory, which is just a big building filled with men and pigs and blood and screams. I put pieces of cotton into my ears when Im working but you cant keep out the squeals. I know pigs from back at Goderich and I know that they are clever beasts, and that they often know whats happening. So these pigs, or *hogs* as the people call them here, as soon as they are driven through the gate in the wall of the factory, they know from the smell and the noise whats going to happen and they set up a cry that warns the next ones coming through and so it goes on and they only stop screaming when the blood is draining from their cut throats and they cant make a sound any more.

Id seen a pig being slaughtered before, of course I had, and

I know that animals have to die to feed us. But not like this. Id never seen, or imagined, anything like this. The pigs, or hogs, go into a run that gets narrower so that by the time they reach us theyre coming through just one at a time. Then two men grab hold of the pig and it gets turned over and they put hooks through its back legs and the hooks are attached to a chain. This chain is hooked onto another big chain that is up by the roof and it circles on through the factory, always moving because theres a machine that turns wheels that makes it move, and there are men in the factory whose job is to feed this machines fire with coal using rusty shovels. As the roof chain moves on the pigs get lifted up into the air by their back feet and the funny thing is that as soon as theyre up in the air they usually stop squealing and struggling and they just look at you but even so theres a man standing a bit further along with a thing like a huge hammer and he swings this up and hits the pig hard between the eyes and this is meant to knock it out but the pigs arent struggling by then anyway and usually it doesnt knock them out because he either doesnt swing hard enough or else he doesnt get them in the right place or something. Then a bit further along a man takes a knife and cuts the throat and for the next few yards as the chain slowly drags the hanging pig along the blood is gushing out into a trough and drains away into a hole in the floor. Someone told me that down below there are tanks for collecting this blood and that they use it for adding to sausages and pies and things like that, but Ive never been down into what they call the basement so I cant say if thats true or if the blood just drains off into the river which is about a hundred yards away from this factory. The rivers full of blood in any case.

Its amazing how fast the blood can come out of a pig.

But its still coming out by the time the pig reaches me. Ive got a knife too and big leather gloves which are to protect me just in case Im careless after working for an hour or two. But like the other men in the factory I am stripped to the waist

254

because it is so hot, what with all the men and all the pigs and the steaming blood and the fire for the chain machine. But if the owner comes round to see how were getting on we have to put our shirts back on, more respectable looking for him, a man in a waistcoat and leather boots.

My job is to stick my knife into the pigs belly just about between its back legs and pull the knife down hard until it touches the ribs. The next man, a few yards along from me, makes some other cuts, then the next man pulls out the guts and they go into another metal basin thing and slither down a hole to the basement. Further along still there are men that make other cuts, that take off the trotters and the head and the tail, that scrape off the worst of the hairs, that clean out the inside of the pig, that take whats left down and cut it into pieces, that pack the pieces into barrels with layers of salt, that roll the barrels away into a storehouse for stacking, that load these barrels onto carts to be taken away.

In this way a pig is turned into meat and begins its long journey to other places such as New York, which is a place you hear about a lot but that nobody Ive met has ever been to. All I know is, they must eat a lot of pig meat there, because these hogs are coming past me all day and there are factories like our one all along the river in Chicago.

Ian says a factory should be for making things, not destroying them. He says it should be called an annullatory, which is not a real word at all. He says the smell, the sounds and the feel of the whole place is like a vision of Hell. I said to him I didnt think Hell would have so many pigs in bits in it and he gave that laugh that he gives these days and he said something about a swines snout and asked me what I was thinking these days about Rachael but I had no idea what he was talking about so I never said anything. Sometimes these days what he is saying isnt making much sense so you just dont say anything and he forgets about it.

One day a man died in the factory just a bit along the chain from me. It was the man whose job was to haul out the guts of the hog and slither it into the metal trough and I never even learnt his name.

The first thing I knew about it was the shouts of the other men and somebody ran over and pulled on the rope that stops the big wheels turning and the chain came to a stop with the pigs, or what was left of them, swinging away, some of them still making a bit of noise and the ones still on the ground screaming and trying to get back out into the sunlight they would never see again.

By the time I got over to where he was there was a fair crowd round him and one man was kneeling down beside him and trying to speak to the man. There was another man standing in amongst the group and he had his knife hanging from his right hand and as he looked on he let the knife fall and the sound of it banging off the floor seemed the loudest thing in the world, despite the noise of all the hogs.

It turned out that what had happened was that this other man, the one with the knife, had just done the slicing cut that was needed to release the guts from the body and as hed done it hed swung his arm away from the hanging pig, being the kind of man who liked to do things with a grand gesture, the others said. And as bad luck would have it this other man, ready to reach in with his red hands and drag out all the guts, took a step back from the previous hog that hed just dealt with and where he moved was the little cut of space where the first mans knife passed through and it caught him right up his arm, right through the big veins there and the blood was pumping out of him and into the metal trough that was already filled with pigs guts and pigs blood and slithering away down through the hole into the basement. The man that was kneeling beside him was talking away to him in his ear and trying to wrap his shirt, that hed ripped off from his waist, round the mans arm but the blood was coming too fast and we could all see the man was going to die there in front of us. He was shaking as if he was cold and his other hand was grasping at the end of the ledge thing that the pigs were moved above but his fingers couldnt reach it and after a while they stopped moving and his arm sank down to the floor. It was as if he wanted to pull himself up and stand straight and just get on with his job, but he couldnt.

Somebody had run for a doctor but by the time he came the man was dead, bled like a pig. We all stood and watched him die because there was nothing we could do about it. It was just an accident. Later on I told Ian what had happened and he had nothing to say about it, nothing at all, as he sometimes doesnt these days.

Thats the sort of place it is. The owner came down and had a look around and had a word with the man whod been swinging the knife and a couple of the other men whod seen what happened and the conclusion was that it was just one of those things that can happen in the world. The body was taken away I dont know where and another man came and stepped in and took over that part of the job and they washed out the trough with buckets of water and within an hour we were back at work again and for the rest of the day I was thinking about what was going on down in the basement where the mans blood was all mixed up with the insides of pig, as if it was all one and the same stuff.

We were down at the side of the river when I told Ian about what had happened. He was leaning on my arm as we walked. I dont know why we were there. In Upper Canada beside a river seemed like quite a nice place to walk and when you saw a river that was the sort of place youd want to go and walk, just the way we used to go and walk beside the sea at Croval all that time ago.

But the river here stinks like nothing on earth and its full of all the stuff that the factories pour out. But the one good thing is that theres not so many people there as there are on the streets

257

so although theres no such thing as a private place in Chicago, beside the river in the evening is not so far off it.

Ian had his hand on my arm. He can still walk fine by himself but hes a bit more unsteady than he used to be and hes got into the habit of walking beside me like this and I dont mind it at all. So I told him about the death and he had nothing to say. After a bit of walking he asked me a question.

How long do you feel you will stay here in this place?

I said, Thats a question Ive heard before.

He said, Thats a question that will always be asked.

I dont know, I told him. If I can put aside some money from the work here maybe we can buy somewhere.

Buy somewhere where? he asked.

I dont know, I said, but not here. Somewhere out in the country again. I cant stand to live here for too long.

He gave that thin laugh that has grown in him as hes got older. Well, he said, youll be working here long enough on the wages youre getting before you can buy somewhere bigger than a shed.

Yes, I said, thats true.

So it seems that this might be the end of our road, he said, with a sad smile.

We walked along for a little while, looking down at the river. In this water you will never see a fish. They might be in there but the water is so thick with dirty stuff that you cant see into it.

Then I said, I hope its not. I want more than this.

He asked me, Do you still think about Rachael?

Id never told him about what happened in the trees after Robert and Elizabeths marriage so there was something important that he didnt know, another thing.

Me – Yes, I do sometimes think about her.

Ian – And where do you imagine she might be now?

Me – I dont know.

Ian – You should find out.

258

Me – Who would I ask?

Ian – Donald Sutherland knows everyone.

Me – Maybe.

I didnt say that Id already asked Donald Sutherland and that hed told me he didnt know the answer to my question. He knows where Callum stays though and hed been telling us that hed be coming to see us soon and sure enough thats what happened today, which Ill come to.

Ian – Its a big place, America. But shes somewhere and somebodyll know where. The Scots speak to the Scots.

Me – Maybe.

So we walked on for a while beside the river of filth beside us. I wondered if this was the moment to tell him about what happened all those years ago at the top of the cliff in Croval. With Ian talking like that, talking about the end of things, it seemed like the right time to say something. But the words died in my throat and I held my tongue, again. [37]

There are pens where the animals are kept before they get taken away to be killed and packed. These pens are another new thing to me. Ever since we left Croval it has been new things and Im wondering sometimes when it will all stop, or if it will.

I was always used to seeing maybe a few animals together. Nobody had more than one cow in Croval. The first reason for that was that there really wasnt any room to have more than that and the second reason was that it was so difficult to get the cows to Croval in the first place that I dont think anyone really wanted the bother of it. You couldnt get a cow down the steps carved into the cliff so the only way was to take a cow to Craigtore and then swim it round the headland on a good day, and more than one cow was drowned that way in

---

37 Another place where there should really be a division in the text. However I like the way that in this section there is nothing to interrupt the description. It all just flows into one. – RM

my years at Croval.

And Im writing this just now and thinking where will I be when the number of years I stayed at Croval are equal to the number of years Ive lived away from Croval.[38] What will I be then? A Scot? An American? A Scottish-American? An American-Scot? Ive met people out here who have been here for their whole lives and they still say they are Scottish. I mean they were born here in America and they say they are Scots. But there are people who have only been here a few years, like me, and they spit on the name of Scotland, because they say that the success they have here beats anything they knew back at home. But they dont call Scotland home. This is home now.

But anyway these pens are so full of animals that when you step up onto the plank at the bottom of the fence beside one, all you can see is hundreds and hundreds of animals backs. They are so tightly packed in that you can hardly see one animal move. What you do see is movements sweep through the pen, like wind blowing across grass. But they cant move far so its not really a movement, more of a kind of shiver that passes across the herd of cows or hogs. There arent really very many sheep here or if there are they must be penned up somewhere else further along the river because its all cows, or steers as they call them, and pigs around here. The air around the pens is just full of dust and the sounds and smells of thousands of animals all crammed up together with nowhere to go. You can see theyre scared but of course theyre just animals so they dont really know whats going to happen to them which is just as well. But sometimes youll see a cows head turn towards you and you can see its eye, white, and it looks at you and you get an idea of the terror its feeling. Its not my fault theyre all in there waiting to be killed but you cant help but feel a bit guilty when they look at you like that. One persons cow back in Croval or Craigtore knows who looks

---

38 I am wondering this as well! – RM

after it, knows who feeds it and takes its milk. Here its not like that. I cant explain, but standing at the side of the pens makes me feel scared and lost. When I was wee sometimes Id climb up the steps in the cliff at Croval out onto the flat land at the top and Id wander away, watching the buzzards in the sky or the skylarks climbing up and after a while it would all get to be too much for me and Id start feeling scared and the next thing I knew Id be scrambling back down to the croft again and inside to my mother. These stinking animal pens make me feel a bit like that, but its too late, of course, to go running back, now.

I should write about where were staying. Its called The Main Street Boarding House & General Emporium which puzzled me and Ian because the street outside is called Johnson Street. But a man told us the street used to be called Main Street and was renamed by a man who bought a lot of property along the street. Although hes dead now the street kept his name which is something to think about. That would be strange, to have people still speaking your name long after you are dead!

Back in Goderich there was a separate building for everything. If you wanted to buy something you would maybe go to the General Store and if you wanted to go to drink some beer youd go to the saloon and youd go to the bunkhouse if you wanted to sleep. The Main Street Boarding House & General Emporium has a saloon bar downstairs and you go up these wide wooden stairs to get to the bedrooms and thats not so good because its always noisy, with people drinking downstairs and shouting and singing with a piano playing in the corner. Theres a door to the right side of the bar you go through to get to another part of the building which is a shop which can sell you whatever you want, like boots or shirts or bread or anything, more or less. In the saloon there are green tables where people play at cards all evening, poker and other games that I dont understand, stacks of coins on the surface beside them being pushed backwards and forwards. You can buy meals in the saloon, steaks or sausages or pancakes or other things. If you want to you can buy women here too because some of the rooms upstairs are kept aside for the girls who work in the saloon. Our room is right next to one of these rooms, where a girl, Lydia, takes up men who have paid her. So that can be noisy too and if Im telling you the truth The Main Street Boarding House & General Emporium is not the place to come if you want to get a good nights sleep but well Donald Sutherland set us up here when we arrived and its cheap and if I *am* trying to get some money put safely to one side then we have to stay somewhere like this. Its all owned by a fat man with a moustache called Mr Murdoch Larkin, who has a gold watch and a thoroughbred horse that hes been known to ride right into the saloon. Murdoch Larkin owns the building and everything in it and all the girls and the barmen and the shop assistant and the dealers at the card tables all work for Murdoch Larkin. He knows what hes doing because under his roof, he likes to say, you can get all you need in this world and of course what he doesnt say is that the money you spend all goes straight into his pocket beside his fat cigars. Sometimes he visits Lydias room and no doubt he wont have to pay for a thing.

The room itself we cant complain about. It is very clean and tidy and a woman who works for Larkin cleans all the rooms every three days and changes the sheets on the beds once a week. There are thick curtains on the window and if you close the window you can hardly hear the animals in the pens down by the river, but on the other hand the animals in the pens down by the river are sometimes making less noise than the animals down below in the bar, Ian says.

The old Croval Ian would have had a lot more to say about this place, but its as if he hasnt the energy now. Some days he just lies in his bed as if he cant be bothered to do anything in the world. Ill go off to work and when I get back hes still there as if all hes done during the day is turn over so his face is to the wall.

Are you all right? I ask him.

He says, Of course I am.

What would you like to do?

Nothing. Im thinking.

What are you thinking about?

Im thinking about a story.

So then he sits up in bed and he tells me this story from the Bible about some pigs. It seems there was this man in a place somewhere called Gadara whose head and body were all filled up with demons who had been sent by the devil to torment him. So one day he meets Jesus who has more power, of course, than the devil, and he gets rid of the demons from out of the man. The funny thing about this story is the way that he does it. He forces the demons out of the man and into a herd of pigs that are nearby being tended by their swineherd. Ian doesnt explain fully, maybe because hes tired, but Im thinking that maybe each demon goes into one particular pig.

Ian says, The whole herd of swine ran violently down a steep place into the sea, and perished in the waters.

So that was the end of the demons and the man recovered and lived a happy life after that.

Ian asks me, What do you think about that? Do you think the swine in the pens are filled with Gadarene demons?

I think a bit. I say, No, but what I am wondering about is why the pigs all had to die. Couldnt Jesus just have chased out the demons and sent them away back to hell where they came from?

Ian shakes his head and replies, It is not for us to question Gods ways.

And what, I ask, about the swineherd?

Ian lies back down and puts his hands over his face and says nothing but gives a deep sigh as if I have disappointed him. He used to love this kind of conversation so I carry on.

I ask, Did Jesus give the swineherd new pigs? And anyway, I can see why the pigs drowned but why would the demons drown, since they wouldnt be creatures of flesh and blood, they wouldnt be breathing, would they, so how could they drown? And why not put all the demons into just one pig and leave the rest alone?

Ian says from behind his hand, This is a parable, Hugh. Do not seek for literal truth in a parable.[39] You look in too deeply.

Well, I dont see it.

Much of what is true cannot be seen, he says.

So that was that time.

Another time when I got back from my work at the factory he wasnt there at all, but the blanket was all crumpled on the floor of the room. I knocked on Lydias door and asked her if shed seen him but she hadnt.

She is a nice person, Lydia, but nothing like any of the girls Ive known before, not in Croval, not anywhere. When she looks you in the eye you feel like taking a step backwards. But on the other hand you also kind of feel like taking a step forward. She has painting on her face so that her lips are redder than they are and her eyes are bigger than they are. Id say shes about eighteen but she can look twenty five. In a way shes beautiful but in another way you know shes not and so theres only so much friendliness you can give her. One time I asked her why she lived her life like this, with maybe ten men coming to her room through an evening and she just shrugged her shoulders and asked me why I lived mine the way I do.

She came with me to look for Ian. She wanted to look in the other saloons and when I tried to explain about him being a minister and how he wouldnt be wandering around the saloons she stopped walking and said to me

Is that right? I never knew he was a minister. He never told me that.

Youve been talking to him?

---

39 Hear hear! – RM

Lydia – I talk to him mostly every day.

Me – When do you talk to him?

Lydia – When youre at work and Im not.

We were standing on Johnson Street, facing each other, a little bit out of breath because wed been walking fast. Lydia wears a dress which is cut very low at the front so sometimes you have to really concentrate when youre talking to her. I couldnt understand what she was saying.

Me – What do you mean you talk to him every day?

Lydia – Why not?

It upset me and I felt a weight of panic bear down upon me, the way a cut tree comes crashing down into the brush, covering everything with its leaves and branches. I didnt want Ian to be speaking to Lydia, or anyone, though at the same time I was saying to myself not to be so stupid, he could do what he wanted.

Lydia – Thats what I like about him. You can talk to him and hes interested in you.

I remembered that was what Id liked about Ian too, the way hed listen to you and make you feel important in what you were saying. I knew that what I was feeling at that moment was jealousy, because this wasnt the feeling Id been getting from Ian, not for quite a while.

Lydia – The only problem is that hell say things to you and then forget hes said them so that the next day hell say them again. But thats just him getting older. Thats what happens. I dont know how many times hes told me the story about the time he set fire to that dead tree.

Me – We dont have time to stand and talk. We need to find him.

And I turned and walked on along Johnson Street, my face burning, because Id never heard this story about the tree. She came along beside me, looking at me with a smile on her face that I couldnt read.

She asked some people she knew as we went along the street, because she knew just about everyone, and I recognised some of the men that Id seen coming out of her room at nights. I didnt like these men very much. They were usually over-confident loud men who would shout and swear with a dram in. When I saw her speaking to them in the street, and the easy way one would lay a hand on her shoulder, or the way one of them kissed her on the cheek after theyd finished talking, some of the jealousy I had in my mind about her friendship with Ian moved over to these men. Its not that Id want to be with someone like Lydia, who is as hard as the stones at the edge of the Middle River, but Im thinking about Rachael and in a funny way Im imagining her in every situation. Im not explaining this well so Ill stop and will try again later.

After one of these conversations, Lydia came over to me and said

Hes down by the pens.

The pens?

The hog pens.

The hog pens?

She rolled her eyes at me and took me by the arm and dragged me down towards the river. There are many hog pens and we went past a good few as we were looking for him. I was thinking, some of these pigs will be coming into my factory tomorrow, so I didnt look at them in the eye. They have sharp wee eyes, pigs, not like the cows with their big blank expressions.

Sure enough we found him after a while. He wasnt *by* the pens, he was *in* one of the pens. He must have climbed the fence and hed forced his way right into the middle of the pen so that the big hogs were pressing up against him, bumping him this way and that as they tried to move about. He probably would have fallen over but there were so many pigs they were holding him up. There was nowhere to fall.

He had his arms up in the air as if he was reaching for some-

266

thing and he was shouting out some words, over the screeching and grunting of the animals in this pen and the others that stretched away on every side. A few small boys had come to watch him and they were perched up on the top rail of the fence over at the other side from where we were. I climbed up and over and pushed my way through the hogs. It was hard work and hot work too because of the fleshy heat of all the animals. Some of them were trying to bite me but it was hard for them to twist round to get their mouths to me so I never got any bites really. It took ages to get right to the middle up beside Ian. I called his name but he didnt seem to hear me. Instead he just kept on shouting out, with his hands and his eyes cast up towards the evening sky. It was just beginning to drizzle a fine rain and there was a steam rising from the animals backs as the light started to go out of the day.

I realised he was giving a sermon. I cant remember the words exactly but it was something like this:

For in the times of trouble the Lord shall hide me in his tents. In the secrets of his great church he will hide me and he shall set me upon a rock. And now my head shall be lifted up above mine enemies.

He was repeating these same words over and over again, as if he was thinking that if he said them often enough the pigs would stop pushing and snorting and squealing and would all stop and listen. I pulled at his coat to get his attention because he hadnt looked at me even once as I was pushing through the pigs towards him. When he did look down at me, turning his eyes away from the heavens, there was no sign that he knew me. He stopped shouting and a confused look was across his face.

I got my arm round his waist and I tried to pull him back through the animals to the fence where Lydia was waiting. It was harder to get back than it had been to get to the middle because there were two of us and there was hardly space between the pigs to push one of these sheets of paper, never mind two men.

Ian never spoke the whole time and he wasnt even trying to help me to get through.

By the time we got to the edge and Id persuaded him to climb over the fence we were sweating and muddy and the rain had soaked our clothes as it got heavier. As soon as he was outside the pen Ian looked at me and said

What are we doing here?

He didnt even remember being inside the pen never mind how hed got there. He knew me again but what hed been up to that day had disappeared out of his head like snow on a river.

We got him back to The Main Street Boarding House & General Emporium and up the stairs and Lydia went away because she had her work to do so that left me alone with Ian to talk about what had happened. I explained to him how wed found him but no number of questions could get him to remember how hed got there into the middle of that pig pen. He couldnt explain. I tried to get him to think about what hed been saying but no. Hed been delivering a sermon to the pigs.

Another time, two or three days after that evening, I came back and he was drunk down in the saloon. He was arguing with the man who played the piano. Ive seen Ian drink wine before. He always had wine in the manse back in Croval and I suppose a few times you could say hed had a few glasses of it and then the words would come sliding out of him a bit more easily and a bit less clearly but Id say Ive never seen him properly drunk before.

The piano man, whose name was Arthur, was standing beside the piano and Ian was sitting on the stool in front of it. The lid was down over the keys and Arthur had his hand pressed firmly down on top of it. Ian was scratching with his fingernails at the wood, trying to get through to the keys.

Arthur was saying, No, youre not going to be playing it. No. Do you want to scare off the customers?

If truth be told there were only three or four customers in

268

the saloon in the early evening time and they were watching the argument and laughing.

Ian was shouting, Im playing! Im playing!

I went over and said, Ian, come away upstairs and Ill tell you about my day at the factory.

He stood up and tried to push Arthur away from the piano. He shouted, I *will* play! I have the training. I have played to the Edinburgh Ladies Association. I have played them Mozart.

This was a name Id heard from him before, someone he thought highly of, like Walter Scott.

Arthur turned to me and said, Take him upstairs, cant you? Ive got my work to do.

We all have our work to do.[40]

I got Ian up to the room in the end, with the customers clapping and whistling as we were half way up the staircase and Ian yelled out over the banister, I have played Ladies to the Beethoven Association!

I got him in through the door and laid him down on the bed. I pulled his boots off and hid them under my bed so that he wouldnt be tempted to wander out again. His breath was stinking of cheap whisky and he was humming some tune or other, maybe one that hed been going to play on the piano.

Why are you drunk? I asked.

I have been drinking whisky, he announced.

I realise that you have, but Im asking you *why*.

The beer is like dirty water and the wine makes the gorge rise. At least the whisky numbs your tastebuds.

And then he fell asleep and he snored away the whole night. The next morning he was a bit foolish feeling and didnt want to

---

40 I like this bit. I wonder, did he speak those words or just think them? The old Hugh would certainly never have given voice to this thought in front of a relative stranger. But I imagine Chicago was toughening him up, and we are beginning to see the development of a more interventionist Hugh. – RM

talk about his sore head or how it came about, at least not to me.

I asked him if there was something troubling him and if that was why he had got drunk.

He said, The world is what troubles me. But I have found that getting drunk has not made it go away.

There was nothing much to say to that, I thought, so I said nothing much. I know that as age and weariness stalks up behind him, he is changing. We change from children to adults so why should we not keep on changing as we begin to move from adulthood to that later helplessness?

But I do worry about what will become of me when Ian has gone, so I dont think about it. You cant go through life thinking about the worst things that can happen.[41]

Anyway, after that I asked Murdoch Larkin if it would be all right if the barmen downstairs didnt serve Ian too much to drink, because, I explained, he didnt always make the best choices about how much to drink. Murdoch Larkin wasnt too keen on this idea at first.

Well, my boy, he said, when Id explained it all to him. If I took that particular route, Im afraid I would become lost in a desert of poverty.

But its just Ian, I said. Nobody else. Im not saying dont serve him at all, but I dont think its good for him to get so drunk.

In the end he said, Well, Arthur has made the identical request, I must admit, and one cannot but bow in the force of the storm. Your wish, my child, is granted.

He made a little gesture with his wrist and hand as if he was a

---

41   And this seems very characteristic of Hugh, a belief that might seem to be the trademark of what we might call nowadays an entrepreneur. It is this spirit that carries Hugh, and others like him, across the world, always believing that something better might be just around the corner. Success lies where you find it: but to find you must seek. And keep seeking. There's another point, too. You can go through life thinking about the worst things that *have happened*, and that's bad too. – RM

lord giving money to a beggar at the gates of the castle. He calls me *my boy* and *my child* but if Im being honest I dont think he is much more than ten years older than me. It is a wonder how he comes to own so much and to be so rich when he is still quite a young man. If only I knew that secret. Ian didnt get drunk again after that though, so at least Murdoch Larkin was true to his word, which is more than you can say for some people.

I think in these pages I have mainly written down what happened to me. I think thats better than me trying to work out what all these events mean. And Im not much older now than I was when I started and certainly not wiser.

But I cant help but learn things. Ive learnt that you cant trust everyone. My mother told me that when I was just a boy and funnily enough it was Callum she was warning me against. But since Ive come across the sea I think Ive truly *learnt* this fact for myself and not just because someone told me it. The way Donald Sutherland deceived us at Pictou taught me that lesson.

But Ive learnt something else, maybe more important. It is that even though you cant always trust people, the world is a certain way and it means that sometimes you have to rely on the people you cant trust and the people you *can* trust cant do anything to make your life better. Im working in Chicago because Donald Sutherland got me this job here. And Ian is the man I love more than anyone and yet he isnt the man I knew when I was younger, just a few short years ago. Now hes relying on me. *He* has to trust *me*. So what Im saying is that trust is important but in the end of the story it doesnt really have much to do with anything really. All that matters is what happens.

But maybe Ill feel different about that tomorrow. Today has been a difficult day and thats what has driven me back to my pages and this is why Ive been sitting all the evening at a table in the saloon writing all this and now the bar has closed and the barman is wiping the glasses and putting them all back up on the shelves behind the bar and looking across at me, wondering when Im going to go up the stairs to my bed.

So I will stop here for today and tomorrow Ill explain more about whats happened. But for just now I just want to write some more words down, because I dont think I can sleep if I dont. Maybe if I put them on paper they can slip out of my head long enough to let me get a few hours of rest. I hope so because I think Im going to need my rest and my energy, because its going to be difficult for me and for Ian.

Callum has come back into our lives today. As I said before weve been waiting for this to happen because Donald Sutherland said it would but we never thought it would be the way it turned out. Ill tell it all tomorrow, after another day of slicing pigs stomachs open. God.

No sign of him today[42] and thats just as well I think because I dont feel I want to see him. Im back in the bar and theres drinking and singing going on and the man is playing a tune on the piano but half the people are singing a different song altogether. So in the end it is just noise. But what happened yesterday is burning in my mind so that nothing, not even seeing Lydia and the other girls go up and down the stairs with their men, can force the pictures of yesterday out of my mind. I wish they could.

He came in the morning, almost as soon as the sun was up and before I had to go to work. My first thought, I have to say, was annoyance, thinking what a silly time to come and visit. I was still in the room, getting my clothes on, when Edgar, who is an old black man[43] who cleans the floors downstairs first thing in the day every day, came and knocked on our door.

---

42   i.e. the day after the previous one. – RM

43   It would have been interesting if Hugh had recorded his reactions on his first meeting with a black person in America, but he didn't. You might have thought that he would realise that such a cross-cultural meeting would be of great interest to any reader in Scotland or America, white or black. But the moment has passed by in one of the shadows that falls between Hugh's episodes. – RM

Theres someone down in the bar wants to see you, he said.

See who?

See you, he said.

Who is it?

He just turned away and wandered off, saying under his breath, Come down and find out if you want to know.

So I pulled on my boots and put my hand through my hair and took a deep breath because somehow in my mind I had the idea that it might be Rachael, although also I knew that it couldnt be Rachael because how would she know where I was staying to come and visit me?

I made my way downstairs and the place was empty, apart from old Edgar sweeping away in the corner. I looked at him and he turned his eyes across to the other side of the saloon and he pointed his finger. It was quiet for once apart from a strange noise from over to one side of the room and it was still quite dark because Edgar hadnt opened up the shutters yet but there was light slicing in through them and laying black and bright lines across everything so it was hard to make out exactly what I was seeing.

In one of the big leather chairs over by the card tables, a chair Murdoch Larkin himself liked to sit in, I could see someone sprawled, with one leg up over the arm and his face turned away. I walked over to him and from ten feet away I could see who it was because I knew the fair hair, I would know it anywhere. He turned to look at me. In his hand he was holding a bird by the legs and this little bird was fluttering its wings and trying to get away, some kind of lark or linnet. He lifted up his hand and the bird was hanging from his fingers and thrashing with its wings to get free and making this noise not like a bird singing, just the noise of fear. Callums face was twisted into a smile and his eyes were on the bird and not on me. Then he turned and I saw he was drunk.

Hugh, he said. Ive brought you a present.

273

And he swung back his arm and threw the bird at me as hard as he could. I put my arm up to shield my face and it struck me on the back of my hand and fell to the floor. I could feel the sharp point where its beak or its claws had hit my skin. I had nothing to say and my eyes found the bird on the floor, scrabbling and stunned.

Is that all you have to say? he said and he laughed, a coarse loud laugh that reminded me of some of the worst men in the Carcair. Ive brought you a present and you cant even say thank you?

Youre drunk, Callum, I said.

Callum – Yes Im drunk. Im drunk as a lord. Wheres the old man?

Me – Ian?

Callum – Who else? Where is he? Get him down. Ive heard hes losing his head.

I didnt answer that. The bird dragged itself towards my foot, its wings fanned out beside it, giving a little chirp as it moved. I wanted to bend down and pick it up but this is a city of cruelty and I left it on the wooden boards.

Callum – Get the old bastard down. Ive some things to say.

Me – Leave him be. Hes sleeping. I think sleepings the best time for him now.

Callum – A madman and a child.

He lifted himself up from the chair and stood swaying in front of me. He was stinking, and not just with the drink but with dirt and sweat as if he hadnt washed himself for weeks. His hands had the filth of ages on them, under his nails. He reached forward and shoved me hard in the chest.

Callum – So this is it, is it? This is what youve come to? Staying in a whorehouse with a mad old bastard waiting for your wee girlfriend to come back?

Me –

Callum – She wont come back. Do you not know that yet?

Shes half way across America for all you know. You fucking idiot.

I should not write down such words. But this is what he said to me. I have to write it down because if I write it down it will stop ringing in my ears. *You fucking idiot* is what he said to me. I never thought to hear these words, said with such anger, from Callums lips. But there they were, in the air of the room, the light and the dark fighting to win the space.

Me – Callum, I always want to be –

Callum – My friend. My friend. I know. You always want to be my friend. Youve followed me to tell me that for years, boy. Trailing after me like a wee dog. Thats all. Well, fuck off now. Im not wanting you any more.

Me – Callum, you came here to see us. *You* came to *me*.

Callum – And now Im here. And now Im telling you. I dont want you following me any more. I dont want to talk to you any more. About Croval or America or Mary Vass or anything. Go away. Leave me alone.

He took a lurching step towards me, his arm rising, and I knew he would hit me the way he hit Robert at the marriage in the woods. But he stopped and his eyes went past me, over my shoulder and I glanced round and heres Ian on the wooden staircase, his hand on the banister and the other hand above his eyes as he peers down into the saloon, trying to make out whos down there in the shadows.

Ian – Callum, is it you at last?

Callum – Its me, old man.

Ian, coming down the stairs, – Lower your fists, Callum. There is no problem solved by violence.

Callum – Is there not?

Ian – But many a one created by it. You must cast aside the past and rise above it.

So what happens then but the bird thats been on the floor, the linnet or lark, takes off into the air. It must have been just

275

stunned and not badly hurt at all because as were speaking now its flying round the room and Edgars trying to get it out, opening up the door and the shutters, letting in the light and the air to try to let the bird out. All this happening while the three of us stand in the saloon with all the anger and all the days gone by between us like a cup of milk gone sour. Why cant a serious moment like this have peace and quiet to act itself out? Why must there always be someone in the background with a towel, flapping like a madman to chase a tiny bird from the building? There is nothing in the world but foolishness and mockery.

Callum looks disgusted at Ian but all the same his hands drop again to his sides. Mind you the hatred is still in his face and his lip curls up in a sneer that is for us both.

He says, Look at the two of you. Is this what you came across the world for? Slitting pigs throats in a stinking factory, and losing your mind in a filthy whorehouse room?

Ian said, Callum, stop it. Youre drunk.

Callum – I am drunk. Im drunk every day. What else to do?

Edgar knocks over a chair and stumbles to his hands and knees.

Ian says, This is not the Callum that I met years ago. The Callum with an open mind and a searching one.

Callum – Ive done my searching I think. Ive found all there is to find. So have you probably. This is the end of it, Ian. Have you looked round this place? Have you smelt it? Tasted the dirt on your tongue? Heard the blood splashing on the earth?

Ian – This is not the end of any journey. The spirit transcends the body.

Me – Were saving to move on. This is where were stopping just now but its not where were staying.

Callum – Do you think that? Do you? And whatll you do with him when the strength goes out of his legs. Look at him. Look in his eyes. Can you not see? What use is he to you now?

Me – Its not a question of how much use someone is, its a

276

question of how much someone believes in you.

Callum – Belief. *I* believed in *him*.

Me – And hes done nothing to betray your belief.

Callum – Look at him. Look at me! Is this what we set off for, years ago? Remember the promises made in the manse?

Me – No promises were made.

Callum – By God, there were. It was the promise that we could leave behind the smallness of Croval and find a bigger world where maybe wed belong and not feel like the shells you crush under your boots as you walk down the jetty. And that fucking book, with its lies.

Ian – You will not speak that way of the good book when –

Callum – Not the Bible, you fool. That stupid book about moving to America.

Me – MacDougall helped us to prepare for –

Callum – He took us by a ring through our noses and led us here. The only person better off was MacDougall himself when Ian paid his pennies out to get the book in his hands in the first place.

Ian – I bought MacDougall from a bookseller in Edinburgh. There were cats that slept by the range.

This caused a little silence and Callum stared at him, then turned to me, his eyes blurred with the drink and red with tiredness, and, I think, with the burning of the guilt hes carried ever since that summer day at the head of the cliff. But this was not the time to say anything about that.

He said, as if he knew what I was thinking, What Im saying, Hugh, is that I thought it would all be different. I thought wed get away from that shit heap under the cliffs and all that happened there and find somewhere that I could just be myself and where maybe I could be happy. I thought it would be different.

I said, Well, it *is* different, isnt it?

Callum – Yes, it is. Ill give you that. Its different the way

277

the rotten corpse of a sheep is different from the rotten corpse of a cow. Its not the difference I was after.

Ian – There were blue leather covers on that book. It must be in the room. Shall I get it?

Me – It fell into the ocean, remember? You had it in your hand when the wind came and

I heard my voice die away. I was looking at Ian and he was looking away round and up the stairs at the room, a frown on his face, and I could tell that Callum was staring hard at me, as if to say *thats what Ive been saying to you, look at him.*

Edgar has taken a broom and is reaching up to poke at the bird which has perched itself on an oil lamp fixed to the wall of the saloon. Nothing is said. He goes to the door and throws it wide so that the light floods the floor and goes back with the broom but before he can do anything the bird takes to its wings and is out through the door into the day and its gone. How Callum got a hold of it in the first place Ill never know.

Really, he says, you have never known me properly and you never will. And you never tried. And you ask me why Im drunk, and you ask me why I hit Robert and why I went to work on the boat at the Lake, and why Donald Sutherland has been a friend to me. You never knew me, even back then.

This frightens me and I get a sudden idea in my head of a darkness inside Callum like a shadow that hides. Ive been thinking about it since he said it. Maybe hes right, maybe I never looked at him closely enough to see what was there, underneath the tempers and the risks that he took. Maybe hes just right. What I see in his eyes is hatred.

Edgars creaking open the other shutters now, muttering away to himself under his breath, shaking his head when the light coming in shows where the little bird messed on the floor. His broom now is scuffing at the boards and his eyes are telling us he needs us to get out so he can get on with his job before the first drinkers of the day wake up and come staggering into the bar, all ready to start again. So our time with Callum is just about finished.

Come in with us, I say to him. Were getting some money together and you could come too. We can forget all this and be all together again.

He says, And Robert? Him too?

Im confused. Well, I say, Roberts married to Elizabeth, so hell not be coming. But we could. We could take some money with us and go west again and see where we get to. I dont know. Maybe a store or a stables or something. Donald Sutherland too, if youd like him to come.

My words are in my ears as if I havent spoken them myself and they are scaring me. Ians not looking at all. Hes scratching at his fingers as if theres ink all over them, but theres not.

Donald Sutherland? laughs Callum, a nasty laugh. Why would I want to have anything to do with him. Hes just a bastard, Hugh, Id have thought youd have realised that by now.

So then I had a choice which was either to point out to him who it was that dragged Donald Sutherland into our lives in the first place, or else to say what I decided I would say, which was nothing.

Ian sat down in one of the seats and leaned forward with his elbows on his knees and his forehead leaning on his hands.

Callum pointed at him and hissed at me, Look at him. Just look. You cant be held back by him, Hugh.

Im not held back, I tell him. Im fine and Ians all right, hes just getting older.

Its as if hes not with us, but there he sits, just a few feet away, rocking a little bit. We both look at him and its hard to connect this Ian with the one we knew back in Croval. Im trying to see a link that takes me from *that* Ian to *this* Ian, but I cant see it clearly. But the thought makes me say

Do you ever think about going back?

Back?

To Croval?

I didnt know I was going to ask that because its not something Ive really truly been asking myself at all.

Callum spits on the floor and out of the corner of my eye I can see Edgar seeing this, an angry but patient look on his face.

Callum says, No. Thats not where I think about going back to.

Well, I say, if we cant go back maybe we can go forward together.

Callum shakes his head and the hatred thats been in his face is smoothed out by sadness.

No, he says. Theres no more going forward either.

He goes to walk out, bumping against me with his shoulder, the soles of his boots leaving little clicks of noise as he leaves. His head is down, his dirty blond hair the last thing Im looking at before he goes off out into the morning sun.

Edgar comes over with a cloth and bends down to wipe up the spit.

Edgar asks, That your friend? He sure aint happy. But he sure is angry.

Me – Hes always been kind of angry. Ever since he was a boy.

But what Im thinking is that maybe I could have done more to spot the unhappiness. I get my arm around Ians shoulders and lift him up and take him to the room and lie him down on his bed. Theres nothing else to do so off I go to work and then come back to start writing about all of this.

That was two weeks ago and Ive not written anything since then because its been hard to find time with Ian not very well and with work. Im just so tired all the time and worrying about Ian, though Im not very sure how to write down my feelings about that. When I lie down in bed at night I can still hear the screams of the hogs and the metal grating and scraping of the chains and the shouts of the men in the factory. When I shut my eyes I can still see it all. It all has a way of stopping you from falling asleep and then youre even more tired.

We havent seen Callum again after that morning. Ive spoken to old Edgar about it and he says that hes heard others speaking about Callum, the mad Scotsman, drunk through the day, through every day, wandering by the edge of the river threatening to throw himself in. Edgar says Calumll stop people on the street to tell them how hes going to drown himself in the river of blood and waste. Sometimes hes to be seen sleeping under a boardwalk or wandering sad from house to house, looking in through windows where families sit down to share their meals and their kinship. Drunk always. How did he get to be this way?

Im sure I could find him easily enough if I wanted to, but somehow I havent been able to make time to do it in the fortnight since he was here. I know this is an excuse, but I really have no strength in my body to talk to him again. Edgar tells me what people have been saying about Callum, and he tells me with a cruel spark in his eye, enjoying seeing me made unhappy by his stories, the way a poor old man with nothing in this world but a broom and a straw mattress likes to see other people learn to understand the world isnt full of fair breezes and helping currents. So Edgar keeps me right with news of Callum, whether I want him to or not.

But today he shouted to me, when I came in through the door after work, my clothes spattered with the pigs blood even though we do wear aprons and take off our shirts, Hey there, Hugh!

Hes waving at me from over by the card tables, which hes polishing up with some oil and a cloth. He calls, Hey! Over here and Ill tell you something.

I trudge over because thisll be a story about Callum that I dont want to hear, the story I most dont want to hear, being that hes done what he was threatening and killed himself. Edgar has a smile on him that for once looks friendly rather than gloating.

What is it? I ask. I need to go upstairs to see Ian.

Ians fine, he says. He was down here in the afternoon laying out the playing cards on the floor. Had to tell him twenty times to shift so I could scrape out the cracks in the boards.

Ian has begun to do strange things like this. One morning, when I was away, he came down and began to carry the glasses from the bar out into the street and lay them on the dusty roadway, which made people angry because of course the horses and other animals come by this way not to mention just people walking there. Nobody wants broken glass underfoot.

So Edgar says, Ians fine. Dont you worry none about him. Ive news for you.

Callum? I ask, with a dark feeling in my stomach.

Edgar shakes his head and gives a happy little laugh, glad to have something new to tell me, No, sir. Weve got someone new staying right here in The Main Street Boarding House.

So I end up in one of the other rooms Ive not been in before speaking to a man I barely know. Hes called Peter MacLean and he stayed in Craigtore for a few years when I was just young, about ten years old. Hed come from another place along the coast because he was marrying a Craigtore woman called Jane MacKenzie, Jane MacLean after that, but when a few years had dragged by hed had enough of her because, so the story goes, she would nag him day in day out and there were supposed to be one or two other things about her too that hed had enough of but they never told me about those because as I say I was only about ten or so at that time, so off he went back along the coast to Rockhill and we never saw him again. Hed be about fifty now. A thin lined face and a beard that was grey and patchy. I wouldnt have known him and he wouldnt have known me but Edgar realised there was a connection between us and thats how we ended up speaking. I didnt even know hed come to America.

The thing was he knew Craigtore people.

It was awkward at first when we spoke to each other, because there was nothing we had in common, except this one question I wanted to ask him and I had to wait until the right part of the conversation before I could say it. He wanted to tell me about all the things hed done since coming to New Scotland seven years ago which I wont write down here but he hadnt made much of a success of himself and maybe his marriage should have told him the way things would go for him. Hed been to this place and that place doing different things and I could write down what he did like a story but Im not going to because there wasnt much to it to be honest. And so hed ended up here in Chicago and he didnt have to do with the animals at all, he was a messageman for one of the newspapers they have here which is where you can get a sheet of paper that tells you about things that are happening here and in other places. I looked at one and I didnt see the point in it. It was just a thing to stop people talking to each other properly. MacLeans job was to go from one place to another passing messages from one of the people who wrote things for this newspaper to the place where the stories were all put together. Its not very interesting.

In the end it came to the point where he started speaking about other people hed been with and other folk from back at home that hed met since hed been there and my heart raced when he said that hed bumped into some Craigtore people in a little place called Waterfield that hed been in a few months ago. He said it was some older Craigtore folk he didnt really know whod just come across to here a year or two back, along with some other people. And there was a young Craigtore girl with them and this was the question Id been wondering about. And what he said hit me like the blow to the pigs skull when it hangs from the chain.

MacLean – About your age, youll remember her.

Me, although I knew this could not be so – Elizabeth Ross?

MacLean – No, Rachael Sutherland and her man.

Me – Rachael Sutherland?

Maclean – Definitely. Red hair? I remembered her from when I was in Craigtore. She was a bonny wee thing then. Good looking now too. I knew her straight away even though the years have gone into her.

Me – Her man, you said?

MacLean – The childs father.

Me – The child?

MacLean – To come. Shell maybe have had it by now. That would be, what, three months back. She was getting big with it.

Me – Married?

MacLean – No, I dont think so, but then its all different here.

Me – Where were they going?

MacLean – Out west, I think, with the others from Craigtore and elsewhere. About eight of them. They wanted to head west where the lands good. Are you going after them? Ask in Waterfield. Someone will know where they went.

Me – You dont know?

MacLean – No, sorry but I dont.

Me – Which other Craigtore people? Matthew Sinclair?

MacLean – I cant remember. James MacKay was one. There was an Alexander something. Alec they called him. Does that mean anything to you?

Me – No. Not really.

MacLean – Oh well. It was only a minute or two I was speaking to them. I never looked closely at who all was with them.

Me – And she was having a child, Rachael Sutherland?

MacLean – Shortly, she was, yes.

He didnt mean me any harm. He was a friendly man in his own way and not to blame for knowing something I didnt want to hear from him. Then he wanted me to tell him all stories about back home, people he remembered and things that had happened and it was only fair that I should tell him when hed given me the one story that he had that could fill my heart with hope and shatter it into dust at the same moment.

This place, this Chicago, is the darkest place in the world

and in my soul there is a darkness growing that will smother me. I wish Id never come here. I wish Id never met MacLean. I wish Ian was his old self.

What should I do? I can think of nothing. I cant leave Ian here and I cant see how I can move on with him unwell like this. Hanging above us like a devil is Callum and I dread to hear the next news of him. So here we stay, waiting on Donald Sutherland to tell us what to do next. Is this what we came for? To be stuck in this shrieking and dusty hell?

Ive written this down because it finishes everything.

I have finished with writing.

These are my final pages.[44]

Well, here I am writing again despite what I put down a few weeks ago. I will write down why I changed my mind, because I want to make it clear to myself. Once I have written this down, though, I *will* stop, because writing takes too much time and doesnt give me time for what I have to do. And now I know what I have to do.

For one week I stayed in our room, hardly bothering to eat, and only because Lydia took me some plates of food did I survive. She made me open my mouth to let in bread and water, and thin slices of cold meat. I swallowed as if it was ashes and dust she was forcing between my clenched teeth.

I lay in bed and never slept. Day or night made no difference

---

44 Three lines like this are scrawled across the page in the manuscript, like nothing else anywhere in Hugh's pages. The lines are scored thick into the paper as if done in anger or despair. I really think he meant never to write again. But a man like Hugh, with a past to get away from and a future to reach, is never cast down wholly, and I like the way he just carries on. – RM

to me. My mind went round and round and backwards and forwards and I couldnt understand why I was lying here in this room so far from home. It was as if I was nowhere and I couldnt bear to leave my room in case no one could see me. And that all sounds stupid now, I know, but thats how I felt, as if nothing was real, nothing Id done and nothing Id hoped for and nothing Id achieved.

Lydia brought me food and Ian sat by me and he wasnt well himself. I cant describe clearly the darkness of those days. I hope and pray they never come upon me again. It was like death and the only thing that kept me alive was fear.

It was if Id climbed one of the trees at the top of the cliff and here I was stuck at the top, nowhere higher to go and unable to scramble back down. So there I perched, stuck and useless, until one day Lydia decided it was time I got back down to the firm earth again.

Get up, she said.

I dont want to, I told her.

Look at yourself, she said. What way is this to behave?

Me – I cant help it. I dont want to do anything. Just leave me alone.

Just leave me alone, she said with a sneer in her voice. How can I do that? Its not just you. Theres Ian to think of too. What if I do leave you rotting here in your stinking bed? Whatll happen to Ian then?

I realised Ian was standing there behind her, looking down at me with a worried look on his old face, his hand up at his forehead. He smiled at me a little, a thin smile, when my eyes caught his.

Lydia said, Are you going to leave Ian to look after himself, or are you going to get up and do what youre supposed to do?

Supposed to do? I asked.

When you came over here, she said, you took Ian with you.

He took us, I said.

286

Dont be ridiculous, she snapped. Look at the age of him. Look at the age of you. Youre behaving like a child.

As I said before, Lydia is only about eighteen years old herself, or maybe a bit more, and what she said made me push myself up into a sitting position for the first time in a week and that was the start of it. She shamed me into becoming my own self again. There is something about Lydia, a strength and a sort of anger that makes you pay attention. Sit up and pay attention, as that teacher back in Croval said to us many years ago.

So what she said there was the start of it and I did do what she said. The more I thought about her words the more I realised that Ian wasnt able to look after himself and that now that Callum and Robert were away it fell to me to do that job. I began to understand that it was a job I wanted and one that I welcomed. It was for him and it was also for me. The more I thought about that the better I began to feel and some of the darkness began to lift the way the sea looks clearer as the clouds burn from the sky on an October morning.

I cant explain this part of it very well either, but I began to feel different. In those books that Ian used to read to us, there would be descriptions of what was going on inside a person, their thoughts and their happy or sad feelings, and this would go on for pages and pages, and here I am and I cant even write down properly how I went from just going along normally until I was down in the dark pit of despair and then how I came back out and joined the world again as if I belonged. It is beyond me, and those books were lies, because it cannot be described.

So let me just put down here that I woke up from a black dream and I rose from my bed and I went out into the streets of Chicago and there I found my direction, when days before I had none.

I turned my attention to Ian. The way Id been in the past week had scared him and he didnt know what to do. He clutched his Bible to his chest and stared out of the window. Murdoch

Larkin had told him wed be out on the street if I didnt go back to work, earn some money and pay the rent. When I looked properly at Ian for the first time in a long time, he seemed to me to be thin and weak, as if hed faded as Id drawn away from life.

I took him out into Chicago and I worked hard to build his strength. We walked and walked, a little bit the first day, then further and further, building up our pace, striding out amongst those noisy Chicago roads. Wherever I could, I would get him to stop and talk to people we came across – a man fixing the harness of a horse pulling a cart load of beer, a woman with a tray of biscuits for sale, a teacher leading a group of untidy children towards their classroom. I was thinking that the more he talked, the more he walked, the more he would return to being that strong and clever man we knew at the manse in Croval.

And the stronger Ian became, the more his mind would return to what it was. The further he can return to what he was the more he can help me, especially by listening. Now that Robert has been left behind and Callum has staggered away from us, and now that Rachael has become someone that I can no longer think about, there is only Ian who can listen to me. So if I one day can turn him back into the man that he once was, then one day I can sit with him and talk about all I feel, and all Ive done and all Ive seen. I can tell him about my mother left behind, about a girl Ive followed foolishly across the world, about a stone that struck rock and earth and flesh. Because if I cant tell Ian all that then there is no one I can tell.[45]

Once there was a road I could see, stretching from the moment into the future. I never knew what would be at the end of it, but I could see where it curved away into the distance, and I liked walking on it. But in the months and years that have gone by Ive lost track of that road, and the leaves and dust have blown over it and the grass and weeds have taken root so that

45 He can tell us. – RM

I can barely see the outline just of where it used to be.

So now Im working again and Im using the money for food and Im making Ian eat meat and drink good wine again, so that I can clear a path through those weeds and place my feet on the road once again.

The more I thought about this, the more I saw that cutting pigs was not my life. In the evenings, then, after Id finished my work and Id seen that Ian was all right and had eaten well, and after wed been out and walked for a while, building up his strength, I went off to find new work.

There was an excitement in me as I did that. At last I was taking things into my own hands, not just letting the currents in the ocean drag me on, or push me back or trap me in a whirlpool. It was new to me and I didnt really know how Id come to this more happy and forward-looking state of mind when only days before I could only lie there with the taste of the pillow in my mouth, scared to open my eyes.

I walked for miles, and into bits of Chicago Id never even seen before, places where dangerous looking men came rushing out from saloons, fighting each other with knives and bottles. They had no ideas for a lost lad from Scotland, and I turned away and walked on. I tried boarding houses and stables. I knocked on the doors of stores and saloons. I spoke to owners of newspapers and seed-crop companies. They turned me away. They told me to come back tomorrow, when the boss would be there. They told me theyd bear me in mind if a place came up. They told me there would be a job in a few weeks time because the business was growing.

So many businesses are growing in Chicago in these new days that there must be coming a time when there is more money here than anywhere in the world.

Late at night, with the moon hazy in the smoke-filled sky and the cries of animals and machines and drunken men and women filling my ears like the salt sea when you dive deep, Id stumble back to The Main Street Boarding House & General Emporium, and Id have a quick drink at the bar and then Id talk to Ian for an hour or two before falling into sleep and then waking up to spend another awful day with the hogs.

I swear I have never been so tired but what kept me going was the thought that all I did served some purpose, working for money, spending to live, living to help Ian, helping Ian to save myself, in the end. And every night I trudged from door to door, my knuckles raw with hope.

One night I met a man standing outside a building counting out some notes that he held in his hand in a fat roll. I didnt know what the building was and I didnt ask him. But a man with a roll of money in his hand is a man who might be able to help, I was thinking.

Good evening, I said, as polite as I could be.

Good evening, he said, quickly pushing the money down into the pocket of his coat and taking off the tall hat he was wearing.

I was wondering, I said, and then my words ran out.

Yes? he asked, sternly.

I just thought, I said, but again my words dried up. The roll of money had scared me as well as drawing me in.

Speak up, boy, he said. If you have come here to rob me you will have to fight me for my money. You are younger and stronger, I can see that, and I have no weapon and you probably do. But I will take my chances to protect my property, despite my age.

I looked closer at him and saw that he was a much older man than Id taken him for in the first place. He had a grand moustache, grey in colour, and though tall, he was past the time of life when men are at their strongest. Maybe fifty years old, I thought. He looked like a nice man, with lines round his eyes that show where he laughs. I took a deep breath and spoke.

I want work, I said. I already have work but I would like something more. Id like something better.

It sounds rude, but those were the words that came out. It worked, because the words made him turn his head and consider me a bit more closely. With an expression of curiosity, he turned to me and held out his hand.

Michael McDonagh, he said. I wonder if I might have something that will interest a young man like yourself.

I will do any work, I told him.

I may be on the watch for someone such as you, he said. Tell me why I should give you work?

Because Ill work hard for you. Because Ill follow you along this street until you do.

He smiled at me. He said, Very well. Come with me.

So that was me working for Michael McDonagh for a week or two. He wasnt quite the man Id thought. He rented out buildings, sometimes just wee rooms in buildings, to people whod come to Chicago for work and the job he wanted me for was to go round collecting this rent money from people. This is not the place to write about McDonagh and the way he made his money, the rooms with no water and no place to cook food, the cracked windows and the rotting floorboards. I worked for him for a couple of weeks and then, with some good money in my pocket I left and did some other jobs. Id had enough of McDonagh when he asked me to use my fists to get payment out of an old Irishman who couldnt work because hed fallen and broken his hip. I wouldnt do that and McDonagh just shrugged when I told him, paid me my wages and told me to go. He said hed find someone happy to do it, and I could spend my life regretting the money Id turned down with my high morals.

But I dont regret it. Now Im doing things I want to do, not what other people want me to do. And theres another job[46]

_____

46 We never find out what work this is, but it must have been a good job, as we find out in the next section that Hugh and Ian stayed in Chicago for some time. Alternatively, he may have held several consecutive posts. Either way, he managed to put enough money aside

waiting for me, so Im not worrying about money any more.

Something else happened about that time that I should write down here because to me, at the time, it felt like another way I was moving on and breaking away from things that had maybe not helped me all that much in the past.

One evening, not all that long after I started working for McDonagh, I was going up the stairs to our room when Lydia caught me by the arm. Shed been waiting for me on the landing outside her own room.

I want to speak to you, she said.

I could see that she was upset about something, but even so, I said, I have to look to see that Ian is all right.

Ive just been with him, she said. Hes fine. Five minutes, thats all.

I went with her into her room. Its quite nice, the room, with red material at the windows and nice furniture and it smells of her perfume, the smell of Lydia. You have to not think about what happens in there though. Its not like any other room Ive ever been in and it makes me feel nervous, but I like it too because its soft and warm.

She sat on the bed and touched at her eyes with the cuff of her dress. For quite a wee while she never said anything, but then she told me that a man that had been with her earlier on in the evening had hit her and sure enough I could see there was a red mark coming at her cheekbone, and also maybe some bruising at her throat.

I dont like this life, she said. I wish there was something more.

I sat beside her on the bed and, building up my strength, I laid my hand on her shoulder and said, Maybe there is something more.

Lydia – What?

---

in the following years to make his eventual escape from "Porkopolis" as it was apparently nicknamed at the time. – RM

Me – I dont know, but I think there must be something more. I didnt think that a week or two ago. You know that. But now Im seeing things differently. You have to decide things for yourself, instead of waiting for them to happen.

I tapped my flat hand on her shoulder to give my words more strength. She stood up and went to the window, pulling the drapes together. The red colour seemed to fill the room and I could hardly take my eyes off it. Her dress was red too, low at the front as usual, her young skin disguised in the rich material.

I hate all this, she said and waved her hand wildly round to take in the whole room, the red drapes, the blanketed bed, me, herself.

Maybe you could move on, I said.

Lydia – Where to? Where would I go? I was born here and this is where Ill end up. But I cant do this for ever. Men dont like it when youre older. Maggie stopped and shes just twenty five.

Me – I was once somewhere and I thought Id be there all the time. Then something happened and also I met someone that showed me how to move on.

Lydia – Ian?

Me – Thats right. He opened up the world for us and thats what I owe him.

Lydia – What was the thing that happened?

I knew that Lydia was not the person I could tell the story to, even though I liked her fine enough, so I said nothing.

What I did say was this – Maybe you could come away with us?

She took a step towards me, the crying forgotten for a minute. She frowned.

Lydia – Where are you going?

Me – I dont know. Somewhere. Well see. But away from this place.

Lydia – And youd want me to go with you?

Me – Why not?

The truth is I suddenly saw that I could ask someone to come with us if I wanted to. It didnt need someone else to decide who was in our group and who wasnt and now that our group was down to two, and now that Ian wasnt going to be making a lot of choices about who did what, well, that all meant it was up to me. Just saying it to her made me feel like Ian, sitting up in the manse, waving MacDougall in the air and pointing at the future.

She sat by me on the bed and looked into my eyes, close enough for me to feel the heat off her body and to see the moisture on her teeth where she was biting her lip. Only Rachael had ever sat closer to me with this kind of feeling in the air. And Rachael was away with her man, the father of the child.

I said it again, Why not? Then I reached up and touched her cheek with my fingers and when she didnt pull away I kissed her.

Lydia – If I came with you, I could be useful. Im able to do more than all this.

Me – I know.

I didnt really know anything about her at all, of course, but I didnt want to be talking any more, not just then. We lay down side by side on the bed, just a young man and a younger woman, and all the other things, collecting scraped rents for McDonagh, and the man whod struck her earlier on, and the singing from the saloon below us, and the old man in the next room waiting for me to come in, none of these things mattered at all. All that mattered were my fingertips touching her skin and her fingertips touching mine.

It was different from that other time, with Rachael at Goderich. Lydia could do things that Rachael couldnt do. Maybe she can do them now, I suppose, but I dont like to think about that. We lay for a while afterwards and talked gently about how the future might be better than the past and the present. All the time, I was thinking about Rachael. Lydia hadnt pushed her out of my mind, not for more than a few minutes, but what a good few minutes they were.

294

But a person can grow into your mind bit by bit, not all at once. The truth is when I was maybe thirteen, I liked Elizabeth before I liked Rachael, the same as Robert and Callum did. But gradually my thoughts turned to Rachael. Maybe, a wee bit at a time, Lydia could push Rachael gently from my mind, I was thinking. Lydias hair is dark and her skin is browner than Rachaels. Her fingers are shorter but have a soft touch in them. Her voice is harsher and she speaks more than Rachael. Rachael always watched, but Lydia doesnt hesitate.

Who knows what the world will throw up? Thats what I was thinking. On the beach at Croval one morning you might find a lobster creel, broken loose from its mooring. On the next morning you might find a branch from some distant forest. You never know what to expect. Sometimes theres nothing but youll never find anything if you dont go and have a look.

I kissed Lydia one more time as she slept and went through to Ian, and he was sleeping too.

So what I was deciding was that it was time to move on again, even though there was a voice in the back of my mind telling me that moving on, moving on could take you right round the world from east to west until you came back to Croval and the old men in the Carcair would look at you as you came in through the door and say, Weve not seen you for a while, have you been away?

But Im understanding it better now, the way standing still is only ever any good if youre standing somewhere you want to be. Its an obvious idea and Im sure everyone would agree with me. But I know that most people, while they were nodding their heads and saying Aye, youre right enough, theyd be standing in a midden gradually sinking into it until the shit was up past their knees, then their waist and then to their chins and up over their head so that you couldnt hear them any more.[47]

---

47 Notice that there is no apology for the profanity in this sentence. Another sign of Hugh growing up? – RM

Heres what I was thinking, the exact thoughts. Id been like a log on the Middle River, drifting along wherever the current would take me. Every now and then Id say to myself, or to someone else, that it was time to change direction. But a log in a river cant turn round and go back upstream, even if it wants to. So thats what I decided. The time for being the dead trunk of a tree was over, thats what I decided. When I was younger, I let others shape my life, and that includes Ian when we were just young and he was the new minister at the manse. Now its time to put that way of living aside. Now that I am older it is time to think like a grown man. I have no children, but its time for me to behave like a parent instead of a child.

And when these thoughts came to me, I realised that to be a father was what I wanted really. I dont think for a moment, or even for a tiny part of a moment, that this has anything to do with Lydia. And I know now that its nothing to do with Rachael, that thought is past. But really I never actually had that thought. My idea of being with Rachael only had to do with myself. What Im understanding now is that it all only makes sense if I start to think beyond myself. Thats what I mean by being a father.

Ian was father to me and Robert and Callum, in a way, and in a way he still is. Now the time has come for me to be a father to Ian, whether he wants that, or knows about it, or not.

So thats what Ill do. And this time I mean it. There will be no more of this writing, because that belongs to the past, the time when I only thought of myself. Now its time to put aside childish things.

Intertitle 5

But of course there *are* more words, despite his promise made in the wake of hearing that awful news of Rachael's pregnancy and once again at the end of the "Chicago" section. In the end he could not resist the temptation to record, though as you'll see there is an incompleteness in the remainder of his manuscript. If he *had* stopped writing after the moment in "Chicago" when he seems to want to grind to a halt, the text would still have been interesting, but I am so glad he changed his mind. It would have been a shame if we had been left with the sense that we could have found out more. Though in reality, I suppose, we are left with that sense in any case, but more of that later. My main feeling for Hugh with regard to his decision to continue with his tale is admiration, given that the next section, "Rocky Bend" contains an event which might have killed his new found optimism stone dead. I do not want to give anything away but there is another hard blow to come. Life is full of them.

Suddenly the style of the text changes and the reason for this quickly becomes obvious. We are no longer reading a diary, if diary is the right word for something maintained so sporadically over the years. Now we are reading reminiscences, penned long after the events described, so he did indeed give up writing for many years. While Hugh the *character* in the next section is still in his twenties, Hugh the *writer* is in his mid-thirties and for the first time there is some distance between the writer, the narrator and the things that happened.

Of course this gap allows for a couple of possibilities. Firstly, we perhaps see a certain amount of fictionalisation, since it seems inevitable that Hugh's memory of what took place nearly a decade ago would be less than perfect. Secondly, I think we can pick up a softening of the narrator's reactions, the way a rock is smoothed round by the constant action of water and time. "Chicago" reveals a tortured soul, crying out as the psychological wounds are cut at that very moment, so that the depression and the excitement seem equally fevered and fragile. Here, though, we have the voice of someone whose wounds have scarred over, to a certain extent (and Hugh deals with this concept explicitly in the opening paragraphs of the section).

But what is lost in immediacy is gained in reflection, to my eyes. Here we are in touch with a more mature and possibly more adult and thoughtful man, less concerned with day-to-day anxieties and more interested in overall shapes and patterns. The writing is less fraught, I think, and this is probably a good thing. I don't think the intensity of the "Chicago" section could have been maintained in any case. There comes a time when you can look back with a certain calm on events which tore you apart at the time. I've found the same thing with myself. Trying to find explanations becomes a hobby rather than a reflex as urgent as the drawing of breath.

So what is this section about? I think it is a key one in understanding the character of Hugh, because here we see him actively engaged in setting up a business in partnership with someone else. It is this section, I believe, which justifies my reading of the text as the tale of an early entrepreneur, rather than the story of someone wandering fairly aimlessly across the disinterested world. Here we see Hugh taking control and actively trying to achieve financial success. And in doing so he speaks directly to us in the twenty-first century, where this urge for success is sometimes seen as something dirty, something to be held in contempt. This tale proves it is a natural instinct, the desire to leave your mark on the world while establishing enough wealth to make you, and yours, comfortable. What could be more human, more normal? Hugh's tale is one that belongs in all generations, one that he, and we, should be proud of, a tale to be told to our children, if we have access to them.

Entrepreneur: someone who takes openings. Someone who sees a door that might be just slightly ajar and confidently pushes through. It is a spirit, a quality, and not one that only has to do with money-making. It is easy to stand in a hall of doors and only notice the ones which are firmly shut, locked and bolted. I have stood in that hall long enough, and Hugh has helped me to see how to watch for that tiniest sliver of light that indicates a handle might be turned, that escape might be possible. This story of an ancestor has shown me that just when you think the world has you trapped, you can find an escape route. Hugh wrote himself out of his trap, in some ways, and I have read myself out. Or I am reading myself out – that might be more accurate.

What I mean is that in this section, more than in any of the others, I began to feel a proper closeness with Hugh. When I first read the pages this was the section that connected most strongly with me and made me see my own tale as part of a long line of tales, a modern-day folk history, which tells not of magic and ghosts and deep dark woods and beady-eyed crows, but of ideas and investment and financial return, and of personal risks taken. I am so pleased to have found this book. So pleased to have found Hugh Ross, though I should have every reason to be angry at him!

I don't think I'm giving anything away when I say that Hugh's business described in "Rocky Bend" ended up unsuccessful. But that is in the nature of business, isn't it? What went wrong with the enterprise was their failure to spot business trends in time to adapt what they were doing (you can read the details for yourself). We all make mistakes like this and Hugh's reiterated 'We did not listen' tolls a gloomy bell in my mind.

My bookshop failed, along with many other things. For a long time my life became unpleasant, and I began to wonder if there was ever to be the kind of life I'd imagined when I was younger. When I lost my husband and my children, and my dream of a family life here in this ancestral house dwindled like a ribbon of smoke in the breeze, I literally could not understand what had happened. The next phase was to work out who to blame. I needed there to be someone whose fault it was that I was on my own. There were certainly candidates, including myself, and my mind went round them obsessively – but nothing was gained, nothing improved by each assignation of guilt, each murderous fantasy.

Well, there is violence too in Hugh's "Rocky Bend" section, though there it does not permeate the whole chapter, as it does in "Chicago". Instead the one key moment of violence becomes a sort of thematic centre to the section, especially when you consider Hugh's reflections on the reasons for it. I must not reveal too much here, but it does seem to me that the question he asks about the actions of Sutherland cut to the heart of humanity: how much of what we do is aimed at benefiting others and how much is pure selfishness? Is there altruism? Is there the possibility of goodness growing from darkness?

It may be that Sutherland is not the most likeable character in Hugh's pages, but where would Hugh have ended up without him? He helped. Maybe he did his best. What else can you do? That point has not always been grasped, but I grasp it now.

We definitely see a strained relationship in Hugh's association with Sutherland. These are two men engaged in a mutually beneficial union, each unable to see, really, what the other has to offer. We, as readers, can empathise.

They made mistakes, and we'll see from the "Big Creek" section that one thing Hugh learned was the importance of entering into agreements that can be relied upon. Sutherland never quite treated Hugh as an equal partner, that much is clear, and there is a lesson here for any budding entrepreneur.

I can see that now, sitting alone in Elgin. I put that clearer vision down to Hugh and his book.

Whatever has gone wrong, at least I did find Hugh, up in

the roof space. I mustn't dwell on my own circumstances, but I am grateful to him for seeing me through this difficult time with his life story. He made errors; so did I. He hit rock bottom; so did I. He recaptured control in his life and this is what I must do. I don't think I really understood success until I read these pages. Success means standing face-to-face with failure and shouldering it out of the way and marching on. Hugh taught me that, more than any novel ever could. He gives me hope, and helps me make sense of my life. I felt, that cold November night, that Hugh was speaking directly to me, as if he had been writing for me, specifically, advising me about forgiveness. He shows me that you have to forgive someone you like. I am Hugh's half-imagined audience: he gives me meaning and I give him it back, in the form of a kind of time-displaced love, I think.

It is an honour to share it with you.

Incidentally, historical meteorological records show that Hugh's reference to a very hard winter places us in 1849.

Rocky Bend

I know now where it was that I was going wrong. I've[48] read more now. There are books here[49] in a library that has built up as officers have come and gone, leaving their belongings behind them. I have had time on my hands now and I have read quite a lot in the past few months.

What I've found is that writers never write in the fury of their emotions but instead wait until calmness has come upon them and then they set it all down. I have read an English poet who says that what a writer has to do is wait until he is *tranquil* and then to think about whatever happened until the emotions of the time come back to life, but only as a kind of shadow or image of what he felt in the original situation. Otherwise, the emotion is too much and he has no control.

And, of course, apart from poets, nobody writes what is true. Instead, everything is stories and falsehood.

So there are two mistakes in what I used to write, more than ten years ago, when I was in Chicago, and Goderich, and on the Lady Gray and in Croval. First, it was all true. Second, I could hardly see, sometimes, for the emotions that blurred my eyes when I picked up my pen. I know I set down that I would never write again, and at the time I meant that with a passion that was consuming me like fire, and indeed I never wrote a thing until this hour.[50]

---

48 Note the punctuation. Maybe Hugh intended to make alterations to the punctuation of his earlier pages but we can't be sure. As I mentioned earlier, it does appear that other changes have been made to the Croval section of the narrative. Whatever else he discovered on his voyage through the New World, we can be certain about one thing: he at least discovered the apostrophe! – RM

49 More about this later – RM

50 This is not strictly true, as we will see. I can only assume that

But I am older now, and I have achieved a kind of peace, and perhaps now is the time to look back on things that happened to me. Gone are the feelings of falling behind with my writing, the guilt of missing out bits of the story, the sense that I wasn't saying all that I wanted to say. Now I am calmer and I realise that no story can be told completely, so there's no reason to be worrying about it.

My decision to return to my pen and paper, I have to admit, is partly due to the dullness of my life here, where days can pass with little of importance happening and you find your mind is in need of a diversion. Maybe it's just that I am old enough now[51] to *understand* a little more. And of course the thing that happened here a few days ago is enough to make anyone think about this world and what happens in it. Enough to make you sit and write it down, to use your pen to think about the meaning of it all, at any rate. The despair I felt in Chicago is nothing when set beside the fear I felt a few days ago, a fear that world was turning upside down and that all my hopes had come to nothing, and that all my journeying was like an empty net pulled from the sea.

When I read back over my pages, however, I see that I must at least begin to account for the years that have fallen in between then and now. I don't believe I have the energy or the desire to try to describe *everything,* because not everything is interesting, and not everything can be remembered. Now, in my *tranquillity,* I must sort out the important from the trivial, something I admit I had no skill with as a boy of eighteen or twenty-two. But how could I have known? This is the whole point.

Now I see, though, that I must begin by writing about a

Hugh at this moment had forgotten about his scribbled notes or else he deliberately means to deceive us. – RM

51 Thirty-four years old, as he points out himself in this section. Not so old at all. – RM

phase of my journeys that happened at Rocky Bend, that town that was not a town, and about our plans that had no shape, and about what became of Ian Macleod.

Why it took us three years to move from Chicago I find hard to explain even now. My good intentions grew thin and starved away. I would like to think that I did not move because I was looking out for Callum, but, if truth be told, we hardly ever even saw him after he came to insult us that day, and after a time we never saw him at all. I worried about what had become of him. I imagined that he might be dead. Certainly he had talked about killing himself and we knew that he got into fights and scuffles almost every day. It would have been no surprise to us if we had received news that Callum had ended his journey with a knife in under his ribs at the back of some saloon near the river. I always hoped that he was still alive and that one day I would see him again and that all our falling out could be forgotten and forgiven and that we could be friends again. But that was a long time ago and much has happened since. More about that in the proper place.

So why did we not leave Chicago? I think it was a lack of push, despite the fine words I wrote there about earning enough to drive on. I found I could not drive us on. I never gave up but there seemed nothing worth pursuing that was worth the energy of starting off again, when we were comfortable enough in the great city. It would have been too hard. I had a few jobs I worked at and we were not short. There were things there that I liked, though I shall not go into detail. And Ian was no worse, no better. Why move him on if that would risk his health? I had a hundred excuses, each one aimed at my own heart.

When I worked in the factory the mood of the place entered into me so that I could do no more than stagger from my bed and stagger back into it. Everything else was a dream, my work carried out in the daze you feel when you drink too much of the coffee they sell there, as if the people and pigs and knives and blood weren't real somehow. I couldn't tell where I stopped and they started. My fingers felt as if they were swollen to a hundred times their normal size and my soul was shrunk to a withered leaf. I'm glad I never wrote it all down.

When I moved on, my mind was full of plans but plans have a way of slipping away with tiredness, a fuller belly and a glass of beer. So even though I felt better, nothing happened. There is nothing much more to tell, except perhaps about Lydia, and that I will not do, as it not right to put such things on paper, not when you have had time to think about them, and to think that it might not be best, or fair, to repeat the events in ink.

But, after three years, move we did. And it was Donald Sutherland that moved us, coming to me with an idea he couldn't hawk to anyone else. By this time he had well and truly given up on Callum, last seen in a street brawl with a woman old enough to be his mother, dirt and grease in his yellow hair and foulness on his tongue. He had to be left behind, even by Donald Sutherland, not known for his morals.

In short, this was Sutherland's idea. As he'd said before and had carried on saying for three years, all the animals in America were coming to Chicago, or so it seemed. Men drove steers and hogs from south and west along routes that finished in barrels full of meat on the riverside in the filthy city. Sutherland said that all along these droving routes wee towns were springing up, places where the herds could stop to overnight and the men could tie up their horses and have a drink and a feed and a mattress under their bones instead of the stones of the land. He'd been along several of these trails, he told us, working out how to make money.

He told us that he'd realised something that would let us make our fortunes. At that time most of the beef came from the south but as more and more people headed west to the land out there a lot of drovers were coming from that direction too. Of course I had no idea then if what he was telling me was true or not, but there was nothing in me that wanted to question it. I was ready at last to see the back of Chicago.

Sutherland explained that there was a new trail growing that came from Iowa and even from the land beyond that, though farming there was dangerous as the native people wanted to push us all back to the sea and who could blame them? Sutherland had worked out that the best route to drive cattle from Iowa to Chicago was slightly northwards and then back south again into the city, because that way the great herds, sometimes numbering thousands of steers, would not come into contact with the drovers from the south, who were known sometimes to steal cows as they drove. So the best route was a curving one that led from the heart of Iowa – which at that time, of course, I'd never seen – up towards a place called Sturgis Falls and then over east to cross the Mississippi River at a place called Dubuque, where the cattle would be swum across the water. All these names of places meant nothing to me or Ian.

As I say Ian was much the same three years after I stopped writing in Chicago as he had been when I was filling in my journal. He wasn't sickening and he wasn't recovering. He had nothing much to say about Sutherland's proposals but then neither did I. If anything he was calmer, as if more accepting of his own forgetfulness and his tendency to wander away at any moment. Or maybe it was me that was more accepting of it, maybe it was me that was calmer, though calmness is not the same as contentedness, and that's why both of us listened to Sutherland. To a starving man a crust of bread can seem a banquet.

Sutherland had picked out a place called Rocky Bend, which lay along the line of this cattle route from Iowa to Chicago. He told us all about it and shortly I too will describe it. The main thing about it, he said, was that it was set in a narrow canyon, so the herds could not possibly pass it by, it had water from three natural springs and a narrow river called Red Bluff River and it was more or less a day's drive away from Dubuque, so the cattlemen would want to rest up there for a night before moving on to the Mississippi crossing. At the time he spoke to us, Sutherland told us, there was nothing at Rocky Bend but a couple of shacks belonging to farmers trying to grow a bit of wheat in dirt that didn't want to help them much.

What Rocky Bend needed was a town, with houses, a saloon, a hotel, a stables, a general store and everything else that the cow drovers could possibly want. This was Donald Sutherland's dream – to make Rocky Bend into a town instead of just a place. He told us how Sturgis Falls was called after a man called William Sturgis who had put the town there in the first place. Sutherland flattered me by saying that one day Rocky Bend would be known as Sutherland Ross City, though from the way he described it even I could see it would be hard to fit a city into the space between the canyon walls he'd told us about.

But who wouldn't want that?[52]

He told us he wanted us to work with him in this project. I don't imagine for a minute that he really wanted Ian along with him but he was wise enough to realise that he wouldn't have me if he didn't have Ian too. Not that wisdom is a word that you would normally link with Donald Sutherland.

Why did he want me? I should have asked that question a bit more often in my head before agreeing to go with him, I think. I think *now*, that is. At that time I was too taken with the notion of getting away, of letting go of my sharp knife at long last, of not hearing those screaming hogs in my dreams.

---

52 The entrepreneur! While in Chicago Hugh stagnated, but what businessman hasn't had a spell such as that? I know I'm in one of those spells at this very time, waiting for the sparkle of business success to blind my eyes again. To read how Hugh's heart was coming back to him is uplifting indeed. It is as if his heart comes back to me. My own will follow. – RM

Donald Sutherland told me that he couldn't do without me, how he needed to have someone he could trust to back him up in his plans, how he felt he had to work with someone that he knew from before, how the Scots are better than the Americans, how he needed a manager for the bunkhouse that he had in mind for Rocky Bend. How he knew that between us we could make our fortunes.

Of course the real reason he came to me with such stories was because he couldn't find anyone else who would trust *him* enough to go in with his plan, and because he knew I'd a little bit of money put aside from the last three years. But, anyway, America is a country full of schemes and plans and quite often you hear of people going off to follow some dream or other, all by themselves. Usually these stories end up with that someone coming home with their head bowed and their pockets empty, or else with a scalped corpse in a ditch beside a log cabin that no children ever laughed in.

We never talked about Ian's role because neither of us could imagine what it could be. That evening, though, after Donald Sutherland had left, saying he'd be back the next day, Ian, who'd said nothing at all much during the conversation, said to me –

Every town must have a church.

I said, What do you mean?

And every church must have a minister, he said.

I said, You're right. This is what you've been wanting, isn't it? This is your good chance.

Every man, he said, needs but one good chance.

There was a glow in his eyes that I hadn't seen for a long time. He smiled his old smile.

I said, It's been a long journey but maybe we're getting towards somewhere at last.

Maybe we are, he said. I think that we maybe are.

It took a bit of time and a lot of talking and some of my well saved money to get us out of the transporting job I was in then[53] and out of the grasp of Murdoch Larkin, who said we owed him two months advance rent for our room. But out we got.

I could write about the journey that we made, on horseback, which I wasn't used to and which hurt me like anything, but I think there is enough in my pages about travelling. Maybe nobody will read all this except maybe myself when I am older. I'd like to think someone else will and I can only hope for that. We had a cart with us in which we had some things we thought would be useful to us, such as nails, a big heavy hammer and some beer.

I could write about what we found when we got to Rocky Bend, a good name for the place which was just a rocky bend in this canyon. Red Bluff River was nothing much more than a trickle at this time of year, which was April after a dry spell. Easter had come and gone and Ian had prayed over our prospects. But there wouldn't be much to write. Donald Sutherland had said there were a couple of farmers there, or homesteaders as they were called, not a word we had back in Croval. But when we arrived on our tired horses we found both of them in the process of packing up to leave. They were two old Danish brothers who had staked out this bit of country, a bit of land on either side of the river. Each of them had all their possessions in a covered wagon pulled by a scrawny horse and these two horses were also brothers the Danish men told us. We tried to talk to them about Rocky Bend and what we should know about it but they didn't want to talk and they headed off east the day after we arrived. They weren't very happy men and that should have told us something.

Sutherland had a wooden board he'd made with *Rocky Bend*

---

53 Hugh never makes any further reference to this job, so we will never know what it was. Never mind. It is just a lay-by on the road to Hugh's future. – RM

City painted on it and he nailed this to a post and hammered it into the ground. We took over the farmhouse on the south side of the Red Bluff River and that was where we stayed in those early weeks. We worked on the other one, on the north side, because it was on the north side that we were going to start building Rocky Bend City itself. The flat land spread for only about half a mile on either side of the river until it came to the canyon walls, so a city it was never really going to be. Such a little fact never held back Donald Sutherland.

We patched up the old farmhouse with some wood that we'd taken with us on the cart and also using wood from a barn on the south side that we wouldn't be needing any more and that we took to pieces. It was more of a shed than a barn and the wood didn't go far. This first building we worked on was going to be the Rocky Bend Bunkhouse and we divided up the rooms inside to make individual little sleeping areas because, Sutherland said, there's nothing a cow driver likes better than a bit of privacy after weeks in the saddle. And we extended it too, because it wasn't big enough for all the trade that we were going to be getting.

Sutherland took the cart backwards and forwards to Dubuque for supplies. We got things going. I'm not going to write about this too much because I don't want to. One thing I've learnt from all the books I've been reading is that they are as much about what is left out as what is put in, so I am leaving plenty out.

I had some money, but Donald Sutherland had more. Where he got it I'm not very sure but there were always rumours about him in Chicago. He would be keeping a brothel, or making money from gambling houses or selling captured Indians as servants or something or other. I did ask him a couple of times about his money and he just winked at me, a cunning expression on his sharp little face. He wasn't a man for telling.

It wasn't just the three of us. There was enough of that

money so that Sutherland could pay men to come out and help us build. We cut some trees that were growing up near the canyon walls near the three springs to help with building materials and pretty soon we had the bunkhouse and right next door to it we'd put up a saloon and then there was a general store and the stables for the cowherds' horses. We built big pens a bit like the ones we'd seen in Chicago and these would be for the cattle when they came later in the year once they'd been fattened up on the grass land away to the west. Ian wanted there to be a church but Sutherland wouldn't hear of it. He said why would the men that came with the steers be wanting a church? I tried to persuade him because I knew how important it was to Ian to have his own place to preach in, even if he did sometimes forget that this was what he really wanted. But Sutherland wouldn't even think about the possibility and as it was his place and mostly his money we couldn't do anything about it and this made Ian sad sometimes. I was the manager of the bunkhouse and Sutherland himself took charge of the saloon. He hired a young lad called Ferdinand Braddle, a shy Dubuque boy of sixteen years, to look after the stables. He got a little pay and he stayed in the bunkhouse free of charge, never causing any bother and hardly exchanging two words with anyone, especially at first. As for the general store, which Sutherland called *The Red Bluff Emporium,* it was meant to be looked after by Ian, but it was obvious he wouldn't be able to do it, pushing up around seventy years old with his mind not running as straight as the river.

So a woman from Dubuque came, Laura Lynton. She was about fifty and had her hair tied up on the back of her head in a bun. Only once did I see it down: when I surprised her in the back room of the store, not knowing she was in there, and she was brushing it out. It came to down past her waist, as white as snow. She'd been a homesteader further west, but her husband had been killed by the Indians and she'd gone back to Dubuque.

To be honest I don't think she knew what to be doing with her life any more. I don't know how Sutherland persuaded her to come, but come she did and she made a good job of stocking up *The Red Bluff Emporium* because she had a sharp eye for what people needed and also for what people might buy that went a wee bit beyond what they *needed* and into what they just *wanted*. She kept herself to herself and I never saw her touch an alcoholic drink in the saloon in all the time she was there. She had strong hands and I sometimes imagined her standing outside a log cabin off to the west, looking out towards where the sun was setting and waiting for her husband to come back, but he never did.

It was funny to think of. She'd wandered out there to find some new life and here she was in Rocky Bend. She'd gone west then back east to Dubuque and then back west to Rocky Bend. It was as if she was caught in a current that wouldn't let her go. Between Croval and Craigtore, right in close by the rocks, there was[54] a funny current that you had to be careful of. If you rowed in too close this current would fairly grab you and drag you down towards Craigtore for about a hundred yards and then it swung round and dragged you back up towards Croval again, no matter how hard you rowed. Then it would slide you back into the same bit of water you were in before and the next thing you knew you'd be slipping back to Craigtore again. It was really hard to get out of and you had to know the timing of it, that you had to row hard just as you reached the Craigtore end of the swirl and then you might get out. Sometimes it took two or three tries before you did it right and you were free.

It's funny to think that this current is still there, it must be. And it must have been there for hundreds of years, thousands,

---

54 This should be "is" but "was" is the word Hugh wrote. The shift to past tense reveals a lot about Hugh's feelings of separation at the moment he wrote down these words. – RM

before ever me and Callum and Robert got caught up in it for the first time and we were there for hours until Finlay Murray came by in his boat and threw us a rope and he was able to haul us out, strong arms that he had.

But Laura Lynton was like this, unable to break free from this east west east west. I remember wondering if she'd be wandering for evermore and also if I would be. What is it that drives us on, that pulls us into places we've never seen, chasing something that we probably cannot have?

You go backwards and forwards in your mind, in your life. One minute you're busy as you can be, hammering in a nail, or digging a hole for a fencepost and then the next moment your ideas are back inside something that happened a very long time ago.

So now one of the chief things on my mind was when, at long last, I was going to talk to Ian about Mary Vass and what happened to her and how I still felt about my part in that.

Sutherland's next job was to head west himself, out into the grazing land of Iowa to meet the ranchers who would be driving cattle to Chicago, persuading them that the Rocky Bend route was the best way for their herds to go. He went armed with money and a pistol he'd bought in Dubuque because there were still Indians in that area that hadn't got used to all these white people and all these long horned cattle. They were used to buffalo but a lot of them had been shot and the Indians would sometimes attack a herd of cows on the move, we'd been told, and take a few steers, kill a man or two. And they'd be quite happy to meet a man with a wee bag of money travelling by himself. So that's what the pistol was for and the money was to tempt the ranchers. Sutherland's plan was to spend money to make money. He called it *an inducement* that he was offering the ranchers. He'd pay them a fee to send their herds our way for the first time and the idea was that once they'd come through

Rocky Bend once, they'd come again, because we'd make it so good they'd have no choice.

You see, he told me when I asked him if he wasn't just throwing money away, once the hands that actually drive the steers come through Rocky Bend and find that they like it, they'll want to come back this way again. We won't need any more inducements then because they'll do the work for us with the ranchers, telling them what a perfect place we've set up here. We'll make this place into Heaven for cowhands.

This was why the bunkhouse and the saloon had to be very good, better than any others, because, as Sutherland said, the cowhands didn't really care all that much about their cows, but they did care an awful lot about their bellies and their heads on their pillows. Ian asked him if he was considering setting up a brothel to cater for another part of their anatomies but Sutherland shook his head and said they could get that in Dubuque or Chicago and from what he knew of these cowboys that sort of thing was something they did when their trail was over, not while it was still going on.

I've been asking them, he said, in Chicago. I've been planning this for years. Trust me.[55]

Ian shook his head sadly and of course his question had been a criticism, though Sutherland hadn't realised it, being very thick-skinned. As for trusting him, well I suppose we did, as if we'd forgotten all we'd learnt of him in the past, but that's human nature.

So off Sutherland went on his journey west, the sleekit wee ferret, and after a few weeks he was back with his pouch empty, telling us of the deals he'd done and how the cattle and the money would soon be pouring into Rocky Bend. He told us he'd only seen one Indian on his journeys, and that had been an old man about eighty begging at the big stone gate of one

---

55 Market research. There is nothing in the world that isn't old. – RM

of the ranches. He'd given the man a couple of coins and he'd spat on the ground but taken the money.

Actually, my memory might not be exactly right here. I can't recall if they called them ranches over in Iowa at that time. That's the name I use now or that I hear used now but maybe they were just farms. It doesn't really matter. But there were these big farms. Rich men had gone and bought out the small homesteaders and joined all the land together to make big farms.

Once upon a time the men of Croval had crofts up in Strathgarrick, then Killarnoch swept them out and joined all the land together to make one big sheep farm that stretched across the heather and burns for miles and miles. Same thing in America. You hear about something once and it seems like injustice. When you find the same thing on the other side of the world it begins to seem like the way things are meant to be.

So we kept on working at getting ready, filling the store up with the kinds of things we thought travelling cowboys would want, guns and bullets, rope, horseshoes – I suggested hiring a blacksmith but Sutherland said no, these men saw to their own horses' needs – saddles, blankets, dried beef, shirts and a hundred and one other things. Laura Lynton set everything out in the log store and chalked up a list of prices on a big black-board behind the counter. In the saloon we had whisky and beer, nothing else apart from water. In the bunkhouse we had wooden frame beds with straw-stuffed mattresses and striped blankets and clean pillows. On the wall of each little room Sutherland hung a painting of Chicago. He'd bought these paintings from a man in the big city who could turn out lots of them, all exactly the same. They made Chicago look exciting, all bustling streets and a bright blue sky above, not my memory of the place at all, not a pig in sight. Sutherland's idea was that these pictures would make the cowboys feel their journey was nearly done and fill them with enthusiasm and hope. Beside each bed was a little table, upon which there was an oil lamp and, because

Ian insisted, a Bible. In the extended building we had space for twenty five men to come and sleep, and they'd get their food served up in the saloon, where Sutherland himself, helped by me and Ferdinand, would dish up fried eggs and bacon with bread and beans three times a day. Sutherland said cowboys didn't need any variety in their meals, all they needed was food.

Because we had space for twenty-five men in the bunkhouse that meant that we needed space for twenty-five horses in the stables, so that's what we had. We carted in supplies of hay and oats for the horses from Dubuque and stored it all in an outbuilding we put up beside the stables. We had water troughs where the horses could drink, so that the cow hands didn't even have to lead their horses across to the Red Bluff River. The idea was to make it all so nice and so easy for them that they would never think of driving their steers any other way except through Rocky Bend and so it would go on until Rocky Bend turned into Sutherland Ross City, by which time we'd all be so rich that we wouldn't know what to do with ourselves any more.

And right enough, as the summer wore on, so the steers and the men that went along with them began to come through Rocky Bend and we were making good money. When there was a herd coming you could hear them before they came in sight. The sound of their hooves echoed up the canyon walls and the sound came round the bend of Rocky Bend and you knew there was another lot arriving.

The steers were fat longhorn cattle, much better cows than the ones we used to have in Croval and better too than the cattle that folk kept in Goderich. Funnily enough they were better too than the cattle we'd seen in the pens in Chicago because of course the steers lost weight and condition as they were driven west to east, and even though there was fair scrubby grazing beside the Red Bluff River, the cows were losing more weight than they could put on and by the time these herds made it to Chicago they'd have lost a lot of the pounds they'd put on eating

316

the good grass of Iowa in the first half of the year. At night they'd be corralled in the pens we'd built up close by the canyon walls and the sound of those dark starry summer nights was of the gentle lowing and constant shifting of hundreds of cattle.

The men that came with them were hard quiet men, friendly up to a point but not really wanting to talk too much to you. They were happy to sit in the saloon drinking whisky after whisky, hardly even talking to each other sometimes. They had the dust of the trail on them and the smell of them was the smell of cattle and sweat. At night they'd fall into their beds and they'd be up at dawn, ready to move their cows on.

They were a different kind of men than any I'd met before on my journeys. They had something in common with the sailors on the Lady Gray, I think, but there was something else about them that was different. They had lines on their face, even though they were young men, because they always had to squint at the sun or gaze at the distance for whatever might be on the horizon, a stray steer or an Indian waiting to attack. There was a seriousness about them.

Sometimes they'd stop off with us again on their way back and then they'd be more talkative, as if the herd had absorbed all their energies and now that they were free of it they could just be themselves. Every last one of them carried a gun, sometimes two. They had pistols and rifles and all of them had a knife that they'd use for a hundred different jobs on the trail. There were times, in that first year, when shots were fired in the saloon, but usually it was just high spirits, or too much spirits, and the trouble would die down again more or less as quickly as it had flared up.

But there was one time when the bullet that was fired was fired in anger and it was a thing that made me think again about Donald Sutherland.

We'd built a wooden boardwalk outside the saloon so that the cattle herders could take their beer outside and sit in the evening sun until it went down behind the walls of the canyon. We set out a few chairs there and I used to like sitting on the boardwalk myself, just talking to the men, if they wanted to, about their life on the trail, about the rich men they worked for, about the women they had fallen in love with, who were quite often whores in Chicago, and that made me think of Lydia.[56] Most of them were born and bred Americans and they liked to hear my stories about coming across from Scotland. The ones that were younger than me made me feel old when I told about our voyage in the Lady Gray and all the miles I'd travelled from home. The ones that were older than me made me feel young when I told them about Rachael and how she was lost somewhere in this wide land. All of them made me feel that at last I was maybe making something of myself because there was no doubt that they saw me and Sutherland as the creators of this place that they liked. As I sat there with them outside the *Rocky Bend Saloon* I dared to think there might be some success in my life, that maybe it might be possible to leave the past behind, and it made me think about writing a letter to my mother, though in the end I never did write one from there.[57]

It was one evening in early August and it was just me and

56 And that is the last we hear of her. – RM

57 This suggests the interesting point that there were other letters, written from elsewhere as Hugh mentions earlier. I don't know how I would begin to track them down, though I suppose the publication of this manuscript may lead to their unearthing. Certainly there were none amongst the papers I found in the attic here in Elgin. I do wish that one might emerge, however brief, since it would silence those who claim that the whole manuscript is a fake. I imagine there will always be doubters, and if a letter were to come to light, I think they would claim I was behind it too. They would add it to the other clues they claim to have found in the text. One professional reader wrote to me claiming to have found twenty three compelling clues in the text suggesting its inauthenticity. I despair. But we live in a world where trust is hard to come by and I think we must live with that, sadly, and just get on. – RM

Ian sitting out there. The sun was warm and I had a jar of beer in my hand. Ian had a glass of red wine, having persuaded Sutherland to buy in a few bottles of the stuff, just for him. It wasn't cheap, because it came from Europe and Sutherland had taken a bit of persuading.

Ian was sitting in the one rocking chair we had out there and I was in one of the ordinary wooden chairs, swinging back to lean against the log wall of the saloon. We weren't talking, just sitting soaking up the last bit of the day's heat. We could hear the sound of the men inside the saloon, drinking and eating and talking in their quiet intense voices.

Ian was calmer here than he'd been in Chicago but he was slowly slipping away from us. I can see that clearly now but at that time I didn't like to think about it, because I didn't want to. He hadn't got a job to do in Rocky Bend, not like me and Sutherland and Laura Lynton and even Ferdinand Braddle. He just drifted through each day, talking about things from long ago, confused by the constantly changing faces around him. Sometimes he thought he was back in Edinburgh and he would get upset if you tried to tell him where he really was, so in the end I never argued with him. He would suddenly get up and say he was going to speak to Robert and I'd have to say to him that Robert was back in Goderich, married, and he'd look at me strangely, completely forgetting that it was him that had married them. In his body, he was a bit better than he'd been, and it looked as if he could go on for years yet, but there wasn't the same strength in his mind. I know Sutherland saw him as a bit of a nuisance, always getting in the way, but I stuck by him. Hadn't he stuck by me, years before? He was just my friend, and of course I had something to tell him when the moment came.

Of course the men that came passing through just saw him as this odd old man, not far off his three-score years and ten, with his white uncut hair and his thin face, and if I'm telling you the truth of it some of them were scared of him and fear can come out in strange ways.

So this one evening I'm writing about, one of the cowherds, a big broad strong-looking man about thirty with dirty brown hair, comes out onto the boardwalk, picking at his teeth with his fingernails, a glass of whisky in his left hand. One or two of his friends were coming out the door after him, stretching and yawning after a hard day in the saddle.

Well, he says, that was a fine feed. Just need to sit down now in the sun and finish off my whisky.

You're welcome, I say to him and I point at the four or five empty chairs along the short bit of boardwalk. I'm writing down what was said as best as I can remember it.

That's the one I want, he says, pointing at the rocking chair that Ian's sitting on.

Now Ian was away in a dream, muttering quietly to himself and he never even looked round at the man when he took a couple of big steps over towards him.

Out the chair, old man, says the cow herder and he gives a little kick with his boot at the curved rocker. He says, That's where I'm sitting this fine evening.

Ian, not really hearing him, because he doesn't when his mind is off in the past, shook his head and turned away.

One of the other men says, leave him be, John, he's harming no one.

He's in my chair, says John, the big man.

There's plenty chairs, I say.

And you keep out of it. I had my eye on this chair. I've been riding all day and now I'm tired and that's where I'm going to sit.

There was silence then for just a second and it was as if everyone was holding their breath. The only noise was the sound of Ian's fingers tapping and scratching away at the wooden arm of the chair, the way he did.

The skinny little man says again, Leave him be, John.

But John reaches over and takes Ian by the shoulder and

320

turns him round so he has to look up into the sun, squinting his eyes so the lines on his face are like the dry stream-tracks at the foot of the canyon walls.

You going to move out of that seat?

Ian frowns and thinks and then he says, They love the uppermost rooms at feasts and the chief seats in the synagogues.

It was the kind of thing he would say and no one would know what he was talking about but nobody minded. This John, though, it made him angry, because he thought Ian was mocking him somehow.

John – What the hell do you mean by that? Answer me straight. You going to move?

But now Ian had disappeared back into himself again, hunched up on the chair and turning away from the big man at his side, dismissing him from his thoughts, if he'd ever been there. So of course John took this as another insult.

The next thing took about one second of time to happen, maybe not even that. John, I never found out his other name, took from his belt a hunting knife with a blade as long as my hand and shining where it caught the sun's low rays and he lifted it up to hold against Ian's throat, his muscles tensed as if he was going to cut.

I don't know if he just meant to scare Ian or if he really was going to kill him, but we never found out. There was a gunshot and the man John fell hard on to the boardwalk and there was blood on the back of his dusty shirt. I looked at him lying there, and I looked at Ian, still sitting on the chair, staring off towards the river as if nothing had happened. And then I looked round to see who had fired the shot, and there was Donald Sutherland standing at the door of the saloon, the gun in his hand pointing now at the wooden boardwalk. It was quiet as if everyone was deciding what to do. I could make out the faces of other cowboys behind Sutherland, peering out to see what had happened.

Then the skinny man, the one who'd spoken before, lifted his hands up, palms facing Sutherland, and he said, Listen, Mr Sutherland, this hasn't got nothing to do with us. He gets like that sometimes. You had no choice. I've seen him kill a man before for less.

The others on the boardwalk, who all must have known this John, nodded and agreed and I realised that none of them were sad to see the big man lying there on the planks, dead as a hog, the bully.

I caught Sutherland's eye but he just shrugged his shoulders and went off back into the saloon. We buried the man the next morning over by the canyon walls, the first man ever to be buried in the town of Rocky Bend. We persuaded Ian to say a prayer over the grave but it was a rambling thing and had nothing to do with the man himself, but who else was there to do it? A couple of weeks later a man came out from Dubuque and went into the back room of the saloon with Sutherland and they talked about what had taken place but I never found out what had been said. Nothing happened to Sutherland because after all the man had been going to cut Ian's throat with his knife.

It made me see Donald Sutherland in a new light and the picture of him standing there with the gun in his hand, and the body on the boardwalk and all the other cowboys standing watching, their shadows up against the wall of the saloon, is stuck in my head.

What I've never been able to work out is this. Did Sutherland shoot the man dead because he was going to kill Ian or because if he did kill Ian then Rocky Bend would become the sort of place where you could cut a man's throat and get away with it? Who knows? But I looked at him differently after that. I'd never liked him, but now I saw him with a mixture of admiration and fear, and I understood better what it was that Callum had seen in him.

It's always good to learn in life, I think, and during this time I was learning a lot about cattle. The herds that came were a mixture of reared and wild cattle and some of them were very wild. At night some of these ones would have to have their hind legs tied together because otherwise they would try to jump the wooden bars that made up the fence of the pen and they could hurt themselves or other cows, kicking out in their anger. We saw a good few cowboys come into Rocky Bend with wounds and bruises where they'd been kicked hard by cattle. Not that they complained about it, it was part of their work.

But the thing that was interesting was the branding and over the years we were at Rocky Bend I got to know a lot of the different brands. The whole point of it was so that no one else could steal any of your steers before you got them to the slaughterhouses in Chicago. Sometimes cattle would wander off from the herd on the trail and there was always the danger they could be caught and taken by someone else and this is where the brands were important and this is where it was quite interesting. Usually the brand had something to do with the owner, such as his initial or initials. But if your name was Hugh Ross and you had a herd of cows it would be a mistake to brand them with the letters HR because it would be the work of two seconds and a hot running iron and suddenly the cow would be branded HB or even BB and you'd never be able to prove the thing was yours in the first place. The dishonesty of people is as inventive as the day is long. So the owners used to try to work out complicated brands that you couldn't easily change, mixtures of letters and lines and symbols and crosses and curves. One cowboy told me that the brand that was hardest to alter in the whole of America was one that went 6666, though it always seemed to me you could easily change that to 8888 or else just add another 6 and make it 66666.

They used to snip the cows' ears too, as another way of showing who owned what. So one whole herd would have the tip of the ear nicked off square and another herd in the next pen would have a triangular piece cut from the very tip. It all had to do with not being able to trust anyone on the trails and though each cowboy ranted and complained about the thieves and rustlers, every one of them would, if they got the chance, steal someone else's steer if they could rebrand it and change the ear cut.

I liked learning the way each man's cows were given their own identity and it made me think about what my own brands and ear clips were, if you see what I mean. I could think of a falling rock that had left a brand on me that I couldn't change, ever. So anyway I used to know about twenty brands or more but I can't remember them all now. It was years ago and that sort of thing goes out of your head after a while.

This is what happened to Ian Macleod, good man that he was. Knowledge went out of his head, draining away into the past as his hands tried to keep a shaking hold of the present.

I don't know how the incident with the knife affected Ian really. It was hard to know what bothered him and what was just him getting worse as the days and weeks and months went by, the way a boat left out of water all summer will shrink so that the gaps between the boards begin to widen and the wood fades to an empty white.

Some days he would be calm, sitting under a tree, talking peacefully to himself. Other days there was an anxiety in him like a sickness and he'd pace up and down, waving his arms, arguing with anyone who came near, tearing at his hair and clothing as if he wanted to be out of his body. No one could go near him when he was like that, and it broke my heart to see it. Sutherland used to say, *Just leave him*. That made me feel even worse, because I knew it was true, and because I felt like a black traitor when I did.

There was the day when he went in the river, one rainy morning in September, the steers all calling out their sad sounds, ready to move on, and the cowboys getting up and coming out the front of the bunkhouse, stretching their arms high and wide, tucking their shirts into their trousers, shouting out to each other their morning greetings, heading towards the saloon for bacon and eggs and bread, me starting to think about the day's work ahead cleaning their rooms and making up the beds and taking one last look down towards the river before going back inside, and seeing Ian standing right in the middle of Red Bluff River, in spate with recent rain, head down, hands by his sides, the rain slicking his white hair to his old head and the current pulling the tails of his coat down river behind him as he faced the current, ready to unbalance at any moment.

I ran down to the bank and a couple of the cowboys came too, partly to help, partly I think because it just wasn't every day you saw an old man standing up to his thighs in a river and a younger man racing down to save him with tears in his eyes.

I waded out to my friend and he turned to me a face that had on it the lines of despair. He didn't always know me in those days but he did then.

Ian spoke, and his voice was as thin as a feather, so you could hardly hear him over the sound of the water and he said, How much longer, Hugh?

I had no answer for him so I just put my arms round his old skinny shoulders, right there in the middle of the river. He was shaking at first but as I held him he slowly calmed and then he laid his head on my shoulder in a gesture that was full of hopelessness and love. I stroked his head.

I whispered in his ear, Not long, Ian, I think. Not so long now.

When we got back to the bank I saw the cowboys had wandered away for their food and only the young stable boy Ferdinand Braddle was standing at the water's edge waiting to help us out.

We pulled his wet clothes off and laid him in his own bed in the bunkhouse and for a little while he was restless, muttering away and rolling from side to side, his hands grasping out towards things no one but he could see, pushing the blanket away from his scrawny chest. We sat down, Ferdinand and me, with the young black-haired boy on Ian's wooden chair and me on the one I lifted through from my own room, until he had quieted down and then slipped into a sleep.

We spoke quietly, so as not to wake him.

Ferdinand – How old is he?

Me – I'm not so sure. Maybe about seventy or so.

Ferdinand – Well, that's pretty old.

Me – Yes, I suppose it is.

We sat for a while, looking at him. I pulled the blanket up a little, up to his chin, because the sight of his ribs and sharp shoulder bones troubled me.

Ferdinand said – You known him for a long time?

Me – Yes, a long time. A very long time.

Ferdinand – I always wondered, but I didn't like to ask. He a relative of yours?

Me – No, just a friend.

Ferdinand – A pretty good one, I guess.

Me – The best.

Ferdinand – And he came all the way across the ocean with you? From Scotland? At his age?

Me – He did that, yes. He's been with me ever since we left home.

Ferdinand – I guess he's done well, the old fellow.

Yes, I said, unable to think of anything to add.

After a bit, the young boy said, I wish I could travel like you've done. From what Donald says, you've been half way across the world. When I get to be your age I'd like to have done something with my life too.

Me – Well, don't be in too much of a hurry. Make sure you

know where you're going before you go.

Ferdinand – Anywhere really. I've been in Dubuque and I've been here. There must be more to everything than just this. I need some more excitement than there is here.

Me – You can make your life wherever you want to. Here the same as anywhere. Let's leave him to sleep for a while and he'll feel better later.

As we went out, Ferdinand Braddle cast his eye back to the old man breathing lightly on the narrow bed. He asked, Do you think he'll be all right?

I told him, It depends what you mean. It always does.

And he shook his head at me the way young boys shake their heads at old men who think they have all the answers and that was me not even thirty years old yet.

Later I sat with Ian again and I decided I would tell him about Mary Vass when he woke up, ask him to tell me what God would think about what Callum had done, but at last I feel asleep in the chair beside him and when I opened my eyes again I didn't feel like it any more.

A letter came from Robert and Elizabeth not long after. It was from Robert, really, but both of their names were on the bottom. I still have it and will simply copy it here.[58] I could write a lot about what it meant to me and Ian but instead I will let Robert's words speak for themselves just:

---

58 It seems to me odd that he did not insert the actual letter itself amongst his own sheets. Why waste time copying it out? Perhaps it is confirmation that Hugh did indeed hope his writings would be passed on and read by someone else. And of course this must have happened, as the pages ended up in my attic and as far as I can tell, Hugh Ross himself was never in Scotland after he finished his account. I wish I knew how it got into my house! Perhaps he kept the manuscript of Robert's letter for sentimental reasons. I'd like to think so – RM

Our Dear Friends, Hugh & Ian,

At last we find ourselves in the position where we can make contact with you, having heard that you are at Rocky Bend. The information came to us from a Scotsman, a Cameron Campbell, on his way back home to Glasgow. He had been working in a place in Chicago where he met in with some cattle workers who told him of your venture at Rocky Bend. It so happens this man from Glasgow had previously met you in Chicago and so the story stuck in his mind, long enough at least for him to remember it when he passed through Goderich on his way back West. On meeting Elizabeth in the General Store here (much expanded since your time), and in conversation chancing on the connection, Mr Campbell told what he had heard and we learnt all. In fact he had few details but we have since found out a little more about your activities, though of course it all seems so very far away. We hope your business is successful and that you are enjoying increasing wealth, as indeed we are. We had hoped to have a letter of you before now but perhaps it has become lost in delivery, as is still too often the case.

Since you were here, we have gone from strength to strength. Our most important news is that we have two children now, a boy & a girl. The boy is Ian, and he is now three years old, and as strong a little boy as you could hope to see. Already he is helping us about the place and it is rare the day when he does not have a skinned knee or grazed palms from some scrape he has got himself into. Our daughter is a beautiful baby of eight months. She is Elizabeth, after her mother & her grandmother and we are as proud of her as we hope she will be of us one day. Words cannot tell how marvellous it is to see these two youngsters beginning their lives on God's earth, and how strange it is that they are starting out so very far from where we, & you, started our own journeys. We hope upon hope that one day you may see our two children, and perhaps in the meantime you may be so good as to say a small prayer on their behalf occasionally.

My time is spent largely on improving our land and attending to our crops & livestock, of which we have much more than ever we had in your Goderich days. I shall not detail the improvements we have made, except to say that God has been kind to us and the money has been coming in so that we are now able to consider the building of a stone house to replace our much repaired cabin. Work on our house has begun and we hope it shall be complete before too long, perhaps before the worst of the winter weather.

Elizabeth, though occupied, of course, with the children, has been earning some extra money in dress-making & repairs for the ladies of Goderich. This all began with a small notice placed in the General Store, and now she finds she scarcely has time for aught else in the evenings. But we are grateful for the money and it has allowed us to make many friendships with ladies & their husbands both in Goderich itself, where now the population is greatly grown, and in the wider area.

As for myself I have taken on some responsibilities within the town of Goderich which may amuse you. The town has established a committee of citizens with the purpose of regulating trade & behaviour within the town's boundaries, as well as advising on the future development of Goderich & its surroundings. We feel that only with good government can we establish a community within which our children can grow up safe & hopeful. We have heard stories that far to the west, where you are, there is a lawlessness that, frankly, would be inappropriate in a polite society such as ours. I am proud to say that I have been appointed the Second Deputy Chairman, and that by a vote of the men of the town. I was flattered by such recognition and I have vowed to do the best I can to further the progress of our home town. I know you may laugh a little behind your hand when you recall the difficult young man who argued over many a passage in the Bible in the manse in Croval and who almost led an insurrection on board The Lady Gray. Suffice to say that I have grown older. My energy is the same as ever but it is directed differently. This may make you smile, I know, but I hope also it will make you respect me a little more than ever you did before.

We have news, too, of Rachael, who has written to us often. We do not know how much you have heard about her since you left. In brief, she left here for Chicago, where she met a man whose name is given as Edward Hill, or Edward Leaney – Rachael herself has been unclear on this. With this man she has had a child, a boy who has been named Jacob and who we believe has taken Rachael's surname, as the two were never married. Rachael, Edward & young Jacob travelled further west with the intention of setting up a homestead, but where we are not certain, since Rachael failed to specify in her last letter to us. What we do know is that her relationship with Edward Hill, or Leaney, was far from satisfactory and her last letter hinted that she may continue her journey alone, or rather only with young Jacob. What has become of her since this last letter we do not know. If you have any news, we beg you to write and inform us.

Mary McIntosh came back to Goderich and stayed with us for some weeks but has returned now to Pictou, though what her occupation is there we cannot be sure. It must be said that our friendship withered a little before we quite lost touch, but this is no place to enter into that.

Well, Hugh & Ian, I think that I must draw this letter to a close, as I can hear young Ian calling for me. At this time of night he is accustomed to be read to. I do not know how much he truly understands but I have been giving him excerpts from *Guy Mannering*. I know, Ian, you will be pleased to hear this. I suspect it is more the sound of my voice that pleases him, but so it often is with storytelling. I recall those evenings in the manse very well!

We devoutly hope that you are both well and that, Ian, your health has improved somewhat since you left Goderich.

We long to hear from you both with details of all of your travels and adventures. We miss you deeply.

We are, always, your affectionate & loving friends,

Robert & Elizabeth Vass

As September drew to its end, Ian took it into his head that maybe he could be a preacher once again, church or no church. Although he would sometimes forget who he was and where he stayed, he could remember every verse from the Bible and it never went out of his mind that he wanted his own place to be a minister of, here in the new land of America. He would talk about it often, usually to himself, and sometimes to the horses in the stable. This is where I will have my pulpit, he would say to me sometimes. Where is this again?

Rocky Bend, I would tell him. One day to be Ross Sutherland City.

Well, here will be my mission, he said, his Bible clutched tight in his bony white fingers.

At first I wasn't sure what he meant by this, since he often said things that led nowhere. You would think sometimes about what Ian had said and the more you thought, the more you imagined you were seeing meaning in his words, but the truth of it is that as he got worse you could look as deeply as you wanted into what he said and you would never find anything, because there was nothing there to find. The words that are spoken to us are like a map, and we follow them to the ends of journeys that can show us the inside of someone else's minds, but in Ian's case the paths on the map often died out in the white paper of nothingness. But the thing is that we like to look at a map and we can make ourselves see routes that aren't really there at all. That much I've learnt.

This time, though, Ian meant it when he said Rocky Bend was going to be his mission. It is still warm in Rocky Bend in the autumn, or fall as the people there called it, because it is the time when the leaves fall from the trees, not that there were very many trees along the Red Bluff River and people said there weren't a lot of trees in the whole of Iowa and when the first white people came they thought that this would mean it would be bad land for growing crops, but they were completely wrong.

Because the weather was still good as September turned into October, it was no surprise that Ian was often out wandering, though usually I kept a pretty close eye on him after the time he went in the water, of course.

But one afternoon I was in the front room of the bunkhouse, adding up figures and counting a fair sum of coins that had been paid to us by the passing men – it was a good and busy time in our little town. There was a sharp tap at the door and in came Laura Lynton, an unusual little smile on her lips.

She said, I think you ought to come and see what your friend is doing.

I stood up so quickly that I knocked the wooden chair over backwards. This was the same chair that I'd carried through to Ian's room when I was sitting with Braddle after Ian waded into the river and remembering that as I heard Mrs Lynton's words made me panic. I hurried past her and out into the sun. My eyes went first to the river again, expecting him to have done the same thing as he did before but there was no sign of him. There was a touch on my arm and Mrs Lynton, beside me, was pointing across to the left, away past the saloon and beyond the cow pens, where there was a small group of cowboys in a circle all facing inwards. In the middle of the circle Ian was standing on top of an upside down wooden box, his Bible tucked under one arm and the other pointing dramatically upwards to heaven. Up high above against the blue sky I could see a bald eagle circling but that wasn't what Ian was pointing at, of course. He was pointing at the Kingdom of Heaven, and he was telling these men how to get there. I brushed Mrs Lynton aside and broke into a run.

As I got closer I could begin to make out the voices. Some of the cowboys, and there were maybe a dozen of them, were laughing and shouting at him, but despite that Ian's voice was raised high and thin above them. He was preaching at them on a passage from the Bible, which I much later found, and he was warning them about their lives.

He said, his voice a thin reed of sound, *And she brought forth a man child, who was to rule all nations with a rod of iron. And her child was caught up unto God, and to his throne. And the woman fled into the wilderness, where she had a place –*

One of the men shouted, Tell us where she is and we'll find her all right.

And another said, We know the wilderness pretty good. We'll find her.

They all laughed that crude laugh that men can do.

Ian fixed them with his eye and said, Mock not. This tale is to warn you. *And there was a war in Heaven. Michael and his angels fought against the dragon, and the dragon fought, and his angels.*

Cowboy – A dragon? What sort of story is this?

Ian – Hush. *And the dragon prevailed not and neither was their place found any more in Heaven. And the great dragon*

333

was cast out, that old serpent, called the Devil, and called Satan,
who deceiveth the whole world, he was cast out into the earth,
and his angels were cast out with him.

Cowboys, laughing – He's here? The dragon's on the earth
with us? Maybe he lives in a whisky bottle &c &c.

Ian, louder – *And when the dragon saw that he was cast*
unto the earth, he persecuted the woman which brought forth
the man child. And to the woman were given two wings of a
great eagle, that she might fly into the wilderness, into her place.
And the serpent cast out of his mouth water as a flood. And
the dragon was wroth with the woman and went to make war
with the remnant of her seed.

As he spoke these words he used his thin finger to point,
which reminded me of a poem he himself had once read to us in
the manse at Croval. When he mentioned the eagle he pointed
again up into the sky where, indeed, the eagle still circled, then
when he mentioned the word flood he pointed over to Red
Bluff River and when it came to mentioning the women's seed
his finger swept round to take in all the cowboys standing in
front of him.

And at last they fell quiet.

So Ian carried on, his voice softer now because it could be,
God gives us these words to warn us. The flood of the dragon,
the serpent, the Devil, is ready to rise and engulf us all. We have
not the wings of an eagle that we may rise to our salvation. The
dragon does not mean to harm us here and now but for all time.
He wishes us to descend with him unto the fiery pit. Some of us
may try to resist but too many go willingly, their sight blinded
by the splendour of his bejewelled scales. And he tempts us on
with drink, and with loose women, and with avarice and dreams
of glory, and with the power of a city of Babel where the cries
of men are drowned by the cries of the dying animals.

They looked at their feet and shuffled about a bit and it was
quiet enough now for Ian to continue in a whisper just, And

those men are you. You are coming towards the latter days when your journey shall approach its end. Be sure your feet are on the proper road and not on the path to Hell, which starts with a gentle slope and flowers by the wayside, but ends with a cliff and sharp rocks.

He didn't need to point this time. As one, the dozen men turned and looked at the cliff at the side of the canyon. They were silent enough now, and so was I. I wondered if he could see into my heart.

And now, said Ian, when they'd all turned meekly back towards him, we shall sing the praise of the Lord. Psalm Seventy-Eight.

They all looked uncomfortable at each other because of course none of them knew Psalm Seventy Eight or any other Psalm for that matter, the extent of their singing being a few bawdy tunes for late at night.

So it was Ian's voice alone that rang out, and even though he was so old then, and his health was going, and he was already many steps down the proper road, his voice still had a thin strength to it, like the ringing of a crystal glass in a dark room. He sang, *Attend, my people, to my law, Thereto give an ear. The words that from my mouth proceed, Attentively do hear. My mouth shall speak a parable, And sayings dark of old – The game which we have heard and known, And us our fathers told.*

And so on, all thirty-six verses I think, but I didn't really hear them all because my mind was thinking that my father never told me any parables or sayings, and Ian was the only father I ever knew, and these thoughts made it hard for me to listen, and to see.

When he was finished he climbed stiffly down from his box, his Bible clutched tight in his hand, and strode off unsteadily towards his room. The men stood for a moment or two then broke off in groups of three or four, talking quietly, bumping past me as I stood there with the damp on my cheeks drying in the afternoon sun, and my past a tightness in my chest.

Well, he never preached again.

The thing is, was his sermon on the box a success? I know it was something he always wanted, to have a congregation in America listening to his words. The pity is that it took him years to achieve, and when he did, he could hardly remember it two hours after it happened. I spoke to him about it when I'd eaten that evening and he was vague and couldn't look me in the eye and I knew he wasn't very sure what I was talking about. I didn't press it with him because I knew he would become troubled if I did. So I never found out how he felt about standing up there with the autumn sun full on his face and a dozen ungodly cowboys listening to him talk about eternal damnation.

The thing was, back in Croval, the old men in the Carcair would moan about him not preaching *enough* about eternal damnation. He came halfway across the world to find his topic.

So if he wasn't sure about what had happened, could you say he attained some success there in Rocky Bend? We all have our ambitions, but are we ever satisfied when we finally meet them on the road? I look back on my own journey and I realise that often I've changed my ambition when I realise that each one is drifting out of reach. Is that a bad thing?[59]

---

59 No. Here we can see, in Hugh, a pragmatism that helps us to understand why, despite all the setbacks along the way, he continually set himself new targets in personal terms as well as in terms of a career. This is the spirit of the entrepreneur. People, such as Philip, would sometimes ask me when I was going to feel I had achieved all I needed to achieve. The implication was that a time would arrive when I would no longer be driven to pursue any more goals. I am pleased to say that this moment has never arrived and I hope it never will. The publication of this manuscript is a case in point. It would have been so easy to have given up when the first two or three publishers turned it down for publication with their badly thought-out questions about authenticity, or when Philip's jealousy (there is no other word for it) urged me to put the pages aside. My response sits in your hands at this very moment. – RM

The thing is that I've reached a point where I hope I know the shape of my life to come, and I appreciate that it is the very first time in my life that I have had that feeling. It is this that has allowed me to go back over my recent years and begin to write them into shape, even though I promised never to write again. But is my life a success? I am thirty-four years old as I write these words, looking back on a time when I was younger, and I find myself looking forward to a time when I am older, and content. Perhaps someone else may see this as a failure of my ambition. I don't know. I hope I am right.

Ian had several congregations in Scotland, none of which satisfied him. He came to America, where the world knocked him over and where poor health hurt him more than I can begin to understand.

Then, in America, Ian found a new congregation at last. It was a small victory and a hollow one, but it was that victory nonetheless. I'd like to think that as he spoke about the serpent and the road to damnation, inside him he somehow knew that he'd reached somewhere that he'd been wishing to reach. I'd have liked, that evening, to have looked into his eyes and into his soul to know if he had felt any pleasure in doing what he'd done, but we cannot look in so far, sometimes not even into ourselves.

That first winter was a hard time in Rocky Bend. In fact all the times after the first summer and autumn, or fall, were hard times, but that first winter was especially bad. I've written about hard winters before, when we were first making our way in America, so I won't give again the details of cold and ice and hunger. At least this time we were in strong buildings and lying on good beds at night, with blankets. This was the worst winter of all, because of what happened. But, to look at it another way, it was the winter that changed my life.

It was a ghost town in the December and January, with just the five of us staying in Rocky Bend. We all slept in separate rooms in the bunkhouse and we ate in the saloon because that is where the food was, but we just huddled in the kitchen where the stove kept us warm. The bar room was a desolate draught-torn space. There were no herds coming through, of course, so late in the year, and there were no more cowboys making their way back from Chicago to the ranches to the west. It was lonely there, after a busy summer and fall. Ferdinand got a bad cold and he passed it on to Ian and the coughing shook his frame day and night as Christmas came and went, and that was the beginning.

We had agreed that when Rocky Bend was quiet through the winter we would patch the place up, improving the buildings and extending the pens. But when the cold weather really came, in the middle of January, we lost the energy and we sat around in our own rooms, or in the saloon kitchen not really talking. Once or twice I took out my pages as if to write but I never did. The memory of how badly I felt in Chicago always stopped me, scaring me in case that mood came back again.

Out of the cold mist one day came a group of Indians. There were different kinds of Indians in that part of America but these ones were Meskwakis, quite friendly, according to the cowboys who'd spoken about them. These were the first we'd seen. There were fifteen of them or about that, all men, ages from twenty to sixty or so.

They were dressed in heavy fur cloaks against the wind, and we saw them coming through the window and went to stand at the door. I was a little scared because you hear these stories about things the Indians do to white men, and white women for that matter. But these were Meskwaki and they simply walked slowly towards us, the little bells they tie to their legs ringing faintly as they came. Their cloaks left their arms bare, despite the cold, and round their upper arms were wound metal armlets.

When they reached us we just looked at each other and nothing was said for some time. Then the oldest of their men held out his hands, palms out, and we understood they were hungry. We gave them some cornflour, some dried meat and some potatoes we had taken from Dubuque. We had apples too but Sutherland never let on. All the time he was passing these things on, he had his pistol in his holster at his belt and they could see it because I saw them looking. There were no weapons between them.

They looked at our buildings, slapping the walls and talking to each other in their own tongue. One of the older men, who wore a porcupine skin across his head covering his hair, looked close at Ian, slumped in a chair with his eyes half-closed and the coughing jerking his body from time to time. The old Meskwaki passed a hand over Ian's face and muttered some words then stepped back. Perhaps a prayer.

When they realised they weren't getting anything more they drifted off, back into the frosty mist. Ferdinand said his grand-father back in Dubuque has told him the Meskwaki used to be a warlike race and had defeated the French settlers who came here first but that now they pleaded for food like common beggars because the white men had killed all their buffaloes and chased them from the best land. Once again I found myself thinking of Killarnoch and how the world is all one.

It was a strange little meeting, and though I had seen Indians before, of course, and saw many after, this is the meeting that will always stay in my head. It was a sad encounter but in the simple silent request for food, and in our giving, there was something noble, I think.

Donald Sutherland always has a plan of some kind and through the winter he had another one. Seeing Ian's lingering sickness, he decided that he would be a doctor, thinking in this way – there will always be people who are sick with money in their pockets. He went to Dubuque one snowy morning and came back the next afternoon with some books that he'd managed to buy there. One was a book that gave instructions about how to pull out people's teeth, one was about setting broken limbs, one was about medicines and the other was a book that gave advice about how to tell what was wrong with someone.

Laura Lynton asked him how he would know which tooth to pull, and he said that if someone had toothache then you would pull out their tooth. But, said Laura, how will you know which tooth it is that is causing the pain.

A sparkle was in Sutherland's untrustworthy eye when he said, Pull out one and if the pain's still there pull out another one, and charge them by the tooth.

He practised on Ferdinand Braddle, strapping up his arms and legs as if they were broken, one time so tight that the toes turned blue and he had to cut him free. And Sutherland invented his own medicine that could be used to cure every illness that anyone might have, especially anyone passing through Rocky Bend that might not ever see Sutherland again. He made this medicine by collecting spring water and mixing it with plants he picked by the Red Bluff River, with a little bit of alcohol and some sugar. He was very light on the alcohol and sugar though as these ingredients cost money. I tasted this medicine for him and it didn't taste of much, and it had no effect on me of any kind, but then I wasn't feeling sick. Sutherland said that the plants he'd used were all mentioned in his book and that it was bound to be a cure for most things, and well worth ten cents a bottle. I wondered if some of these hard men that came through Rocky Bend with their guns and their knives might be back a few weeks later looking for their money to be returned, but Sutherland said not to worry, since if they were really sick the chances are they'd either get better, in which case they'd put it down to the medicine, or else they'd die. And if there wasn't really anything wrong with them in the first place, then how could they say the medicine *hadn't* worked?

He didn't look like a doctor, he looked like a weasel. He gave

340

some of his medicine to Ian at the start of February, and I agreed to it because by that time he was in a bad state of health. It was hard to make him swallow the stuff from the bottle and it made no difference to him. The next day he was just the same, lying in his bed, his eyes half-closed, his head turning backwards and forwards weakly on the pillow.

I was so worried about him, because he hardly talked at all now and he never left his bed and he didn't even pick up his Bible to look at, which was not like him. When March came round and there was no change, I persuaded Sutherland to send to Dubuque for a doctor, and Ferdinand carried the message there when he went to visit his parents in the town.

The doctor came the next day, a young man with thin hair and little round spectacles that kept slipping down his nose. He wore a big black coat that he never took off while he examined Ian, if examined is the right word for less than a minute spent by Ian's bed. He laid his hand on Ian's forehead and touched his fingers to the side of Ian's throat. He lifted Ian's eyelids and peered into the eyes. He laid his ear to Ian's chest. Then he wrote something down on a little sheet of paper, which he tucked into his pocket.

Well, he said. Well, well. He has a congestion in his chest. Plenty of fresh air. Steam is good for the airways. When the spring weather comes he'll pick up.

I told him about the other symptoms, the forgetting, the strange behaviour, the way he didn't know his own face sometimes in the mirror, the panic this brought to him, the way he could not rise from his bed.

Yes, said the doctor, well that can happen with old age. What is he? Eighty years old?

About seventy, I told him.

Well, seventy, it's not young, is it? The spring weather will brighten him up, but if not, send for me again.

He took two dollars for his visit and for his expenses and

341

I was tempted to take ten cents off for the hay his horse had been eating while he looked at Ian, but I never.

So that was the doctor.

I took to sitting by Ian's bed all through the day, and I pulled my bed through to his room so I could be with him at night too, hoping he would brighten and I would be able to talk to him at long last. I had to lift out the little table to make space, because the rooms were not built for two beds. All night I'd lie, listening to his troubled breathing, and whenever it faltered I felt my heart pound in my ears and my eyes strained in the darkness to see across the narrow room. When he breathed normally again I felt my muscles lose their tension and I sank down into the mattress, with sleep a continent and an ocean away.

Sometimes in the darkest hours of those March nights, Ian would talk, but it was impossible to make sense of what he said. The words flowed out with no real story to them, just mentions of things that had happened to him, all unconnected. I listened hard to see what he might be saying, trying to make meaning of his words, but I failed. On the cloudy nights when there was no glimmer of moon or stars through the expensive glass window, it made me wonder about all the words we speak. What meaning is there? It troubled my heart to lie there and think that way, and to feel something of my Chicago mood creep back into my soul.

Some nights Laura came and sat with him because, if I'm telling you the truth, I was getting so tired I couldn't think straight myself, and sometimes when I was talking to Ian and he was answering back in his own wee world, it was hard to say who was making less sense. I would go and sit on a chair in the empty saloon, with my head down on a table and pray for sleep to come, which sometimes it did and sometimes it didn't.

By the end of March he was skin and bone, unable to keep down even the thinnest soup that we made for him and pressed to his dry lips. His hair was falling out on the pillow and I stroked his head and I read to him from the Bible when he was awake and I stared at his face when he slept until I knew it as well as my own, better probably, because I'm not one for looking in the mirror all day the way some people do.

Laura said to me quietly one morning as we stood by the river's edge looking over to where the sun was rising over the cliff, You know he hasn't long left?

Don't say that to me, I said, a whine in my voice that I couldn't keep out.

Laura – It's true, though. You must prepare yourself for the day. How long have you known him?

Me – Forever. Longer.

When the day itself came, I actually thought he was getting a bit better. His eyes opened brighter that morning, a clear April morning, with plovers calling. I heard, through the open window, a trumpeter swan fly overhead. He looked round at me as if he hadn't seen me for a long time, as if he'd swum up from some great depth, as if he was reaching the end of some uncertain voyage.

Hugh, he said, his voice like crumpled paper.

My heart leapt. I said, Ian!

He smiled and when I took his hand he returned the pressure, but weakly. I offered him a little piece of bread which I'd been about to eat but he turned his head from it impatiently.

What are you doing here? he asked.

Why would I not be here? We've been worried and I've been sitting with you. We wouldn't leave you on your own when you're not feeling well.

Ian – No, I mean *here*.

Me – Rocky Bend?

Ian, frowning, concentrating hard – Portobello.

I felt the hope I'd had a moment before drain out of me like the sand running through an hourglass. My words dried up.

Ian – Where's Peter? Has he gone now?

343

Me – I don't know, Ian. Where would he have gone?

Ian – Away to the city. I don't want to be left alone.

Me – You're not alone. I'm here.

Ian – But where's Peter?

Me – Peter'll be back soon, you wait and see, just. He wouldn't leave you for long.

Ian – Will he bring me anything back? When he comes home?

Me – I know he will. What would you like him to bring you?

Ian – Books. I like it when they bring me books.

Me – When who does?

Ian – Anyone. I like it when anyone brings me books.

Me – Why do you like books?

Ian – Because they can show you places you've not been to. Foreign islands and Spanish deserts!

We sat in the quiet for a while, with Ian every now and then lifting his head and peering anxiously at the door, waiting for it to open. But he was too tired, too worn out after all the years and in the end he let his head fall back on the pillow.

He says, I hope he gets here soon. I think I might be asleep when he arrives.

I say, No matter, Ian. I'll wake you up when he comes.

Will you, he asks, his eyes wide. Do you promise to?

I nod and reply, Of course I will. Why would I not? Is there anything else that I can do just now?

No, he says, thank you. And he gives a decisive shake of his head. He says, No, I'm fine now that I'm home.

And with that he shut his eyes and turned his face to the wall and took one deep breath and then no more. I laid my face beside his and I cried for him, and for the father I'd never known, and for the friends I'd lost along the way and for the distance between me, alone in America, and where I came from, and for the story I held inside me that I'd always meant to tell him and now here it was too late. I don't know how long I was there, sobbing by Ian's body, but after a while I realised that

344

Laura Lynton was with me and her hands were on my shoulders and she was pulling me very gently away from the bed.

Come on now, Hugh. It's for the best, she told me.

How can it be for the best? I asked her, angry.

That's you free now, she said. Now that he's died you're free to do what you want. Like it or not, it comes to us all.

At the time I thought she was talking about death, but maybe she meant freedom. She took me in her arms and held me like a mother and over her shoulder I gazed on Ian's body, trying to look in to see his soul as it departed, but I saw nothing.

And freedom was the last thing I felt. I felt my guilt sweep round me like a flurry of dry leaves and now there was no one to talk to about it. I'd always hoped that Ian would tell me that I wasn't the worst man in the world.

That afternoon we buried him up by the canyon walls, near the grave of the man who had been going to cut his throat. I said some words from the Bible, from Mark, but I could hardly say them, my throat was so full of fear. We prayed over the grave and then trudged back to the empty buildings of Rocky Bend, and nobody had anything more to say.

So that was Ian MacLeod, the best man I ever knew. He took me across the world and then he left me and I miss him to this day. I don't know if he achieved what he wanted from his life, and I don't know if he ever regretted coming across the world, but I'm glad he came with us and shared with us his wisdom and his kindness and his friendship. He was a part of me and everything I do is to please him, even now.

The months of that year wore on, and people began to come to Rocky Bend again. At first it was a few cowboys who had wintered in Chicago, only heading back west when they knew there would be more work to do on the ranches. They told us stories about the city, how it still grew, about murders that had happened, about scandals involving the city's rich men and low-life women of ill repute, about the Galena & Chicago Union Railroad and how soon the railroad would be used to transport steers across the land much quicker than driving them. We didn't listen to them, so caught up were we in our Rocky Bend dreams. I would ask these men if they'd heard anything of Callum or of Rachael, but of course they hadn't. It was a big city and they told us that there were thirty thousand or more people living there all the time with thousands more coming and going and others that weren't really meant to be there at all, so maybe there were fifty thousand people living there, more people than you can think about. So why would they have heard of Callum? One lost soul amongst so many?

And Rachael, I knew from Robert's letter, was already further west with her child. She was my only plan. Where Ian had been there was a dark space in my heart.

Our next visitors, at the start of the summer, were some of the ranch owners, or the foreman who organised their cattle drives, come to look at Rocky Bend and to think about the way they would drive their cattle in the months to come. Some of them had driven steers our way the previous summer and had come to talk about rates and to see if they could do it cheaper this year. Sutherland resisted but when they said they could easily go another way he found he had to cut the prices for a bed in the bunkhouse and a meal in the saloon and a pen for the cows. Of course once word got round they all wanted their prices cut and, true enough, you couldn't charge some of them one price and the rest something different. It wouldn't have been fair, not that Sutherland was ever too bothered about fairness, but he knew if he didn't match all the prices they'd just go some other way. They told us there were other routes and other posts like ours springing up, further south. We didn't listen.

One night I was in the saloon, as I often was in the months following Ian's death, with a beer in front of me, when a man came and sat at my table. We spoke for a while about nothing very much, the falling price of cattle, the way the hard winter had slowed up the feed growth, the way that there were so many ranches springing up now that you couldn't rely on hands to show loyalty and stick with you. I couldn't be bothered, if I'm telling the truth, with his moaning, but I was polite because men like him kept us afloat in this hard sea of life. He was a foreman for a ranch called the Long T, and their brand was a sloping line with a cross at the top like a T leaning over to the right and they clipped the ears at a diagonal too. They'd driven a small herd through us the year before and he was back to see if they would do so again. His name escapes me now. Maybe I never knew it. I can't even conjure his face to my mind, no matter how deep I look. I remember the conversation, though, because in the end, and after two or three more sour beers, I managed to turn it to the subject of Rachael and young Jacob Sutherland.

So didn't it turn out that he knew them and that she had worked on their ranch which was over to the west near a place called Storm Lake, which this man said was a very beautiful part of Iowa territory but sometimes bothered by Indians. Rachael had been there the previous year, working as a cook for the cowboys.

I asked, So when you were here last year, she was at the Long T?

He said, Yes, she was. I recall her because she had a son Jacob, like the one you're speaking about. Must be the same girl.

I asked, fighting off the beer, And her husband? Was he working on the ranch too?

He said, There wasn't no husband. She was on her own. I think the boss took pity on her when she showed up. All alone like that, her and Jacob. Pretty girl, red hair. Nice little boy, quiet like.

I said, That's her. Is she still there?

He shook his head. No, she moved on before the winter set

in properly.

Heading where? I asked.

No idea, he replied. She just up and left. West, though. Or south maybe. There's so many going that way now, with the gold and all.

What gold? I asked him.

There's been gold found, he told me. Down in the south west, in California. Didn't you hear that yet? Everyone knows about that.

Of course I had heard about it, because lots of the cowboys were speaking about it and talking about how they could make money easy down there instead of wearing themselves out twelve hours in the saddle every day. I don't know why I asked him *What gold?*

I said, And do you think that's where she's gone?

He shrugged. Maybe so. There's some women go down there but it's mainly men folks. The women that go, well, mostly they're whores and I doubt that young Jacob would be much use to her in that line of work.

I didn't like to hear him say such things. I got him to promise to try to find out what had become of Rachael and to get a message to me through one of the cowboys when the Long T herd came through at the end of the summer. But as it turned out the Long T herd never came through because they took a route to the south, a cheaper and quicker one.

And this was the problem. Our Rocky Bend was in the wrong place. As usual, Sutherland had rushed into deciding what to do and his idea that owners would want to drive their cattle north then south didn't make sense, even though where he picked was a convenient place for corralling cattle and well supplied with water. There was a better route, in fact more than one better route, off to the south, and other men had realised the same thing that Sutherland had realised, which was that there was money to be made from this annual flow of steers from west to east. We even found out that one cowboy who'd been through Rocky Bend the year before had gone and set up his own station further south near Cedar Rapids, taking the steers across the river at Lyons. He'd picked up some tips from us, one of them being that he could offer money to owners to come through his station.

So that year wasn't as good as the year before. The ranch owners had, as they would have put it, wisened up. There were choices in front of them and the Cedar Rapids to Lyons route promised more, partly because there was a railway supposed to be going in down there so in the end it would be a route that owners could drive across or be transported across. We knew nothing of that then, just fifty or sixty miles too far north.

There were fewer herds coming through and that meant fewer cowboys. Fewer cowboys meant fewer coins handed over in the bunkhouse, fewer meals sold in the saloon, fewer things bought in the general store, fewer horses stabled with Ferdinand.

Sutherland's answer should have been to have packed up and moved on, but he was a stubborn little man, and he decided we should sit tight, even though by September it was clear we were never going to make our fortunes camped beside the Red Bluff River.

He pushed hard with his new job of doctor, talking to every man that came through the place, wheedling away with his furtive wee face, trying to persuade them that they had something wrong with them, that they weren't feeling their best, that they had aches and pains they just hadn't really noticed, that they could feel a summer fever coming on, that their gut was all dried up, that what they really needed was a bottle of Sutherland Ross Tonic at ten cents.

One night he told me that he was considering putting something in their food to upset their stomachs, just so he could sell more of his medicine. The only thing was he wasn't sure what to put in the stew. He said he'd already tried some of the plants that grew down by the river, but nothing seemed to have much effect. I told him this was wrong and he told me to grow up and then we were hardly talking to each other, and not for the first time.

I spent more time with Ferdinand Braddle, helping in the stable, though to be honest my help wasn't really needed. Ferdinand was good at his job and there weren't that many horses to groom and feed and water anyway. But I liked his company better than Donald Sutherland's and I realised that I'd only put up with Sutherland for so long because I was distracted by Ian's illness.

He was a hopeless little man, Sutherland, at last I realised. He'd aged in the last few years and there was a good bit of grey in what was left of his greasy black hair and the lines on his shifty face were deepening. Although I'd never liked him I'd always thought that he had a certain energy, a horde of ideas to set loose against the world. I never liked these ideas when they escaped from the dark pit of his mind, but I always had a grudging respect for them. But now I saw his ideas were as foolish as the next man's. There we were, hoping to build a city in our names in the middle of nowhere and here it turned out we were completely in the wrong place. Couldn't he have realised that earlier? Shouldn't he? My dislike for him grew as I saw him following a cowboy one day, pleading with him to buy one of his bottles for eight cents, just eight, maybe seven.

When October came, Laura Lynton had had enough too and she left to go back to Dubuque, still caught in her whirlpool. It was a cold farewell. She wasn't someone who became close to you. Maybe life had taught her that, but she packed her bags and left one morning, sitting straight-backed on the cart that Sutherland had bought before and that he now sold to her for a pittance. So she was gone and so was our way of restocking the store and the saloon, but Sutherland said we'd enough put by until the end of this season and that we'd get a new cart in the next spring and that in the meantime we could take a horse into Dubuque for any small amounts of stuff we would need.

Even Ferdinand could see that was madness and he told Sutherland so and then they fell out over it too and Sutherland told Ferdinand that he could leave as well if that was the way that he felt, that just the two of us could easily manage the stables as well as the saloon and the store and the bunkhouse.

So one night Ferdinand and I were in his room, packing his things, such as they were, into a cloth bag. He was going to move on, but west, not east.

You should be coming with me, he said. You've travelled far enough already, you should travel away from here too.

Maybe so, I said, taking from the wall a drawing he'd done of the river and tacked up there. I folded it and laid it in his bag. I said, You're maybe right. But what about Donald?

Ferdinand – You owe him nothing at all, do you? In fact he owes you money, I'm sure. I guess you don't get the share you're entitled to.

Me – What does it matter, though?

Ferdinand – Maybe nothing. But you could get out of here and make a new start in the west. You could work on one of the ranches. Or you could come with me.

He was heading overland to California, looking for gold. He'd had a letter from some distant cousin who was there already, trying to get Ferdinand to come too to help him to get the yellow metal out of the rock.

He said – You're not so old. You could come to California and we could get a place there and pan gold. Then maybe, I don't know, we could buy a hotel or something.

He trailed off, not very sure what he would do with the riches he saw growing in his mind's eye. He was only a boy, much like the one I'd been when I was only a boy.

I asked, Why would you want an old man like me along

351

with you?

Although I wasn't old at all, he made me feel so, with his bright eyes and his blurred dreams.

He said, Why not? You've been good to me while I've been here. You listen to me. We don't have to stick together for ever. Just till we get started.

I had an image of a time decades ahead, me lying on a narrow bed and Ferdinand sitting beside me with his hand on my brow.

I said, No, you're right, we could split up at any time.

He said, That's right. And maybe you'll meet that woman you talk about.

I muttered, Maybe I will.

So that was that agreed and the next day we headed out west on a couple of horses we'd bought from some cowboys who were on their way back to their ranch. They had spare horses because some of the men had stayed in Chicago to overwinter, though that doesn't really matter.

As we turned the bend in the canyon, I looked back to see if Sutherland was standing by the saloon, watching us go, but there was no sign of him. I was surprised by a little feeling of disappointment. Time used up together should mean something, even if you don't like a person much.

I don't know what became of Rocky Bend. It might be still there for all I know, but I doubt it. If the truth be told, I think it would have just slipped away. As for Sutherland, who can tell? I haven't seen him since those days, and I don't really expect to see him ever again, though they say that bad pennies have a habit of turning up. I don't want to see him again. He belongs to the past and it is always so important to keep your eyes focused on what is ahead, or else all you can see are the shadows that trail behind you.

So we turned the bend in the river and that was us on our way.

352

Intertitle 6

A short section deserves a short Intertitle, like one of those ones in a movie that simply says "Later that day..." or "Meanwhile, on the other side of town..."

There is nothing to note about the following section apart from the obvious: that Hugh compiled these notes well *after* the events mentioned ("described" would be too strong a word), and all we have are these scribbles that form the general shape of what this section would have looked like had he ever got round to writing them up into a finalised form. It is intriguing to think about what some of these jottings actually mean (I have put in some footnotes to help where possible) and how Hugh might have expanded on them. Of course the "Rocky Bend" section was probably produced in the same way, written up from notes based on memory, but for some reason that we will never know, he did not develop this "Big Creek" part of his tale in the same way. I have comment to make on this later, but there is no sense of giving any sort of game away. Not that I am sure what exactly the game is in the first place.

I am almost embarrassed to mention that, as earlier, I was tempted to cheat and considered writing the notes up myself, to create the illusion of one continuous narrative, but I'm pleased to say that this idea never got beyond the stage of idle speculation. I do have a sense of morality, and while it would be tempting to involve myself in Hugh's story by writing some of it, mixing our literary DNA for posterity, my honesty would not allow me to do so. Those who question the authenticity of Hugh's story might do well to consider that if I had wanted to manufacture anything about the narrative, the "Big Creek" section would have been an obvious place to start.

I do have a comment about this section, however, if you would be good enough to bear with me.

The Gold Rush is a metaphor for the American Dream, one that is so familiar that it has become cliché. While Hugh is not quite a "miner, forty-niner" (nearly, though) he is a very recognisable figure from the pages of history as he pursues the yellow metal in the rocky streams of California. It is interesting that in the "Croval" section his mother uses desire for gold as a metaphor for Hugh's desire for success of any kind across the ocean. What is remarkable, I think, is the way that Hugh has bounced back from the despair of the "Chicago" section and the bereavement in "Rocky Bend" to embark once more on an attempt to make something of himself. I like the way he takes Ferdinand Braddle under his wing. It makes sense to have some protégé to nurture so that all the eggs are not in the one dropped basket, but that is another story. I like the way he shows us that the only way out of solitude is to seek the company of others. It is an obvious point but not one that I've always understood.

Haven't we all searched for metaphorical gold? The details of Hugh's search are obscured by the lack of detail but there is enough here to fascinate, and this is why I decided to include these pages in the volume. It would have been easy enough to leave them out. But would it have been fair to Hugh to do so? We all want our lives described as fully as possible, and I apologise for including some of mine in this volume. I would like to think that one tale illuminates the other.

So "Big Creek" is not much more than a glance at an important stage in our narrator's journeying, but a glance is better than a pair of closed eyes, if you see what I mean. I have enjoyed working on this section, as it has given me a chance to be more directly engaged with the story than at any other point.

Big Creek

– details about setting up Joint Stock Company[60] – arranging money and people – visiting, persuading – laying out plans – ranch owners – arrangements for travel, buying wagons, supplies – disagreements amongst Company members – withdrawals – new people – list everyone in group with words about each[61].

– advice received about travel in spring and how after discussion decision to travel December to March through winter weather – my points about this – advantages of early start in gold country – but against this dangers of winter travel, discomfort & danger – two more withdrawals, especially write about withdrawal of Ernest Gillingham and what this meant for us all[62] – setting off in December in heavy rain – wrong time but hopeful – sullen atmosphere – missing Ian's advice – something about Croval and setting out to sea in bad weather.

– camping at River Fork Ranch – food and care from Mr Smith & Mrs Smith – entertainment provided by the children & their music & dramatic show – food, describe – last feeling of homeliness for four months & better weather, cold & sunshine – on leaving, talking with ranch hand worked previously Long T Ranch – confirms Rachael moved on to California with Jacob

---

60 It seems that many prospectors took this approach, pooling resources to finance the journey to California. Hugh is always reticent about his finances but we can assume there was a little profit from Rocky Bend. It would have been interesting to know the financial agreement, later dissolved. In this section I owe much to the information I gleaned from the *Land of Golden Dreams* exhibition at the Huntington. – RM

61 Who these people were we can only speculate. Cowboys? Ranchers? Who knows? We may assume that it was a male, or predominantly male group, but their faces and names are forever lost. – RM

62 I assume this Gillingham was a major investor in the project. I have researched as far as possible but can find no record of the name anywhere, either in Iowa or California. – RM

– at River Fork following Long T – half the world heading to California & very like a flood or like a flock of birds or flock of sheep, point to be made – journey started so long ago on MacPhee's cart now joining the journeys of others as if destiny – death of old Stephen[63], not surprising but sad – reduced to eleven.

– details of journey – but not too many words here as much written previously on travelling, though earlier different, boat &c[64] – lightning storm on crossing ridge and fear, loud noise of the thunder cracking in our ears – horses terrified & bolting – rounding up next morning – all goods soaking wet and dispersed when wagon turned over but collected again – the spirit of determination – pushing on – sickness[65] striking, close to death but all survive – something about sickness on board Lady Gray, the cost of journeying is illness as if removal from comfort harms the body – river crossing with water so high horses swimming, heads lifted high and wagons in danger of drifting away – some goods lost – all survive – brief account of difference in land as further south, landscape, animals, plants, weather &c &c. Snow in drifts and extreme cold, too cold to think properly, just surviving. No sign of Indians, despite warnings of GJ[66].

– Ferdinand's broken leg when wagon turns on rock

---

63 This must have been hard, so soon after the death of Ian Macleod, and it would have been interesting to see what Hugh would have written here. It is hard to escape the feeling that his story is often one of loss – though also of gain. Same as everyone. – RM

64 This is interesting, showing again that Hugh is now conscious of writing for an audience – or maybe he is simply weary of the repetitive nature of long traveling, or writing about long travelling. – RM

65 Contemporary accounts often mention cholera as a threat on these overland journeys, so this may well be the sickness referred to. Such sickness seems to have stalked Hugh across the globe. – RM

66 Another mysterious reference. There are no GJs anywhere else in the narrative. – RM

– attempts to set – Donald Sutherland's book, can't recall –
dangers of not paying attention – the pain of the injury – wagon
wheel broken beyond repair, attempts at replacing but failure
of this &c – FB feverish at night but gradual improvement –
pain of wagons jolting on rough trail, FB crying out, wishing
he had stayed behind, Dubuque – eventually walking again but
not easily – thinking about Rachael travelling this same route,
though perhaps route further west first then south – idea of
seeing her again, awkwardness, nervousness, some little anger
&c – perhaps talk with Rachael about MV. More on journey,
quick description of final stages through February and March,
weather improving somewhat.

– end of March – arriving at American River – visiting
Sutters Mill – tell story of how gold found here as reported to
us by various miners, soldiers &c – Marshall[67] – disappointment
of lack of opportunity in this area – all available sites used up
or taken – already many gold seekers in area – we are a year
too late according to some – asking about Rachael but not
possible, like finding one stone thrown in the sea from jetty at
Croval – some words on my mother and what she would think
of me here chasing gold and whatever else – dent to ambitions –
numbers in group down to eight with three moving on to city.[68]

– section on equipment for gold searching – write about
pans and panning, long toms[69], sluicing &c – section on how

---

67 James W Marshall, who reputedly made the first discovery of gold
at Sutters Mill in January 1848. Marshall himself had completed a
journey – he was a carpenter from New Jersey and had moved west
to work in John Augustus Sutter's sawmill. Another story of altered
pathways and unexpected arrivals! – RM

68 Presumably San Francisco. See below. – RM

69 A long tom was a sluicing device which was used by gold miners in
California. Essentially it was simply a long box into one end of which
dirt was shovelled and water sluiced through. The heavy sediment,
which would include any gold in the deposit, was taken out at the end
of the day and panned. A long tom required at least half a dozen men

this done, hard work, back ache, frozen hands, cuts and bruises from rocks rolling in current – other methods not here but later, starting small – sleeping in tents on rocky ground, more uncomfortable than during journey despite cold – no time to build cabin – compare with Goderich – thinking about Robert and his town and family – FB much better but leg still painful, describe his nightly troubles, unable to sleep for discomfort but working very hard in panning – friendships.

– asking lots of people about Rachael but still no sign of her or her son – one rumour she is working in a saloon in Placerville[70], determine to try to find her, though told people move on from one place to the next so very often – too much time spent asking about Rachael, not enough time panning – disagreements in group – discussion about dissolving JS Company and withdrawing remainder of money equably – advantage freedom, disadvantage no helping to share work – much discussion, give points made on either side – eventual decision dissolution – FB stays with me – once more losing people.

– conversation with Michael Munro from Chicago – describe time he stayed in Main Street Board Hse & Emp – arrived California after sea voyage – describe his journey, Cape Horn, privations, seasickness, storms &c &c, arrival in Bay of San Francisco[71], his impression of the Golden Land – memories

to work and this was another reason for the joint stock companies. Working together in this way conferred a great advantage over the individual miner. – RM

70 In fact this town was not called Placerville until 1854, which shows for certain that these notes were not made until Hugh's time further south in California. The town was originally known as Dry Diggings or Dry Diggins, referring to the method used to extract gold, where soil was dug dry and then taken to water for panning. Later it was known as Hangtown, because of a lynching that took place there. Eventually the citizens decided on a more respectable name. – RM

71 Most gold-seekers took the oceanic route rather than the overland

of voyage on Lady Gray, peculiarity of two different voyages to the same place – section reflecting on the meaning of such voyaging – nearing thirty years old, people here aged forty appear to be fifty, people here aged fifty appear, mainly, to be dead, use this phrase.

– section on gains so far, sense of hopefulness – small bag of gold dust stolen – search for culprit but impossibility of knowing who could be to blame – anger and despair – darkness reminding me of Chicago – starting again with nothing – trying to find another place as Big Creek increasingly empty[72] – working twelve hours a day or more just for a few grains of gold and hundreds, thousands of men all along river doing the same, and along every river, like ants in a nest – FB for returning to Iowa territory and working on ranch but persuaded otherwise.

– now section on bigger workings – advantages of groupings, companies, loose arrangements, big investors with money to spend on paid labourers, Chinese, Indian, black men – hydraulic washing – shaft sinking – tunnelling – turning the river – use notes written then[73] – how all these methods turn the land into something else – find reference in Bible from Revelation about the latter days and the effect on the land we live in[74] – all soil washed away in some rivers – further down stream seas of mud – gold scarce & not to be had by single men working with pans

---

route Hugh preferred. Travelling by sea was, perhaps surprisingly, safer, and more predictable. – RM

72 i.e. of gold. – RM

73 A revealing phrase, easily overlooked. It shows that Hugh did indeed write more, despite his promise when disillusioned in Chicago, and then again when feeling more optimistic in that city. Whatever notes he made in California are lost. – RM

74 Perhaps Revelations Chapter 11 Verse 18 – "And the nations were angry, and thy wrath is come, and the time of the dead, that they should be judged, and that thou shouldest give reward unto thy servants the prophets, and to the saints, and them that fear thy name, small and great; and shouldest destroy them which destroy the earth." – RM

and long toms – Killarnoch again – repeating patterns, not too much on this, mentioned before.

– another winter – taking over TR's cabin – cold weather affecting FB's leg – snow and halt to working – dreary time – stupid gambling and more money lost – wishing for spring – FB limping and increasing poorly – not sure about being able to work when better weather comes – find doctor in Placerville but says nothing to be done, remembering DS and his attempt to be a doctor – who can be trusted? – no sign of Rachael in Placerville in any saloon or any other place – cold dark nights – birds calling in the dark like spirits.

– section about the contrasts between hard work and idleness – common belief in California that those who work hard are rewarded and those who are idle fall into poverty and failure – compare with back in Croval – sometimes hard work has no reward and sometimes success comes to those with no moral strength – DS – religion, IM, Robert & E for example and so on – we work harder every day and now no chance to go to ask about Rachael of anyone as no time – FB's health not so good, a sickly child still, longing for the big find that will let him go back home – comparisons.

– story about Ferdinand, the whore and the thorn bush.[75]

– the growth of the Golden Land – by end of year they say one hundred thousand people all digging, sluicing, panning, mining for their lives – five times what it was two years ago, they told me, too many people – competition between groups and between individual men for the best spots – get back from day panning and belongings in disarray and scattered, with clothes torn up &c – fist fights and other violence happening every day – drink – venality and selfishness and greed – also men together

---

75 It is interesting to speculate here. The story is obviously still very fresh in Hugh's mind years later as he does not need to elaborate with notes. – RM

sharing drinks in the evening laughing, joking, telling stories &c – Carcair – talking of everything but not talking about the way it all falls apart around them.

– journey south on advice of MM – three days – possible other things to do in this land – FB needing to be away from hard labour and no rest – south into farming land – huge herds of cattle – remembering Rocky Bend – thinking about cattle raising – miners further north will not grow food and they have to eat – changing plans as often before – FB keen on change but tired out by expedition south.

– Placerville – searching again for word of Rachael but nothing – talking to some of those with money about possibility of dealing in meat – one man offers to put money into plans and then as about to finish talking, maybe sign sheets of paper &c mentions he knows Rachael when I say I've come from north part of Scotland – says she has gone a bit south, talked about looking for work down there – must have been close to where she was when on way to see cattle herds & on way back – different feelings – decide not to sign sheets as now different prospects – most hopeful time for a long time – explain feelings, longish section – resolve to stick to gold panning for a while – make stake and go south with money in pocket for possible future prospects &c.

– background, setting the scene with description of all different nationalities – Mexicans, Chileans, Chinese &c – fighting & violence – white men against paid labour, seems unfair – black men and Indians pursued out of area, even if working for someone – some here as slaves, further disagreement – describe some of these fights – give personal opinions – explaining to FB – talking to Chinaman about his life, not really understanding – telling him about Scotland, him telling me about China – reflect on wideness of the world – further letter from Robert.[76]

76 Lost, of course. – RM

– setting up of vigilance groups to bring order to mining land – refuse to take part, also FB – examples of these groups and what they do – hanging of Frenchman who stole horse, call this lynching – most people accept but some speak out – stay quiet to try to build up stake but diff. & dangerous – FB for confronting group one night when they come to take black man thought to have knifed another – place of violence, my feelings on it, memories of IM.

– Rev Wm Speer[77] on behalf of Chinese and others – meeting in Placerville – large hall, describe, crammed with men – Rev Speer talking about humanity and all together – shouting – punching – riot nearly – try to speak to Rev Speer after meeting broken up but cannot get near to him – my impressions of him and how he seems, like IM when younger – more memories of IM and how he led us from a barren place and how this Wm Speer trying to do something different, change barren place into better place – so many ways to move from one life to another life.

– at meeting in Placerville many pamphlets handed out with Rev Speer's ideas – other pamphlets and leaflets and letter sheets – describe some of them, the words and especially the pictures of the Golden Land – truth and deception – writing home to my mother – thousands of words printed, speeches & songs & politics &c – another idea for getting some money put aside would be to be a printer of such leaflets as they are in demand by every man and all willing to pay 1c or 2c for a sheet of paper with a hundredth of the value[78] – but where to start such

---

77 The Reverend William Speer seems to have been a most worthy man, fighting tirelessly for the rights of ethnic minorities in California at that time. In particular he defended the Chinese population against some shocking barbarities. – RM

78 Once again Hugh's entrepreneurship comes to the fore. What else does this chapter show but a man determined to make some money using his own strength and his sharp wits. He is a lesson to us all,

a venture and how?

– visit San Francisco – major city of the area – describe the bay – scene setting – ships in harbour – ships turned to buildings – city growing round the edge with tents – new arrivals every day – commerce – buildings bigger than Chicago – many types of men – a constant movement – describe contrast with Croval and the land at the head of the cliff – thinking of all the men and women and all their different stories – wondering if my story will end in a city like this or in a quiet place – not sure which to prefer – is this a question for us all, move towards noise or move towards quietness?

– the fire in San Francisco two days after we get there – on the hill looking down on the city – flames half a mile wide – one blanket of flame – men shouting – horses screaming and racing through the streets from burning stables – the sound of the fire and the buildings crashing down – orange & red, black night, pillar of fire, pillar of smoke &c – morning bringing rain & desolation – by midday new tents and work already beginning on pulling down burnt buildings – the city healing itself – in all my travels this the most amazing thing – men destroyed and resurrecting – men like gods, or devils – the city eating the land around it – three weeks living in SF with GH on Hepburn Street at the corner with Archibald Street.

– something about politics and Presidential Election perhaps – perhaps not – voting and so on – important for California – first vote after admission – think on this and decide – or else keep to the story instead and leave this out – decide later – not sure of all details.

– the whole Golden Land destroyed really – rivers ravaged & raped – poverty & failure – contrast greed with the growth of the city – one a good and one an evil – but same impulse to improve – working together and working alone – San Francisco,

especially if we see the making of money as metaphorical. – RM this is how the world goes – decision to be made – third answer to question – madness & disorder, another new life – journey still not over.

– somewhere to the south an army outpost and work available, we are told – but first steps must be taken to start journey there – FB in agreement – leave behind this dirt and anger and unquenchable grasping for wealth – start over again – Rachael in this direction in any case – end with description of pulling belongings together, shaking a few hands, goodbye to MM, another soul left behind along the way – memories of Ian Macleod – setting out – empty pockets again.

Intertitle 7

And so at last we come towards the end of the story, though the end of the story is just exactly what this is not. The story ends, it's true, but there is no "closure" as those irritating self-help books would say. I know people like neat endings. I suppose it all dates back the childish sound of "… and they all lived happily ever after" and the satisfying thud of a book being shut conclusively. It's not how the world works, is it? We think we're going one way, looking for one thing, and suddenly we find out we're going somewhere else, finding something completely unexpected.

It's enough for me to say there is work for you to do. What are the facts? After completing the next section, named "Fort Tejon" by myself for obvious reasons, Hugh must have gone back and written up the "Rocky Bend" section, and, I think, produced the notes for "Big Creek". Thereafter something stopped him from doing more, writing up the notes and filling in the gap of years that exists between "Big Creek" and "Fort Tejon", and for which not even a scrap of paper lay in my Elgin attic. You will have to decide for yourselves, as I did, what it was that led to his final abandonment of the recording of his life. After 1857 Hugh Ross disappears from the pages of history. Any attempts to trace the rest of his story have been futile so I have no idea of the shape his life took after the events described in the next section. It follows, therefore, that we have to speculate, but without the satisfaction of ever finding out if our speculations are accurate or wholly off the mark.

The following section sees Hugh further south, but still in California. In the missing years, hugely surprisingly[79], he has joined the American army, though there is no hint of any kind

---

79 To me – perhaps another reader might have seen it coming.

of combatant status in the ongoing Indian battles. How this
came to pass I have no idea, and Hugh doesn't explain, probably
imagining that he would cover these events in some never-to-
be-started section.[80]

My guess, and it can be no more than a guess, is that he
saw the army as a means of personal advancement, following
on from the disappointing failure of the search for gold hinted
at in "Big Creek". We know that Hugh is always on the look
out for a way of "making something more" of himself, to use
his own words. Perhaps the fact that he could not strike it rich
in the gold fields of Big Creek led Hugh to pursue other means
of moving himself onward and upward.

By 1857, however, it has to be said that Hugh Ross hasn't
taken the army by storm. He is just a simple hospital orderly in a
minor Fort set up in 1854 to provide a buffer between the white
settlers and the occasionally rebellious Indian population, a Fort
which, as you'll see, occupies only a tiny place in the history
of America. The only hint of leadership potential he shows is
his willingness to keep Ferdinand Braddle under his wing, and
if I'm telling you the truth, as Hugh would say, there's not too
much about Ferdinand in the pages dealing with Hugh's stay
at Fort Tejon.

I suspect the presence of Ferdinand provided Hugh with
some security and comfort as he moved from the gold fields
to the Fort by whatever mysterious route he used. It can be
reassuring to have somebody with you on your journey, though
sometimes we have to do without. Anyway, we're getting to the
end of the story.

Selling up when my business began its downturn was the
hardest decision I ever made, maybe, but at least it allowed me
to return from Aberdeen, and at least it allowed me to buy the

---

80 Not that Hugh really divided his writing into sections, as I mentioned previously.

house in which I discovered Hugh's testament. It's a big old empty house, and I am glad I found something in it, though what I found was not what I had expected to find. I felt good about coming back to within a few miles of my birthplace, and once we got here I thought, *Now that we're home, everything will be all right.*

But Philip had his own ideas, and so I am here alone, although I do, of course, have Hugh. The children are with Philip and that's a battle I should have fought harder and might yet, if things don't work out. I know we're always the last to see our own mistakes, always the first to see the mistakes of others.

When mistakes happen (this is the conclusion I have come to) it is not just because of *me*, or *you*, or *them*, or *him*. Me and mine, you and yours: these are the ideas that make life incomprehensible. Reading this story with its revelations about my ancestor have helped me think again about how it all joins together. Who to blame for the mistakes in my life? And, more importantly, how to accept that mistakes are what make life what it is? Things go wrong and you can do one of three things. You can rant against the world, you can carve your guilt into your own flesh or you can just agree to see that mistakes give impetus. Life is a packet of errors, sent anonymously through the post.

This is not to say my hopes are dead. Far from it. I am sure I will think of other ways to make money. Most entrepreneurs have business failure behind them and business success ahead. And I will think of other ways to build my family once again, the way so many people have to. It is just a question of seeing clearly the direction to take, and it is interesting that much of this next section of Hugh's narrative deals with the issue of tracking and identifying correct directions.

But, to get away from myself and to return to the purpose of these Intertitles, I ought to give you some guidance about the next section and your reaction to it. What ought you to look out for here?

Firstly, I would say you ought to think carefully about the character of John Xantus, a minor but not insignificant figure in the world of natural history, though, as you'll see, he would certainly have disagreed with my evaluation of his worth. Hugh never quite explains his feeling of connection to Xantus, nor his reaction to the incident of the squirrel hunt. And it seems to me that Hugh's feelings of guilt regarding the grizzly bear are not justified by the description of events offered, though perhaps this is because Hugh has not given us a complete account of what was said and what exactly happened. There is no doubt, however, that Xantus is a key figure in this section.[81] I wish there was more about him. I wrote a lot of footnotes about him, and about other things, in this final part of Hugh's story, but I have removed them all. No distractions. But I think someone should write a book about John Xantus. Maybe *I* will, one day.

Secondly, the reader might consider the apparent absence of any sense of connection between Hugh and the other men in the Fort. While some conversation is reported, there is none of the camaraderie one might expect to see in this all-male environment. Why this might be I can't say. Perhaps, by this time, some disillusioning event had given Hugh a sense of distance. I can understand that. I well remember the feeling of isolation when my so-called Team Members decided their perfectly adequate wages were insufficient to prevent a strike. Bonds can be quickly made but once broken they are hard to repair. It may have been so with Hugh. I don't sense animosity, just a lack of engagement. It may be a case of once bitten twice shy: it is just that we never did really see the bite in the first place. Or maybe his mind was just elsewhere.

---

81 The letters that Xantus sent to Baird from Fort Tejon are available in print, and though dry they make an interesting read, I found. One intriguing aspect of reading his letters, for me, was provided by comparing Hugh's account of certain events with that of Xantus.

Thirdly, the whole Reed's Ranch aspect of this section is of interest to anyone who knows the age-old stories we love to believe. The thirty four year old Hugh, panicking a little, as you do when you see the horizon receding when you thought you were getting closer, gives much significance to this Ranch and its people. He quite simply sees the appeal of the familiar and tries to entwine that with his desire to become "something more". Nothing could be simpler, nothing in the world.

Fourthly, Callum. I will say no more than that the man surprises to the very end.

Fifthly, I am not sure if I ought to remind the reader not to be critical of the text's inconclusiveness, touched on above. As I mentioned, we all like *shape* in our stories (fictional or real) and we like to try to impose it if it is not to be readily found. That temptation will strike you as you come to the end of these pages, but I would urge you to fight it. Don't seek for meaning in the dust of the final words of Hugh's memoirs. Do not try to impose a significance on the fact that there are no words after his final ones. Do resist that human urge to wrap, to recap.

The importance of this text is not to do with one man's life. It is not a tale of one man's search for happiness. I repeat, it reaches across the years to speak to *us* about our *own* lives, and the shapes we try to find within our *own* experience. Bear this in mind. It has given me new energy: maybe it will be the saving of me. You can never know what would have happened if circumstances had been different. I can genuinely say, however, that finding those yellowing pages in my attic caused a flicker of flame amongst embers I had thought were dying. I may yet flare brightly. That is what I take from this text: I must.

And so I am finished at last. This project for me is ended, my annotations and intertitles all complete. If the sales of Hugh's book benefit me then that is a pleasant by-product of the months I have spent in his company, poring over the scrawled handwriting, piecing together the occasionally disordered pages.

It has been a privilege.

The time I have taken to read and understand this book, to step back from the tangle of my personal life, has clarified my vision. I wanted to feel one way but I have ended up feeling another. We should always be prepared for that. I started exploring my family tree as a way of turning my eyes from my present situation, but when you find these characters in the past, these real people, your reaction is not what your expect, now how you feel you *ought* to react. All you have to do is take that openness and shift it into the present day and then maybe you can live again.

I was born in the small town of Forres in 1970 and my father John MacPherson was born there too, in 1931. His mother, called Alexandra, my grandmother, was born in Nairn in 1906. She was a MacKenzie, becoming a MacPherson by marriage to Anthony, and at one point they stayed in this Elgin house for several years. Alexandra was the fourth daughter in a family of eight, all fathered by Richard Mackenzie, husband of Ann Main, who was born in 1878. She was from the coastal fishing village of Hopeman, a few miles from Elgin. Ann Main's mother Rebecca had her only daughter at the late age of thirty-eight. Rebecca was born in 1840 in Elgin itself. She was born there because her own mother, Catherine, ran away from home with her husband-to-be Peter Main. They settled in Elgin and had six of a family, three boys and three girls. Catherine was born in 1815, and before she was a Main she was a Vass and before she came to Elgin she was from Croval. Mary was her mother.

So now I must turn away, and try to start my life afresh, seek a new direction. I, like you, must say my farewells to Hugh and take the first steps down the next path that opens up ahead, chasing something new.

I forgive Hugh Ross, because without forgiveness there is nothing.

Fort Tejon

So, after all this time of moving from place to place, and after the army not being sure exactly what to do with this lost Scot, I ended up here, at Fort Tejon, as I'd hoped. It's a lonely place, up in the hills, at the head of a canyon that's greener than you'd expect for this part of America, full of oak trees and scrubby brush. It reminds me a bit of Rocky Bend but without the river and the bend.

They gave me a job in the hospital as an orderly, and Ferdinand's job was sweeping out the barracks and the hospital and anywhere else that needed sweeping out, including the stables, and that was the one place he actually wanted to sweep out, because he likes horses, probably a bit more than he likes people. I'm glad they kept us together because for a time they were going to send him back east again to Fort Riley, which he would have been happy enough about, but I'd have missed him, I know.

It was hard to persuade them to send me here with him, the one place I wanted to go, but it worked. I told them Ferdinand's parents had been killed in an Indian attack and that I was his legal guardian and no one thought to question it because why would you make up a story like that? I've learnt that dishonesty can sometimes be important. He was old enough, of course, to look after himself perfectly well and he had no need of a legal guardian, being in his young twenties, but because I told them that, these army people thought there was something wrong with him and he wouldn't be able to manage being sent some-where else. You can create a world for other people, even if it is false, maybe especially if it is. They thought this Fort in the middle of nowhere was a good place for a Scot and a boy who couldn't look after himself. But to me this place is the centre of the world, now.

We came to Fort Tejon on foot, me and Ferdinand and two other young soldiers sent to replace ones who had run away. As I said, it's a long way from anywhere and they'd had enough, on the look-out for some more excitement, I think. We came down through Grapevine Pass, with Grapevine Peak towering away to our left, on the east. The names are right, because all across the hillsides there are vines growing with small sweet grapes on them. Not at this time, though, the time I'm writing, January 1857. I've been writing for years, on and off, and now I've come to this part of the story, which I will tell without giving anything away. I didn't know there was a story, not really, despite all I've written in the past. I was just writing then. Now I'm finishing, writing the end part of the story that went from Croval to Upper Canada to Iowa to all over California. It was in the autumn that we came and there was a warm breeze blowing down the Pass, as it often does. I thought I'd never seen a lovelier place. A clear little burn ran beside us and I stopped to taste the water and it tasted like hope. There was greenness and the leaves starting to turn. There were birds in the air and of that there will be more to write as I go on. I put my arms round Ferdinand's shoulders, a lightness in my heart.

I said, Well, Ferdinand. Here we are.

He smiled at me, but I knew he was not as happy as me. He wasn't sure where his journey was heading, and I know he resents being just part of my journey. I hope he will be free soon. Perhaps he will return to Dubuque, where his parents may still stay.

As we came down the slope to Fort Tejon, there was a lightness in my heart because not far from Fort Tejon are several ranches, and one of them is Reed's Ranch, and on Reed's Ranch there are cowboys and fencers and all sort of workers and one of those workers is a cook and nursemaid and her name is Rachael Sutherland.

Good storytellers set the scene. As we walked down towards

the camp we saw a bustle of activity, men in uniform walking horses, others exercising in the parade ground, others smoking clay pipes on the steps of the two main barrack buildings on the south east side of the Fort. On the north-west side of the parade ground was the hospital, where I was to work, a big wood and adobe brick-built place, like all the rest, with a sloping roof. There was a granary and store-houses, a blacksmith and a guard-house, a bakery and the grander officers' quarters. This was to be our home, and its inhabitants watched us curiously as we made our way past the first buildings and into the main parade ground, the open area at the heart of the Fort.

I don't know if we expected to be met by the Chief Officer of the camp, but we certainly were not, though the figure that did approach us was distinctive enough, and looked authoritative. But more of him shortly.

We were shown into the barrack room where there were lines of beds more or less side by side. It was a thought, to be starting again with so many new people. There were about forty dragoons at Fort Tejon when we arrived but there are fewer here now. It changes from time to time. Some get sent away to other posts and some just go away. There always seem to be some who have had enough of this army life and just wander out of the Fort. No one bothers too much to stop them because you can always get new people if you put your mind to it. People like us, ready for their next new life. It's all the same for everyone, that's what I've learnt.

Some of the dragoons were in the barracks when we walked in, about half a dozen. They were wearing their pale blue-grey trousers and they had on their darker blue jackets, unbuttoned mostly, the orange piping at the edges and at the collar standing out. They had their hats on their beds beside then, the little cockade of orange feathers strange-looking to my still-Croval eyes. They watched us as we were shown to our beds, away over by the far corner, two beds beside each other. Nothing much was said, just a few murmured greetings and a couple of mild insults about new men. I said I was pleased to meet them and one of them said

A Scottish fellow?

Yes, I said, a while ago now.

He said, How long ago?

Sixteen years.

He gave out a whistle. Then he said, And now you reckon you're an American, right? You reckon you're an American in the United States Army, am I right?

I nodded. I said, I suppose I am that.

Well, he said, standing up and putting out his hand. Pleased to meet you. My daddy was a Scotsman, from Lochgilphead, so I reckon we're sort of kin.

This was Alan MacKay, six foot six inches tall about, with a grip as strong as any you've ever felt, a scar down the right side of his face as if he knew how to fight and win, and a man I thought would be right useful to have on our side in the barracks of Fort Tejon, except he ran away the following day and no one ever heard from him again.

We left our kit there and then we went over to look at the hospital. This is where he works, the man who was showing us round. His name is John Xantus, or John de Vesey, or John Xantus de Vesey, depending on what mood he is in and who he's talking to. He told us as we walked across the parade ground that Xantus was his real name and de Vesey was his army name but I never really understood about that.

He is a tallish man with a look of importance about him, a pointed black beard and a moustache that sweeps away on either side, the moustache of a man who loves to look well to other people. His hair is thick at the sides but starting to go on top, like mine, but you could tell, even at first glance, that it mattered to him. His eyes are dark and intelligent, his nose is long and his whole face and posture and style tell you of good breeding, the way you can always tell a good horse from the tinker MacPhee's. John Xantus is one of the oddest men I have ever met, friendly and bad-tempered, hard-working and lazy, trustworthy and completely dishonest and he is an eternal puzzle to me, and, I suspect, to himself. I liked him right away as he showed us round. He is about my age, perhaps a little younger, but somehow he seems older than me. I can't explain why that is. I miss him now that he's gone too. I could write a lot more about him, but he's not the main character. There are only two main characters. Me and Rachael.

This is the hospital, Xantus said as we went in, and his accent was not American or Scottish. It was later we found out that he was a Hungarian, which is someone from the country of Hungary, which is somewhere away to the east of Scotland.

I looked around. There were half a dozen beds in the big empty building, and none of them occupied. There was a bucket sitting in the middle of the floor and beside it on the ground lay a broom. Xantus is the other hospital orderly and I suspect the bucket and broom had lain there for a long time, as had the pile of crumpled blankets lying on top of one of the beds. Getting his proper job done is not one of the strengths of John Xantus de Vesey.

This is the hospital much quieter as usual, he said. But nor is it full ever of people. I think there is work perhaps here for one orderly and not two, but your arrival, Mr Ross, fills me with many pleasure as now I may be released to my true vocation. Perhaps to be some of the time out in the woods and beyond. This is what I prefer much as working in here.

This made no sense to me at the time, though very soon it did. I asked him how long he had been at Fort Tejon.

Not long, not long, he said, wistfully looking out the window at the parched parade ground. And soon I will be gone from here, so soon as Mr Baird secures my move to some other place more amenable. Or else, he continued with a flourish of his hand, it is easy for me to go to Bolivia. Or Peru. Or Chile perhaps. Nothing may stop me from pursuing my own collection, no Ten Broeck, no Blake, nobody.

He fixed us both with an icy stare. We said nothing.

After that Ferdinand went off to see the stables and so I was left in the hospital building by myself, working out what I had to do.

For a while I just looked out of the window, out across the dry reddish-brown slopes and up into the groves of oak trees that seemed to be everywhere. I had a sort of peaceful feel about me at that time, not a feeling I have a lot. It was as if the world had stopped moving and it was just me with my elbows on the narrow window sill, gazing out into a landscape that for once I seemed to belong in. There were birds hopping around on the ground just beyond the fence that marked the edge of the compound, finches or some kind of blackbird. I thought back to the seagulls of Croval, and the noise they made as they curved down to the foam of the waves and up away again into the grey sky. For a moment I was both there and here, and I liked that feeling so I held it in my mind for as long as I could, until, with a sigh, I straightened up and looked around me.

It was obvious the hospital needed someone to pay it a good bit of attention, though I wasn't sure exactly why that was, not at that time. I know now, right enough. It wasn't exactly dirty but it wasn't exactly clean either. I took the broom and, starting at one end, I began to brush up the dust and the leaves that had blown in through the open windows. It was strange, to be working in someone else's building like this, a bit like being in Chicago, but here it was calm, and quiet, and I wanted to be here. For the first time in a very long time, I felt my life had slowed down a little bit, like the rock that was pushed from the high cliff and that plummeted down, then bounced across the land until it rolled and came to a stop down near the water. I've had enough of plummeting, I think, and now I know who

I can at last honestly tell that story to.

After I'd swept up I straightened the blankets on the beds and put blankets on the beds that didn't have any. I had no idea if I was meant to do this but, well, I had to do something, and that seemed like a good thing to do. There was a cupboard at one end of the room and when I pulled open the doors I found medicines in bottles made of brown and green glass, all mixed up together. I mean the bottles were mixed up, not what was in them. Some of the bottles were lying on their sides and some had leaked their contents a little from their glass stoppers. I set them upright and tried to arrange them in a more organized way. On two shelves I put the clear glass bottles, on two shelves I put green and on two brown. Within each shelf I had no idea about how they should be ordered so I decided not to worry about that. I cleared up some spills with a scrap of cloth I found in a small room leading from the main *ward,* which was the word Xantus used.

I discovered later that this wee room, which has in it a table and a chair and piles of papers and letters and such-like, is the room of Dr Ten Broeck, who is the surgeon at Fort Tejon. More of him in time. There is also another small room at the other end of the ward, which was the room where Xantus would sit, avoiding the hospital work he loathed. But Xantus also had a spacious set of two rooms in the officers' quarters, the strangeness of which I shall describe in the correct place.

I do not propose to spend very long describing my work in the hospital in the months between then and now. It was dull work, on the whole, and it would be dull to write about and more dull to read. It was cleaning and organizing and running at the command of Dr Ten Broeck to fetch this or that. It was tending to the needs of the small number of patients who entered the doorway of the hospital through necessity.

But the hospital at Fort Tejon doesn't have a lot of patients, so I was never exactly busy. The dragoons are a healthy bunch of men, not given to illness in this dry climate, and the most common cause of there being someone in one of our beds is a broken limb, caused by a fall from a horse, for example. We have had one gunshot wound while I have been here when a young recruit accidentally shot himself in the calf, or so he said anyway. I have changed a few bandages and I have spooned thin soup between the lips of one or two men. But this is not a hospital where duties take up your every minute, though I know there are many hospitals like that in the busier army posts and in the cities like San Francisco.

Working in Fort Tejon hospital leaves you time to do other things, the things you would prefer to do, really. And I knew that before ever I came, and it was one of the reasons I sought this post. It was why Xantus came here too, or one of his reasons. And he was happier than before once I had arrived because that meant he had even more time to spend in the service of the Smithsonian Institution in Washington, away across towards Scotland. So I could find time here, if I needed to, and before all that long, I did.

Although she hadn't replied to the letter I sent from the city, in November Rachael made contact with me at Fort Tejon. A note was delivered to me along with the camp's other mail. I have copied it here.

Dear Hugh

I was pleased to hear news of you in S Francisco, and I don't know how you knew I was at Reed's Ranch, but so I am. In your letter you told me that you were going to be in Fort Tejon and I don't know if you have gone there at all, but I write this note in case you have. If not, then I don't know what will happen to my words, perhaps they will find you somewhere else.

Jacob and I are at Reed's Ranch still. We have travelled a long way, the two of us, and so have you. I had decided that it would be the best thing if we did not meet. I thought it would be best to continue with each our own lives. Yet also I thought that if I have a friend here, so far from home, I would like to see that friend.

What passed between us, years ago, is past. My life has taken on a different shape now but that is no reason why we cannot yet be friends. I think that I would like to talk to you, and that perhaps we could compare our stories.

Do you ever think that it is strange? That we should come across the world like this and end so close together by chance when we could have ended a thousand miles apart. Because of this, I have decided that I think that we should meet. I would like you to talk to my son and tell him tales of the home that will never be his home. You were always good with your stories. Perhaps we can talk of the others we have left behind. I was sad to hear that old Mr MacLeod had died. Perhaps you will tell me about that.

I do not wish to be cruel, or to give you hopes that cannot be fulfilled. Companionship is as valuable as any other emotion – this I have learnt. I hope that you will understand and that perhaps you will visit me, or if that is not possible I can visit you at Fort Tejon. I do not know about your army responsibilities. It may be, I know, impossible to arrange this visit. If so, or if you do not agree with what I have said here, perhaps you could reply by letter and that will be the end of the matter. I do not wish to meet if it will put you to inconvenience or if it would be in conflict with what you feel in your heart.

We are both well. I hope you are the same.

Yours very truly

Rachael S

This was not the letter I wished to receive, but I convinced myself, the more I gave it thought, that it was better than no letter at all.

In short, I arranged with Major Blake an afternoon during which I was excused duties in the hospital building, so that I could make the six mile journey to Reed's Ranch. I thought about writing her a letter to tell her I would come, but after several attempts I gave up the attempt, unable to find a form of words that pleased me. I decided that I should arrive unannounced, and that way I would be able to gauge Rachael's reaction to me more accurately.

I walked. There were horses in Fort Tejon that I could probably have made use of. Not one of the officer's fine horses, of course, but one of the ordinary pack animals that were used on occasion by the sutler and others, not much better than MacPhee's nag. But I have always felt foolish and uncomfortable on horseback and I decided that my arrival at Reed's Ranch should be as dignified as possible, and that it would be best if I could still walk a little without pain when I got there.

It was a cold day, but the big snow comes later to Fort Tejon, and it was dry at least, though a strong wind nipped my ears as I made my way to see them. They tell me some years it's very hot at this time, but we were in a bad spell of weather. The manzanita and sagebrush was flattened down towards the ground, but my mood lifted upwards as I crossed the ridge and scrambled down the dry rocky slope towards Reed's Ranch, which was exactly where Xantus had said it would be when he pointed his long thin finger to the south east. He knows his way around these lands, John Xantus. As I made my way through a little copse of leafless oaks I took off my gloves and blew on my fingers and slapped my body with my arms to get some life into me and made my way up to the arched gate in the fence. Reed's Ranch didn't look to be the biggest ranch in the world, and it was all fenced, I later found out. There were steers in a pen across to my left and I could see others wandering more freely away in the distance, seeking out the winter grass.

I decided there was no need for me to introduce myself at the big house so, like any other worker might, I went over towards the cookhouse, where smoke was coming from a stone chimney and being whisked away by the wind. I stepped up on to the wooden porch, my army boots clicking on the boards. I had on my thick blue army coat too, with the collar turned up against the cold, so I probably wasn't that easy to recognise when Rachael opened the door in reply to my thumping on it with my fist.

She frowned for a moment, looking at me, placing me, then all expression left her features briefly, before she smiled a tired smile and threw the door open, beckoning me in with her hand.

Rachael Sutherland. I've known her since she was a child like me and here she was now, in front of me, a grown woman, with lines of weariness on her face but with that red hair that sticks in your mind, with here and there a strand of grey now that was never there before. She was wearing a plain brown skirt and her shirtwaist sleeves were rolled up to the elbow. She was still slim, young-looking in a way that a few lines and a few grey hairs couldn't touch.

Come in then, Hugh, she said. Keep the cold outside.

I stepped into the room, which was the kitchen. I later found out the canteen part was on the other side where there was another door. It was warm, with the stove burning away. For a second the image of Mary McIntosh came into my mind and I thought that Rachael was maybe about the age now that Mary had been then, in Pictou. She'd asked me what I was chasing. I could smell the smoke in the room but not any food cooking.

Sit down, says Rachael, pointing to a chair near the stove. She says, I didn't know if you'd be coming or not. Or when. I didn't know if you'd have seen my note.

I saw it, I tell her. And here I am.

Well, she says.

Well, I say and then the two of us are tongue-tied and I suppose we're both thinking of before, in Goderich. She's standing beside my chair and I feel a bit clumsy, with my big coat on so close to the fire and yet I don't want to take it off because I don't want her to think I'm taking it for granted that she wants me to stay for a while to talk, and, in fact, she doesn't.

She says, You came at a bad moment, Hugh, because Mr Holland is just going to be taking us away to Lebec in the cart to get stuff.

I can't think what to say, so I ask, What kind of stuff are you getting?

We need salt, she says. And we need sugar and some other stuff for the fences, Mr Holland was saying. He says we're always needing more nails, it's never-ending.

This is not the conversation I had pictured in my mind, so I try to bring it round. How are you, and Jacob? I ask.

This sounds very unnatural to my ears even as the words come out of my mouth and I have a strange sensation of being separate from my own body, as if I'm looking down on myself, sitting sweating uncomfortably on my chair while she stands beside me, her red working hands on her hips, with a sort of laugh on her face, as if her ears think it's very unnatural too, that I should be here, talking to her like this.

Ask him yourself, she says, and points over to the corner of the room.

I look where she's pointing and realise there's another person in the room that I never saw when I came at first because my eyes were for her just. There's a boy, about ten years old, sitting on a stool over by the door through to what I later found out was the canteen. In his hand is a pencil and he's been drawing something on a sheet of paper, but as I look at him his gaze is not on the paper but on me, a childish curiosity on his features. He doesn't have Rachael's red hair but there's a sharpness in

382

his eyes that is all Rachael.

He got up and came towards me, his hand stretched out. I rose awkwardly, and we shared an oddly adult hand shake. I couldn't think of what to say to him at all, so I said, I'm Hugh, Jacob. I'm a friend of your mother's from long ago. Are you going to Lebec too?

He said, Lebec is named after Peter Lebec who was killed by a grizzly bear twenty years ago. But when he was eaten by the grizzly bear there wasn't anywhere named after him so he was killed nowhere. They called the town after him so he could have died somewhere. My mother hasn't told me about you.

This last sentence was aimed at his mother, as a question. I let go his hand and looked at her. She had a flush on her cheeks, at least. I thought about telling him that I'd heard the tale of Peter Lebec and that he had actually been killed where Fort Tejon now stands, but I didn't.

I said, to spare Rachael, It was a very long time ago, Jacob. Maybe she forgot.

Jacob frowned. There was a little silence. Rachael Sutherland and Hugh Ross, side by side, a thousand thousand miles from home, not looking at each other but instead concentrating as hard as they possibly could on a little boy who was standing in front of them trying to work out why his mother and her old friend weren't even speaking to each other.

So that was all of my first meeting in California with Rachael because a moment later the door opened and in came Mr Holland, Reed's Ranch's storeman, a solidly built man of fifty-five or more, bald-headed and red-faced, and after some quick introductions, Rachael got her own heavy coat, and Jacob's, and off they went in their cart to Lebec to buy salt and sugar and nails and other stuff, leaving me standing by the gate to Reed's Ranch, my hand raised in a farewell wave and my heart lurching with uncertainty.

Why can we never say the things we ought to say? I know I

383

never said to Ian what I should have said to him, or to Callum, or to Robert. Or to my own mother, come to that. And here I was, having spoken to but not really spoken to Rachael, and all I had ahead of me at that moment was the cold trudge back up over the ridge and into Fort Tejon, the place I'd come to so that I could come over the ridge in the first place and speak to Rachael.

As the cart went out of sight, I felt all alone, like the last leaf clinging to an autumn tree, and I started walking as fast as I could, soon breaking into a staggering run. By the time I got back to the fort the sweat was pouring from me despite the cold and my calves were sore from the heavy hem of the coat whipping against them. I went into the hospital, and scrubbed the floor until my knuckles were raw from being scraped off the wood, and my tears bled into the soapy water.

The very next morning, as if he knew that I wanted to stop thinking, Xantus asked me if I wanted to come collecting with him. I said to him that I didn't understand what he meant.

I am collecting specimens, he said, for the Smithsonian Institution in Washington.

This was the first I ever heard of that so I had to ask him to explain and he told me about how this was a big building and inside it are all the animals and birds and insects and snakes and fish of America, all there so that a record can be kept of what lives where.

I am collecting in southern California, he said, on behalf of that most famous man Mr Spencer Fullerton Baird, more renowned as any man in his field, secretary assistant at the Smithsonian Institute. He has arranged my presence here for the collecting of specimens.

He paused dramatically, and opened his arms in a wide gesture.

Me – I don't know what you mean. How do you collect these creatures?

384

Xantus – Shootings. I go to the country and I have shootings of the animals and the birds. Follow.

He led me over the parade ground to the officers' quarters and into his two rooms. One of his rooms was simply furnished with a bed, a small table and a chair, but to my amazement the other, much larger room was packed full of all sorts of dead animals, some of them just skins, some of them small piles of bones, some of them split open and stretched out on a wooden bench, others stuffed and set on their feet to look like they were alive again. There were finches, hawks, snakes, badgers, owls, blackbirds, mice, buzzards, woodpeckers, squirrels, deer, hummingbirds, sparrows, ravens and even a small grizzly bear. And many other things I had never seen before. Seeing this room made me think I had never seen anything before. I thought of Chicago where the hogs were killed, and slit and chopped and packed until there was nothing left of them. This was different. Only life was missing from these animals and the stuffed birds were created so beautifully they looked as if they might burst into song and fly about my ears. It was one of the biggest rooms I'd seen in Fort Tejon, apart from the communal rooms, and it was full of these animals.

Xantus, proudly – I have been already been so pleased as to send already three boxes to Mr Baird in Washington with my earlier specimens.

Me – I can't think what to say.

Xantus – My work is to collect, my ambition is to collect. I am an officer, no orderly, I. But here, to have time to collect my specimens for Mr Baird, I must be orderly. Dr Ten Broeck, he does not understand this, and for this reason I am often unhappy in my duty.

Dr Peter Ten Broeck seems to be a very skilful surgeon. I find him always friendly and, although he spends much time on the coast, he does his job well, as far as I can see. He is a plump clean shaven man in his middle years, with perhaps a little too high an opinion of himself, but in other ways likeable enough. He has a deep and smooth tone to his speaking with that friendly sounding American voice. I had already worked out that Xantus and Ten Broeck despised each other with an intensity that went as deep as the old Carcair hatred of Killarnoch. Now Xantus explained why.

He said, Always, this man Ten Broeck is standing in my way, hampering my collecting. Always is he telling me I must work in the hospital, be ordering medicines from the city or dressings, be washing and cleaning. I am an officer and only in this temporary way am I orderly John Xantus de Vesey. And who is this Ten Broeck?

He paused, bristling with anger, drawn up to his full height, jutting his bearded chin at me. I realised I was expected to respond.

Me – He is the surgeon.

Xantus – No! He is a nobody. In his eyes my collecting, it is useless. In his eyes Mr Baird he is worthless. Ten Broeck is a blight on my work. He has told me I must not discharge a shotgun within three miles of Fort Tejon. This is madness, I think so. But he will not stop me. I am made of a material that cannot be torn by a man such as this.

He held his temper upright for a second or two, and then his shoulders relaxed and he smiled at me. This is John Xantus. One second there is a fire in his eyes and then the fire is replaced by a spark. He took me by the shoulders with his delicate hands.

Xantus – So, Hugh Ross. This afternoon we will go and we will collect.

Me – But didn't you say you couldn't shoot your gun within three –

Xantus – Today we use no shotgun. But I will shoot my shotgun wherever I wish to shoot my shotgun. Let him stop me. Mr Baird is more my inspiration as Dr Ten Broeck.

He spat the name out as if a fly had ventured into his open

mouth. He stared at me intently for a moment, his face just a few inches from mine. I thought he might kiss me on both cheeks, as I had seen him do once to Major Blake, the Fort Tejon commandant, which Major Blake had not liked, but instead he just nodded decisively, once, and strode out onto the parade ground.

So that was my introduction to the feud between Xantus and Ten Broeck and many times since that day I have stood between them on several occasions, defending the one to the other, listening to the complaints of the one about the other. They are like two brothers who have fallen out, or two friends who have.

So that afternoon Xantus and me headed up Grapevine Pass, about two miles to the south-west. The weather was better than it had been the day before and the air that blew down the Pass was warm and pleasant. This is not the main story so I won't go into detail about how we found and shot what Xantus said was a Mexican Woodrat. He said Mr Baird would be pleased.

I asked him, But didn't you say that Major Blake told you not to fire your gun within three miles of Fort Tejon? Won't he be angry?

He smiled broadly, his white teeth smooth and even. He said, sharing a secret, Major Blake tells me I must not shoot *shotgun* within three miles. So I fire pistol! Now he will tell me not to fire pistol also, but in the meantime I have good specimen of Mexican Woodrat. In my letter to Mr Baird I will tell of your important involvement in this capture.

So that was my first collecting expedition with John Xantus. There have been many more since then, but Xantus tells me that the spring and summer are the best times for collecting. I'm not sure what will be happening then, and John Xantus has gone now in any case, but I am not giving anything away.

When I told Ferdinand Braddle about our collecting trip and about all the dead and stuffed animals in Xantus's rooms, he laughed.

He's mad, he said.

I don't think he is, I said.

Who else has a room full of things he's killed? I understand hunting, but why would you want to skin everything and stuff it? Even snakes, you say?

Even snakes, I answered.

Mad, said Ferdinand. I reckon you can't argue with that.

We were in the stables and he was working away at one of the officer's saddles, softening and shining the leather with saddle soap. They gave him more jobs to do beyond sweeping, once they'd realised what he was good at. He was coming to like his work at Fort Tejon, the routine of it, the way a hot and sweating horse could be groomed back to sleek calmness. He told me he liked the way his day was shaped for him by others. It stopped him worrying, he said. I can't help feeling this is a little bit weak, but he is young yet and he'll grow. There was a time when I was content to return to my mother's house every night and follow her rules like law. But even so, I did feel it was my duty to Ferdinand to talk to him about other possibilities, ones that lie beyond just doing what someone else wants you to do.

Xantus has an obligation to a man away across in the east, I said. He is collecting animals for a huge gathering of all the animals and birds and everything that lives in America.

Why? asked Ferdinand, pausing for a second in his work. Why would anyone want to do that?

I told him everything Xantus had told me on our hike up Grapevine Pass, about the grand building in Washington, a building that would hold all the knowledge of America so that the people who lived in this huge place could begin to under-stand it all in one, instead of as a thousand different places not really joined to each other, if you see what I mean. Ferdinand said it sounded like the ship that Noah built that Ian used to ramble on about in Rocky Bend sometimes, and I suppose he was right, except all the animals are dead in the Smithsonian Institution. If I'm telling the truth, I don't really understand how this can work. That river in Chicago, the tall trees in Goderich, the hoses shooting dirty water at the rock in Big Creek, the dusty slopes that rise up behind the stables at Fort Tejon, what joins them all together? I don't know. But then people say I'm Scottish and all I ever knew was one little corner. I never knew Edinburgh or Portobello or any of those other places. And there are thousands of places in America I haven't been, and that I'll never go to. So although I've *come* to America, I haven't really *been* to America, if you can see what I mean. Not in the way I could say, when I was Ferdinand's age, I've *been* to Craigtore. Maybe one day I'll go to Washington and see all of Xantus's animals in the glasses cases he's told me about. And he says it's not just him collecting, but lots of other people too. It must be the biggest building in the world. And Xantus was collecting in other places before he ever came to Fort Tejon, like Fort Riley, and afterwards of course he went to the coast to collect fish from the sea and so on. All this I told Ferdinand, except the last fact because I didn't know that part of it then.

What will you do after Fort Tejon? I asked him.

Ferdinand – After?

Me – When you've had enough of life here, I mean. What will you do?

Ferdinand – Maybe I won't though. I like it here now. It's peaceful.

Me – Before, you told me you were missing Dubuque.

Ferdinand – I know. But you settle, don't you?

I laughed, because my life is a story that shows that Ferdinand is wrong. I said, What about family?

Ferdinand – I suppose I have left them behind. Didn't you do the same? You told me this was growing up.

Me – I know, but that's not what I meant. Don't you ever think about having a family of your own, meeting a girl and settling with her, maybe having a son.

Ferdinand – Not really. I'm young. Did you ever think that way?

Me – You make me sound too old to think that way now.

Ferdinand – Well, older than me, in any case. I reckon I might do that some day, but not for a while. I'm liking what I do just now.

Me – But where's your direction, your *plan?*

Ferdinand – Like Mr Xantus, you mean?

Me – Well, he knows where his life is going. He has a good story to tell.

Ferdinand – Does he?

Me – Well, he hasn't told me it all yet, of course, but I think he does. He comes from even further away than me, from the east part of Europe.

Ferdinand – So?

Me – His story has *direction,* even if I don't know what it is. Think of that journey, across Europe, across the sea, across America.

Ferdinand – Why does your life have to have a journey in it? Why can't you have a good life even without a journey? You just say that because *you've* travelled so far.

Me – Maybe. Maybe so.

Ferdinand – So what is his story then? Xantus, I mean. How come he's here?

Me – I'm not sure, but I'll ask him about it.

I suppose there must have been something resentful in my voice, because Ferdinand smiled at me before speaking again.

He said, I'm sorry. You know that what you say is important to me. I just want to understand and I think you can help me. I know there's a part of me that just wants to do the easiest thing, here. Polishing saddles, sorting out the harness, dealing with hooves, grooming the horses. It's easy. I know there's a laziness in me, don't think I don't. So I do want to hear what you think.

I didn't mean to be difficult. Part of me knows you're right.

I put my hand on his shoulder to show I wasn't annoyed, even though I was, a little bit. I said, It's all right. You're allowed to be young. I'll speak to Xantus and then I'll tell you all about his journey and then we can decide what yours is going to be.

I left him there in the stable, pleased we were still friends, but a bit worried too, in case my direction now was just to show the direction to someone younger. I went to bed that night with my thoughts on Ian MacLeod.

I never really got the whole of the story of John Xantus, and it was not really his fault, but mine. My head was full of Rachael, so full that other things fell away from me the way the land grew small when we sailed away in 1841.

I did ask him about it, though, one important day as we sat under a tree in the parade ground and he began to tell me about how he'd served in the Hungarian army as a young man. One day I'll write down what details I have about this man, but not just now. He asked me if I could guess what he did when he was captured during some war with Austria that they had, when for some reason he'd joined *their* army.

I didn't answer right away, because I was distracted by the sight of Rachael Sutherland walking towards us from behind the mess and the kitchen. She was by herself and her eyes were fixed on me. She had a woollen shawl around her shoulders and her pace was firm and purposeful. I gave some vague answer to Xantus.

Well, he said, his eyes flicking from me to Rachael as she approached us, Xantus has decision to make. Xantus must escape, I think so! Chased by Austrian soldiers on horseback with guns and swords, many times I am almost caught and executed by the Austrians. Many times. On one time I am hiding in a cave in the Austrian mountains and the soldiers are no more further away as this woman here is to us. But Xantus, always he escapes, and as he escapes sometimes he must fight for his life and he has to kill five, six, ten men from the army of Austria. But at last he is in Hungary and then I enlist in the great army of Hungary, the Royal Artillery. So John Xantus is the only man to be serving in two armies at war! Remarkable!

By this point in the story, Rachael had reached us under the oak tree. I stood up, dusting myself down, and so did Xantus, clearly irritated by this interruption to his life story. I introduced them to each other and hands were shaken.

Rachael said to me, Hugh, I've come to apologise for two days ago. I could have stayed. Mr Holland could have gone to Lebec by himself.

Before I could speak, Xantus, all gallantry, said, My dear lady, no apologies must come from one so pretty. No lady is ever in the wrong, I think not. The complications in life come from the male of the species. I am just telling Mr Ross about my mission in the war between Hungary and Austria! A tangled time! The army of Hungary tell me I must go back to Austria and you may ask me why they would want me to do that. You may ask me.

I looked at Rachael and said, Why did they send you back to Austria?

Xantus – I cannot tell you. Even now is such a secret that it must not be told, not ever.

Rachael – Hugh, I wonder if I can speak to you for a minute, alone.

Me – Perhaps we can walk a little. Mr Xantus, thank you for sharing your adventures with me. I would enjoy hearing more about them.

Xantus, following us as we began to walk away across the parade ground – Of course you enjoy to hear my story! But do not think Xantus is wishing to stop his account. No! In Austria I am captured most unfortunately and they are charging me for deserting and running from their country.

He was a step or two behind us, and we quickened our pace

a little. I didn't want to be rude to Xantus, but I did want to speak to Rachael and I wanted to hear what she had to say. I was pleased she had walked all this way, just to talk to me.

Me – There is no cause to say sorry, Rachael. We are close by each other here and we have so much that links us. I thought we might be able to talk sometimes.

Rachael – I think I was rude to you. And I think maybe you felt Jacob was rude to you as well.

Me – No such thing.

Xantus, catching up – Will they execute Xantus? Of course, no! I am here! I am trained lawyer and when they bring me to trial for desertion I argue my own case. No execution for John Xantus.

Rachael – It's just that we move from one place to another, and our lives change.

Me – I know.

Rachael – In my letter, I didn't mean that –

Me – It's all right. When I wrote it was just an idea that maybe –

Xantus, laying a hand on my shoulder – Instead, they are sending me to Asia. Asia! A land of many strange creatures, very much stranger as any other part of the world. So there Xantus is building his knowledge, always building, until I am becoming one of the important men in natural history. But Asia is not where I must live. No! Soon I go to America and for many months I am trying hard to find my directions.

He paused, and stopped walking, his hand to his brow as he remembered this difficult time. Rachael and I hurried on. We were now two hundred yards or more beyond the camp, on the way up Grapevine Pass.

Rachael – And then there's Jacob. He changes all things.

Me – The person I am talking to is you.

Rachael – I've made my own way, Hugh. It's been hard, and maybe I've not always made the right choices. But here I am, with Jacob. It was all years ago, when we were closer. I don't know what it means any more.

Me – Closer?

Xantus caught up, still speaking. I'd missed the first part of what he was saying.

Xantus – So being a good piano player, and a tolerable draughtsman, I procured an honourable support by teaching for a short time.

Rachael – Are you curious? About Jacob? He is a part of me now.

Me – I did hear about him, when we were up in Iowa.

This word broke through the barriers of Xantus's attention.

Xantus – Iowa? Iowa! This is where I go! But not at first. I travel to Louisiana and I meet Dr Wagner and Dr Agassiz and I meet Duke Paul William of Wurtemberg and all of these great men say, Of course! Xantus is a first-class man of natural history. These men of science they all together pay for me to begin my collecting, in Minnesota. You have been to Minnesota, Mr Ross, my dear lady?

We told him that no, we hadn't been there. Rachael leaned close and spoke quietly to me, her warmth brushing my face so that my heart beat faster and my breath came quicker. I could smell her skin, fresh and clean and reminding me of an upturned boat on the beach at home, reminding me of being sixteen years old, all innocence.

Rachael – I do think of you, often. Don't think that I don't. But sometimes we just have to make our own way. Everything is so complicated. Sometimes it all feels as if you can't breathe. Do you understand me?

Me – Yes. Of course.

But what I'd thought was that Rachael was someone who might help me to breathe more easily. I'd never thought that she was stopping up my breath.

Rachael – So I came here to say that to you. I hope that we

394

won't lose touch with each other. Not again.

She hooked her arm through mine and leaned in to me in a way that was at once sisterly and exciting. I never knew my sister. Another one left behind along the way, but not my fault. I felt my heart breaking.

So, joined to me, but still distant, Rachael turned to Xantus and said – Your story is interesting, Mr Xantus. Where did you go from –

Xantus, beaming at her – Thank you, kind lady! From Minnesota, I go to Iowa. Yes, Iowa! In Iowa there is a place with the name New Buda and here there are many Hungarian people to be found there. All Hungarian people in America seek for other Hungarian people, share their words and their food, like home but in another country. You have been to New Buda, Mr Ross, I trust?

I explained that I had not.

Xantus, frowning – No? Very good place, but also not a good place, with many cheats and swindlers living there. In New Buda I own some land, better as any other land in the town of New Buda. My land is called section thirty six, township seventy, range twenty seven, but in my mind the land is called Xantusia, called with the same name as the species that will be called with my name one day when my natural history works are complete. But there are those who try to steal my land. I have written many times to Mr Baird in Washington and he will help me to reclaim my land. I have lost my homeland and I have lost my American land also. But Xantus will reclaim, I think so. For now I join the army, with my new name, de Vesey, but one day I will reclaim my homeland.

Rachael – That's a sad story.

Xantus smiled again, his flashing smile, and said, There is never a better story than a sad story, unless it is a story of success and fame.

Rachael – I think the first kind is more common than the

second kind.

Me – Ian once said to me, *Fame is no plant that grows on mortal soil*.

Rachael – What does it mean?

Me – I don't know. It just stuck in my mind.

Xantus – It means that long after you are gone, people will still talk of you, and hear the name John Xantus.

We stopped and there was a feeling of sharing some idea between us, standing half way up the Pass, looking back down towards the Fort. Rachael leaned into me again, and I could feel her softness against my side, my unreclaimed homeland. Together we strolled back down to the parade ground. So that was that day.

As November drifted on towards December another letter came from Robert. I read it and took it to Rachael to read down at Reed's Ranch, but she had got a letter of her own and she knew everything that was in my letter already, though she was interested in the letter that came with it, of course. This is what Robert said.

My Dear Hugh,

We were both greatly saddened to hear of Ian's death. I have longed to write to you ever since the news came to me, but for these past few years I have not been aware of where you are. Since that letter you wrote to us from Rocky Bend I have been trying to establish your whereabouts. Your letter alarmed us, not just because of your account of Ian's death, but also because of its disjointed meaning and sense. When no news of you could be found, we feared the worst. Rachael's news that you are in Fort Tejon has reassured us that you are alive and well, and perhaps it is not presumptuous to say that we hope that the army has given you a stable footing in your life. I hope you do not think such a comment impertinent – I simply mean that for many years now, it seems to Elizabeth & I that you have led a rather drifting life, and it would be wrong to say we have not worried about you.

Now that you are installed at Fort Tejon, perhaps we might begin a more regular correspondence. We hope that this can be so. With that in mind I shall cut this letter rather short, with the full intention of writing another before too long, I trust, in response to one from you. I may briefly tell you, I hope, that we are all well here. Young Ian is growing into a fine strong lad, dark coloured like me. He is a great help to us around the place and we dread the day when he will move on and start a new life on his own, or with some girl with whom he will build his own family. But that is for the future and we must not worry. Young Elizabeth is a pretty wee thing, a credit to her mother, who is well and asking after you, of course. As for myself, I am now the Chairman of The Goderich Citizens' Committee, and have been so for three years now. As such, it has been my duty to preside over many improvements and expansions to the town, of which we are more than proud. I wish that one day you might visit us here. What stories we would have to tell each other! What memories we could share!

It would be such a pleasure to us if you would write back and inform us of all your travels and adventures and to give perhaps a more detailed and less imaginative account of the death of our good friend Ian MacLeod.

My main reason for writing is to include along with this sheet a letter intended for you. I shall say nothing about it, for I do not wish to prejudice your response. However, I would wish to know what you feel as you read it. Perhaps you could include that in your letter to us. I know it is too late, but better that you read it than

never know.
Ever your friend,
Robert V

Tucked in along with Robert's brief letter was another, much longer one. I unfolded it curiously and this is the letter I read. I write it down here because now I know what must be said and I know who must hear it. I have come a long way to set these words down.

Dear Hugh,

When Robert told me about Ian's death, I was brought to my senses. I could write here all that I remember about him. The stories that he told are still with me. The books that he shared with us in the manse still are alive in my mind. The ideas that he gave us I still struggle with, even now. Hardly one day goes by when I do not think of him, when I do not speak to him in my imagination, asking his advice, seeking his approval.

And yet what I remember the most is how I spoke to him the very last time I saw him, in that place in Chicago, that saloon. This is what burns in my head, when I close my eyes to sleep. I was drunk, yes, I was, but that can't explain to me why I said what I said, why I did what I did.

I have long ago remade my friendship with Robert. He is one of many I have treated wrongly in my time. I have learnt, I think, that the world cannot turn any way but one way. Nor can I make it spin in any other direction. So I have shaken hands with Robert, I have kissed Elizabeth on the cheek, and though we will never be what we were, at least the sourness has been sweetened. Their children are a constant sign for me of what I have missed in life. A fool and his future are easily separated.

But Ian Macleod, he is gone now and I can never

undo what I did. He was a kind man, and he shaped my life for a while until the time when I decided to shape it for myself. I have always been running after something new, and never have I known what I ran after. Without him, I would not be here. Without my rejection of him, I would not be about to do what I must do.

And as for you, Hugh, what do you think of me now? What stories did you hear of me in Chicago? If you will not shake my hand across all this space and all this time I will never know. I understand I was cruel to you, that I belittled your dreams. I could say the drink spoke through me. I could say the devil was in me and using my tongue. Or I could tell you the truth, which is this. I meant every word that I said. I looked at you then and I thought you were nothing. I thought it was weak of you to work in a factory killing pigs, feeble.

I think back to the Hugh I knew as a boy, the Hugh that was part of every adventure we got involved with, who tempted me against my judgement to do things that later I knew I'd enjoyed. You were a boy who took chances, such as coming to America, and you took us all with you. You showed me drink in the first place, not that I blame you. You took us out in my father's boat when it was too rough. You were the boy that always wanted to go to the Carcair to argue with the old men. When we pushed that rock together off the cliff you scared me half to death but at the same time I was excited. Our friendship was the very shape of my life. And there you were in a packing factory in Chicago, with nothing in your mind but your day at work and your bed at night. What was I to think? It made me weep, the emptiness of your life.

I know you'll say that it was me who broke up the whole thing in the first place and that is true, I can't say it's not. Why did I leave Goderich? It was too small. Why did I come back when it was Robert's wedding? The lake was too small, backwards and forwards on that boat, and the future had grown too small. Something broke in me. And so to Chicago, looking for somewhere bigger and at first it was. But Chicago too tightened on me like a rope around my neck squeezing the life out of me. There was nowhere wide enough, that's what I learned. You can run for ever, but it always catches you up, the smallness of the world. Yes, I was drunk. Yes, I chased bad women and I fought and many other things I can't bear to write down. I was swinging out, my fists all blood, my eyes blackened, my nails split and my muscles aching, trying to beat to death the walls of the world all around me.

And in the end it came to this. I stood by the edge of that dirty river because there was nowhere else to stand in a world that had narrowed until I was balanced on the head of a pin. Maybe if the waters closed over my head and filled my throat and my lungs and my heart I'd find space at last. Sometimes we have to go somewhere to find out where to go next. I jumped. I tasted the foul rotting taste of the blood and waste that your factory and a thousand others drained into my mouth. I sank and turned in the current and my arms floated out and my eyes were shut and this was the end. Nobody pulled me out. Nobody saw me jump in.

Hugh, I touched the bottom with my fingertips and when I did I pushed myself away and up and I opened my eyes and saw the sun through the dirty water and I reached for it with my hands and my arms and my soul. I wasn't ready to die. I don't know why. When I broke through the surface the first thing I saw was a bird flying high above, an eagle or a kite or something. I could have risen from the water and soared into the sky to join him.

I went to find you after that. I wanted to say sorry,

for all I'd said and all I'd done. But you'd gone by then. I told myself that it would happen one day, that we'd meet, you and me and Ian and I'd list all the stupid things I'd done and you would forgive me, take my hand. I wandered for a time, in Chicago and elsewhere, but the destinations of my travels are unknown now. I stopped the drinking, gradually, and now I am free of it, I think. I went to Goderich and here I met Robert and he told me what he knew, and then I understood that everything had changed. Ian has gone and you are still here and all I wish is that we might be friends again.

But I could not stay in Goderich for ever. It is all fool-ishness. America has no answers for me, for any of us. My berth is reserved for the fourteenth of June. I don't know what I will find when I go back, but I hope they will welcome me. Croval will have changed, I know as much. Perhaps they will forgive me for ever going away.

Until I go I am in Pictou once more, staying in a hotel that doesn't charge too much and that lets me pay my way partly by helping with cleaning and washing and doing a turn in the garden. I do not ask that you give up what you do now, whatever that is, but only that you come to see me here, and things can be once more at ease between us.

Of course I have no address to send this letter to, but I shall post it to Robert, and when he discovers your whereabouts he will send it under cover of a letter of his own. I hope it will be in time.

Yours in apology

Callum Ross

16th March 1855

So he'd gone. I read the letter fifty times, and each time none of the words in it changed at all. I went to Reed's Ranch and talked about it to Rachael, and she cried, quietly, which probably stopped me from crying, although I wanted to. I asked her if she wanted to go back too but she wouldn't answer.

I said, I don't mean do you want to go back with me, just do you want to go back at all?

But she shook her head and wiped away her tear and pointed over at Jacob. She said, He's an American boy, you know that? Like Robert and Elizabeth's children. This is a new place we're making.

She let me take her in my arms for a minute, but then she pushed me away.

This is daft, she said.

I know, I said.

But I didn't mean it. I didn't mean it at all and it is my curse to never say what I really mean.

So that was Callum's letter and in it was something I never ever faced and just writing it down in these pages has been the first good thing I've done for a long time. One day it will be read by someone else and that will be an even better thing. You try to escape but you can't because the thing you're escaping is yourself and the thing you're chasing is also yourself. In the end it all comes together. I see that now, but when the letter came at first it confused me a lot.

I couldn't decide what to think about for the next few days. Sometimes a thing happens that makes you wonder about every single thing you've ever done. It makes you wonder about every single thing you're ever going to do. I mean most of our lives we just go on from day to day. Things happen to us and we make things happen to other people, but during all these events we never think too much. Maybe we can't think too much. But after that letter, and after seeing Rachael's reaction, I couldn't turn my attention to the real world at my feet. My head began to live in the past and the future, and it made me unhappy. It was like having a book and not being able to read the page you were on, only the ones you'd read already or the pages still to come.

The first thing that broke me from this mood was John Xantus asking me and Ferdinand if we wanted to come with him on another of his collecting expeditions.

Today, he said one morning as we ate our breakfast in the mess, a kind of porridge and a strong black coffee, Today, we go and we hunt grizzly bear. We find big grizzly bear and we kill him, take him back to Fort Tejon. Three men can carry him back, I think so.

I'd seen his room and his specimens already, of course, so I said, Don't you already have a specimen of a bear?

Yes, young bear, he said, smiling. To this bear there is attached a very interesting story. I tell you of this young bear one day. But today we hunt big grizzly bear and we shoot him.

I looked along the table, where Major Blake sat at the head, his cold eyes surveying the untidy men under his control. I suspect he had hoped for something better than Fort Tejon, and maybe he'll achieve that yet. He's still young enough. I whispered to Xantus, What about Major Blake? He won't let you shoot your shotgun and –

Xantus interrupted me, saying loudly, Ah no! Major Blake has received a letter from Mr Baird and so too also has Dr Ten Broeck. The Major and the Doctor are very supportive of this my collecting. *Now* they are.

I glanced back at Major Blake and caught him just looking away, a look of utter contempt and hatred passing across his face like a cloud across a grey sky. Ferdinand was laughing. To him it was an adventure, but I was beginning to think I'd maybe had enough adventures in my life.

Off we went again up Grapevine Pass and over the hill up towards the north west, Xantus with his shotgun held confidently in his left hand. He was happy and smiling, glad to be away from the hospital. I was nervous. It was near the middle of December and Xantus had heard from a trapper who'd been through the Fort that there were grizzlies wandering in that area. One of the other soldiers had told me that in the winter the grizzlies would sometimes come down into the Fort because they were hungry. He said the previous winter one had come and had shuffled up and down the parade ground for two or three hours, with all the dragoons in the barracks, staring at it out of the windows, trying to guess what it would do. In the end Major Blake had returned on horseback from wherever he'd been and the bear ran off. There were stories about children being attacked in some of the outlying ranches and then of course there was Peter Lebec. I was thinking it might be better not to find a grizzly bear at all, just in case Xantus missed it, or, worse still, hit it a wee bit.

There was a dusting of snow on the ground and our breath came out in clouds in front of us as we laboured up the slope. I didn't see how we'd be able to pull a fully grown bear over this hill if we got one, but Xantus would hear none of it.

He said, Yes! Three men very strong. Slowly we pull.

I'm not writing down the whole story of that bear hunt, how Xantus shot one and how when we came to try to haul it up through the rocks to get it up over the hill, we could hardly budge it.

Xantus said, Just these rocks. If we get him over these rocks, then it is easy to pull him up to the edge of the hill and after is easy over down the other side, I think so.

I replied, I don't think so. At the speed we're going now it'll be dark by the time we get twenty feet further.

Xantus, irritated at me, said, No! We must try! This is my best specimen for Mr Baird. We must pull him over the hill and to the Fort.

I had an idea, and said, What if its mate is here somewhere and the dark falls?

Xantus brightened. We shoot her too! he said. Two specimens is better as one.

And he took hold of the bear by its ears and tugged. I tried to grab it by the fur around its neck but it was sort of greasy and my hands slipped off. I was tired and annoyed and the day was coming towards its close and it all seemed pointless to me, away out in the middle of nowhere trying to lift a dead bear the weight of a horse over a hill. I said so and there was an argument that I shall not write down here. It ended with Xantus stamping away up over the hill and down to the Fort, leaving a flurry of dry snow in his wake. Ferdinand and I followed more slowly, glancing back over our shoulders in case the bear's mate really was likely to seek revenge.

The whole story seems to me to have a meaning that I can't quite find a way to put into words, but maybe I will one day. By the time Xantus went back the next afternoon, with a horse and six dragoons, the coyotes had been at the corpse and the skin was too damaged to be of much use to Xantus or Mr Spencer Fullerton Baird at the Smithsonian Institution. Xantus blamed me for this so our relations had become a little bit strained.

But I had other friendships to be thinking about. I went back to Reed's Ranch and spoke to Rachael about the letter again. We sat out on the rockers on the porch of the cookhouse, wrapped up in coats and scarves, so that the men inside wouldn't hear us. Rachael had in her arms the one year old child of Mr and Mrs Reed, a fat baby with astonished eyes called Amelia who was thrust into Rachael's arms whenever her parents had something of more pressing importance to attend to such as a whist tourney at a nearby ranch or a musical show in Lebec. It was too cold for the baby on the porch and she was just beginning to cry.

I said, Should we go back, do you think? Do you think we should all go back to Croval?

Rachael – I'm not from Croval, you're forgetting that.

Me – No I'm not. You know what I'm meaning. It's just that I always thought Callum was the man to drive things on, but then it all went wrong, and now here's him off home. I mean, what if it's all a mistake? What if we should have never come here?

Rachael – But we did come here and now this is where we live. We talked about all this, Hugh. We talked about all of it already.

Me, miserably – I know.

Rachael – Don't be so weak. You've done so much, all the different places you've been, the people you've met, the money you've had in your hands.

Me – And lost again.

Rachael – If you can make that money once you can make it again.

Me – I've lost interest, I think.

I told her the story of shooting the grizzly bear and the more I told it the more it seemed to me like one of Ian's parables.

No, she said, It's just a story about that madman Xantus shooting a bear.

I asked, But do you not think it's like a symbol of what I've been doing for the last fifteen years?

No, she said. Why can't it just be a story about killing a bear?

Me – I don't know.

Rachael – I don't mean to be bad again, but it's too cold for Amelia. I have to go inside with her, you know. And the men are in there, Mr Holland and all the others. They already think there's something between us. Best if you go.

I drew up all my courage into my throat and said, And is there nothing between us?

Rachael – There is indeed, but not what you want it to be. I won't send you away from my life, Hugh. Not again. But I think what's past is past and what's now is now. That's what I think.

Me – But things change. Can't things change sometimes?

She said nothing and, surprised, I glanced across at her. She was staring straight ahead, a muscle in her jaw clenching and unclenching. My heart stuttered.

I said, Can't they?

She looked at me then and there was the tiniest nod and then she was up and away into the cookhouse. I fairly ran back to Fort Tejon, as if I was fifteen again and rowing like fury from Craigtore round to Croval.

My spirits were so high I ran straight to Xantus's quarters, to apologise to him for my behaviour when we'd been hunting the bear. I realised I'd been childish and sulky, and I wanted to tell him so. Rachael's little nod had made me feel more like an adult again, as well as more like a child.

I found Xantus seated at his desk, staring morosely at a letter. He looked up at me with eyes red enough to make me wonder if there had been tears there a minute before. My determination shook like the surface of a horse trough in the wind.

I'm sorry, I stuttered. I hope I'm not interrupting. I just thought –

Xantus waved the letter at me and said, Mr Baird, still he has not arranged for my boxes and the materials I need. Mr Forbes has betrayed me, I know this. Never will I see my boxes, I fear. Where will they be? How can I continue? I need eyes! I need eyes!

This left me silent, because I didn't understand what he meant. Some of the old men in the Carcair, who were really Gaelic speakers, sometimes said strange clumsy things when they tried to turn their thoughts into English. I think Xantus was trying to express some Hungarian emotion, and I couldn't work out what it was. I changed the subject of the conversation.

Mr Xantus, I began, I was wanting to say sorry for not helping more with the bear. I know how disappointed you must be that you've lost this specimen. I am sorry I was not more help. I didn't understand. I knew you already had one grizzly and I thought that would be –

Xantus – Ah! My baby grizzly. Is not the same. A mature specimen is worth so much more to the Institution as an immature.

Me – I'm sorry. I should have tried harder to help.

Xantus – One day I tell you how my baby grizzly ate Ten Broeck's dog. Not today. Too sad. Too angry.

I left him with another mumbled attempt at an apology but by that time he had sunk back down at his desk, his red eyes reading again the letter, whatever was in it, and I don't think he heard me. We never spoke again really about the grizzly bear the coyotes got to, though sometimes he hinted to me about the way I'd let him down.

At the end of December I'd been working in the hospital one afternoon when there was a surprise for me in the barracks. I was tired, because the hospital was busier than usual, with people suffering from coughs and colds, and one or two who had hurt themselves in falls, because the weather had turned icy and snowy and it was easy in the windy dark to miss your footing and turn your ankle or worse. There was one man who'd been wounded in a scuffle with an Indian. So Dr Ten Broeck had kept me and Xantus busy through the day, bandaging and cleaning and dispensing potions and pills, though what good they do I'm not sure, and I am sometimes reminded of Donald Sutherland and his bottles of splendid tonic.

So when I hurried across the parade ground and into the barracks, bundled up against the snow that was blowing flat in my face, I wasn't expecting to see anyone I knew apart from the soldiers. But there was someone sitting on my bed in the corner, and the soldiers all looked at me when I went in, and fell silent.

I must have just stood there for a moment, because one of the dragoons shouted at me to shut the door. It was cold enough in the barracks anyway, and the stove couldn't fight against the draught from the open door. I walked across the room to my bed and sat down on it. We talked quietly, and soon the conversation grew up again like the corn in spring, so that it hid me and Jacob, because that's who it was, as we sat there, talking shyly, my fingers grazing the rough blanket, my eyes on

408

the boy beside me.

He explained that his mother was at that moment in the officers' quarters. Her employers, I found out later, Mr and Mrs Reed, had been invited to speak to Major Blake to discuss supplying Fort Tejon with beef to see us through the hard winter months to come. They had taken their little Amelia with them, rather than leave her in the ranch as they were so attached to her. This seemed funny to me because half the time they never paid her any attention at all. But that had meant Rachael had to come too, and she didn't want to leave Jacob behind either, and Mr and Mrs Reed had agreed he could travel in the snowy carriage too, but only on the condition that he waited in the barracks and Rachael told them this was fine, because Jacob knew me and I'd look after him until it was time to leave again.

The thing was, I didn't really know him, and even if I had, I wasn't used to speaking to ten year old boys. I asked him how he was and he said he was in good health. Then he asked me how I was and I told him I was in good health too. He asked me what I did in the Fort and I explained about the hospital. He asked if he could see the hospital and I said no. He asked where the doctor was and I said in his own quarters. Jacob wanted to know why the doctor stayed in different quarters from the rest of us, so I explained about that and how some people are more important than others and get better rooms, though I still don't really understand why *Xantus* got better quarters. He'd told me he'd been an officer before, in Fort Riley, but I can't see how that could be true.

Jacob said, Are all these men your friends?

I looked round the dragoons. There were about fifteen of them in the barracks at that moment, lying on beds, smoking, playing cards, reading books, just sitting. I said, Not really.

Jacob asked, Where are your friends then?

I said, I left my friends behind, I think.

He asked, Where did you leave them?

I laughed, sadly. I said, A few different places. I've been careless, I think.

Jacob – Was my mother your friend?

Me – She was once, and maybe still is. I hope so.

Jacob – Did you and my mother have an argument?

Me – I don't think we did.

Jacob – I've heard her having an argument with people.

Me – Well, I don't think we really had an argument about anything.

Jacob – Why aren't you still friends then?

Me – I hope we *are* still friends. What do you think about that, Jacob?

His face was serious, his light brown eyebrows creased up in thought. He said, I don't know, really. When I have an argument with one of the boys on the ranch I usually fight them.

I told him I was tired of fighting, but of course he didn't know what I was meaning by that. We spoke then about what he liked to do, the school he went to in the mornings, the things he learnt there, his favourite ranch dog, the food he liked best, the lizard he kept in a box until it died and lots of other things. We were deep in conversation when his mother appeared in the barracks to get him, flushed from the cold and from being a bit embarrassed at being in this big room full of strange men. She stood at the door and beckoned to Hugh. He went to her without even a backwards glance at me and I felt a little skip in my heart at that, for some reason. Rachael lifted her hand, just a little, to wave to me as she went out with him.

One of the men said, as the door closed, That your sweetheart, Ross? and there was a snigger of laughter round the barrack room.

They are mostly younger than me, these men, and I never know what to say to them, or how to laugh at their jokes. I lay down and thought a lot about Jacob and his visit.

I was looking in him for some sign of Rachael, if you understand what I mean. Somewhere inside Jacob is Rachael and I was trying to see where. The hair wasn't hers, I was thinking, it was Edward Hill's or Edward Leaney's or whatever his name really was. When I looked in Jacob's eyes I could almost see Rachael there but I wasn't sure. It wasn't the colour that struck me, it was something else, a way he used his eyes, darting quick glances at you, then looking away. Something too about his hands, always moving, touching his face, his knees as he sat, each other, that was Rachael. Or the way he leaned back on the bed, still sitting up but with his arms splayed out behind him, his palms down on the blanket, relaxed but tense, a shape to him that recalled to me Rachael at fifteen on the jetty at Craigtore, her bare feet touching the surface of the clear green water just.

What would it be like to have a son? To see yourself there, every day?

All of a sudden I had an image of myself, years from now, lonely and tired, with no one to speak to about what's happened to me, no one to tell my stories to in the evening to help them to fall asleep, with that safe feeling that I would be sitting over them. And in my mind that sad feeling was mixed up with my memories of sitting by Ian as he lay close to death in Rocky Bend, and I thought of him buried in his grave under the cliff, with the cold snow falling softly upon him.

I was thinking, what if all this means nothing, what if it's just a list of things that happen to you, one after the other, not really joined together at all, until eventually you run out of things to happen. I had to turn away towards the wall so the dragoons wouldn't see the tears in my eyes and laugh at me. Rachael could see her own past there in Jacob, and in him she could see her future, as if the past and the future and now all were happening to her at the same time when she watched him playing with the dog in the yard at Reed's Ranch. Who would I look at when I was an old man, sick in some damp bed far away from home? These are the thoughts that were going through my mind as I thought about Rachael and her son travelling back through the dark in Mr and Mrs Reed's carriage.

There are only so many thoughts you can have before you have to start thinking about something else. You can only think about having a son for so long when the truth of it is that you haven't got one at all. So I tried to put these thoughts out of my head, lying there, and I fell asleep, hours later, thinking about the small bear and the doctor's dog, trying my hardest not to think about not being a father to anyone.

I wasn't sure who to ask about this, so the next day I asked Xantus. I don't know what I thought he would be able to tell me, but I didn't have anyone to ask about anything, not since Ian died.

He'd asked me, kind of reluctantly, to join him on another collecting trip. This time we weren't going up the Pass but down to the area not that far from the little town of Lebec, where he'd found some special kind of squirrel living amongst a huge pile of rocks in a wood.

He said, This time is not like the bear time, I hope so. This time we work very good together, much more good as last time.

I said, trying for a smile, Well, at least they should be easier to carry back.

He glowered at me, saying, Not so easy to catch, I think, however. All of our wits must be alert and our hands always ready to pounce.

When we got to the wood, he showed me where we would be waiting for the squirrels. He'd found a place in amongst the rocks where we could hide. He'd rolled one big heavy rock away from its place, and this revealed a sort of cave amongst the jumble of stone that we could crawl into. There was just enough room for us to lie, face down, side by side. He pulled some branches across the front of the opening so the squirrels wouldn't see us. Through a gap in the branches he pushed the muzzle of his shotgun.

It was freezing cold, and even though we'd taken blankets with us to lie on, I could feel the chill of the rock and earth below us start to eat into my bones as soon as we took up our positions. I couldn't move to get any warmth into my blood. I tried to pass the time by talking. I asked all of these questions over the following three hours, with long cold silences in between each question.

What kind of squirrel are we waiting to catch?

Why are they so rare?

Have you ever had a wife? Or children, even without a wife?

Don't squirrels sleep through the winter, like bears are supposed to?

What do you remember of your own mother and father? Do you miss them?

Are you as cold as I am?

Have you ever left friends behind on your travels?

Won't the squirrels smell us hiding in here?

Do you do your collecting so that you'll be remembered?

All these questions but the last, and others I asked that I've forgotten now, were met with a pointed silence, or a brief instruction to be quiet. But when I asked the final question he turned stiffly in the cramped space and looked at me intently.

Xantus – To be remembered? Yes! Of course Xantus will be remembered. There will be birds and other creatures named for me, Xantusia. My name will live for thousands of years.

He said the word *thousands* as if it was *tousands*. I asked him if this was why he did it, for all these people that would live thousands of years from now. It was hard to think about.

Xantus – No! Of course not! So stupid. I collect because knowledge must be growing, always growing. My name will live, but Xantus is nothing, knowledge only must grow.

Me – If you had a son, would he carry on your collecting?

Xantus, with a clever smile, pleased with his idea – My specimens are my children. Mr Baird, he is the godfather.

413

So I was none the wiser, and I had the feeling that my questions hadn't raised me very much in Xantus's esteem. We lay there for another lonely and quiet hour, then he swept the branches aside and wriggled out from the cave, brushing the frost from his trousers in a sudden temper, and we went back.

When we got back to Fort Tejon, a little warmer because Xantus walked so fast in his bad mood, Dr Ten Broeck was waiting for us at the door to the hospital building. It was late afternoon and the light was beginning to fade out of the sky and the doctor cut a commanding figure as he stood on the top step, framed by the open door. Breathlessly, we stopped at the foot of the steps.

Dr Ten Broeck pointedly pulled out a watch, examined it closely for a moment or two, then returned it to his pocket. He said, slowly and seriously, I believe, Mr Xantus, that we had arranged that you would be here at two o'clock in the afternoon so that we might examine together the inventory of medicines and supplies. You are inexcusably late, sir.

Xantus said, his bad mood still burning inside him, I have important tasks to perform, for Mr Baird. Had I completed my task earlier I would have most certainly and immediately returned to count the little bottles of medicine with you, I assure you. But my collecting, this is my most important responsibility. I apologise for saying this thing to you, but nevertheless is the truth. Today I am collecting the black California squirrel. This is the fact.

Dr Ten Broeck – I suggest, with respect, that the black Californian squirrel is not the highest priority in terms of your employment in the army, sir.

Xantus – Mr Baird is fully supporting my activities and –

Dr Ten Broeck – I do not know your letter-writing Mr Baird and I do not care who is or is not supporting your activities. What I do know is that I have a hospital to administer and my work is hindered rather than helped by your presence at Fort

Tejon. Mr Ross. Perhaps you would like to explain how Mr Xantus has lured you away from your duties, which today, I think, included several cleaning tasks.

So here it was again, a moment when a friend escaped from my life. Not that, I suppose, John Xantus was ever really a friend. But there was something I liked about him, even after the thing about the bear. He caught my attention in Fort Tejon, someone who stood out, the way Callum had stood out when I was a boy, or the way Ian stood out when he arrived at Croval, the way even Donald Sutherland stood out. The way Rachael does.

I said, I'm sorry, and those words felt like a betrayal. I should have said something in defence of John Xantus, odd man that he was. Instead I hung my head and crept into the hospital, brushing past the solid figure of Ten Broeck. I am ashamed of myself, but I went and meekly got my broom and began to sweep the floor between the beds. I could hear the raised voices at the door for a minute or two more, but I couldn't make out exactly what was being said. Then the door to the hospital crashed shut, and the doctor stamped through the ward and into his room, muttering away to himself.

Later that evening, before going to sleep in the barrack room, I went to see John Xantus and I tried to apologise to him. He was packing his clothes and papers into a trunk. Through the open door to the other room I could see his specimens, waiting to be boxed and sent away.

He waved away my apology with that strange foreign kind of gesture, his arms flapping politely. He said, No, Mr Ross. There is no fault to you. Dr Ten Broeck has, in every turn, attempted to despise and despoil my best efforts here. Him I blame entirely. Yes! Never have I met such a man as him, and even when he received Mr Baird's letter, still he is preventing me from doing this work I must complete.

He put two white shirts into his trunk and threw some

books in on top.

I said, Well, I'm sorry. I should have said a word in support of you.

He stopped his packing and looked at me, a smile on his face, his eyes bright. He said, No. Ten Broeck, he hears no words. He hears only the words from his own mouth, I think so.

And with those words, Xantus threw his arms around me and embraced me in a grip so tight I could not breathe for a moment. Then he thrust me away with a farewell wave and turned back to his possessions.

I wandered away across the parade ground and into the barracks. In the morning he was gone, leaving me detailed instructions about how to package up his remaining specimens for delivery to Mr Baird, a task I did not relish.

So that was John Xantus. I hear he has gone to the coast to help with a scientific survey of the tides, and to collect any fish that Mr Spencer Fullerton Baird hasn't got yet. It would be like him.

That leaves Ferdinand Braddle and the thing about Ferdinand Braddle is, he's just a young boy. I know that I was the same once, and when I was that age I relied so much on someone older listening to the things I had to say, giving me advice, laying out my path for me. I know that young and old must talk together. Maybe there will be a day, one day, when I feel I know and understand enough to pass what I know on to someone else. Maybe I don't understand yet what I already know, if you can see what I mean. If I'm telling the truth, I still feel like a child in the world, as if all my growing is still ahead of me. So much has happened and still I can't tell if I'm going the right way or not.

What I mean is that, still, I miss Ian. I still wish that he was here to talk to me and tell me that what I am thinking and what I have done is right, or wrong, or somewhere in between. I don't mind which. I just want to know. Sometimes he would laugh at my words, but it was never the hurtful laugh of mockery. It was a laugh that showed me my errors and always he would follow it with words that set me right. He took me *here,* to America, and now he's left me high and dry. Like the last tree in the clearing at Goderich, like the boy pulled from the crowd of immigrants by Neptune's men, like the steer that wanders from the herd and stands alone by the side of some slow pool, head bowed but not drinking.

So what I was thinking then, and am thinking now, is what would Ian say to me if he was here, beside me, in Fort Tejon, his mind still as clear as it was in Croval back in 1841 when I was a boy and the sun was still high in the sky with the seagulls calling over surf for ever.

The day that Xantus went away, I wanted to ask Ian so many questions. I was wiping the windows in the hospital, inside and out, smearing away the dirt blown up by the frosty winter winds. Work like that, it only needs your hands and arms and the power you put from your muscles to the cloth. Your mind is free, whether you want it to be or not.

Ian, I said, in my head just, Why does everyone go away out of my life?

Well, Hugh, he'd say, sitting in his big chair by the fire in the manse at Croval, a glass of wine in one hand and a brown leather book in the other. Well, Hugh, it's like this. The thing you have to remember is this. This is the most important thing to think about. Here's what you must never forget.

I could imagine it all so far, but no further. *What* did I have to remember? *What* did I have to think? I could hear his voice in my head as clear as ever in life, but I couldn't put *his* words into the voice, only mine.

I asked him, What about Rachael? She's the only one that's left. How do I make sure she doesn't disappear again? She's close by and at the same time not close by.

Ian replied, You've known Rachael for nearly thirty years. What does that mean to you?

I said, I don't know. Not really.

Ian said, You've been across the ocean after her, you've trailed across America after her and here you are. You've caught up with her at last. Now what are you going to do?

I said, That's what I'm asking *you*. What am I going to do?

Ian asked, What are you going to do?

I asked, What do you think I should do?

Ian – What do you *want* to do?

Me – That's what I'm not so sure about.

Ian – That's what you've got to decide though.

Me – Is there a book I can read that'll help me?

Ian – There always is.

Me – What's it called?

But he just laughed again, and faded from my eyes and all I was looking at was a dirty bit of thick greenish glass and my own hand upon it and in my hand a dirty cloth that I'd held in my hand the day before and would hold again the day after. My fingers red raw with the cold.

I can't explain why the leaving of John Xantus hit me like a blow to the stomach. In my head I was bent double and struggling for air, the breath driven out of me. I needed somewhere to lie and sob, to shut my eyes tight and wait.

Once, I saw a fox in the woods up above Croval. It was lying right at the edge, just in amongst the trees. I thought it would run as I went up to it, but no, it just sat there as I got closer and closer. When I got right up to it, only a few feet away, I could see it was an old fox, its red fur tinged with grey, its eyes watery and blind, a sore in its side where a bite had gone bad. There was a tremble in it as it sat there, waiting. I should have taken a stick to it, put it out of its pain, but I hadn't the strength. I touched it with my foot and it stiffly got up and hobbled slowly off into the trees until my eyes lost it in the shadows and I never saw it again. Sometimes, over the years, that fox has come back to my mind and I wonder what sort of death it had, in the end.

That was me the day that Xantus went away. All I wanted was a few words, but there was no one there to give them to me and I didn't know what to do.

But a new year came, again, this time the year 1857, and I'm almost up to date with the story. It's almost now.

I went to bed on Thursday the 8th of January with nothing very much on my mind apart from what I would say to Rachael when I spoke to her next. What else was there to think about? This is the way I have lain my head on my rough pillow in the past few weeks, forcing myself to fall into sleep by repeating imagined conversations in my head until my mind can't take any more, and I drift away to dreams.

But that night was a bit different, because that was the night I made my decision, once and for all time. At last, I'd decided what I would do, because there comes a point where you really have to, and I'd already spoken to Dr Ten Broeck, who has been much more friendly since John de Vesey Xantus has gone away, to ask if it would be all right if I went to Reed's Ranch the following day, Friday, in the afternoon. Dr Ten Broeck thought about it, smiled in his gruff way, because he knows what's been on my mind because Xantus told him, and said it would be all right, so long as I worked hard in the morning, and came back into the hospital in the evening to do some cataloguing. He has discovered that I can write quite clearly and he wants me to collect together the scattered pages of treatment notes and to arrange them all in a catalogue. He is particularly interested in injuries to the limbs, breaks and sprains. He says he will write a book on this subject, because he believes he has some new ideas about the treatment of swollen tissues. I am reminded of the absent Hungarian, but of course I don't say that.

So on the Thursday night, when I laid my head down, I wasn't just thinking about an imaginary conversation with

419

Rachael, but about a real one, one that would happen on Friday afternoon. But that wasn't to be, because of what happened, at least not exactly the way I had intended.

That meant I couldn't sleep, of course. All through that long night I lay with my eyes open in the dark, going over my questions, my answers, my hesitations, my promises. I could hear the other men sleeping soundly all around me in the barracks, their breathing like the waves you could hear all those years ago on the Lady Gray when we sped across the water, trying to sleep in the shut-in deck, all of us emigrants together. I envied them their sleep, and in the dead of night I was lying wondering about their dreams, hearing Ferdinand crying out softly in some quiet nightmare, the groans of men far from home, the sighs of those who remembered, asleep, a time when their lives were held new in their hands, like a fish freed from a dripping net.

Outside the owls called back and forth across the oak trees and the vines, and a dog barked in the distance. The air above my blanket was cold and pressed me down. I have never been so awake. All through the night, as the hours crept by, I worried that I would be too tired to do my work in the hospital and that I wouldn't be allowed to go to Reed's Ranch. I tried to shut my eyes tight, tried to fool myself into sleep, but nothing would work. I can't recall a night ever, and I've had many nights when sleep has been hard to reach, when I've been so full of the sense that something important was about to happen.

This might be the way I give meaning to that night, now that I know what was about to happen, but I don't think so. I really did lie awake all night watching the sky through the window, half covered by the dusty curtain. I really did find my heart beating hard and fast for hours on end. I really did feel the cold slip away to be replaced by an uncomfortable warmth, as if the earth had changed its story.

In the morning, with all the men still fast asleep and the sky not quite showing the beginnings of the light of sunrise,

420

which comes about half past seven o'clock at this time of year, everything outside was silent. Owls don't call all night, no bird does, and the animals sleep too, true enough, but suddenly I sensed that all was quieter than it should have been. There was still the sound of the soldiers in the barracks, all fast asleep. It must have been about six o'clock in the morning. I don't know. I strained my ears to hear any sound from outside but nothing came. It all seemed strange, eerie.

Quickly and silently, and I don't even yet know exactly why, I got out of bed and pulled on my trousers and shirt, and hauled my heavy jacket around my shoulders. Carefully, so as not to waken anyone, I unlatched the door and went out, pulling the door shut carefully behind me.

I stood in the middle of the parade ground in the dark. It was a clear night but there was no frost. An odd warm air had come in through the night and I realised I didn't need my coat at all. I took it off and laid it over one of the bars at the corral. My eyes were getting used to the dark, or else the first movement of dawn was beginning, but suddenly I realised that all the horses behind the fence were standing stock still, heads up, ears pricked, not looking at me, but up towards Grapevine Pass.

I turned and strained to look up that way too but there was nothing to see. There was no early bird singing, no sound of any animal scratching in the brush. No breath of wind. I felt the hairs rise on my arms, and, despite the warmth, I shivered. I had a most odd sense of being separate from myself, as if I wasn't really there. I looked at my hands and they were trembling a little bit, but they didn't seem to be my hands and I couldn't connect them to me in my mind. This frightened me and I turned my eyes away from them and looked up at the silent sky, just colouring from the rising sun.

Something made me begin to walk up Grapevine Pass. I don't know what I was thinking I would find up there. I just went. Soon the light began to show itself away to the east. Not a bird crossed the sky. It was as if I was the only thing alive in the world and as I turned to look back at the Fort, I had this sudden sense that I was all alone, and a panic surged through me that, I'm sure, had its roots in my tiredness after my wakeful night. I don't know where else the blood surge in my ears came from, or why my legs felt weak as if I could hardly stand.

But then the noise I could hear wasn't from my pounding heart any more. There was a low and distant rumbling coming from the head of the Pass or beyond. It was like thunder but the sky was clear. I turned away from the Fort again and tried to see what might be causing it, but there was nothing to see.

I didn't know what to do. I could feel the vein in my throat pulsing hard and there was a sickness in my stomach that came from nowhere. I had fear building up in me, fear with no particular cause. There was a feeling in me that something was terribly wrong and all at once I knew I had to get to Reed's Ranch to warn Rachael. I broke into a run, but before I had gone twenty breathless paces I fell to the ground, though at first I didn't know why. I got to my hands and knees, blood coming from my mouth where I'd hit my face on the dirt. There was a dizziness in my head and when I tried to stand up I found I couldn't do it. I staggered off to my left and found myself again on the ground, this time falling hard on to my left side, hurting my shoulder as I landed.

The thunderous noise was coming closer, a rushing in the air that seemed to come roaring down the Pass towards me, surrounding me. And it was added to by the strangest noise I can remember hearing. The horses in the corral began to scream, their teeth bared, rearing up and pounding down with their hooves in the dirt, milling and barging and struggling to leap the high fence, the sound of them like one great creature in pain as if its skin was being scraped from its flesh. The air filled with birds, bursting from the trees and brush, screeching and flying in every direction. As I looked up at them it seemed

422

as if the world was sliding and turning under me and I began to crawl towards the Fort, knowing I couldn't get up, my ears full of all these sounds and under it all this huge roar, like the end of the world. I think I began to cry, not knowing what was happening, crawling on bleeding hands and knees to get to Rachael, six miles away. It was the Day of Judgement, and I would get what I deserved. The horses screamed as if in the Devil's fires.

All at once I was thrown over again, on to my face, the taste of dust on my lips. I raised my head and the rocks in front of me seemed to be swimming away from me, then rushing back towards me. The noise was all around me, in me, and I could feel the earth bend under me, trying to throw me off. A tree across to my left tore itself from the ground and flung itself across another, taking it down too. I turned my head and saw the stream to my right leap into the air in a flurry of foam and stone and then, a madness, the water began to flow back up the hill towards the Pass, leaving the stream bed below impossibly empty.

There were shouts from the parade ground and I looked to see the men running from the buildings a hundred yards away from me. The noise of their yelling added to the thousand other noises I heard and the sight of them falling and lurching against each other added to the thousand strange things I saw. The barracks building tore itself apart in a cloud of dust. The hospital swayed from left to right and folded in on its heart, just as Dr Ten Broeck appeared at the door, dragging the one patient behind him by the hair, down the steps, just as they vanished from sight. The corral fence splintered and the horses tumbled and rolled from their pen, a wave of hooves and manes and screams, knocking men over who could hardly stand on their feet. The bakery burst into a confusion of dirt and sparks from the oven.

Then the strangest thing of all. From behind me, up the Pass, a crack, a foot wide or more, slit its way down towards the Fort, the earth parting in the way a stone might split with frost. The crack passed me and raced through the parade ground, ripping through the officers' quarters and beyond, away towards Lebec. Where the crack sliced through the land stones and earth were thrown up as if the world was opening from inside, as if it was the crust of a loaf being broken open by a huge pair of invisible hands.

It was like a dream. It was like terror, turned into something real. Ian had told me the stories from the Bible about how the world would come to its end, and I thought this must be what it would be like, and I knew that in a moment I would have to account for the worst of my sins.

I think it must have lasted less than one minute, but of all the things I have described in my pages, it seemed to last the longest. There was blood in my mouth and my arm ached as if it had been kicked. I got to my feet and found I could stand, that the world had stopped moving. I looked at my feet, scared to look at anything else. In that minute of fear the most extraordinary thing I saw was the small fish that lay at my feet, cast there from the stream thirty feet to my right. It flapped feebly, eye staring up at me, mouth opening and closing as it died.

I ran down to the parade ground, where the others were starting to get to their feet, dust themselves down. Nobody was saying very much, but men were staring at each other, patting each other on the back, putting an arm around someone's shoulders, just checking they were still alive, sort of. Men went round, seeking out their friends, shaking hands, congratulating each other on not having been killed. One man was just sitting in the dust, crying quietly, rubbing at his eyes with the sleeve of his coat. It was one of the oddest scenes I've ever seen, I think.

A couple of dragoons went off after the horses that had broken free which were standing half way up the hill, blowing hard and prancing nervously on their tense legs. Two more men went over and began to put the corral fence to rights. Another man was trying, uselessly, to raise the flagpole, which had sheared off at the base. It was all going back to normal – birds were singing, the noise had gone and the stream was running just as it should.

I looked round me at what had been Fort Tejon. There wasn't a building that wasn't damaged in some way and the hospital and barracks were rubble and dust. The sun was properly up by now and the low rays cast odd shadows behind the broken walls, shadows we'd never seen before and which made the Fort seem like anything but home.

Major Blake was going round, trying to get the men organised so we could have a count. It took a few minutes to get us all lined up in the parade ground, nervously looking at the deep scar that ran by our feet, waiting for demons to leap from it. When we counted off it turned out that there was one man not present and the Major told us to start with the barracks, using our careful hands to clear the collapsed walls, trying to find the missing soldier. We soon had a sweat up, and there was a quiet urgency in what we did. We were all thinking that it might have been us under the pile of shattered adobe clay. I was wondering what it was that made me get up and leave the building before it fell. Even Major Blake helped, his jacket off and his shirt sleeves rolled up, his hands dirty and his hair full of dust. Dr Ten Broeck was dealing with the casualties, out in the open because of course there was no hospital any more, no beds to lie them in.

An older dragoon working next to me was saying, I've been in an earthquake three times now and that's the worst. I was in one in Los Angeles, and I was in one once near San Francisco, but that was just a shaking of the ground so you staggered a bit. Nothing like this one. This is the biggest. Hope I never see another one like this one.

So that was the first time ever I heard about an earthquake

and I wondered what Ian would say about it, and then I was thinking that Ian had never been in an earthquake and here I had been, and I wanted to tell him about it, so there was a tear in my eye, again, as I tore at the wreckage. I could feel my fingernails split and crack as I scraped away, hoping not to feel dead flesh under my fingertips.

We'd been working for maybe two hours, and we were just beginning to wonder if there was much point in carrying on, thinking Major Blake would be telling us to stop any minute, that it wasn't worth it, when the missing man appeared in the parade ground. It turned out he'd been in Lebec. He'd sneaked out of the Fort last night and gone to see his woman in the town. He said that Lebec wasn't too badly damaged and he couldn't believe that Fort Tejon had been so wholly destroyed. He said the crack in the ground went as far as you could see, away to the south east. We were annoyed at him, because we'd just spent two hours looking for his dead body, but at the same time we were pleased to see him because if we hadn't been it would have meant we'd have preferred it if he'd been dead under the ruins of the barracks.

Nobody hurt here? he asked as we all crowded around him.

Just you, one of the men said. You were crushed under the walls of the barracks. If you hadn't come back just now we'd have been burying you before you'd have known what happened. Maybe you're a ghost.

It was good to joke about it, because the morning hadn't felt very much like a joke.

Well, he said, I'm feeling well for a dead man.

He patted himself on the arms and body to show how real he was and we laughed, a nervous snigger that came from seeing the world ripped in half and still being here to talk about it, and laugh out loud about it at that.

Well, one of the other men said, there's a few cuts and a broken leg or two. He pointed over to the shade by the trees where Dr Ten Broeck was laying out the injured men, fussing over them with bandages, holding a canteen of water to their lips, gently stroking their foreheads.

Not too bad, then, said the man who'd been in Lebec. There's a few buildings damaged in Lebec but I never heard of anyone hurt especially. You've had it bad here. It came right through here, didn't it? It carries on down that way and maybe it's as bad down there or worse. I hear there's a woman dead over at Reed's Ranch. A beam fell from the ranch roof. I heard it from a Paiute on the road. He said the steers stampeded there too, all sorts of problems.

My voice sounded as if it came from a thousand miles away when I said, Who was it that died?

He pursed his lips and shook his head, saying, I don't know. That's what I'm saying, I just heard from an Indian. He wouldn't have known. Why, do you know anyone over that way?

Yes, I said. I know a Rachael Sutherland. You didn't hear that name said, did you? Rachael Sutherland. That's her name.

No, he replied. I'm telling you, I only heard that a woman died. It might not even be true. Ain't the Indians always lying? He might have just said it. Don't you think so?

But I didn't give him an answer. As he was speaking I started to move backwards out of the crowd and just as the last words fell from his mouth I turned and started to run. I glanced over my shoulder once, and what I saw was a scene from a nightmare, Fort Tejon bathed in the morning sun, utterly destroyed, the group of men standing staring after me.

And so began the longest journey of my life, much longer than those journeys from Croval to Cromarty, Cromarty to Pictou, Pictou to Goderich, Goderich to Chicago, Chicago to Rocky Bend to Big Creek to Atascadero to Bakersfield to all the other places that led to Tejon. It seemed to last forever.

My legs were heavy and I could feel the bruise deep in my arm from where I'd fallen when the earthquake struck. Out of breath, I felt the pain surge into my shoulder with every heaving breath. I tried not to think as my feet pounded on, every step a jolting crash through my bones. I stared at the ground as my feet hit and hit, and once again, as I'd found just before the earth split open, I couldn't find a connection between my limbs and my mind. It was as if I was in another body. I could see myself running and running, hurrying to Reed's Ranch to see what had happened to Rachael.

In my head, two voices spoke, warring with each other. One said, She's dead, it's all finished. The other said, It isn't her, it could be anyone, it might be Mrs Reed, or any of the women on the ranch, it can't be her.

The first voice – Why can't it be her? Just because it's you that's running towards her?

The second voice – Why must it be her? Just because I have had other hard blows?

The first voice – This is the way the world goes. You go from one place to another and when you get to the end there's sadness waiting for you.

The second voice – I want there to be no sadness this time.

I shut my ears to them, listened instead to the thump of my feet on the ground, the sound of my breathing, the beat of my blood in my skull.

It was six miles and it was the longest journey I ever made, although I think it took me much less than an hour. I ran most of the distance, though at times, I remember, my hands were grasping at the rocks on the slope ahead.

At last I came over the ridge and ran and slid down to the ranch where nothing looked different, the way a fever can kill and leave the body untouched as it lies under a blanket, dead. I slowed to a walk, wanting to be there but yet not wanting to arrive. In through the gate of Reed's Ranch I went, to meet my fate. There were men away across the fields, rounding up cattle. I went up the steps to the cookhouse and stood for a moment with my hand raised, ready to hammer on the door.

I was thinking, This is what it has come down to. All these miles, and here I am knocking on a door to find my future.

I thumped the wood with the palm of my hand and took a step backwards on the porch. Nothing happened for a long time, and all I was aware of was the bustle of things going on round about me on the ranch. Horses were being led from one place to another, a man was working at the broken wheel of a carriage, men were standing in small groups, scratching their heads, looking round at places where the fences had come down. I was worrying someone would come and challenge me, tell me to go away, they were busy enough without some stranger coming and getting in the way, did I not realise that this was no time for a social visit? Then the door opened and there was Rachael peering out into the midday light.

I said, You're alive.

She laughed at me, saying, Well, so I am. Why would I not be?

I said, red-faced and not just from running, I was told that you'd died. Well, that someone had died. A woman had died. I thought it might be you.

Rachael said, more serious, It's not me. But someone did die. The wife of one of the vaqueros. She was in the barn and a rafter fell on her. I didn't know her, but it's sad.

I wasn't sure what to say.

What was it like at the Fort? she asked. Was anyone hurt there? Are you injured?

Still standing at the door, I told her about the Fort, missing out the part where something told me to run and warn her, just before I was cast to the ground. I suggested that we walk for a little while, away from the buildings. The old soldier at the Fort had told me that sometimes a few hours after an earthquake the ground would shake again, like an echo of the first shock, the way the words in the Seal Cave would come back at you again and again. I was worried that if we were in the cookhouse we might be killed, even yet.

We went and walked by the fence, watching the men herding the steers back together again, using the horses to push them back into one safe group. The air was filled with the noise of the men's shouts and the lowing of the cattle and this noise was the background to our conversation. As we walked Rachael ran her hand along the top rail of the fence.

I asked her if the earthquake had scared her and she said yes, it had. I asked her if it made her think how easy it would be to die, and she said yes, it did. Turning from her and shutting my eyes for a second, I asked her if, during the minute or so it had lasted, she had thought about me at all and, after a minute she said yes, she had.

Was Jacob scared? I asked.

He was, she told me. He wouldn't stop crying at first. Then he went quiet and wouldn't speak at all.

This place is too dangerous, that's what I think, I said.

Everywhere is dangerous, she replied.

I told her about what the old dragoon had said about how the earthquake comes back and also how other earthquakes would come along, some time in the future.

It's not a safe place for roots, I said. A tree was torn up in Grapevine Pass and thrown into the air and you know fine that our roots are less deep here than a tree's roots.

This is the way it always seemed to be with Rachael, me saying something that was close to but not exactly the thing I wanted to be saying.

She said, But where else would we be, me and Jacob? I've had enough of moving.

Somewhere else, I said. We could be somewhere else.

We could? she said, stopping and leaning back against the fence. The sun was behind her and I had to squint, making me feel foolish when I spoke.

I said, Yes, *we* could. We could go somewhere. Back east or further if we wanted. We don't have to stay here forever. You don't. *Where* are we here, really? *Who* are we here? That's what I've been thinking.

There was a pause and she looked at me closely. She said, What else have you been thinking?

I've been thinking about John Xantus, I said. Chasing across the world from Hungary, wherever that is. Coming here and not being happy. Moving on and not being happy there either probably.

Are you saying you want to go back to Croval?

I don't know, I said. But I've learnt that coming to all these places hasn't been what I thought it would be, not that I knew what it would be when we set off fifteen years ago or whatever it is.

Sixteen years ago, she said. Sixteen years in the summer, for you.

Sixteen years, then, I said. I don't know really what I was expecting to see when I went to look at other parts of the world. But I haven't seen anything really. Nothing I couldn't have seen at home.

She looked away, up to the ridge. She said, Do you ever wonder about the ones that never came? Like your mother.

I told her I did.

She said, So what are you going to do? This earthquake has shaken you really, hasn't it?

Of course, but I was thinking about all this before, I said, on and off for a long time. Since Chicago. Since before then.

Will you go? she asked.

We could go, I said, and I reached over and took hold of her arm. I meant to take her hand, but her hands were folded in front of her and I wasn't sure what would happen if I tried to prise one free, so I just put my fingers on her elbow and took a step closer to her.

Back to Scotland? To Croval?

Maybe it would be best for us, I said.

Us? Me and you? And Jacob?

That's what I was thinking.

She pulled away again and started to walk briskly along the fence, away from the ranch. I stood still for a moment then hurried after her. We talked as we walked, both of us quickly a little bit out of breath.

She said, sharply, You don't know anything, Hugh. Or you wouldn't even suggest it.

I told her, I don't mind. And no, I don't know anything. I don't. And I don't need to. About Edward Hill.

Edward Hill?

Or Edward Leaney. Whatever he was called.

Leaney! she said, spitting out the name. That bastard. I left him far behind.

What I'm saying to you, I said, is that it doesn't matter. Where we've been doesn't matter, just where we go now. Me and you and Jacob. It doesn't matter about Leaney.

She stopped again and faced me. She said, You think that Leaney is Jacob's father?

I felt helpless, as if another earthquake had come. I said, weakly, That's I was told. That's what Robert said in his letter.

What letter?

He wrote me a letter when I was in Rocky Bend. He said about Leaney.

Yes, she said, that was what he thought. That's what I told him when *I* wrote to *him*. It was easier. I told Robert and Elizabeth I'd gone west with Leaney and maybe we'd get married. But I was done with Leaney long before. You don't stay with someone like that.

So, who then? I asked. But you don't have to say if you don't want to. It's the past. It can stay there.

It was Callum.

Callum?

That's who it was.

Callum? I thought it was Elizabeth he liked.

It was Elizabeth he liked. But it was me he got.

So Jacob's Callum's son?

That's who.

I didn't know, I said. I never knew that.

No, she said. You wouldn't have. Now do you want to go anywhere with me and Jacob?

I took a few steps away from her and gazed back at Reed's Ranch, fixed there in the cold January California afternoon. I thought I could just make out the boy sitting on the steps of the porch of the cookhouse. Then I turned back to her and said, See this earthquake we had?

Yes.

What a story to tell him, one day. I could tell him how I came to be there at Fort Tejon and what I saw there. How I saw a stream flow backwards, and a tree jump out of the ground.

I don't know, Hugh, I don't know.

I went up to her. I said, I have a whole story to tell. It's mostly written down already. Maybe I could write out the rest and read it to you, the two of you. If you want. It could be a story for Jacob. I'd write it for him.

Would you?

Yes, I would.

And when I said it, that's when I knew it was the answer. That's just what I would do. I knew Rachael wasn't going to give me a reply there and then, standing half a mile from Reed's Ranch, with the steers calling out in the distance. She was never one to tell you right away what she thought. I knew I'd have to be patient. I came back to the Fort and worked on this writing of mine. And now that I've taken my story up to now, and it's taken me days, I'll go back and make the rest of it right, and maybe one day, if I've time, I'll get it all finished and I'll tell the whole thing to them, if we can be together somewhere, making something more of ourselves, I'll tell it to Jacob who is Callum's son but could maybe be mine. Maybe I wouldn't have time, though, if we were together, because, If I'm telling you the truth, most of this writing I've done because I'm lonely. So maybe, if Rachael says yes, maybe I'll just put it away, however far I've got, wherever we are staying, and never turn to it again. I don't really know what I hope. I'd like to have it all finished, and neat, but maybe it won't be like that. That would be all right. But at least I've brought it to the most recent part of the story now, the part where I'm waiting for her reply. And maybe I haven't always been truthful, but maybe that doesn't make me a bad man, I don't know.

I walked back to Fort Tejon that day, happy and scared, following the crack in the earth to the tent where I'd be sleeping. I was thinking ahead to a time when Jacob would be my son, when he would call me his father, when he would confess, one evening, maybe, something sitting heavy in his heart, knowing I would not judge him, just as he will not judge me.

I saw Fort Tejon as I reached the ridge. It was broken apart, a mess of wood and brick, but already I could see men working here and there, using their strong hands to put things right. I went down to help them.

So that was that day.

Two Ravens Press is the most northerly literary publisher in the UK, operating from a six-acre working croft on a sea-loch in the north-west Highlands of Scotland. Two Ravens Press is run by two writers with a passion for language and for books that are non-formulaic and that take risks. We publish cutting-edge and innovative contemporary fiction, non-fiction and poetry.

Visit our website for comprehensive information on all of our books and authors – and for much more:

- browse all Two Ravens Press books (print books and e-books) by category or by author, and purchase them online at a discount on retail price, post & packing-free (in the UK, and for a small fee overseas)

- there is a separate page for each book, including summaries, extracts and reviews, and author interviews, biographies and photographs

- read our regular blog about life as a small literary publisher in the middle of nowhere – or the centre of the universe, depending on your perspective – with a few anecdotes about life down on the croft thrown in. Includes regular and irregular columns by guest writers – Two Ravens Press authors and others

- sign up for our monthly e-newsletter, filled with information on our new releases and our authors, with special discounts, giveaways and other offers.

www.tworavenspress.com